MYTH

ANGELA K. CRANDALL

Arcadia Publishing
ISBN-13:
978-0692610879

ISBN-10:
0692610871

Kindle Edition
ASIN-B016P42VXI

Arcadia Publishing
First Edition
Cover design by Toni Kerr

Special thanks to:

Toni Kerr for designing my book cover. Jaime Goodrich for her expert editing advice. My husband for his helpful idea's and the Robot Review Club for encouraging me to continue working on this project. Last, but not least thank you to my friends, and family for your continued support.

Chapter 1

(Sunday night, Starla)

I walked by the houses, staring up at the round moon that lit up the night's sky. College and the night shifts at work had been continuously dragging me down. Stepping up to the apartment door, I began digging for my keys in my purse as I glanced up to see an elderly couple heading towards me. I smiled.

"Um, miss? My wife and I hate to bother you, but we locked ourselves out of our apartment. Can we use your mobile to call someone to open it?"

He had graying hair, an adorable smile, along with mismatched socks. She looked a bit younger, a little more stylish. They were cute. I tried not to laugh. Mobile, who called cells that these days? Yeah, most likely he wasn't dangerous, but you never could tell. Little old men can be sneaky. I tried to hide the chuckle under my breath at this thought.

"Thanks, gal," he said graciously, taking the phone from me.

"Glad to be of help. I'm Starla. My family and I just moved in," I said, shaking his hand.

"You look a little young to have a family," he replied, examining the phone.

"I'm in school. I work part time over at the diner down the street."

1

"Earl, you know Denny's. He cracks me up... always forgetting things," said the old woman.

"You'll forget things too when you're ninety!" he exclaimed, holding the phone to his ear.

"Yes, yes, Fern and I locked ourselves out again. Can you meet us upstairs at apartment 201? Yeah, thanks," he answered, handing me back my cell phone.

"Earl, why is it you cannot ever remember our keys? I asked you to do one thing," nagged the old women.

They started to bicker back and forth. I turned away towards my apartment, shaking my head.

I opened the door and dropped my purse and backpack on the floor beside me. I clicked the lock to its secure position, not sure if anyone was home. Our dog Fritz came trotting up to me as he barked. He licked my hand a few times before heading into the kitchen, probably to find his food dish. Gosh, I needed a quick shower. Grease from Denny's kitchen coated my hair. I leaned against the wall, looking at our stairwell. I could use a drink. I'd better get cleaned up since Molly said she would go out with me tonight. Slowly I climbed the staircase. Suddenly, out of the wall, small round metal spigots spring out, spraying me with water. Instinctively, I jumped back.

I took my glasses off and wiped them on my shirt, placing them back on my face. "Hey, Mom. Are you home? Megan? Did someone set off the sprinklers smoking again, or something?" If so, I'd not seen a system resembling this before. No one answered. The unrelenting water sprayed onto the staircase and began forming a puddle in the entry way.

There was no fire, no need for this. There was nothing in sight to force the gadgets back into the wall. I searched the sides of the spigots for any buttons or devices that might shut them off. I clicked on what appeared to be a star. A whirring sound started up, blowing warm air out from where the water had emerged. No explanations, no reasons.

Ahh, nothing to be alarmed about, I guess. Maybe I'd overreacted. I opened the door to my room, and my cell rang.

"Starla, are you there?"

"It's me," I said. "Who's this?"

"Jenson, I tried to call you earlier but..."

"Oh, yeah, I worked tonight at the diner. I'm home now. A minute ago someone set off the sprinkler system. Strange spigots shot out of the wall, and now there's water everywhere! I'm not sure what I would have done if I hadn't figured out how to shut it off."

"Hmm, that does sound wacky. I was just trying to contact you, ah, never mind, it's not vital."

"It's OK, what's up?"

"Just be careful. I got a feeling earlier today I was being followed."

"I will, but you know you've had these gut feelings before, and zilch happenings," I said.

"Make sure to call me if you need anything."

I assured him I would, and hung up flopping down on my bed. My clock said 7:15 p.m. Just a little nap. It had been a long day. Curling up, I laid my head down on the pillow and drifted off.

Shuffling my covers off my feet, I pushed them to the end of the bed. I stretched out my limbs and noticed the open window. A faint light shone throughout the red flowing curtains. I jerked back, startled. It was only the wind outside. Scooting up against the headboard, I allowed myself to relax. What time is it? I reached over to turn on the light near my bookshelf. I froze. A dark figure stood inches from me.

My instincts kicked in, adrenaline, fear, then dread, leading to confusion. *A chase, so you want to hunt me?* The figure moved a bit closer. I slowly inched nearer to the open window merely a few feet away. My heart was about to fly out of my skin. I leaped toward the ceiling a few feet from the ground near the windowpane. Putting my hands underneath it, I pushed up. It was stuck! Grabbing hold of the encasement, I searched for an object to break the pane. Nothing, I smashed my fist into the glass over and over again, unbreakable!

I stopped, trapped. A quick tug on my dress pants, nobody visible before me, no one who could have...

I fell, no, was forced, or pressed down. I splashed hitting water. I couldn't breathe. I felt claustrophobic, a small space, a basin? No, a cast iron tub. Was I dying? Who would have wanted to kill me? Minutes passed, and I opened my eyes to the ceiling above me. I must have been in shock. I couldn't move. What had happened? Was I already deceased? Pushing my mind to compel my limbs to function, I pulled myself out of the water and shook myself off. I gasped for breath and placed my hand where the side of the tub would be. Blanket! I'm sitting on a blanket. My bed covers still at my feet.

It was a dream, a very lucid nightmare. "Get up, find your glasses, and get that shower," I ordered myself. The clock on my bed stand read 10:15 p.m. That drink with Molly would have to wait. Hearing my stomach growl, I realized I hadn't eaten since my break at work. Now my eyeglasses, I didn't remember taking them off, nor putting them on. I moved around the room inspecting shelves and other areas where I might have set them. Glancing towards the doorway, this time not one, but two figures stood there. Their red eyes glowed in the darkness.

"Suppose you weren't hallucinating. You don't need eye glasses. That's why you don't wear them. Have you tried out that special power we gifted you with, my dear?" said the strange creature.

"I need my glasses. I'm not sure who you are, or how you got into my home!"

"Have you chosen?" he asked.

What was he talking about? Chosen what? The other figure stood silent, not moving, just scanning me with those beady eyes. It reminded me of a rat I used to have. Mother had to give it away. It freaked me out.

"We've been monitoring you for a while now. You weren't aware of this?" said a female as she stepped out of the dimness, visible, attractive. I shook it off. Where was my phone? I needed to get help, and call Jenson.

"No need to call anyone. You have to make the choice," he said.

Are they vampires or werewolves, I thought.

"Mixed breed," said the lady before me.

I could fight or run. I didn't have any holy water, stakes or silver bullets on me. I wasn't Buffy, well not exactly. I'd seen the show like a zillion times! Now, I was stuck in this position. Did I have a super power? What about that dream? Had it meant

5

anything? Perhaps it had been a premonition. I'd had them before we moved.

"Come on now, we haven't got all night!" he said.

All around me, I suddenly heard laughter. *Did I choose?* I gave them my best squinty face. Heck, I wasn't sure what else to do. It had worked for Samantha in Bewitched. I almost started laughing. Then my face began to twitch! Subsequently, a jolt of pain hit my abdomen, then spread throughout my body. I felt it against my cheeks as if something was pushing against them, emerging out of my face. Whiskers, I felt whiskers! My arms jutted out in front of me, no longer hands, but paws! I grew furry back legs that replaced my human ones! I opened my mouth to speak. The noise that had escaped my lips resembled nothing I'd ever heard before. It was similar to a scream or a shriek if you could even describe it. I looked up at the strange vampire wolves who'd harassed me. They held their ears with their paws, aggravated expressions displayed on their faces.

This was my chance to escape, I thought. I couldn't focus on what, or who, I was until I did.

The door to the downstairs remained a jar. Arching my back, I jumped, leaping over the two jerks and raced down the stairs. At the bottom, I gazed up at the front door. *I have paws, paws? No, I don't have time to fathom this. I'd once watched a cat open a door.* I stood on my hind legs and then stumbled. I listened, nothing yet. I stood back up holding the doorknob with both paws. I moved it from side to side. *Damn! I'd locked the door. Jenson, where the hell are you? Do you know about this?*

My ears perked up, listening I could hear them upstairs moving about. Were they looking for something, or did they want me? Choose. What had that meant? I scanned the landing for something to help me escape and caught a glimpse of myself in a nearby mirror.

I was a fox. What could foxes do? I had jumped up to the window casing; maybe I could hop onto the table against the wall? Was it just a dream? I heard them running. They must be heading downstairs. There was no time to get that key, or even try. I didn't look back, but headed left towards the kitchen. Thank goodness we were on the ground floor! Going into the kitchen, I trotted near the dining table. I remembered the doggie door, we'd put in just as Fritz bolted out of the laundry room. He stood his ground with angry barks. Gah! Fritz! I hope they leave you alone, I thought, staring back at the tiny Shih Tzu. I quickly exited the room via the doggie door as my pursuers entered.

Chapter 2

(Tri)

"Starla, Starla are you here?" I cried. I pushed open the front door, flinging my keys on the hall table. "Go check upstairs and find out where your sister is at. I'm going to start our dinner. See you in the kitchen, sweetie."

"Mom, she said she was going out with Molly tonight after work, remember?" said Megan. She leaned against the railing to the upstairs hall.

"Oh, that's right, dear. Well, go clean up, then come down and help me set the table. It will just be the two of us." I sauntered into the kitchen and switched on the light. Fritz sat shaking in the corner near the laundry entrance. "Oh, Fritz, what's the matter? It's only me, you silly dog," I said, bending down to pet him on the head. A low growl started up in the dog's throat; he tensed up, glaring at the entryway behind me, ready to attack. I twisted round to face whatever he'd been barking at, finding nothing behind me. "Fritz, what is it? Did you see a ghost or something?"

Megan bounced into the room, sliding in her white socks towards the dining table. "Hey there, Mom!"

"Megan Lindsey Lee! What is going on?"

"Sorry, Mom just having a bit of fun," she smiled, grabbing a cup off of the counter. She filled it with water from the tap, proceeding to drink.

"Fritz almost gave me a heart attack. He was cowering near the laundry room when I came in, then he started growling, but there was nothing here."

Megan shrugged. "I thought I heard noises upstairs. It could just have been my imagination again. I wasn't going to worry you about it. Remember the old house? How we use to hear things all the time?"

"I do, let's not talk about that now." I opened the cupboard above the sink and began putting away the groceries I'd purchased. "Megan, please start the oven for the frozen pizza. Then go turn all the lights on, look around, and see if anything is missing. After that, we're going to call your sister. This isn't sitting well with me right now."

(Starla)

As I ran along the sidewalk far away from the complex, snow gleamed on the ground like the stars above me, before me lay a city. It wasn't as bad as L.A., but it still held cars, traffic lights, and busy streets. I hoped that mom and Megan would be OK. I shook my head standing there. What would they think of our new tenants, or would they have left after my exit? Searching up and down the road I tried to figure out which way to go. Everything was new to me. I'd just lived here a few weeks! Even if I could change back to my human form, I had no cell phone, and no clothes! My worst nightmare! The college was behind me. Jenson lived a few streets down.

"Hmmm?" I looked again left and right trying to get my bearings, using landmarks having never in truth paid attention to street signs. Swiftly I trotted towards homes, which appeared most familiar to me. A wing and a prayer is what my mom always said when I followed my gut instincts and went with it. Glancing up into a nearby window a girl studied, in the other people watched TV, and here I was. I had not yet tried to speak, so I did. "Jenson, are you here?" I could still talk, well what do you know, "Hot Diggity dog!"

"No, you're a fox!" A small five-year-old boy looked straight at me.

"Shhh, do you know Jenson?"

He gave me a wide grin and then patted my head. I was a bit annoyed.

"I do, he lives in that blue house." He points to it. In the driveway was Jenson's old red beat up car.

"Why thank you, squirt. Please do not tell anyone you spoke with me. Hmm, please?" I gave him pleading eyes.

He shrugged as he walked away. I heard him exclaim to himself, "Who would believe me anyway?"

Myth

(Tri)

"I don't know where your crazy sister is, Megan, I called Molly's. She never got ahold of her after work. When she gets home, she's not going to be happy. I'm at wits end with her. I know she can be adventurous. This is why we moved! No more mysterious, no more strange events. She was just going to be a normal college girl."

Megan sat at the dinner table and stared at her cold pizza. "Mom, don't worry. She's probably just off with Jenson somewhere. All those puddles down the steps lead me to believe she hopped in the shower and washed her hair only to head out to Shimmer's. You know she usually leaves a note. Did you look?"

I moved to the table to sit with Megan, fumbling with a few napkins. I picked up a piece of the cold pie and began eating.

"Mom, maybe we should call her."

I set down the pizza to look at my youngest daughter. "Your sister can take care of herself, but why would she forget her keys, cell phone, and purse? She never leaves without them. What worries me is Mr. Fritz was growling when I got home. It didn't look like we had an intruder. No forced entry that I could see. Springville is a mid-size town pretty safe now that. Well, never mind."

Megan took my hand and squeezed it. "If she's not home in 24 hours we can call the police. After we finish eating and clean things up, you should give Jenson a call. OK?"

I got up and hugged my daughter.

"Thank you," I said.

"It'll be OK, mom."

(Starla)

I sprinted to the house, checking for any signs of Jenson or his folks. A large oak tree stood in the yard. I'd rest there until I figured out what to do next. I needed a moment, then maybe I could plan my next move. What had I been thinking about when shape shifting into a fox? Was it possible this was a permanent transformation? The vampires said to make a choice, was this my choice? I shook myself all over. Afterwards, I stood on my hind legs and stretched out my long fox arms against the tree. The full moon hung low tonight. I looked up at it longingly. How could I make myself panic? That's the last emotion that had occurred before...

My whiskers started to pull inward; my body began to shake all over. "Ouch, help someone, please!" I rolled onto the ground. My fur vanished within me, revealing my human skin and hands. Laying there I checked out my body, everything seemed intact. I was exposed as I feared. Naked! Great, here I was at Jenson's in my birthday suit. The last thing I wanted him to think was...

"Hey! What are you doing out here! Starla, why don't you have any clothes on?" said Jenson's sister.

"Bring me your bathrobe, then Jenson, and I'll explain, but only to you and your brother. No one else should be involved in this. We can't talk out here-someone might be listening."

"OK, paranoid much?"

"As of this evening, yes, very paranoid," I said to Sage, as I used my hands to cover myself.

"Go behind that tree and don't come out til I bring you some clothes," she said as she headed back to the house.

"Oh, I will, you don't have to worry about that!"

Jenson's room appeared to be a jumbled mess of clothes, sports equipment, and books. He called it organized chaos. I hastily explained to him what happened as my eyes surveyed the rest of his room. A computer and the internet would be helpful. I sat down on his cluttered bean bag, pushing items onto the floor.

"Starla, how do you wind up in these odd situations? I'm glad you found the house. The previous time it was tricky trying to locate you. Especially without you being able to give me any street names."

I gave him my best geeked out smile, as I rolled my eyes. "Why would vamps, let alone a mixed breed of them, be after me? Why would I change into a fox of all things?"

"You said you screamed. It irritated them enough for them to plug their ears, giving you time to run."

"I ran alright. Do you suppose my mom and Megan are safe?"

"Umm, about that, you'd better call. My Star Wars collectible has been off the hook tonight!" Jenson exclaimed, gesturing with his hands for emphasis. "Here, I'll even dial the number. I hope you're not in deep poo."

He handed me the phone, and I waited for an answer.

(Tri)

"Mom, the phone!" yelled Megan. "It's probably her, want me to grab it?"

Starla had better be somewhere safe. "No, I got it. Go back to cleaning up that room of yours or no movie night!"

She better be safe. I had been de-cluttering my closet in hopes of soothing my nerves. I wondered if my mother ever had it this tough. I took my cell off the dresser and hit the green button.

"Starla?"

"Mom, I'm at Jenson's. I'm really, really sorry!"

"Couldn't you, at least, have left me a note?" I said, annoyed.

"Mom, please just understand this once that I cannot explain it. I came home and the sprinkler system went off. Did you see all the puddles on the floor?"

"Megan mentioned something about that, but it didn't look like sprinklers caused it. Are you sure you're alright? Did you hit your head on anything today, dear?" I asked, as I riffled through the bureau.

"No, I am fine, really I am. We have an assignment to do for an upcoming project. I may be here late. Is that going to be a problem?"

I loved my daughter. I tried to understand my daughter and needed to give her space. I kept repeating the things I'd been told. I should not reveal anything too soon, or become too worried, or panic.

"OK, but call me if you need a ride home. Be back by one a.m. at the latest please." I stated sternly.

"Yes, mom, and if not I'll call ok?"

"One a.m.," I snapped and slammed down the receiver. I prayed they hadn't been here.

(Starla)

I wanted to laugh, how the hell am I going to tell my mother I changed into a fox, that two vamps or wolves were preying on me, maybe for months. I hung up the phone.

"So did your mom lose it?" asked Sage, while she stood in the doorway.

"No, it's cool for now."

"Oh man, you honestly turned into a fox!" Sage laughed. "That is so outrageous," she exclaimed, and skipped into the room.

"You're not to tell anyone about this, my little princess," I said as I tickled her.

"You two really need to stop messing around. It's almost midnight, and your mom's orders were to be home by one. It doesn't give us a lot of time to figure this shiz out." Jenson turned on his computer. "I don't want you going home if it's not safe."

"You're right, come on Sage, you should go to bed. Jenson will fill you in later." She pouted, then hugged her big bro and me, goodnight.

Thank goodness she had found me. I sure wouldn't have wanted his mom or dad to discover me naked and cold on their back lawn. I shivered again, considering it. How would I have explained myself? They definitely would have called my mother. What would she have done?

"Lost in thought?"

"Huh," I shook my head a bit in an attempt to bring myself back to reality. "Is this, could it be somehow connected to our myths and studies class? Bits of research, we've dug up on foxes forced me to re-examine their role in our world. Could they really be guardians? Jones claimed some of them were. The guy, although well versed, seemed out there. My first instinct, subsequent to changing form, had been to scream in rage, shriek, and run. What do they want from me? What is my purpose in this? The only vampires, I ever encountered were on the television show Buffy until tonight. They said they knew me, they'd been watching me."

"That tattoo on your arm, is it still there?"

"Yes, since birth." I pulled back my shirt sleeve on the right side of my upper arm. The paw print remained, similar to three small peas with a big blob below it. I repeatedly thought of a cat or dog print when inspecting it. Mom had claimed it to be a standard birthmark.

"Do you believe she'll continue to argue it has zilch to do with you now?" He drummed his fingers on the computer desk, disturbed. My mother didn't hate Jenson, but she wasn't fond of him either.

I shrugged, and then looked him in the eyes. "Jenson, I don't know. Why would she cover something like this up?"

"To protect you, these crazies could want to use you as a weapon, or worse."

"A weapon, what kind would I be? They laughed at me during my transformation. That is, until my scream left them reeling in an anguish of pain." I stood up and stretched. "Now explain to me what this has to do with our research?"

Jenson pulled out a binder from the drawer underneath his desk. He opened it up to the first page. I rubbed my sweaty palms on my borrowed jeans, scanning over his shoulder. Witty, trickery, there was a lot of information about foxes around the world.

"Which one am I?"

"I have yet to see you in your fox body, or how you interacted with those creeps. It will be hard to tell from your brief encounter with your err new self."

"My new self!" I exclaimed shoving him playfully. "I am still me. I'm just more super."

Jenson laughed, "Yeah, you've always been pretty super."

He patted my arm. I gave him a little push, urging him to get up so I could take control of his laptop. He smiled at me, the queen of his computer. I'd used it frequently since I'd moved here. Mom claimed the library was best for studying. She didn't want me up all night chatting with friends. What friends? Jenson and Molly

17

were the only people I knew, personally. The rest were in passing or acquaintances.

"Starla, focus on the research, it's twelve thirty!" Jenson pulled up the beanbag and sat next to me.

I hurriedly typed in, can a fox be a guardian over animals, into the search engine. A long list popped up before me. Immediately I clicked on the website referring to a fox as a spirit animal. Scanning it, I looked at Jenson, "Care if I print this out?"

"Go ahead."

"We should start a folder, print out all the information we can about foxes. This is going to take longer than one night to analyze." He nodded. I hit the print button and gave Jenson a troubled look.

"We'll work this out; it could be to your advantage. Those things," he shuddered, "they left when you screamed; this article you are printing claims you may have magical abilities. They either want you as an ally or to scare you. You've had a lot of crazy stuff happen, but never this. How did being a fox feel physically?"

"Strange, a sense of freedom, but mostly fear overall. The crowd I ran with back home would be envious. We regularly talked about spirit animals, guides, and mystical beings. It made my mother terrified. She warned me not to mess with the stuff. It's why we moved here." I stood up and pushed aside the comfy swivel chair.

Jenson reached from his seat, pulling me down to him, into a hug. I returned the favor briefly, then nudged him away.

"Don't start getting all ga-ga for me. You know with all that is going on..."

"Yeah, the last thing you can handle is a relationship," he grumbled as we stood up. He handed me an extra jacket that had been thrown on his bed. I put it on, a bit big, yet it would do.

"Jenson, I have school, work, and now this!" I said, throwing my arms into the air.

"Please let me walk you home."

I rolled my eyes at him as I slouched against the wall.

"Come on, your mom would approve. You know how overprotective, she can be. If she finds out about this..."

"Hell will freeze over."

"Yep, and then what will happen to all the baddies?"

"They will come back to earth to torture us, and we'll have to fight like Buffy," I sighed.

"Ok, now let's get you home. We'll just have to keep our senses alert," he warned.

Jenson took my hand. I shoved it away. Then we stepped out into the night.

Chapter 3

(Monday)

I swung my backpack behind me on the way to Myth class, supposedly based on local legends, but no one knew if it was historically accurate. My glasses had never been recovered. Did mom notice this morning? I exhaled out into the air, an anxiety held within me. Things were going to change sooner or later. At least, Jenson would be in class today. As I nearly tripped over this speculation, my hands flew out to stop myself. Were my shoes untied? Yep. What ever happened to Velcro? It made everything easier. Yeah, I was that old!

"Hey! Where were you last night?"

I finished tying my laces and turned to see Molly, her brownish-blonde hair in waves. She wore jeans and a simple green sweatshirt. My best friend was not the style police. I almost chuckled, standing up to lean against the white brick wall.

"What happened, and where are your glasses?" she asked.

"I had some pretty strange things go down last night."

"Strange, as in?" she asked, walking up to me.

"You remember when I told you about my old high school?"

"You mean how you were practically comparable to Buffy, but no big bads, well similar to Buffy anyway," she said.

"Yeah, anyway, after dealing with work, as usual, I came home. This silly old couple had locked themselves out of their unit

20

so I lent them my phone. That's the normal part of the night. Once inside, Fritz greeted me. When I attempted to go upstairs, the sprinkler system turned on. I didn't even know we had a sprinkler system!" I continued my candid details of the evening's events as we headed to class.

"So you don't need your glasses anymore?"

"I guess not, I made my way to Jenson's OK without them."

"My imagination's running rampant with your details. You naked in Jenson's yard!" she exclaimed, and then laughed. "What did your mom say when you got home?"

"Nothing, thank goodness. She'd already turned in for the night. I don't suppose I'd want to reveal what occurred. You know how my mom has been about me, and mysteries, now and in the past." She gave me an understanding glance as we entered the class.

I took my seat next to Jenson, Molly joined us. He pushed some papers towards me.

"Your mom's been hiding something from you. You're either going to be ecstatic or very angry."

(Tri)

"What did you tell my daughter? Why were they in my house? Dan, she is not ready for this! We had an agreement. You would not send them until she'd completed college. I was adamant about that. Afterwards, she'd join you. Not now, when I finally have her level headed again. Look how long it took me to convince her that the tattoo was just a birthmark!"

I ranted on the phone with my ex err Starla's father. It had been years since I'd seen him. The girls knew little about him. It hadn't been right, me denying him access to his offspring. It had been the only way to keep them safe.

Megan wasn't like Starla. She was different, and the time would come when I'd have to let go of her too. I'd just wanted to hang on for as long as I could. While listening to Dan, I remembered the day it had happened. The scene kept playing over in my head days after it materialized.

"Mommy, it looks like a fox's paw. It can't be just a birthmark!" Starla had been pushing my buttons at five years old. One of her friends in kindergarten had pointed out that her birthmark appeared to be a fox paw.

"Honey, it's just a blemish. Many people have them at birth. It'll probably eventually disappear."

"Mommy, it glowed! Cal said she saw it, mom! She wouldn't lie!"

"Honey, maybe she really thought it glowed, but observe how the light reflects onto your arm."

Starla had looked up at me with her big eyes. It hurt to have to lie to her. I didn't want to do it, but she was only five. Finally, I convinced her. It took me a few years to do so, but by age seven, she'd stopped asking.

"Honey, are you there?"

He hadn't called me that in years. "I'm here!" I snapped.

"I'm sorry this is so aggravating for you. I wouldn't have sent them if this wasn't so urgent. We need her help. You recall all the times she solved those mysteries in high school, the ones you didn't want her getting into?" he asked.

"That was you?"

"We didn't exactly set them up. We needed them resolved. She happened to be at the right place at the right time. Analyzing the current problem now with regards to your emotions, be grateful she's learned to figure things out on her own. She needed to discover some of her abilities. You've seen her becoming stronger, and that glow you once tried to hide will no longer stay hidden. We cannot wait any longer. I'll need to be re-introduced to her soon. If not, she could be in danger. Tri, please hear me out on this. I do not want our daughter's life at risk. I have honored your request for her protection for 19 years. This cannot continue."

I hung up the phone. I'd have to mull this over. Maybe Dan was right. I needed to evaluate her safety, the security of our people. This Jenson boy she'd been seeing better understand the situation about to occur. If only I could stop their friendship. Damn! I remembered being a teenager once. Falling in love with Starla's father, created an ache that would not cease. It seemed so long ago.

(Starla)

A loud slam startled me. Mr. Jones made his way past our tables.

"I guess now would not be a good time," I said to Jenson.

"Probably not, stick 'em in your folder. We'll deal with it later."

"OK."

Mr. Jones meandered towards his desk. He shuffled through a stack of boxes. "Ah, here it is," he mumbled to himself picking up the round reel. "Now class, this film isn't very new. Pay close attention to this legend in particular. Recall when we discussed the findings of fox appearances in Hunters Park. The killings of men that once took place there and the one that occurred just a few weeks ago. Be careful around the campus don't go wandering in parts near the wooded area leading to the park." He turned down the lights, and the projector began.

What killings? I hadn't heard of any. Neither had Jenson or Molly, they would have told me about it. As I slumped down into my cold hard seat, the room fell silent. Not once had we watched movies or any sort of motion picture during the semester. The discussions were the basis. Mr. Jones didn't care for technology. I made a note of the old school projector with its long reel in my notebook. This film appeared as if it had been spliced together, or repaired. Where had it come from?

The mythology and folklore of the Kitsune Fox beamed out in its loud, old-style sound. A cassette tape player sat off to the side. Mr. Jones had to start it as the film began. The pictures on the screen were cartoon-like in black and white, women luring men into the woods.

"Where did he get this film?" I whispered to Molly.

"Who knows, an archive? National Geographic's never covered it in their magazines," she replied.

"It reminds me of a website someone put up. It seemed totally suspicious. I couldn't even get an IP address on it. The legend focused on exactly this!" Jenson pointed to the screen.

The women on it had begun to seductively dance, taking the young man in her arms. Without warning, her torso began to change into the form of a fox.

"They would lure men away in female form, make love to them, then kill them, or possibly let them go," Jenson interjected.

I hid my face away from the screen and listened to the audio: *Kitsune is the Japanese word for fox, and these spirits represent knowledge and enlightenment. They are common in folklore. These intelligent beings possess magical abilities, which increase with age as they gain wisdom. They are able to take human form; some use it to trick others, but not all. Some of these foxes are faithful guardians, friends, lovers, or wives. The rise of the legend arose when humans and foxes began living close to each other. Kitsune are said to grow up to nine tails the older and wiser they become. Some people make offerings to them like they would a god. Stories of fox wives bearing children occur in folklore; they can acquire physical or supernatural abilities.*

The hair on my arms started to rise. My heart pounded as if it were going to dance right out of my chest. Deep breaths, relax, breath, relax-- I kept at it, attempting to calm down. Then, before I lost it and went all foxy on my class, I got up and left for the bathroom.

After getting myself emotionally back together, I proceeded to the cafe, my favorite place to unwind, no one bothered me. Our college consisted of local high school graduates who'd soon transfer. I didn't know most of them. People came and went, often. Finding a table near the back, I sat and sipped my slushy ice lemon water through a purple straw. The little green umbrella in it sat off to one side. I'd needed something girlie for a change.

"Are you OK? You just bolted out of there, even Mr. Jones seemed worried," said Molly. She sat down beside me. I played with my little umbrella. It was green. I loved green.

"Is this about Jenson? You two have gotten awfully close," she pressed.

I took her hand, and she pushed mine away. "You always worry about what people think," I said.

"I'm not worried."

"If it is any consolation to you, I was only seeking a little comfort. You're my friend, right?" I asked.

"Sorry, I just don't want..."

"I'm not going to out you to Jenson, if that's what worries you. I'll also answer your question. I do have a tiny crush on him, but right now, is so not the time! I mean, why would you even ask that?"

"I care about you, alright?" said Molly. "I don't expect you to care back, but I'm doing my best. I just want to see you happy. Things were going pretty good. The three of us hanging out, then everything gets all mysterious."

"OK, if you don't want to help just say so, if you're freaked out, you can stay behind if whatever it is, goes any further."

"I saw those papers. Jenson showed them to me. Have you seen them yet?"

"No, where is he anyway?"

"He had to go home, or so he said."

"It's almost four." I pointed to the clock near the barista's station. "Mom, will want Megan and me home for dinner. It's the one night we're forced to do family stuff."

"You don't sound too thrilled."

"Lately, I've had a gut feeling Tri; Mom is going to throw something big at me. I don't know what, a new responsibility or expectation. You might call it a hunch. I'd make plans, but you remember what happened yesterday evening."

She gave me a sweet look that said yeppers. I pushed myself away from the table, stood and picked up my drink before turning to leave.

"Don't forget your knapsack." She handed it to me.

"Thanks, I'm... I'm sorry about earlier. I shouldn't have said anything, knowing how sensitive you are about it."

She brushed her hair behind her ear, and I leaned in for a hug. She returned it.

"Thanks, Starla."

"Your secret's safe with me, but when you're ready to open up, I've got your back."

Chapter 4

Having missed my math class, I curled up on my bed to deal with the last assignment. One that wasn't as entertaining as Myth class. I laid my head against the pillows, staring out the window. Squirrels chased one another, bickering back and forth. They had it easy. All they had to worry about was gathering nuts for the winter, creating babies, raising them, and trying not to end up as road kill.

There take that, you evil arithmetic problem, I thought, finishing the last one. If I flunked out of college, this would be why. I placed my notebook on top of my pile of books and tossed them aside onto my nightstand. Should I open the folder Jenson had given me? No, he'd probably want me to wait until he and Molly were here.

Still, my hand reached for the binder. Why is this so difficult? I drew in a deep breath and let it out. My best friends, I was lucky to have them. Lately, though between work, the other night, and then today with Molly, I wasn't sure where I fit. Sure, it would be easy to cozy up to Jenson. Molly was a sweet girl. I'd hoped she would find someone, or else, at least, be comfortable enough to be herself. I didn't want her to have to hide. It just wasn't fair to her. I picked the binder back up, looked at it and set it back down. Not recognizing why it was eating me up inside.

Myth

I had taken all the board games out of the closet. I'd begun to heap them on the kitchen table. Mom called it the dining area, but it was in the kitchen after all.

"Mom, Jenson and I are just friends. College is my main focus right now. There's no time for that lovely dovey stuff, and yes, as far as I know, I prefer boys, so we don't have to go over that!"

"What has gotten into you lately?" my mom asked, extracting some cookies out of the oven.

"It's called independence." I watched her set down the cookie trays to cool on the stove.

"You're headstrong, just like your father," she answered.

"Where is he by the way? It's not like he's called or sent postcards in the last few years."

"You know your dad; he never was especially interested in you, girls." I hated lying to her, but tonight she would find out just how invested her dad was.

"Mom, let's not talk about it. Could Molly and Jenson come over? I'm tired of it just being us." I went to reach for a cookie and thought better of it.

My mom gave me a smirk, fiddled a bit with the cookies she'd placed on a plate, and then finally answered me.

"Given that we're just playing board games, okay," my mom replied.

"Thank you, Mom! This is great. I'm going to go call them. We have some important business to take care of before some 'serious Jenga' tonight." I gave my mother the quotation marks trying to be funny. She just rolled her eyes back at me. We had that kind of connection, love/hate that is. I loved my mother, but I was me after all.

An hour later I opened the door, inviting Molly and Jenson in.

"I can't believe you talked your mom into having us over. She rarely lets you have friends over for family fun night!" Molly said.

"Yeah, something must be up for her to be allowing this," I giggled like a kid. I'd been so serious this afternoon, now I felt giddy just to have my two best friends over--talk about mood swings. I hoped this excellent atmosphere would last.

"I think you two have been drinking either too much Mountain Dew or you've hit your limit on espressos," said Jenson.

I laughed at him. "OK, you can hang your coats in the closet, and your boots can dry on the register if you want," I said, pulling open the closet door.

Molly and Jenson handed me their jackets as they removed their boots. I hung them up and then turned back to them.

"Come on, our living room is right through here," I pointed and they followed.

"So," Jenson said.

"No, I haven't peeked inside the folder yet. I assumed you'd rather be here when everything is exposed."

"Well, where is it?" they said in unison.

"In my room, but mom will want to serve us cookies, and to play Jenga with us. I did tell her we had some stuff to take care of before, so I might be able to sneak it past her."

"It's better to start the night out on a light note, and end on a da da da dum!" said Molly.

"Yeah, you're probably right."

We were about to sit down when mom popped her head in the doorway.

"Hey guys, let's go into the kitchen. Then we can start the games and have snacks." She turned, leaving us to follow.

I got up and led them to our dining area. On the table sat popcorn, pretzels, chocolate cookies, and some cola. Wow, Mom really went all out. Now where was my sister? I turned around and bumped right into her.

"Hey, why don't you guys sit down, so we can actually, kick off a game already?" she whined.

Mom smiled at us. It had been ages since I'd had friends over. Megan had met them, on one of our few trips to the mall. Another one of mom's pet peeves, she believed our society spent too much. Money should be saved for college funds.

We all took our seats. My guests surveyed the pile of board games, sitting to the right of my mom.

"So, who gets to choose the game tonight?" I asked.

"Jenson and Molly are our company. Instead of playing Jenga, as usual, let them decide."

I glared at my mom like I want to kick your butt; sis stayed silent. No, nothing, no rebuttal from mother. Molly pointed to the Game of Life while Jenson shook his head.

"Monopoly?" asked Jenson. He pulled it off of the bottom of the stack.

I put a hand to my head. Jeez, Jenson, really, we'll be playing all night. Molly said nothing, even though she knew we had pressing matters.

"Alright, but I get to be the little dog," I said.

Jenson opened the box. He handed me the game piece, allowing his hand to linger on mine briefly.

"Let me set up the board and be in charge of handing out the houses," declared Molly.

"Banker," Megan chimed in.

Mom gathered up the fake bills and placed them in front of each of us. We'd begun to munch on the array of goodies.

"Hey Molly, why don't you go first." suggested Megan.

She picked up the dice and tossed them on the table top. She rolled six and began moving her piece when the door bell rang.

"Mom, we're not expecting anyone. Are we?" I asked.

"Honey, give me a minute. I'm going to go get the door. Maybe it's Fern. She was over yesterday in need of eggs to bake a cake."

I looked over at Molly, "It's the old couple who locked themselves out the other night. She's pretty stylish; he's kind of cranky."

We'd only met a handful of neighbors in the few weeks we'd been here. Yes, it was not an unfriendly place, but it wasn't Green Acres either. I heard my mother at the door, she let someone in, then I saw him.

Dad?

He waltzed into our dining room. He looked good, official, like he was on business, wearing dress pants, a white shirt, and a green tie. His hair was graying now, a sandy pepper color instead of ash blonde. Megan's jaw dropped a mile. Dad hadn't come to visit since she was a baby. He claimed that he hadn't a clue how mom had gotten pregnant, seeing as he'd been supposedly absent for months on end. Mom swore up and down she was his, and father accepted it.

"Sorry to interrupt this gathering you have going on," he said, sitting down in the empty chair next to mine. "Are these your friends?"

Well, duh said my brain.

"This is Jenson, and my friend Molly. Maybe you know, since here you are. Mom moved us from L.A. because, well, I got into too much trouble."

He mussed my hair and grinned. Mom stood there watching us with her arms crossed. She wasn't happy he was here. I wondered if her actions were real, fake, or...

"I'm not going to say this is a standard dad call," he spoke. Jenson glowered up at him, brave Jenson.

"Sir, are you here about the crazy stuff. The rumors of bizarre occurrences in Hunters Park? I've been doing research on that and err..."

"Actually, I am. A group I work with is investigating a death in the area. We're sure it's an outside source."

I knew Jenson wouldn't out me to my family about my, err, fox problem. How could we keep it a secret? Was I the secret, did I belong to someone else?

"What do you mean by 'outside source'?" I asked

"I cannot believe you're involving children in this, Dan!" My mother's hands rested on the table as she intently stared him in the eyes. It was mom's death look. He ignored her for the moment.

"I'm going to be in and out of this area for a while. Maybe you guys could keep an eye out? Your mother is against this, of course.

I'm unable to divulge specifics, but as soon as I am we'll be in touch. Jenson, here are some newspaper clippings I'd like you to look over. In fact, in the next few days, you'll be given clues to decipher. They might not necessarily be directly from me, but you'll receive them. Tri confirmed you have mad skills with that computer of yours. Starla, mom said you took some defense classes last year at the gym before you moved, good girl. Now then, Molly you might want to look into that. It could be useful even outside of this case," said Dan.

"Dad, you make it sound as if we are going into battle. You show up here after years of abandonment. Now you want our help, more importantly, my attention? I know I've solved a few mysteries. Who put hair in my best friend's sandwich, missing students, and then there was that one time..."

"Starla, I know of those adventures."

"Who told you?" I blurted, looking squarely at my mother. Was she the culprit who revealed my secrets?

"Never mind that for now," he said.

I stood up from my seat, anger swelled inside of me.

"When have I ever asked anything of you? And when, father, have you done anything for me?" I screamed. "Something is and has been going on for years. I've known it since my tattoo glowed-- and mother, you denied it. All of you have been hiding things from me. Jenson and Molly, let's jet, Megan if you want to come with us, then let's go!"

"Starla, we should hear your father out," stuttered Molly.

I was angry, angry enough to out my friend right there, but something pulled me back from doing so.

"I need to take a walk before I say, or do something I regret. Don't follow me! I'll be safe." I grabbed my cell phone and got out of there fast. The last thing, I needed, was to change into a fox in front of them, but they probably already knew about that too. It made me wonder, what else they were hiding from me.

The Sunshine Cafe had a dark yet pleasant atmosphere. You'd probably call it a spectrum of the in-between. The booth chosen by the waitress was faded at the corners. After ordering fries, I stared out at the setting sun until my food arrived.

"Here ya go, and your cola. Let me know if you need anything else," she said.

"Thanks." I picked up the ketchup, pouring it on the side of my plate, and proceeded to swirl my fries around in it. When was the last time dad showed up? My mind could not form an answer. I tried to conjure up a reason this was happening as I sipped my Coke, then played with my food some more. Was I fooling myself? Should I have accepted my dad wanted to be a part of my life? That he'd been spying on me for years or maintained contact with mom concerning me? Then there was Jenson, so eager to help my father with whatever task he gave us. I still wondered what was in those files from years ago, ones my father hid from me. I picked up several fries, stuffing them into my mouth. That was more like it, salty fried goodness.

"Are you doing alright, hun? You've been sitting here messing with your food for a while. It's good to finally see you eating," said the waitress.

"Tough night, it could be worse, though. I'll just finish up my fries and let you clean up."

"Take your time, hun, take your time," she replied.

She trotted away and I did a double take, was that a wolf's tail under her skirt? Shaking it off, I thought it couldn't be, probably just nerves. I took a deep breath in, exhaled out as I'd been taught to still myself. Oh, I'd forgotten that. I'd been little, so small. Mom and dad talked to me about getting worked up, not to panic, that I must stay calm at all times.

"Ring, ring," the diner door opened. I glanced up to see a straggly fellow, dark hair, lanky, wearing a shabby gray overcoat. He strutted to the counter, sat down and ordered a cup of coffee. I continued eating my fries. False alarm, I thought perhaps my friends would have come after me. In retro-spect, they could be collaborating with my parental units back at the apartment while I sat here sulking.

It was better I had left. There is no telling what would have materialized if I'd stayed.

(Tri)

The newspaper clippings were spread out on the table among the games we'd meant to play. I looked around at the three of them. It was just like Starla to exit when things were about to heat up, we were in the kitchen after all. I tried to contain my anger. This was not the time to go Mommy Dearest on my daughter's friends. She was mad at her father. I understood that, being angry with him also, but couldn't see how to keep him away from her much longer. The cat would eventually have to be let out of the bag, so to speak. She'd only left to keep from losing her temper in front of her friends.

"Dan, explain to Jenson and Molly how you want them to help out. Then they should go look for Starla," I said.

He then began instructing us, "Concentrate on any odd suspects you might find lingering around campus, or in the park. I don't want you to enter Hunters Park after dark. It's bad enough that I'm asking you to do this. Now, Starla is going to be exceedingly useful in this investigation. She's done this before. We had some problems a while back with a few children who'd gone missing from their homes. They were recovered before..."

"Before what," said Molly?

"Starla stopped them from being taken. She sensed something bad was going to occur, so she walked them home from school. Once there she told them not to leave their homes, making sure they locked their doors behind them. She was very young, five years old. The last year, hmm hmm hmm," he cleared his throat. "The last year we were together," he spoke, eyeing Tri, "We didn't realize she'd had any abilities at her birth. After this incident, I started calling her my little medium."

Dan smiled at me. I guess he wasn't going to reveal her secret yet. Maybe he didn't sense it was safe for her friends. No, he couldn't assume they would reject her, could he? He'd also left out the part where she'd come home and told us the name of the suspect along with a description. We'd called a hotline, anonymously, leaving his name. Soon after he'd been apprehended outside of a local store, she'd described in her vision. We'd told her they were just bad dreams, waking dreams from a lack of sleep, but following that she sorted out how to use them. They'd come and go. It was how she'd solved a few of the mysteries in high school, but not all of them.

"Do you know who's behind this?" asked Jenson.

"No, son, right now I only know what I've read in the papers. I have an idea of who it might be. A group I'm familiar with. They're pretty rowdy actually, not to be trusted. I am unable to point blame until physical descriptions of the suspects are released, or revealed. If the authorities find any physical proof, it might connect them to the location. If there was any evidence discovered at the scene, it has not been released to the park ranger."

"Yes, but who are they?" asked Molly.

"Once we have certain particulars, I'll let you kids in on the full picture. Until then you're on a need to know basis. It's for your own safety, including my daughter's. Do you understand?"

"Yes, for now, we do, sir. If anything happens, how do we reach you? Your cell number or home phone?" asked Jenson

"Here's my card, but only call if it's extremely urgent. I'll be investigating further. Don't forget, I'm counting on your assistance in this. Now go find my daughter."

He got up from the table and slid his chair into place. Suddenly he embraced me; drawing back, startled I gazed at him. "Take care of our daughter, watch over her friends. I'll be in touch," he said.

Then I watched him walk out the door.

Chapter 5

Sitting in the diner's booth, I pushed my empty plate away, surveying the scene. The strange man had ended up getting his coffee to go. I hadn't seen a soul enter or leave since. My life was beginning to feel like a bad episode of the Twilight Zone. I'm not talking vamps this time; I'm talking, the old television show, black, and white before Technicolor existed.

My Coke sat half full. I drank the watery sugar substance, then set my glass down to dig my phone out of my pocket. It read, "No missed calls." I pushed my flip phone back into the pocket of my jeans. The waitress sauntered back up to the table. Her name tag said Sue. I hadn't paid much attention to it earlier.

"Here, let me get you some more soda. Don't you have anywhere to go?" she asked.

"More soda is good. I'll just sit here a spell. Then take the trail back to my abode."

She stared at me as if I'd just come out of an alien spaceship while she refilled my Coke from her plastic pitcher.

"Whatever floats your boat, dear, make sure you're gone by ten. That's when we close up for the night."

Peering out the window, I spotted Jenson, strolling in beside Molly. They looked pretty stern.

"Oh, more customers, I best get some menus ready!" she said, running off to fetch them.

Jenson and Molly came up to my booth, "Are you guys going to eat? Sue is delighted to have more customers. It's just been me, and some weird guy getting coffee to go," I said glumly.

"Starla, we have things to discuss. We better order a round of something caffeinated. Your dad laid down some heavy information on us," replied Jenson.

"What did he say?"

"Quite a bit, have you had any visions or waking dreams lately?"

"Not that I'm aware of. Those experiences ended with our recent move. Unless the dream the other night was a precursor to those vamps showing up."

"Make a note of that," replied Jenson.

He and Molly scooted into the other side of the booth.

Sue stepped over to us with her order pad, a pencil in her hand. "Are you, kids going to have anything else? If not, I have to ask you to leave due to loitering laws."

"Give us a round of Espressos, whipped cream, and be generous," said Molly.

"Alright, we close at ten, well, I'll make it ten-thirty, but then you, kids need to sca-doodle, Ok?"

"Fine by me," I replied.

After Sue dropped off the espresso's Jenson laid out one measly article my father had left. *Heavy-information? This really didn't seem like much.*

It was dated February 19th, 2004, only about a week old.

He pushed it over to Molly, "Read it out loud, quietly."

"Martin Du-Vance a senior at the Shady Lane Community College suffered fatal injuries in an attack around nine p.m. on the 19th of February. It appeared as if an animal of some sort had mauled him. The victim had deep teeth penetration in the neck area along with several wounds to his abdomen and facial features. Identity was confirmed by dental records in correspondence by means of a special unit group wishing to remain unidentified for their protection. Police ask that at this time you refrain from visiting Hunters Park during the evening hours after sunset. If you do, disciplinary actions will be taken."

"What is this other entire jumble of papers?" I asked.

"My findings and an additional folder containing research completed since the night you turned up at my house as a fox. Are you're prepared to hear this?"

Molly picked up the folder, handing it to me. I scanned its contents. "This doesn't tell us anything we don't already know. It explains the visions I've received in the past during dreams, or waking ones. I thought maybe I'd gone crazy until I solved mysteries using them. Occasionally, when enemies are near, any kind, I see things happening in my head. It's not 100% accurate. The other obstacle is, it cannot be turned on and off at will. It just occurs. Does this signify me as a guardian of sorts?"

"You are a part of a clan, not sure what one, but some sort of Fox clan or alliance. I'd wanted to tell you in class. Jones doesn't have great timing. Those vampire wolves may have come to make you choose to align with them before another group gets to you. Possibly the real reason your dad came tonight. They may not have known this part of your life has been hidden from you."

"What?" I said.

"Your abilities, here look at this," Jenson pulled out the file she'd seen as a child in her father's office.

"How did you get this?"

"It was among the clippings your dad gave me. Perhaps he misplaced it? I read it on the way here."

I should have been furious, but all I did, was nod in response. "I'm not sure I want to see them. Good news or bad news?"

"That depends on you. I mean, you've known your special most of your existence, right? Don't you want to know why? I would."

Molly pulled the file towards her. Then pushed it on over to me. "You should open it."

I nodded, looking down at my empty cup of espresso. "Did anyone bring a notepad?"

"Yes, here it is." Molly slid it across to me.

I picked up the notebook and began to scribble. I heard someone clear their throat and I looked up. Our waitress set the check down on the table. Jenson took it mischievously.

"My turn, since you usually foot the bill," said Jenson, reaching into his pocket for his wallet.

Molly smiled. She knew Jenson crushed on me. My best friend understood my heart well, often teasing me that he and I should be a couple.

"OK, but just this time," I protested.

"I'll treat on the next occasion," Molly blurted.

Lately, they'd both been acting like I lost the lottery or something. Be thankful you have good friends, I scolded myself. Molly tapped the folder lying next to me, getting impatient.

"OK, I'll open it!"

On the right-hand corner of the paper was a picture of me. *When had dad gotten this? Did he know what all my abilities would be? Below it: "My findings: visions, dreams, ability to predict some future events currently. Starla may gain the capability to wield magic if properly trained by the clan, one miserly page.*

"This is pretty redundant," I said, closing the folder.

"What? It shook me up," Jenson croaked.

"Sorry, most of this I've already experienced. It doesn't explain my tat any further either."

"Are you disappointed?" asked Molly.

"No, only frustrated it didn't reveal my position in the clan."

Our waitress waltzed up to our booth. "I hate to end your little investigative party, but it's ten twenty-four. This gal is going to soak her feet tonight if ya know what I mean."

Jenson politely gave her a twenty and told her to keep the change. You should have seen her face light up. Our espressos along with my last order were pretty inexpensive.

"Let's get out of here," said Jenson.

They grabbed their things as I put on my coat. Then we made our way towards the exit. Looking back, I thought about the wolf tail I'd seen on our server. Nah, probably just my imagination.

Jenson held the door open for Molly and me.

"What were you jotting down back there?" she asked as we left.

"Oh, just some notes, questions requiring answers to solve how, and why Martin was killed. We could assume he's an innocent bystander, or he might be involved. We'll need to do some poking around."

"Research online at my house tomorrow," inquired Jenson. I gave him thumbs up.

"We need to roll, like fast. See you later, unless you want a ride," said Molly.

"Um, yeah, I'd better let you drive me," I answered.

"Let's jet," replied Jenson.

Chapter 6

(Starla, Tuesday)

I'd just woken up, soaked sheets from my bed stuck to my skin. A man was running in the woods. Who was it? I reached for my notebook on the nightstand, then set it down beside me to begin the meditation. Had it been a vision? Taking a deep breath in and out, I slowly brought myself into balance. The stress in addition to negativity simply melted away. I pushed my legs into my chest, and then stretched them out in front of me, as far as I could reach. Afterwards, I brought myself into a cross-legged position. My hands lay on my sides with my eyes shut. I let them come again; images, flashes of light...

Was it Martin? He quickly wandered down a path of green pines. There were no other trails, but that which was in front of him; on each side pine trees framed the path. It looked similar to Hunters Park. Was it? He gazed back from where he'd come from as if someone had followed him and then picked up speed, running to the side. I saw a shadow, but could not make out the silhouette. A rather large animal; nevertheless it was difficult to determine the species. It could have been a wolf or a bear, maybe even those hybrids who visited me! I observed the creature attack him from behind. It pushed him into the dirt. He tried to push it off himself with no success, subsequently, he kicked the shadowy image, momentarily distracting it. It wasn't enough. Then it grabbed for Martin's throat...

I opened my eyes, not desiring to see the blood gush from his throat again, attempting to make out more details that occurred earlier. Meditation after a dream or vision could every so often lead to new imagery or fine points otherwise missed. Picking up my pen, I wrote down what I had experienced.

Laying down my fountain pen, I reminisced... Wicca in junior high, this moment reminded me of that. It was all Willow's fault. That red-haired girl from Buffy was wicked cool! That's when meditation hit a nerve with me. I by no means spoke to my mother about it. She would've found it rather cultish. Wicca's a practice of respecting the earth over all else. Many still believe Wiccans worship the devil. It's a matter of perspective. Various groups use meditation, Native Americans, Buddhist monks, even the western Christians, but the way they meditate varies.

I slid out of my bed, pulled the covers up, and fluffed my pillows. What to wear? Then I should go downstairs for some breakfast. Picking up my jeans off of a chair, I threw them on. My green shirt, where was it? Oh, I spotted it in the hamper. Rats! I'd just have to wear the blue one hanging in my closet. I grabbed it and put it on. Slamming the closet door, I remembered Jenson and Molly wanted to see me today. I raced downstairs to get a bit to eat before heading out.

Two hours later...

"We were worried," said Molly. I'd just entered Jenson's room. She appeared as if she'd been ready to call me on speed dial. "What took you so long?"

"An unexpected vision emerged." I sat down in the overstuffed chair, noticing the map on the wall. They were the clippings dad had given us. Jenson was in his captain's chair ready to take on the internet. He had this grin on his face. *Gah, don't gush, don't gush.* Molly was on his bed among books of myths, culture, plus a few Marvel comics. She flipped through them. I considered giving her a quick squeeze, not sure why I felt the need for affection. Jenson was right there, after all. Why did I keep denying my feelings for him?

"Can I get that notebook of yours?" Jenson knelt beside me, placing a hand on my shoulder. "You OK?"

"I'm just lost in thought," I said, grabbing it out of my pack, then scooted over so he could sit by me.

Jenson opened it, skimming the pages where I'd jotted notes and sat down. I glanced at Molly, now hunting through one of our textbooks, a highlighter in her hand. I wasn't sure how it was going to assist us.

"Have you considered Martin might be involved with a gang, does he have any enemies, who were his friends?" Molly pondered looking up from her book.

"You and Starla are on the same page. She's got all that written down," he answered, holding up the notepad.

"Ah, we need to find Martin in the student directory. Technically, we could have had classes with him and never knew," I replied.

"Good idea. We do need to be, a bit discreet," answered Jenson.

"What about a web page? Most students are starting to use them now. Check Google," suggested Molly.

Jenson leapt up from alongside me, nearly knocking me to the ground as he scrambled to get to his computer. "I got this!"

Molly and I observed from the sidelines. Jenson typed in Martin Du-Vance into the search engine. After he typed in the address, an image of adorable cuteness popped up on his page.

"This page is basic. He used HTML to set it up. It claims he lives in Willow Brook. That's a subdivision a few miles from here." Jenson scrolled down to several pictures of Hunters Park. It described hikes for beginners and warned people to stay on the trails. "Nothing unusual there for someone interning for a Ranger's position."

"How about his hobbies?" I asked.

"Umm, here it is on the last page. He enjoys fishing, hunting, hiking, and reading books. Note, check out the book club on campus to see if he has any acquaintances. No friends are listed," observed Jenson.

I pushed away from the computer area, pacing back and forth. "Maybe we should visit Hunters Park today. It's only, what, one o'clock," I said, staring at my wrist watch.

"First explain that vision thingy you had," insisted Molly.

"There was a path of green pines. Martin was running on the trail away from a shadowy image. He tried to escape his attacker. I couldn't make out what assaulted him. If we go to the site, perhaps I'll find a connection?"

Jenson nodded in response, "We have to start somewhere."

I touched my arm, vibrations; did I just feel my birthmark, vibrate? Lingering near the door, I watched Jenson and Molly get their things together so we could leave.

"Ready?"

"Sure," I said, grabbing my own pack.

"Who's driving, or are we hoofing it?" asked Molly.

"I'll drive," said Jenson. "You two can be my co-pilots, and we'll need some snacks!"

"Snacks, what about lunch? Girls cannot survive on snacks alone," said Molly.

"We'll pick up something on the way to the park, and then eat there," I said.

We hurried along the path, the wind blowing fiercely while the sky threatened rain. I shivered, "This is it, right where he'd been attacked," I said. I held my coat tight to me, not sure of what I expected to find. The area had already been scoped out by local law enforcement. If there was anything left, it was certainly long gone by now. *Giving up is not an option, something could still be here.* I tried to shake off the voice in my head. Jenson and Molly had already started to explore the perimeter.

"Fox prints, should we follow them?" asked Molly.

Kneeling down to get a closer look, I scoured the ground for clues. The paw prints much resembled that of a dog. "These could be fresh tracks, but it's hard to be sure," I said, brushing the dirt off my pants. "OK, let's see where these lead."

The prints guided us in circles on both edges of the pine trees, leading us out into the street where the park ended.

"It just stops," I said to Jenson.

"What about going into the forest?" suggested Molly.

"I didn't see any prints leading into the trees, and my dad said to stay safe. Our best bet would be to go to the ranger's station. It's that way." I pointed behind us. "We just ignored it coming in. I wanted to go to the precise site of my vision. It sure didn't tell me much. When my paw print vibrated earlier, I thought it meant something."

"When?" asked Jenson.

"Right before we left. I was talking about the green pine trees, considering it might hold meaning. It's glowed before, but never vibrated-- why would it just react to things with no purpose?"

"Your clan!" exclaimed Molly.

"Shh," Jenson covered her mouth with his hands. "We don't know who is out here. Anyone could be listening. There could be shape shifters," he said, slowly removing his hand from her mouth.

"Sorry," Jenson, she whispered.

Out of the corner of the trees came a quick swishing sound, something was running towards us.

"Back up, now," I called out.

All of us took a few paces backward into the pines. The deer leaped out of the woods, across to the other side of the trees. Trotting after it was a wolf. It paid us no mind, just kept on racing after its food. There was a chance it was one of the hybrids. I mean, heck, in Buffy, Angel had survived on animal blood, so why not here in the midst of real life? Me, on the other hand, I wasn't ready to dive into that world yet.

"Come on guys, ranger's station," I prodded. "I'd rather not run into any blood-sucking enemies today."

I took Molly and Jenson's hands, not caring if we looked geeky. The sun began to set behind us. After what happened to Martin, risk taking wasn't on my agenda. I felt safer being physically connected. Listening, I heard our stomachs growl. We'd missed lunch. No one could compromise on anyplace to get food for one thing; on the other hand, all of us were low on cash.

I looked at Molly, "I'm sure that my mom won't mind if you both join us for dinner tonight," I offered as we approached the ranger's station. "Ha, look at him, lazy man. He's sitting in there watching TV!"

"Doofus! He's viewing monitors of the forest," said Jenson. He gave me a playful slap on the back.

"Oh, how do you know?" I asked.

Jenson shook his head and knocked on the front door. What would we say? It wasn't like we knew Martin, we only knew of him. Man, were we ever going to look shady.

"Let me handle this," urged Jenson.

I scoffed. Yep, that was his ego talking. I'd just let him have the moment, why not?

The ranger got up from his desk, heading towards the office door; his name badge said, Mike. Hmm, that was a nice name.

"Hi, I'm Ranger Mike, . Can I be of any help to you, kids? I have pamphlets on the trails if you're interested. I can even take you on some tours of the paths sometime. Right now it's almost six o'clock. It's getting late and dark. If you're interested, though, let me know." He turned to grab the pamphlets mounted to the wall. "Here you go, anything else?" he asked.

"Yeah," said Jenson. " We have a few questions to ask you."

"OK, what kind of questions?"

"We heard about Martin Du-Vance. We went to school with him and are a bit concerned."

"I understand, but you should let the police take care of this," Mike replied.

"Maybe you know my dad, Dan?" I asked, figuring it was worth a shot.

"Yeah, he was by here the other day with some detectives. Are you Starla?"

"Yes, I guess I should have introduced myself."

"He told me if you came by to give you this folder and to call him. Now, I know you have solved other mysteries; furthermore, I'm not to reveal anything to you just yet. Call your dad, it's urgent. Then meet me back here tomorrow. Do you have classes?"

"It's Wednesday, but Molly has church," I replied, taking the blue file from him.

"Well then, after church, if it's possible. Here's my card. Once you talk to your father, I can clue you in on the park, how things work here, including--"

He stopped short, looking around to see if anyone was listening, gathering us close. "Things go on here I'm not allowed to talk about unless you're part of the circle. There are many circles or groups. I'll discuss it with all of you. When you are approved later. You kids get along now, stay together. I don't want anything to happen to you. I've heard good things about you, Starla. You'll make a great addition to the team. Damn, did I just say that?"

I smiled at him, "You sure did," I answered, patting him on the back. "It's OK, I'll call you." I took his card as he handed it to me.

Chapter 7

We sat at the table and devoured massive amounts of spaghetti.

"Mom, this is great, exactly what we needed after our long day of exploring and investigating. Ranger Mike, needs me to call dad. It's necessary for the case; however, I know you're not thrilled about us being involved."

My mom gave me a compassionate smile. "Honey, you know I loved your father, sometimes I think I still do. We just have different ideas about what's best for you." She sighed, "I am starting to think, and I hate, to say this, but he's right. You're not a little girl any longer. Please remember to keep an open mind when you call him." She glanced at my friends, then back at me. I waited for her to continue, but she went back to stabbing her spaghetti.

"So, where's Megan tonight?" Molly asked.

"Oh, she's off with Carol, a new girlfriend of hers. They wanted to check out that old roller rink," Tri said.

"Have you guys ever been to one?" I asked Jenson and Molly.

"When we were kids Molly and I used to hang out there, but it's been a while."

"Yep, we'll have to drag you there when we're not on a crazy mega mission," Molly quipped.

I laughed, and scooped up large amounts of noodles into my mouth, taking time to observe the smiles on the faces around me before swallowing my food. It felt good to be relaxing. Any second it could change-- the phone would ring, and wham! For the moment it was peaceful, but it wouldn't last long. It never did, for me.

I grabbed Jenson's hand under the table. I'm not sure what made me do it. He smiled at me without a word. It was better that way. I didn't want Molly to feel bad. She must be lonely. I wanted to hug her, give her comfort, but I also didn't want to make her upset or give her the wrong impression.

"How are things with you?" I asked, looking up at Molly.

"Hmm, I don't know, church isn't what it once was for me."

"Everything changes. It doesn't hurt to explore other religious beliefs. You might find a place you fit," Tri responded.

"Ma...Maybe," stammered Molly in a shaky voice.

I patted her on the back gently. I realized her family stood firm in its beliefs. She would need a lot of support from us. I pushed my plate away, "Mom, should we wash the dishes?"

"Nah, you ought to phone your father. Go, and I'll finish things up. Molly, I'm not sure when your curfew is, but Jenson you need to leave by ten, please."

"Yes, ma'am," he said.

We exited the kitchen before mom decided to change her mind.

Cozy up in my room, we sat with the door ajar. My mother had it in her head that something wild and crazy just might occur if it was closed. Sigh, I hadn't even thought about messing around with a boy. Frankly, school, my family, and chaos had taken care of that. Now at odds with myself, I sat with my cell phone next to me. I continued to watch it, confident it would ring so I didn't have to make the call.

"Starla, just call him! It's almost ten. Jenson will have to leave soon," said Molly.

"I know, I know."

Jenson gave me a sympathetic gaze. It had been fine. I'd geared myself up to call him, and then wham! Moving forward would mean accepting this reality. Could I allow my father into my life completely? This could either change my entire existence or bring it to a close. Grow up, I thought and grabbed the cell and hit speed dial. It rang two, then three times, and then click he picked up.

"Hey, Starla put me on speaker. Is everyone there?"

"Yes, dad," I said, putting the speaker phone on.

"Now, what happened? Did you go see Mike? Is there any new evidence?"

"Dad, Ranger Mike refused to pass on any specific details. He said we had to be approved. What does 'a part of a circle' mean?"

"There are several groups, we call them clans. Each group has their own territories protected by a guardian. Be honest with me. Have you had any eccentric visitors recently?"

"Eccentric isn't the word for it! The night I had leads me to believe you've lied to me my entire life. I'm not exactly sure this is something we should talk about in front of my friends."

"Starla, they're already involved. Now, enlighten me."

I recapped my dad on the night's events when I'd met the vampire wolves, along with my experience of transforming into a fox. He listened and seemed grateful Jenson had been there for me.

"Now Starla, just do your best not to panic," he chuckled.

"Dad, um, you put me in these situations. Why?" I demanded.

"Hunters Park is the hub for a fox clan, one you are part of. Ranger Mike, has had to infiltrate into other divisions. We suspect that someone from an outside clan killed Du-Vance."

"What? Was Du-Vance, part of Starla's clan?" Jenson asked.

"Yes, and recently we deduced he tried to create a peace treaty with a not so diplomatic group. At this time, we're not sure why, but we are attempting to find out. There are a lot of assumptions, but no answers. Mike has been leery of who enters and exits the park during moonlight hours. It's when our clan is most active. The vampire wolf hybrids have been assisting in protecting us. That is why they contacted you, not to hurt you. However, they assumed I'd told you about our heritage. It upsets your mother. She's never trusted Lance and Shellena. I'll call Mike and give him the go ahead. He'll set up a time for you to meet your clan."

I shuddered--, alone? No, not without my backup. Yeah, I trusted Mr. Mike the Ranger, but how long had I known him, ten minutes maybe? It wasn't as if my dad was releasing all the data at once. He was giving me small pieces, tidbits of what he wanted me to know. It really pissed me off!

"On one condition, Molly and Jenson, you said they're already involved. You've planned for them to be here during this conversation. I want them by my side throughout this entire process. I don't want to be unaccompanied."

"OK, fine," he stated, and the phone clicked off.

"Huh, disconnected?" I set the cell down on my nightstand and stood up.

"Well, he sure as heck didn't give us a lot to go on, did he?" asked Molly.

Tears filled my eyes, "Yeah, tell me I'm a part of a clan, as if I didn't already know from his notebook, after that chuckle at me, and then act like I'm going in solo! What a bright idea," I replied sarcastically.

"Now wait, maybe your dad got interrupted. Do you actually believe he'd hang up like that?" Jenson asked.

I pouted, "I don't know, in fact, I barely know my dad at all. This is the first time he's shown up in years. One day he packed his things. He told my mother to take care of me. There was no discussion, apparently she knew how to raise me better than he did. It might have been over all this crap going on now. I'm a fox and a part of a clan, one I get to meet tomorrow," I smiled through my tears.

"How do you feel?" asked Molly.

"Confused, excited, scared, and unsure."

"It sounds about right," said Jenson.

"What about your sister, if he left?"

"I ask myself that all the time. Possibly dad came back for a late night rendezvous or my mom is very sly."

At that instant, I considered my mother must be a fox, but if I was part human, was my dad? I shook it off. One of them was a fox, and one a human. I had that sorted out in my mind. I'd have to let it sit.

"I've got to go, or your mom will kick me out. It's after ten," said Jenson.

I hugged Jenson, then Molly.

"What time do you get out of the church?"

"About one, pick me up from there, please, you and Jenson?"

"Sounds good, I'll just walk you both out."

I trotted down the stairs. My friends followed and we said our goodbyes. Slowly, I shut the door behind them.

Chapter 8

11 P.M. I stared at the clock and hugged my teddy bear tight. Mom had offered to stay with me until I fell asleep. Um, no thanks, not at 19 years old, if I'd been normal I'd be checking my e-mail. I threw the bear across the room. It bounced off the wall to the right of my bookshelf, knocking off the blue folder; papers flew, gravity pulled them to the floor.

If only Molly didn't have to attend church. I turned on my lamp, hopped out of bed, nearly bouncing to the floor. I pushed out my hands onto the cold wood beneath my feet. Gosh, it felt good to stretch out, the ground felt nice, maybe it was the fox coming out in me? I wasn't even in that form. I brought myself back up to the upward dog yoga position. What was in that folder the ranger had given me? I didn't remember putting it on that shelf.

I shuffled over to it, picking them up. They were numbered, I noticed dates, faces of missing people, and where they had been attacked. It went as far back as 1977. I put them back in order debating whether I should continue to go through them. It must have something to do with this case, pieces they considered might fit together with Du-Vance's death. The only difference was these people might still be alive somewhere. Well, it couldn't hurt to study them...

A picture of a skinny tall boy with light brownish hair was displayed on the left-hand corner of the page. It read below:

<u>Lang Orion</u>, Male went missing February of 1977, he was 19 years old, and his family said he'd been out for a walk in Hunters Park. Friends from school claimed that Lang went there hoping to catch a glimpse of a few fox's, wolves or similar animals. He'd been studying mythology and wanted to be a historian who specialized in local legends. There was nothing currently in print to prove any supernatural animals existed, but gossip spread, when a sighting took place by a few local students. They thought they had seen an image of a lady running in the woods who mystically transformed into a fox. The police re-assured these pupils that it had been a hallucination due to sleep loss and peyote, a herb usually used in Native American tribes they had obtained from a friend. The students denied obtaining the natural drug. Officers didn't know why these students were left unharmed. No names have been released for their own protection. (He would be 46 now, I thought.)

The ranger had made notes in the margins. Why would the officers use the word "unharmed"? Disappearances did not mean a fatality. Who could have taken Lang? If I wasn't myself being protected from my clan, could I have helped them? Was this why my mother left? I saw nothing else written so I turned the page.

Hmm, this person, I did a double take. She looked almost like... *No!*

A girl with golden blonde hair stared back at me, trim, yet curvy, big brown eyes just as I had remembered her. We went to kindergarten together when I was five back in L.A. The memories were fuzzy. A bit blurred together. Our parents were close... were they? We used to talk about dreams, fears, and hopes. Little girls create imaginary ideas, worlds, and friends. We were only five then. She had moved three years later in 1994.

Myth

<u>Cal Summers</u> In May of 1997, Cal would have been 11, it claimed she was playing in the park when she swore to her mother she'd seen a lost dog wandering among several pine trees. Kris Summers told her daughter to come along, leave the dog alone. Cal quickly turned away from her mother, running towards where she thought she'd seen the animal. A bit old to be chasing a dog, I thought. Kris at first searched for her with no results. Later she returned to the ranger's station where Dale, an older gentleman, called the cops. Not a trace of evidence had been left behind to prove Cal had even been in the park. Kris filed a missing person's report for her daughter after 24 hours. Police consulted her at the station. A party was formed to search for the girl. Summers claimed her daughter must have been kidnapped, but the police found no signs of a struggle.

It's 2004, that was seven years ago! How could Martin Duvance be tied into this? He wasn't 19 years old. Usually, criminals followed a pattern. How odd, peculiar, even, but it could be a coincidence. Chills started to creep down my back. Looking up, I realized I'd left my window opened; setting down the files; I stood up, quickly to shut it. The moon held an eerie glow. I placed a hand on the window, staring out into the night. The trees swayed in our yard, everyone was in for the evening apparently. A few cars were parked on the side lot beyond our complex. *Martin why did you die, yet these people lived? Are they still alive? What is their secret? Is it one someone else wants to be kept?* My hand felt for the lock and latched it.

Now back down on the floor I turned the page to Martin's file. Twenty-nine years old? That seemed pretty mature to be in college doing an internship. Why hadn't Mike mentioned it? I fingered the picture in the corner as a wave of nausea hit me. Gradually moving my body to the floor, I enjoyed the coolness radiating off the wood. What about his family? They must be worried. Did Ranger Mike, have facts on them? No notes in the margins. I wanted answers. A few more pages lay beyond this one. Perhaps there were files on his Dad, Mom, and did he have any siblings? Rascal, the name was at the bottom of the page following it was his current address, nothing else. Had he been questioned? Did he know anything or care about this man?

Getting my bearings, I sat up. My bathroom was to the right of me. One nice thing about the small room I'd gained. Still not quite myself, I slide across the floor to it, and stood up. Once inside I used the sink to steady myself, I hit the light and turned on the faucet. I let the cold water run over my hands, wetted my neck, then my hair, grabbed a Dixie cup, filled it with water, and drank. That was the best water I'd ever had. What had made me so dehydrated? Too much caffeine before bed? Was that why I was still up? Flicking the light switch off, I picked the documents up off the floor. I sat them back up on the bookshelf and placed my teddy bear on top of them. My hand lingered on my bear. I remembered when I believed he could protect me from all things, just like my father, and mother. Those were the days.

Now, back in bed, unanswered questions still weighed heavily on my mind. The case alone was not my only concern. My friendships were changing. I was changing. Snuggling down, I tried not to think. I'd thought enough, for one day. It was time to drift, to be calm, to let my worries float into the sky and give them to a higher power. I would worry again when I awakened.

(Wednesday)

Bright rays of light illuminated into my room through the curtains that framed my window. No, it can't be morning. I pulled the covers over my head to drown out the sun. My alarm had already rung several times. It finally got the hint, shutting itself off automatically.

"Starla, breakfast," my mom hollered.

Food was the last thing on my mind after being up so late.

"Starla, you know mom is calling you," said my sister. She stood in my doorway in her blue flannel pajamas with pink bunny slippers. She slid one off and threw it at me.

I caught it and sent it right back her way, hitting her on the leg. "Score," I sang out.

I pulled my covers off of myself and jumped up to grab the robe lying on the floor. Before I could retrieve it, Megan tackled me to the bed, instantly a tickle fest erupted.

"Stop, stop!" I snickered, pushing her hands away from my armpits and belly area.

"Give up yet?" she asked.

"Yes, I give up."

Megan got up, slid off the bed giving me a mischievous grin, "You'd better come down for breakfast."

"Definitely, once I'm dressed." I tossed my robe aside that I'd never put on. I got up and pulled items out of my dresser. A pair of faded blue jeans; they were old, yet do-able.

"Are you going to wear those?" she asked.

"Yep, and this old green T-shirt will do. I'm just going to the park later today. Is mom, angry?" I asked.

"Not really, she's just dealing with stuff, you know with dad being back. It can't be easy for her. I assume she still loves him. I'm not sure how you see it. If only you'd seen the way they hugged. You'd already left in a huff that night. I wasn't supposed to be watching, but I'm a good spy, sis. Let me know if you ever need me to help you, alongside your friends."

"You might be on to something there. We'll just have to wait it out, observe what happens. I haven't been around much. Homework never seems to end, then this? I didn't expect to be..."

I stopped. Did my sister even know what was going on? Did she know I was a fox? Clearly she knew about the mystery, so that must be OK to bring up.

"I heard mom talking to dad on the phone. She mentioned a clan. What is it? Do you and I belong to a biker gang? What kind of word is clan anyway? We're not bears, are we?"

"Nope, we're not bears," I answered her. "It's just a group I'm meeting for the assignment dad gave me. You don't have to be worried."

"OK," she shrugged it off.

I touched her shoulder. "Sis, I'd been hoping we'd get some time to spend together after the move. Then with me, starting at Denny's I got caught up in making money to help mom with my tuition. Things have happened to me, I never expected to. Jenson, I really like him yet I'm not sure if it's right. Then out jumps dad with this mystery he wants me to solve. I just want you to know I'm still here."

She rolled her eyes at me and I pulled her into a hug.

"Please don't get mushy in front of mom. I don't want her to think that we're best friends," Megan chirped.

"No way!" I replied. Then shoved her playfully. We shot down the stairs like tornados into the kitchen.

"You girls are definitely up to something today," my mom noted as she sat down at the table.

I pulled up a seat, grabbed for the cornflakes and placed them in my bowl. I munched on them without milk. "Not really. We just haven't gotten our sibling rivalry in lately. I wouldn't want you to think we're best buddies. Not happening."

"Nope," replied Megan.

My mom grinned as if she knew differently.

We ate breakfast in silence, that's how we liked to conspire. We weren't against mom. It was just that some things were better left unsaid. Mom hadn't always stayed at home with us. When we were younger, we relied on each other. I trusted my sister even if there were times we fought. I'd never had to be concerned when it came to her having my back or likewise. She may have been younger, but at times, she'd been wiser.

Chapter 9

Damn Jenson, where are you? I stood outside, freezing. My game of Bejeweled on my flip phone wore thin. I switched it off to check the time, almost one thirty. Where could he be? This wasn't like him. In all the years I'd known him, he'd been adamant about arriving on time. Absent-mindedly I scanned pictures taken weeks ago at the college orientation. It was just before my job at Denny's began. I considered calling Molly when her parent's car pulled into the drive. Jenson sat next to her in the back seat. Jenson and church, I scoffed.

My heart raced with fear. Were they together? Why would they be? Molly wasn't interested in boys, was she? She said goodbye to her parents while Jenson stood off to the side wearing a confused expression on his face. It sort of matched his clothes, a purple tie over a blue dress shirt and jeans. Not exactly church attire, but who was I to judge?

Once Molly exited the car, I grabbed her sleeve and pulled her aside privately.

"Give us a minute," I said eyeing Jenson. Molly's parents lingered in the driveway.

"What's going on with you? What's wrong?" she asked me.

"You can't keep this up, you need to let go. When are you going to tell your folks, what's going on with you?" I asked.

"What about you and Jenson? Are you going to keep leading him on? I've seen all the signals. You're not up front with him. I just invited him to church, what's so immoral about that!"

She was upset, and frankly, I didn't have a response for her. She was right. I lowered my eyes, feeling her hand on my arm. She took her other hand and gently pushed my chin up so I could see her face.

"I care about you too, but I have to keep them at bay somehow," she said, looking back at her parents as they pulled out of the driveway.

"Do you know what my church does to people like me? It's not pretty. I'll end up at one of those pray it away sessions, in group therapy, or they could even send me away," she gulped. "It's just until I can get out on my own, until then I have to act like Jenson and I are..."

She trailed off when she observed Jenson staring at us. I wondered if he thought we were going to kiss. What? Boys are like that, at least most of the boys I knew. Maybe they had changed since high school. Who knows?

I pulled her into a quick hug.

"Honey, does he know?" I asked. "We can't both be giving him mixed signals."

"He thinks it's just a friend thing. I've dated guys and can't stomach it anymore."

"Tell Jenson, he'll understand. It won't be nearly as scary as telling your parents. It surprised me he even went to church with you today."

"OK, but promise me that eventually you and Jenson... When I see you guys together it makes my own heart melt. That's to say the least," gushed Molly. We smiled at each other, our heads touching, giggled a bit, then separated, glimpsing where Jenson stood waiting.

As I waved him over to join us, I asked Molly, "Now how are we going to get to Hunters Park?"

"We're going to get my car," Jenson interrupted. "Are you girls done?" he asked, annoyed.

I felt the tension inside me grow. I wasn't angry at him, more hurt than anything. Jenson and I had disagreements, but he had to understand that sometimes Molly needed me.

"How was the service?" I said, moving closer to him.

He fidgeted with his clothes a bit, "I need to get out of this outfit. It's not very comfortable. Are we supposed to meet your... them at any certain time?"

"Nope, we'll just head over to your place so you can change, swing by that coffee shop near the college, and we can eat on the way."

Jenson started walking ahead of us. We followed.

"Hey," Molly said. She grabbed Jenson's shoulder. "Don't be angry with Starla. I needed to talk to her about something. I have a lot going on right now. We need to concentrate on this. I promise we'll fill you in later."

He looked at her and kept moving forward. I heard him mutter under his breath "OK." Slowing down, he let us catch up with him.

"Church was OK; I've heard it all before. I don't know how you deal with it every Wednesday," he said to Molly.

"It's not that bad. I mean, if you think about the unconditional love, grace, and peace and understanding part. I like to think someone is up there watching over us. The fire and brimstone that is spoken of at times there, not so much."

I stared out the window, admiring the sunshine that gleamed throughout the trees, leaving shadows on the pavement as we passed. I touched the molding on the glass. Then felt the car turn as Jenson pulled left into the Rangers station. It appeared deserted until I spotted a few cars in the lot. A moped, pretty cool, I thought. Pink too, sweet! Who did it belong to? The license plate had a fox paw on it, but other than that it was the usual Springville plate.

"Did you call Ranger Mike?" asked Jenson, parking the car next to a blue Tempo.

"No, I never had time, after you and Molly left it was pretty late. My teddy bear got more sleep than I did, in spite of his ability to fly across the room."

"So--," said Molly.

"Teddy bears don't just fly across the room," Jenson interrupted.

"OK, I threw the bear, Mr. Teddy deserved it, he was supposed to comfort me and he didn't! It made me angry that I couldn't sleep, also sort of afraid someone from the clan might show up. Doubtful I know, but possible. I hit the files on a shelf in my room. As a result of Teddy's adventure, flying papers went falling via Mr. Gravity. So I ended up digging around where I shouldn't have."

"Any new information?" asked Molly.

I realized Mike was jogging towards our vehicle. Great timing mister, I thought as I unbuckled my safety belt.

"Yeah, as usual, it will have to wait, or we'll have to discuss it with Mike. I look forward to you both being cleared for take off."

"Meaning?" asked Jenson.

"That you and Molly have been OK'd to be a part of everything involved in my new life. Not only the mystery, but my new identity, or old identity, I'm not sure which it is."

Mike rapped on the car window. Jenson rolled it down.

"Hi, how's it going?" Jenson asked.

"Good, you never called," he said, eyeing me.

I felt guilty, but it was an honest mistake.

"Sorry," I said, getting ready to open the car door.

"I have some donuts and coffee up at the station. Starla, did you go over those files? I thought maybe you might have gotten a chance to look at them. I know I never asked you to, but I just sort of assumed you being your dad's daughter and all."

"Teddy had an adventure and on that journey, I decided I ought to look at the archive."

"You are a strange girl," Ranger Mike, replied, shaking his head.

"No, she is just awfully witty," said Molly and grinned.

"Oh Starla," Jenson sighed, giving me a side glance, then busted out in laughter.

We exited the car en route to the station. Ranger Mike, must have thought we were all nuts.

"Here we are," the ranger opened the door for us to step in. The room was fairly small. Straight ahead was the viewing area for the park. It had a few seats. Monitors sat on a low hung desk attached to the wall.

"The refreshments are over here," he said, leading the way into a large conference area. "Let's sit and talk about our current circumstances. I want to fill you in on what I couldn't yesterday. Starla, your friends have all been given the OK to help you."

"Thanks," I said, sitting down. Jenson and Molly followed suit.

"So, you don't want to discuss the files I found first?" I asked, reaching for a ring of yummy glazed goodness. I began to eat, and my friends helped themselves to the varieties at hand.

"I need to fill you in on how the park works. You can't just be wandering about wherever you wish. You see, your clan lives on one side of the pines. The other side is wolf territory."

"That must be why we saw that wolf, but he leaped out of the woods chasing after a deer. Was he coming from his territory, or the fox?" asked Molly.

"Oh, they are both allowed to cross lines for hunting purposes, but preying on each other is forbidden while they share the same habitat. My rules, not theirs, but they have managed to live by them so far," he replied.

We nodded in response.

"The vampire hybrid wolves? Now where do they live?" Jenson piped up. "I can't imagine they are too far away if they found Starla."

"Ah, Shellena, and Lance have their own story. The wolf pack they once held a partnership with abandoned them once they, uh..."

"They were bitten by vampires!" I said, in my excitement.

"The pack they had belonged to was a sorry bunch anyway. I didn't much care for them. I'd only met them once, and it wasn't pleasant. It was during a festival called "The Peace of Difference." That is where I encountered them attempting to create conflict. I had to break up the brawl before it got out of hand. In the case of the wolves, we have three different packs in the area. Trinity is a pack of three. They mostly keep to themselves. The Crusaders tend to watch over the park in subtle ways. I don't see them often. They only contact me if necessary. Shellena and Lance pretty much stand alone as allies of ours."

"The wolves that live on the other side of our fox clan, which are they? What can we expect from them?" I asked.

"The Crusaders live across from us, most of the time they are cooperative. We've had some issues of fights between the clans." Mike took a sip of his coffee then set it down. "Things actually had calmed down. That is until Martin Du-Vance's body showed up in our woods. The first thing I asked myself, is who is to blame?"

"They could be outsiders. We cannot assume the clans here had anything to do with it, can we?" asked Jenson.

"I suppose you're right. You have the file I gave you as well as the newspaper report. Currently suspects are limited. Your father, Starla, is one of the best investigators we have. The police do their best to work with us. I've tried to get your mom to join for years, but she's still being stubborn."

"Have you spoken with Martin Du-Vance's father? You have to ask yourself what the connections are between Martin and the clan. If he was an active member, is there a reason he may have been killed? If you don't call his father in for questioning, then what have we got to go on? The reason I ask is because I saw no file in that pile pertaining, to his dad, except for a current address. The odd thing is the papers never mention any living family members," I probed.

"It's pretty taboo on our end. Rascal, that's what Du-vance called his dad. He said he was a pretty private person. I know for a fact he asked the papers to only state what happened to his son. He didn't want to be publicly involved, considering this an incredibly private matter due to his circumstances. Dan, I mean your father, has spoken with him briefly about this tragedy. I know little about Rascal except for what Martin told me while on duty here, divulging few details. I have no clue how they might fit together. Du-vance said after his mother died things changed between them. They grew closer than they'd ever been before. Then about a year later his father became involved with a woman. Martin said it was the happiest he'd ever seen him. Then all of a sudden she broke it off. Du-vance had no clue why this woman would want to hurt his dad. The only other detail I recall Martin sharing with me was the pride his father felt when he told him he wanted to become a ranger. He was learning how to protect the clans' territories and to observe humans around him and others who could prove fatal to our existence. We have few human allies."

"That's all we have to go on?" I asked.

"For right now," stated the ranger, getting up to remove the empty donut box from the table.

"I can't sit anymore," complained Molly.

"Me either," I replied.

"About that, do you kids want to take a stroll around the grounds?" Mike stood up and stretched.

"I thought I was going to meet my clan today. What about the other people in those files? I still have a lot of questions." I shot up out of my seat, "I knew Cal Summers!"

Mike's eyes grew wide, his jaw dropped.

"Yes, we attended elementary school together in L.A. I was five. It shocked me to see her in the missing person file. She may have been a part of my clan. These missing kids must have connections to Du-vance; he ought to have known something. Was he trying to find them, and someone found out?"

Chapter 10

"Starla, if you're going to meet with your clan today, you must do it alone. I'll go over the police reports I was not yet permitted to disclose to you. I can't make any promises when it comes to giving you answers. You wanted your friends with you, I get that. Right now even with the approval of the clan, things are pretty unstable with some of our members. If I send you in there by yourself, they'll be more at ease. I'll be here, observing from afar. Heck, your friends can stand on the outskirts near the entrance, but going by yourself, shows bravery. They truly admire that kind of thing." He looked over at Molly and Jenson. "How do you two feel about that?"

"He's right, you should go. Why would he send you out there, if something was going to happen?" questioned Molly.

Jenson shook his head. "I don't care if it's in the middle of the day. Martin Du-vance is dead, we have missing people, and you want to send my girlfriend out into the woods alone! Nuh uh, I don't think so, mister."

"Jenson!" I exclaimed.

"You are a girl and my friend. Plus, I care for you, but we'll talk about it later, in private," he stated firmly.

"I'll go. I'm not pleased about it," I muttered, giving him an angry stare.

Mike instructed me. "When you get to the clearing, sit cross-legged, meditate. Find yourself, your center first of all. I realize you've only transformed through being startled, or was it panic? Anyway, they will be watching."

"So not only do I have to go alone, but I have to transform into a fox?"

"Yes, that way they know you're who you claim to be. It's the only way," he concluded.

My friends hugged me goodbye. I shot the ranger a bit of a dirty look. I didn't hate him; I was just upset.

The pine trees smelled fantastic. Thankful for the cold weather for a change, I hurried along and hummed to soothe myself. It was a crock, this entire "meet them by yourself" crap. If, that was how it must be done, I would do it. Reflections swirled in my head, taking over. I let them run wild. I'd really stunned Mike when I'd told him about Cal. I'd never forget the expression on his face. If only he'd given me more answers. My only choice was to admit we'd hit a dead end until new evidence presented itself. Still, I needed to find out why my tattoo, or clan print, acted the way it did. Each step I took seemed to push me one step back.

I was in the middle of two lives, one I'd always known as a human and then myself as a fox. Was I scared? A little. Breathing in the sweet aroma, I took in my surroundings. It was just as it had looked before, big tall pines on either side of the trail. I sat cross-legged in meditation, pushed my arms out in front of me, flexed my fingers and moved my wrists as if I were making them dance. I brought them down to the ground, jamming my hands into the earth as I had my paws when I'd run to go to Jenson's that night. Slowly rising up into my throat, the panic rose. I can't say it felt any more pleasant this time than before. The transformation started from my torso and worked its way out. My whole body ripped inside out. I saw them, foxes started to trot out one by one. How many were there? I continued in pain until my last whisker set itself in place.

Then I glanced at the clothes I had been wearing lying next to me. They'd been torn in places my fox body couldn't fit into. I backed up as if to leave when one of them stepped forward towards me.

"My name is Star. Please don't run, I too am both human and fox. Please listen, hear me out before choosing to go."

I nodded in response, and she continued.

"I suspect with your arrival you've agreed to help us. Nevertheless, I do not wish to assume you'd want to live here, being accustomed to your home. You're entitled to both lives as a clan member and a human. Where you choose to reside is yours alone. I've experienced many who have come and gone. We each have our specialties."

Star bows before me. I gave her an odd expression, but am not sure what it is, since I have not seen myself as a fox in my bathroom mirror.

"Specialties?" I asked.

"Yes, I am sort of a gypsy rare amongst our clan, but I traveled with shamans for a while, learning about natural medicine, herbs, and how to heal my people in combat if needed... I did this for a bit, and it is still in my blood. You see my mother and father..."

She turned her face aside, I noticed her bringing up her paw to wipe away a tear or clean something out of her eyes.

"We were all training to be healers. We planned to split up into diverse clans to offer our members protection in the North. I'd intended on somewhere in the Lower Peninsula in Michigan. My parents sought to work in the cities of Detroit. Our clans were incredibly vulnerable there. They searched for people similar to you and me. I'd warned them with all of the gang influence, it would be quite difficult if not impossible. A pack who called themselves the Bandits, dangerous wolf-hybrids, were among tribes we feared the most."

I leisurely stepped closer to her as she told me this account. It must have been difficult to open up to me like this. A complete stranger, it took a lot of guts, I thought as she continued.

"While they left for Detroit, I traveled to a small town named Charlevoix. So serene, quiet, stable and the clan there, amazing! Not all of us were halfsies, but at the time, I'd chosen to reside among them. We integrated into the lives of humans, but for me, it didn't last. An anxiety of uneasiness seemed to grow the longer I remained in tranquility. One of the clan members noticed this, someone who lived near Dead Man's Hill, a scenic overlook. This boy offered to help me go back to Detroit to be with my parents."

"What happened?" I asked, growing impatient.

"When we got to Detroit, I didn't even know where they lived. We went to some of the suburbs like Royal Oak and Southfield. Their parks are industrial, without many places to hide. We located my parents amongst others massacred in a park named River Rouge. It's one reason we've had you stay hidden." She shook her head from side to side. "It shouldn't be this way."

"Is this why my mom and dad split up? What do you expect from me?"

"Deep down, you know. I heard that Shellena and Lance visited you. They weren't supposed to do that. I'd told them to wait. They're always in a hurry to take things into their own hands. Dan tried to convince your mother it was time. You'd just gotten into town and I had spoken with him about how he would tell you. I didn't want you to find out like that. I'm grateful to Jenson and Molly for standing by you. Jenson could have turned you away. He didn't. Hang on to that boy."

"If I choose to be a fox, I won't be able to be with him will I?"

"Starla, look at your mother. It doesn't have to be like that."

"What is it like?" I asked, and looked around at the others observing our discussion.

"Ask your mother, now for the matter regarding Du-Vance's case. We're afraid his death may be related to his father's relationship with a clan member: Nuria, a girl who ran off."

"How would that fit? What about the missing people, Lang Orion and Cal Summers? Perhaps Du-Vance was connected in some way to them. If so, maybe whoever killed him didn't want them found," I interrupted.

"Good point, that's something we'll take into consideration." Star gestured towards a fox with dark reddish markings. "Starla, this is Eva."

"Hello, I am she," she said, stepping forward next to Star.

What a beautiful fox, how strange?

"So you are a suspect in all this?" I asked. She ignored me.

"You have a gift. The tattoo on your arm can sense things."

"So, it's not like I know what half of it even means. I'm still trying to determine its purpose," I replied.

"Cal Summers is my daughter."

"This isn't right. Cal's mom's name is Kris and she's human! What did you do with her?" I demanded.

Eva laughed, "Nothing, it's the name I go by in human form."

"My dad, he knew Cal was like me?"

"Mmm hmm," she replied.

"DAMMIT," I said, doing my whole pacing thing, shaking out my fur in anger. "I knew it! I just knew that there was more to our friendship than my parents let on!" I prepared to leave.

Star nudged me softly on the shoulder closer to where Eva stood. "Just listen to her before you run off," she said.

"OK, Star."

"I realized you'd be distressed," said Eva. "When Cal disappeared, your Mom and dad decided to make the split. Dan moved back to Springville to start investigating for us. We didn't give you any details, you were only twelve. Tri was especially worried about you. Nothing had ever been recovered from either Lang's or Cal's cases. Martin was an especially curious human, more curious than most. A lot like his dad. He kept to himself."

I continued pacing.

"Please do not go in anger," she pressed.

She could sense my urge to bolt. I had a habit of doing that when I got heated. It wasn't like I was going to turn into a fox since I'd already transformed. Would I turn back into a human, though? Panic rose in my chest and I blacked out.

Myth

"Starla?"

At the mention of my name gradually I regained consciousness. I shivered uncontrollably in the snow, not able to figure out why. The clan members were gone. Where was that voice coming from? Oh cripe, I thought and gazed upon myself. I sat in the middle of the forest without a stitch on!

"What was I thinking? How the heck am I going to get back to the station without freezing or being arrested?" I asked myself.

Molly stepped out of the clearing. I stood up and covered my body with my hands.

"Here, I brought you these," she said, thrusting the grocery bag at me.

I sighed, relieved, "Thanks! You saved me from massive frostbite." I speedily put on the clothes, boots and coat.

She snickered, "You owe me one. Kris gave me this note to give you." Molly pulled it out of her pocket.

"She was here?" I asked.

"Eva gave it to me when I arrived. You'd already blacked out. Don't worry, I wasn't scared. Be concerned about Jenson, he said you need to talk. You're to meet him for dinner tomorrow, after your shift."

"OK, kind of cryptic if you ask me," I replied.

"Jenson can be mysterious. Come on, we should head back to your house. Aren't you going to read that note?"

I opened it and read it silently.

Starla,

Cal would want you to have transportation. After all, you're helping to solve this case. You'll find her pink moped in the parking lot. It has a fox's paw on it. Make sure you keep in contact with us. If your tattoo lights up, contact me at this number. I know it's strange, but you'll get used to it. We'll talk again soon,

Take care

-Kris.

"You know that pink moped I saw in the parking lot?" I asked Molly.

"Yeah," she responded.

"We get to ride home on it," I beamed, in good spirits.

"Your mom will have a fit!" exclaimed Molly.

We made our way back towards the station.

"Yep, isn't it wonderful!"

"At least, you're happy about one thing, I saw everything. Jenson, he took off, something about his folks needing him to mow the lawn."

"That sounds just like his father," I answered.

"Yep, let's get back to the station, and then head out."

Chapter 11

The ranger assured me I'd be fine, driving home. After a few spins around the parking lot, I'd felt pretty comfortable. I had a driver's license already, just no car. Mom's rules: earn your own money, buy a car. Smiling, I pulled up to the back of the apartment complex and parked the moped next to the shed. Made it, maybe my sense of direction was getting better. I leaned back against the tree, looking out at the small landscaped yard. We'd had a few warm days, odd? Molly had been mumbling about them in my ear all the way back to her house. Today, wandering into the woods there'd been little snowfall. Later, at the Ranger's station, it came down in heavy flakes. Then on the way home, well, it filled our yard. I wondered if it was something mystical. Megan stepped out of the entrance.

"You better get inside. Dad's here, and we're going to have a family dinner," she said.

"Oh, is this something new?"

"Beats me, but they looked pretty cozy earlier. Maybe he'll stay this time," said Megan.

"Maybe, just don't get your hopes up, sis."

Megan turned, walking towards the back door. She opened it for me, and we arrived in the kitchen. Mom and Dad were sitting at our dining table. It seemed as if everyone had been waiting for me.

"Are you ready to have your favorite meal? Well, one of them anyway," said my mother. She got up to set down an extra plate on the table and then sat back down opposite my father.

"Of course," I replied. I meandered over to the table and pulled out a chair sitting down next to my father. The food looked really good; meatballs in the pasta and sauce, meatballs were a rarity. Mom claimed that too much red meat would give us all high cholesterol, leading to heart failure. She must be in a good mood. I took my napkin and placed it, in my lap.

"So, how was everyone's day?" I asked.

My parents just stared at each other. Did they want me to speak or start the conversation so they didn't have to?

"Well, your father and I've come to the conclusion you're ready."

"Ready for what?" I replied.

"A car," piped up Megan.

"Um, that is sort of going to be a problem," I said, picking up my fork and swirling spaghetti.

"Why is that?" asked my father.

"Kris, errr, Eva is letting me borrow Cal's moped to get around for right now. Besides, Mom, you always said how most cars aren't particularly fuel efficient. This is-- oh, and I have a helmet. Mike made sure of that before I rode it home today. I had a quick lesson in the parking lot at the Ranger's Station."

"You what!" exclaimed my mother, setting down her glass of water.

"Now, Tri, I'm sure it's fine. Ranger Mike, wouldn't have let her ride it home if he didn't think it was safe."

Megan and I smiled at each other as they argued. I could tell she was in shock, knowing I'd seen Cal's mother. No one spoke about it openly, but I was sure she knew.

"I guess the moped is alright for now, but your dad is taking you to get a proper license tomorrow after your shift at work."

I chewed my food, swallowed, and said, "I can't, I'm supposed to meet Jenson for dinner. He says it's pretty urgent."

"Does it have anything to do with the case?" My father questioned as he swirled a piece of bread in his sauce.

"It has more to do with us," I admitted. It wouldn't sit well with either of them, but would come up sooner or later. I took a deep breath in then let it out, waiting for someone to explode, shout or say something to the effect that Jenson and I shouldn't date or that I had too many things on my plate right now.

"Fine," said Mom.

"OK, then I'll just take you on a different day, but I want Jenson to pick you up at the diner. Mom will take you to work after class. How did the meeting go today?"

"I met Star and Eva," I said, glancing at my sister.

"That's good. Did you get the information you needed?"

"Bits and pieces I'll have to try and fit together," I replied.

"Ah, when we go to get that moped license we'll need to discuss the case in more detail," he concluded.

My sister was in the dark about my whole fox experience, and I didn't want to bring it up. Sure, she would have to find out eventually, but until then I preferred her not to.

(Dan)

We're finally alone, I thought. Starla had left to work at the diner, and Megan claimed she had homework. I cleared the dishes from the table, observing my wife, remembering how I'd seen her in such confusion when we decided to split up. A lot of people assumed we were divorced. Friends had started asking me afterwards when I was going to start dating. I'd tried, but I just couldn't take my eyes off her.

"Are you going to be OK?" I asked Tri.

"Jenson-- what do you think of him?" she said, laying her hands on the table in front of her.

"Nice boy, Starla likes him. I know you have your reservations about her and relationships." I poured her some more wine.

"I don't know why. It's not like she's ever been wild. I mean, look at us? I can't really compare her and Jenson. My parents found out when..."

"Starla was on her way, you never told them," I interrupted her.

"Then it was really too late, mom got sick, then dad went soon after that." She took small sips of the wine. "We left even though some of our members were mixed," she reflected.

"I accepted your need to live among the humans, and I am human. How odd is that?"

"Not as odd as me," answered Tri.

I kissed her forehead, brushing her cheek with my forefinger. "Just give her time, be there for her if she needs you. Let me know when you want me here."

"I will. You should go. I have to get some shut-eye," she said, getting up to place the empty wine glass in the sink. "Oh, and make sure to lock the door behind you."

"OK, Mrs. Librarian," I answered, turning to leave.

(Starla)

"Hey, Starla, get that Grand Slam out to table one!" shouted Gina.

I grabbed the hot plate, picking up my tablet to take the next order. It was turning out to be a wild night at the old diner. It seemed everyone in town was out on a Wednesday night. Briskly walking over to the table I set down the food.

"You had the eggs, sunny side up with a hint of salt, hash browns, and two pieces of toast?"

"That's right, young lady, don't fret. I see they're keeping ya on your toes tonight," said Mark.

"Yep, they sure are, but it's almost the end of my shift," I answered, then smiled setting down his plate of food.

"Could you please get me some more coffee and cream?" he asked.

"Why of course! I'll be back in a jiffy," I turned around to see a crowd of people lined up waiting for tables and zig-zagged through them on my way into the kitchen. It wasn't often this town was in such a bustle.

"It certainly is hectic, what do you suppose is going on in town?" I asked another waitress as I slid past her, reaching for the coffee pot.

"Not sure, nothing I know of. Maybe everyone is tired of being cooped up. People don't go out much in the winter here. It could be a meteor shower tonight. Sometimes the folks will come get a bite to eat, and then go over to the college observatory to watch."

"Ah," I replied.

"Here and take this milkshake to table five. You need any creamers for that coffee?" she asked.

"Yep, give me four, it's Mark, he likes his creamer," I said.

"Good thing you remembered, the last time I didn't, and he gave me hell."

"Are you new?" I asked

"Marla."

"Nice to meet you, Marla, I should get this order out."

And that is how most of my night went until Jenson arrived. *What was he doing here?* I was just taking off my gross apron in back when I saw him grab a booth to wait. Gina gave me a grin, and then nudged me.

"Your boy toy is here."

"Don't call him that."

"What do you want me to call him?"

"Right now, he's just my best friend. That is for now. Things could change, not sure yet."

She winked at me as I punched out at the time clock.

"Hey Don," I hollered at my manager.

"Yeah," he said. He'd been reading the paper.

"I'm outta here. Jenson just showed up. Could we get some service, please?"

"Sure, give me a minute. I'll get you your discount too. Thanks for all your help. I'm not sure what's gotten into this town!" He set down his paper and started to get up from the small desk in the corner of chaos.

"Me either, but it's good for business," I replied.

I took my jacket off the coat rack and swung it over my shoulder, making my way towards the booth. He looked nervous as he played with the silverware beside him. He spotted me heading his way. A brief smile formed on his lips as he set the silverware aside.

"Hey," I said, to him, sliding into the booth. "Weren't we supposed to meet tomorrow night?"

"Yeah, I didn't want to wait... too afraid I'd... Are you hungry? I mean, why wouldn't you be hungry since you've been working all evening," he stammered.

"It's OK, and yes, I'm famished. One of the waitresses will be here soon. Then we can order," I said, taking his hand, hoping it wouldn't make him more uneasy. I meant it as a comforting gesture. For a few minutes, we just sat. I took notice of his blue eyes and dark brown hair. It was mostly his sad smile that left me sullen. I felt his hand slowly slide off mine onto the table, grabbing for the ice water sitting next to him. He took a big gulp right before he began.

"I'm going to try to be serious. This isn't the easiest thing for me to say. Our friendship is valuable, but it's time we acknowledge there's more to us than that. It's those looks you give me, a hug, nudge, or the way you push me playfully aside. It's not sisterly, and fear is keeping us from taking the next step. Yeah, we could mess it up, but if we don't try what then? What can I do to make you more comfortable with the idea of dating me?"

Comfortable, wasn't I already at ease with Jenson? What did I fear? Was it seeing what my parents had been through, or what if the friendship was better than the relationship? In spite of all this, I wanted to tell him no and yes. What about all the times my mom told me my studies came first. Now knowing I was part fox, could Jenson handle that? Not just my transformation but everything tied to it? I rubbed my forehead, feeling a bit of a headache coming on.

My voice shook a bit, "How about we try it, and see what happens. It can be kind of a trial period." It wasn't what I planned on coming out of my mouth.

He didn't smile, frown, or get mad; instead he said, "I guess I can't argue with that. I mean you're willing to give us a chance."

I saw our waitress coming over.

"We should order something now. My stomach is starting to rumble."

"Good idea."

We ordered what we always did. It felt a bit different. I wouldn't call it a first date.

Mom hadn't questioned it when I got home so late; in fact, she was sleeping so I wasn't going to worry. I'd break the news in the morning about Jenson and me dating. What was unusual had been that he hadn't asked me about the fox clan or brought up anything related to the case. Possibly he had wanted a normal evening.

Instead, we chatted about college. We'd moved on to some new ideas in our myth class: unicorns. It was so off base even for Mr. Jones. We shook our heads and had chuckled at it. I grinned, thinking how Jenson could really make me laugh. He had held my hand all the way through our conversation, opened the car door for me before escorting me home, and then last, as he said Goodnight at my doorstep we'd embraced.

I didn't want to let him go. It felt right. No kiss, yet. I never kissed on the first date. It would happen. I wasn't like other girls, but was hopeful Jenson wasn't like other guys either.

I snuggled down into my comforter to get some sleep. Tomorrow I'd need to deal with my mother and another day of college classes. As comfortable as I was, I still couldn't shake what I'd learned about Cal's mom as well as who Cal really was. Should I go back and talk to her again?

Chapter 12

(Thursday)

Was I dreaming? Someone was touching my arm. My eyelids fluttered open. My mother curled up near me on my bed. A smile on her lips--maybe she changed her mind about Jenson and me? The impression I always received, had been one of disapproval of us being together in any way, other than a friendship. Before she could speak, I pushed myself up to sit against my headboard unsure of what would pass out of those lips. We'd already had the birds and bees talk. I'd just never gotten that far with anyone. I rubbed my eyes and pushed my hair back.

"Morning Mom, I didn't think about waking you last night. It was a little after one when I got in."

"I knew you'd get in late. Thanks for letting me sleep, but I would have liked to talk to you," she said, pushing the stubborn hair out of my eyes that kept falling forward.

"It was a good night. Work was crazy busy. We were thinking maybe it was another meteor shower, but when Jenson and I left, we didn't see anything falling from the sky."

My mom laughed, "Well, it was a full moon last night. I don't know how it affects people. I tend to stay up late, do dishes, and when I was a part of the clan we would have meetings. It was usually about how to protect ourselves from others. Did they tell you any of this yet?"

I shook my head, and my mother continued.

"We had a few guides who came from other tribes. Alliances, we called them. I had to leave all that behind. I thought you'd be much better off raised as a human, not knowing your heritage. It was a fight your father and I often had."

My mom sighed as if her heart had been broken.

"Is that why you are so leery of Jenson and I starting a relationship? Mom, it could be so much more complicated than this, you know?" I rubbed her back and pulled her into a hug.

"I admit I've been the overbearing mom, one who doesn't want her daughter to grow up too fast. When I last spoke to your father regarding issues going on with the clan, I'd been against what they had planned for you. Then last night after you left I had to take a step back. This includes you and Jenson, but it's not only that," she pulled away to look at me.

"I never imagined that Kris would lose Cal. It made me even more skeptical about ever telling you where you came from and who you are. I disassociated myself from everything running from my identity."

My mom began to shake violently. Was she going to transform? She began taking deep breaths.

"I have to pull myself together."

"Mom, is Megan my biological sister?"

I knew then I'd said something wrong, watching tears slide down her cheek.

"Mom, I"...

She pushed the tears out of her eyes, wiping the snot against her sleeve.

"It comes all at once, a wave bringing to shore all the things hidden, inside my ocean outward into the light. That is why I was worried about you hiding things from me."

"Mom, what did you think I'd hid? I pretty much lay my cards on the table most of the time."

"You're right, you've told me quite a bit except your father revealed to me, you're changing into a fox, then explained to me why Fritz had been upset. Allies of ours, vampire-wolf hybrids, had come to warn or was it to protect you? Maybe it was both."

She got up from my bed, opening my closet door. What could she be looking for in there? Did she want to borrow my clothes?

"I had it hidden in here somewhere." She moved aside clothing, scouring the shelves, "A few pictures at the time of your birth when I was in the clan, including an old diary of mine. I considered maybe someday when you were old enough, I'd give it to you. I don't know if it will be of much use. Ah, here they are way in the back of the secret drawer."

She walked over to me, setting them on the bed.

"Thanks, Mom. It still doesn't explain Megan."

My mom took my hand, then sat beside me.

"Megan isn't a fox. I don't know why or how it happened. It does from time to time occur that an offspring of ours only has the genetics of a human. I don't know what to do. I've seen a few gifts within her spirit. They're not the same as yours and mine. She is extremely bright which is why she has never struggled in school. I suspect somewhere in my lineage there was a gypsy because she tends to want to travel a lot. Remember when she wanted to go anywhere in California just to get out of L.A.?"

"Yeah, although how do you know that's what it is? She hasn't really wanted to be uprooted since."

"Well, maybe you're right, maybe not. Time will certainly tell as we gain our abilities at various maturity levels."

Tired of being in bed, I got up and began to scrounge for some decent clothes to wear for the day.

"I'm really glad we had this heart to heart. I just hope it's OK that Jenson and I are dating."

My mother did not look shocked, nor did she appear impressed.

"If it makes you happy, honey. Jenson has always been a good friend to you so if he can be more, then I hope it works out. If you have any questions regarding being a fox and him being human, it would probably be best to ask your father first."

"We've already talked about sex, mom. If it's any different now that I'm a fox/human, maybe even a hybrid of one of the two, well, if it comes to that I'll be coming to you for advice before it happens."

I wondered how my mother would take that. I didn't know many of my friends who were willing to discuss sex, or the possibility of it, with their parents before it happened, especially pre-marital sex at that.

My mom just gave me a wink, shutting my bedroom door. I guess she was OK with the fact I'd be coming to her if need be and not my father. Go to dad, about sex? I shuddered at the thought, "No way in H E double hockey sticks," I mumbled to myself as I got dressed for the day.

I had tucked away the diary and photos in my nightstand drawer before leaving the apartment. I'd check them later privately. Man, I should have left earlier. Cars whizzed by in a rush to get to their destination. I'd decided to hike to school since I needed the license to drive the moped. It was quite brisk outside for the end of February. This book club would be a good thing for me. I had considered joining when I'd seen the posters prior to the Du-vance mystery. It would also help me, maybe meet a few of Martin's friends. The school was just up ahead, good, not much further to go.

"Hey, you there, aren't you in that myths class?"

I stopped. He sounded out of breath as he tried to catch up to me.

"Starla, right?" he asked.

"Yeah, that's my name," I replied, eyeing his shaggy brown hair, and hazel eyes. He was built, unlike Jenson. I almost had to slap myself.

"I'm Owl. It's nice to meet you."

"Really, like the animal?" I stifled a chuckle.

"Don't laugh, it's my Native American name," he explained.

"OK, so, um, what's up?"

"I have wanted to say hi since the beginning of the semester. Is it too late to join your crew?"

"My crew-- I didn't know I had one?"

"I think it's pretty cool that you hang out with the non-conformist types."

"I'm not sure you would call us that. Let's keep walking. I don't want to be late for this book club thing. Then we both have a class to get to."

94

"OK, but I overheard you and Jenson talking about Martin. I can help you. He was one of my friends."

I gave him a puzzled look. We continued on to the front entrance of the building.

"Martin was a very private person. I can tell you what you need to know," he insisted, opening the door for me.

It's nothing like trying to investigate only to run into people just willing to hand out information, I thought as we entered the hall.

"OK, um, sure, why not," I said.

He stopped in front of me, putting his arms up and blocking me against the wall near a door. What the heck, I barely knew this kid! Who did he think he was? I inched down the side of the wall, maneuvering myself out from his grasp and slipped out under his arm. Then I started running down the hall. He ran towards me, hollering to stop. I did, once I got to the door of room 224. There in front of me was a decal of a raccoon reading a book. Owl was still right behind me. I turned around to face him.

"Look, we need to talk. You think you can solve this on your own. It's dangerous, it's not going to be as easy as all of your other little mysteries," he hissed.

"First of all you need to start treating me a lot nicer. Second, I'd like to know, how you know that I can solve mysteries, and third my boyfriend Jenson's not going to want you in on this if you treat people this way."

"Boyfriend," he said, befuddled.

"Jenson and I are dating, as of yesterday."

"OK, as far as this case I just want to point out how essential being discreet is. Martin was on to something, I know that. He had a few articles, but they are at his house. I am not sure how to get them. I've gone over there to see his dad a few times since his death, but he won't allow me up in his room. You'd think he'd at least give me a memento. He was my best friend," he whispered, slumping down to the floor.

"I understand. A little consideration, though, goes a long way," I answered, placing my hand on his shoulder.

Now how are we going to get his dad to listen to Jenson, and I? Did I have to get my father involved now? I wondered.

"Still want to go in?" he asked, interrupting my thoughts.

"I don't know. I'd like to, but with all this..."-I drummed my fingers on the door. A student who must have heard me opened it.

"Hey, we're about to start. You don't have to stay for the entire meeting. At least pick out a book or two. Today we'll be discussing *"To Kill a Mockingbird."*

"That's my favorite book," I replied.

How peculiar, I pondered, shaking my head. Owl and I walked into my first book club meeting. I had a hunch he and Du-vance had been to many of them. Owl may have been good looking, but he sure didn't know how to handle himself around women. If he did that to all the girls who he wanted to either court or solve a shenanigan with, well.

Chapter 13

"That sure felt like high school lit all over again," I said as we left. Glancing down at my watch, I saw we had a half hour til Jones's class began. I pointed to my clock, indicating the time.

"What do you think about the next book?" I asked

"Great book, I've read "*The Heart is a Lonely Hunter*" a few times now. I imagine you'll appreciate it," he said.

"Do you want to head to the cafeteria? I could use a Coffee. Then we can discuss what's going on."

"Sounds good," we rambled on in silence, colorful posters advertising housing, used books for sale, and the upcoming dance caught my eye. Had Molly seen them yet? It hurt to think about. I had Jenson, and who would she, could she ask to go, if any of us went. Unexpectedly someone took my hand from behind me, Jenson. Deja vu? Or was it my fox self kicking in?

"Do you know Owl?"

He gave Jenson an awkward grin. They shook hands and did the fist bump thing.

"Good to meet ya man, what's up?" said Jenson.

I took it that they knew each other, or maybe they were just being friendly?

Owl grabbed the side of Jenson's shirt gently tugging him off to the side. I rolled my eyes as I listened to him explain what he'd told me earlier.

"So are we cool?" asked Owl.

"Yeah, let's just get some milkshakes, Starla can have her coffee, and we'll chat about Jones's class for now." Hastily we headed in that direction.

"What about Martin?" I asked.

"Shhh, we'll discuss that in the library after class. I have a few notes in my locker," snapped Owl.

"Why didn't you tell me that before? You said Martin's dad had all the articles," I whispered.

"I had to make sure you were trustworthy."

So, I was being tested, how I didn't exactly know. Owl seemed a bit off. Could we trust him? His Native American heritage could be helpful as he'd have some amazing insights on folklore and myths. Did he know anything about Lang? What tribe did he belong to? Was he aligned with our clan?

"When you're ready to spill, don't hold back. We have questions and you may have the answers. I'm not going to put them off for long, Screech," I chided as we entered the cafe.

"Is that going to be his nickname?" Jenson moved towards the aisle where the shakes were sold.

"Yep," I said, grabbing a cup off the stand near the filling station. I observed them both fill up their shakes.

"You better watch out for that one, Screech," Jenson said, trying out his new nickname. "She is as sly as a fox."

Jenson winked at me as I filled my cup. A sudden flutter crept from my stomach into my throat. Then it dropped. Where was Molly? She was usually here by now. I glanced at my watch again. Class was in fifteen minutes. Seriously, had it taken us that long to trek here?

"Have you seen Molly at all today?" I asked Jenson.

"No, but she should be in class." He turned to Owl, "These two girls are attached at the hip. I swear I can't go anywhere without them."

"Isn't it a good thing? You have two pretty girls on your side. I've seen your friend Molly. Is she single?" he asked.

I glowered at him, handing the cashier at the counter money for our drinks.

"Um, she's not interested in dating anyone right now." I answered.

"Bad break up?" he replied.

"Um, yeah, something like that," I lied, snagging my coffee and scurrying off.

"Where are you going?" Jenson demanded.

"Weren't we going to talk?" asked Owl.

"I'm going to class."

They watched as I left the cafe.

I pushed open the door to the classroom. Molly sat in the back corner at a small table. How unusual? She usually preferred being front and center. It was the last place in the room I'd imagined she'd sit. I pulled out a seat and sat beside her. She didn't even seem to notice as she scribbled something on a piece of torn off paper. I pulled her myth book towards me. I'd seen it a number of times before, had one just like it. I flipped through it, then set it back down next to her. We'd found ours at the used book store a few weeks before classes had begun.

"Molly, hey, are you OK?" I expected her to look up with tears streaking her cheeks. I was afraid maybe her parents had learned the truth.

"Um, not really, I'm trying to determine how I'm going to manage to pay for my own place. Being at home is like being under investigation. I had to get out! They carry on about finding me a suitable husband. Endlessly I remind them my studies are more important than guys. Then to top it all off the other day I saw someone I really like, but..."- Molly shook her hand aside like she had to just let it go...

"That's really unfair. What's her name?"

"Maine. I haven't asked her to the dance yet. I'm not that brave."

"Perhaps you could work for the Ranger. Rent out a cabin?"

"I don't think Hunters Park has cabins, nor would my parents approve of that. I might have to borrow Jenson for church next week. It's either that or possibly stay at your house for a bit. At least for a few days?"

"That can be arranged. Would you consider allowing a new member into our circle? His name is Owl. Jenson seems to like him."

"Oh, you mean that guy who sits behind you in class?"

"Yes, that guy."

"He's alright. How's he going to help?"

"He knew Du-vance."

"How?" whispered Molly.

"On my way to probe the book club that we discussed he ran after me terribly out of breath. He'd been observing us since the beginning of the semester. A bit creepy if you ask me, calling us non-conformists and asking to be a part of our crew. After he tried to interrogate me, I was ready to flee. Instead, we ended up at the book club meeting together. No one there had any details on our victim. They knew of him, that he liked to read, but he came and went. Owl was the only member he held a relationship with outside of analyzing books they'd read. It seems those two were close. He called him his best friend."

"Where's Jenson?"

"Oh, he and Owl are at the Cafe." I pointed to my mocha, and then pushed it over. "You want some?"

She took a few sips, handing it back. I downed the rest, then threw it across the room into the waste basket.

"Are we going to involve Mr. Jones?"

"I'm actually considering maybe we shouldn't. Owl claims he has all this great material."

"Does he have a plan, when are we going to meet up? Du-Vance's dad, are we going to cross-examine him?"

"Whoa, take it easy, those are a lot of questions. In order to examine Du-Vance's Dad, we need Owl. He says he knows his father."

I turned myself around in my seat to see Owl and Jenson strut in. I patted Molly on the arm and then gestured towards them. She gave me, an oh, gosh, look, "Yes, it is about time for a girl's night," I chuckled.

After class, we hurried to the library, chatting on the way.

"Listen to that storm outside!" said Jenson.

I peeked out a window as we passed through the main doors exiting the building. Large flakes of snow drifted down from the sky. More snow? "I am so not ready for this. Is the climate always in a constant change here?" I asked Owl.

"Yes, most of the time. My friends and I always joke if you don't like the weather, wait five minutes, it will change."

"Ironic, since this place is called Springville. Is there much of a spring following winter?"

Jenson grinned; he knew how much I enjoyed conversations with new people. I felt him place his hand in mine.

"It depends on the year. It varies. You might have to go back to L.A., city girl," he joked.

We neared the entrance to the library. Molly raced ahead to the large glass door, and we slipped inside. I placed a finger to my lips demonstrating we needed to be quiet. I'd seen several students get kicked out of here before. We passed several groups studying, reading, and a few were on their laptops. My friends followed behind me. This was the place to be if you needed to cram or get away for a bit of R and R.

"It's probably best we sit somewhere in the back then," whispered Owl.

Molly nodded, proceeding onward. The rest of us followed her to a medium round table near a window looking out to the grounds.

"Jone's class was off topic today. Did you notice that? What's with all the gossip about vampires? Is he in fact, that desperate to gain interest or trying to reinforce the idea they exist here?" Jenson asked.

They do exist here, I thought. Had Jenson forgotten Shellena and Lance? If Owl wasn't here I'd remind him. Was Owl, a new suspect, friend, or ally? So far I wasn't quite sure.

"He keeps bringing up subjects closely related to this case. I know that much. What I don't know is about you," I said to Owl.

"I recognize you, Starla," he replied.

"How's that, are you an undercover agent spying on me?"

"It's simple; Native Americans respect myths, legends, and folklore. It's a part of our community. Our God is different. Many of our tribes have more than one God. A lot of times, he or she is called the Great Spirit. We acknowledge your kind. It doesn't mean all of our people do, but the group here is united with all clans in this area. It's how I met Du-vance and his father. We have an open pow-wow to the public every year. He helped me get acquainted with the campus during orientation. This was to be his last year, and he would have taken over Mike's position."

I nodded. "Someone had been afraid of Martin taking over. During this time had he designed any changes that would have affected the clans or our allies in a negative manner?"

"None that I'm aware of. The crusaders are not fond of fabled creatures mingling amongst humans. It wouldn't have caused them to wage a war though."

"What tribe are you from?" Molly interrupted.

Owl fidgeted in his chair. "Mixed, from many, I'm not certain of my origin; at birth I was adopted into a Caucasian family. How did I learn about my past? How did I end up going to pow-wows in the first place? To answer that, my adopted parents stayed very involved in the community after my placement. This is very rare. They sought out a group of Native Americans who would accept me. I attend meetings, gatherings, and pow-wows as I have mentioned."

Not sure how to respond, I remained silent, touching the window pane, my mind drifted to Molly's dilemma. Who was this

Maine she admired? I hadn't seen her around. Gah, I was scheming in my head again. How could I help her? I placed my hand back on the table, scraping at some gum that had been discarded.

"Listen did he have any siblings, he didn't know existed? What about his father's lover? Why did they break up? Could she have been implicated?" Jenson interjected.

"I know only what Mike has disclosed to me. That Du-Vance's father found someone fell in love, and then she broke it off," he insisted.

"I acquired files on missing people. It's a reach, but maybe Martin was searching for them. If I'm on the right track, he may have been eliminated. One was named Lang Orion and the other Cal Summers. Have you ever heard of them?" I inquired.

"No, catch me up to speed," he replied.

After sharing a brief overview of my findings, I asked him, "Where are the articles you wanted to share with us?"

He pulled out some papers from his folder that sat on top of his myth book. It didn't appear new to me. The articles before us contained several on the Native American pow-wows, new rules since Du-Vance's death, and another on college curfews. I sorted through them a bit, and then passed them around for each person to study.

"We should probably get going," Owl suggested.

"You're right, let's go talk to his father now," I said, pushing my chair aside. "It can't wait any longer. The only predicament is how are we going to get to him in this?" I asked, waving to the raging winter wonderland outside.

Chapter 14

Holding hands we trudged further into unfamiliar territory. We must have appeared to onlookers like children who'd lost their way in a blizzard. The snow came down thick and heavy. It hadn't been particularly cold earlier when I'd left the house this morning. Nothing compared to the chill in the air that currently took its place. It had turned so dark that the streetlights flickered on. I'd called my mom to let her know I'd be home late prior to leaving the library. I didn't exactly tell her why, and she hadn't asked.

"Molly, will your mom be alright with this?"

"I called her remember? I'm staying over at your place, correct?"

"Hmm, OK." With any luck mom wouldn't care. She adored Molly. Picking up speed, Owl moved ahead, preparing a pathway through the snow for us to follow.

"Come on, a few more blocks to go. Then we can go in and get warm," he said.

"What if Rascal turns us away? He might not be fond of unexpected visitors, especially given how secretive he is," said Jenson.

"It will be fine, he trusts me. We have an understanding," declared Owl firmly.

If I could have transformed into a fox, withstanding weather conditions wouldn't be dreadful. The issue being I couldn't stay a fox. Naked in a snow storm, heck no! I laughed at the thought.

"What's so funny?" asked Molly.

"My foxy ability, with it this wouldn't be so awful," I said, signifying the white flurry around us.

"Um, yeah, and when you go to change back?" Molly glared at me with her eyebrows up.

Then we laughed. Owl immediately focused on our exchange.

"I'd be in my birthday suit, I'd freeze. Don't you realize what happens to humans when they alter from one shape to another?" I asked.

Owl just smirked, shaking his head.

"Starla tends to be a bit witty; you'll get used to it. I suppose her sense of humor as well as her confidence caused me to be captivated," Jenson yelled over the howling wind.

I blushed even in the harsh conditions.

"Molly, are you alright?" asked Owl.

"I'm still here," she sighed.

I hoped Owl wouldn't push, and at that thought I heard him reply.

"Good."

Stopping to catch my breath, I saw the subdivision come into view. The homes appeared run down and in need of repair; several could have used a new coat of paint. There was an air about them. Something I'd been unable to pinpoint. This part of Springville had definitely undergone hard times. We crossed the street where a large hill lay before us.

"What a strange neighborhood," said Jenson.

"Shhh, we need to get up the hill. Then take a right. Rascal lives on the corner of that street," urged Owl.

"Finally someone else who goes by landmarks," I muttered under my breath.

I concentrated on putting one foot in front of the other. The blizzard raged on, swiftly diminishing visibility. Owl climbed his way to the top of the hill. Jenson was not too far behind him while Molly and I staggered further back.

"We're almost there, Molly and Starla, come on! The wind is really picking up!" yelled Jenson already half way there.

I stopped, shutting my eyes. Wind and snow stung my face. Molly took my hand guiding me up to the top, and then pushed me to the right where Owl had said to go.

"Look, here we are. Open your eyes," said Molly.

In front of us stood a two-story stone house, with several small round windows. An old blue rusted Ford pickup sat in the driveway. I lifted my fist to knock on the door. Owl stepped in front of me and nudged me over to Jenson's side.

"You'd better let me make our introductions," whispered Owl. He knocked and we waited. Someone bustled about inside, perhaps they were putting away dishes? Then we heard a clatter of plates crash.

"Gol darn it!" yelled a voice from within.

The door opened, revealing a small man five feet tall, dark shaggy brown hair, and hazel eyes with glasses. I took notice of his raggedy blue jeans, a white T-shirt barely visible under his old blue flannel. Nice, old school style.

"Owl, what brings you here? What on earth are you doing out in this crazy weather?" he wondered, staring at the four of us standing out in the cold. He waved us in without a word. We shuffled through a hall entrance, took a left and arrived in a tiny kitchen.

"You kids have a seat. I'll sweep up these dishes. I wasn't expecting company this late at night. Give me the details or at least a good reason for bringing your friends by. What is it, you need?"

"Go ahead, sit down," said Owl. We'd been standing, staring at the wall to wall, rows of china, trinkets of old tin cans, cola bottles, and what looked like jars of preserves.

"It's not just the women folks that can, kids. So what do you want? You must want something," Rascal remarked as he swept up the mess.

"I want to introduce you to Starla, Jenson, and Molly. I met Starla today at the college," said Owl as he sat down next to Molly.

Rascal acknowledges us by means of a slight bow following the introduction.

"So I guess you know about my boy being killed. It ain't any secret tis all," he replied. Then sat down in the empty seat next to Owl.

"Well, I hope you kids are being safe. I'm aware Mike the Ranger said he had someone named Dan running this. Is that the reason you're all here?" he inquired.

"Yes, I'm his daughter. Owl suggested you might be able to share your insight with us. It could direct us to the killer."

"I wish you kids wouldn't get mixed up in this. I hate to speculate and blame without much knowledge, but I sense it has something to do with those wolves in Hunters park. If not them, who?" he asked, holding up his hands gesturing.

"What we want to find out is why your son was there. We've determined he interned for Mike and would shortly take over his position. Do you have any clue why someone would harm your son? Did he have any enemies? Was he searching for something, information, or maybe even someone?" I asked.

Mr. Du-vance took several deep breaths, then set down his glasses. He picked them back up and cleaned them off only to place them back on his face. Molly sat strumming her fingers on the table, Jenson appeared deep in thought, and Owl had out a notepad. I wasn't sure if I should say anything at this point. Several minutes passed. Rascal got up from the table, walking over to the fridge and removed from it five cans of cola.

"Do any of you want glasses for these," he said, holding one of them up.

"No, we're fine," said Molly.

"Now this is going to take a bit. Allow me to clear my head," he replied, taking a seat. "It's important I give you as many facts as I can muster up. My son mostly kept to himself. Owl, you realize this as you've been the only person he's confided in. I doubt my son even dated anyone. That boy," he said with a grin. "He loved his work among the Park Ranger. Any other time he had was spent on book club or science projects. Let me tell you about a strange experience. It isn't easy on my emotions to conjure up the past. The world may paint men as detached creatures, but eh, I'm not one of them," said Rascal.

He came back over to the table, setting the cans of Coke in front of us. I opened mine, taking sips. The clock on the wall read seven-thirty five. I was getting hungry, but my mother taught me, it's impolite to invite myself to dinner without being offered.

"Once my wife died, despair took over, engulfed me in mourning. I couldn't stand to see couples together of any kind." Rascal let out a long sigh, "then one night I happened to stop in at the diner. The one I saw Starla in a few nights ago. I thought you looked familiar when I saw you at my doorstep tonight. I go there occasionally to reflect on the past. I never stay for too long, just pick up a coffee, scope the place out, hoping maybe she'll decide to return to me. Anyway, I had gone in for a burger and soda. I sat down as usual, ordered, and waited for my meal to be served. It was quite peculiar as if fate stepped in when I needed someone the most. She just sat down at my table. I mean, how many times does a gorgeous woman just non-chalantly walk over to a booth, especially to sit or introduce herself to a guy like me? I still question her motives at times. Nuria was her name."

Nuria, wasn't that Eva's sister? I wondered.

Rascal continued, "That was what we did for a few months until things got serious between us. We'd meet for burgers every night that Martin had a school activity. As I said he was into science, book clubs, and those types of things. I mean, had it been an event for parents to attend I'd have been there for my boy."

"Anything suspicious that you noticed about her, anything off?" asked Jenson.

"Once we were having dinner, it was late, almost midnight. She seemed like she was in a hurry to leave, but wouldn't tell me why. It was the night we got in our first fight. I told her we shouldn't keep secrets from each other. Her response, some secrets need to be kept for everyone's safety. If you knew me, what I am, you wouldn't love me. I told her nothing could change how I felt concerning her. I admired her relaxed attitude, that she let her hair go wild, wavy; the way she'd go on about books she'd read for hours reminded me of my son and my wife. She reminded me why I choose to live. No longer could I seclude myself, instead she urged me to immerse myself in things she established as intriguing. She held a great interest in government affairs, people's rights and social justice, maintaining an ability to see the world in a broader perspective."

"What happened the night of the breakup? Is that stepping too far ahead?" I asked.

"Owl, can you grab us some crackers out of the drawer, and get out some cheese. I know we're on a roll, but I keep hearing your stomachs growling. When did you kids last eat?" asked Rascal.

We all gazed back and forth at one another. Then I piped up.

"I know I haven't eaten since breakfast. Then I had a coffee before, book club."

"Ah, so you did think about going to check that out huh? Is it for your love of books or the investigation?" he asked.

"I love a good book now and again. The problem is with college, I don't get much time to read anything on my list."

Rascal chuckled, "That's what my son told me after he started school."

Owl got up and began severing us. It looked as if he'd been here many times. Once he placed all of the fixings on the table in front of us Rascal continued...

"Martin only met her a few times. She'd light up a room with her charm. Then at our two year anniversary, she dropped a bomb. She told me we couldn't see each other anymore. Devastated, I entered back into the seclusion I'd established after my wife passed. I recognized this woman's independence. I'd leaned on her extensively. Perhaps my weakness drove her away. She constantly had to leave before midnight on the night of the full moon. I suspected her involvement with a clan. I never asked her, maybe I should have. The other thought that crossed my mind, possibly she was pregnant. Why would she disappear? Wouldn't she have wanted to start a family, to get married? Then again, she repeatedly discussed her feminist ideas, her plans, and perhaps I would have held her back. She could have put the child up for adoption if she had been. I didn't see her ending it. I don't know. I just don't know," he stammered.

Owl got up placing a hand on Rascal's back. Then he drew him in to hug him.

"I know it will never be OK, but we're going to try and find her for you. She may have some answers. Do you have any idea where she might be? Did you ever go anywhere with her? Was the diner your only meeting place? Did she ever come here?" he asked, letting him go from the embrace.

Rascal shook his head.

"Did she ever come here?" I repeated.

"No, never, we stayed at hotels, hung out in Hunters Park, went for hikes out near Stream Lake. There's a cabin on Outlook Point just outside of Springville where the woods start up. It's state land. She called it her home away from home, implying a brief stay. She never did tell me where she was from exactly. I should have known a relationship could not last in the midst of secrets between us. I'm just a hopeless romantic who had a notion that one day she would reveal everything to me," he stated.

"What about interests, did you share any?" asked Molly.

"She invariably spoke in relation to the world and current events as I mentioned above, also justice. Then again, she may have been an underground agent. All I have are speculations. I shouldn't put all this on your young shoulders, but I trust Owl. He's like a son to me."

"Don't you have any pictures of her?" I asked.

"No, every time I asked her, she refused to be photographed. I found it strange but I didn't push it," he responded.

I nodded, then got up from my seat. I picked up the plates, preparing to help do the dishes before we left.

"No, let me get those." said Rascal.

He took the plates from me shuffling over to the sink. Then set them aside.

"Did Nuria ever talk about someone named Eva?" I pestered.

"No, why?"

"I met her the other day, Nuria's sister. She said she knew you and her sister had a relationship, but offered no additional tips regarding the matter."

"Well, it sounds like she knows just as much as the rest of us. I can't tell you anything regarding her. This is the first time I've heard of any of her family members. She never spoke of them," he answered.

"It's getting late, why don't you take my truck and see that everyone gets home safely," Rascal instructed Owl.

"Alright, sure thing, should I swing by afterward? I'd need to crash here for the night. If you don't mind it would give us time to go over the particulars of what may have happened to your son or Nuria? It's almost ten."

"OK, if you wish. Just do me a favor. Be safe out there. I'm glad to have met you in spite of the circumstances. Please maintain a low profile. I don't want this leaked to the press."

"Of course," Owl confirmed.

"Can we talk to you again?" I asked.

"In due time, if you uncover anything contact me, but only if it's urgent."

Then, with that we were walking out the door without any more pleasantries. I believed Rascal had had enough of the past for one night. My only desire was to uncover the truth. Who had killed his son and why? Then maybe we could stop anything else horrifying from occurring.

Chapter 15

"Do you suspect that Du-vance went looking for Nuria?" I asked Owl as we rode back in the truck towards Jenson's. The snow had let up a bit. Scanning the road, I could tell the plows had been out. It put my mind at ease. I slouched in the soft, worn-in seat. The truck's tires trudged through the white drifts as we passed the main intersection.

"That's a good theory. It was getting so late," he said, shaking his head.

"Tick tick tick, time waits for no one," I commented.

"If he knew how broken up, his father was over her, he probably went searching," said Molly.

"And if he stepped into the wrong place, at the wrong time, he could have been attacked, whether or not she was a secret agent," Jenson suggested.

I noticed Molly playing with her necklace. It must have been new. I'd never seen it before.

"Where did you get that?" I asked.

"A friend, you haven't met her yet," she said, tapping her hand near her heart. Then she placed it back on the door handle of the vehicle as if she might have to make a great escape.

"How are you doing? You said a while ago you'd clue me in on a few things going on," spoke up Jenson.

"We have all this going on. Starla is here for me right now."

"Maybe you shouldn't push her. Let her tell you whatever it is when she's ready," said Owl.

Jenson started hitting the interior of the car seat with his fist. I could tell he was getting angry. His face turned red. It looked like smoke would start coming out of his ears if she didn't open up to him.

"I am your friend too, and I would like to know what the heck is going on. You invite me to church as friends, but then hold my hand. You know that Starla and I are dating now. It doesn't add up. You've been acting pretty strange. Please tell me what is going on!"

Molly hung her head a bit low. Owl pulled the truck off to the side of the road. I assumed he wanted to give Molly a moment to get herself together. She wasn't sobbing, but tears crawled down her cheeks, falling onto her jacket.

Once the truck was stopped, and in park, Molly wiped away her tears, and looked directly at Jenson.

"I don't know how else to say this. Owl, I don't know what you'll think. You just came into all this today. You might even throw me out. I've been trying to hold this back. I've tried to bury it deep down inside, but it... - won't go away."

I could feel her trembling beside me. Why did Jenson have to do this? I guess Molly could have said no, told him it was none of his business. Maybe it was best that she told him, I couldn't imagine him shunning her! If he did, I couldn't be his girlfriend or friend. Molly grabbed my hand, but I didn't push it away. She needed my comfort and support. If it was her or Jenson, well Jenson would have to go.

"Jenson, Owl, I'm ga...ay," she stuttered.

They just sat there stunned. I hugged Molly. I didn't want her to feel alone. I could not envision the guts it took to do that. I knew she'd been hanging on to it as long as I'd known her.

A few minutes later Owl and Jenson joined in and embraced her.

Owl spoke up, "What about your parents, will you tell them?" he asked.

"I don't know what I'm going to do. My family is the epitome of perfect God-fearing folks. I... That's why I took you to church Jenson, for protection," she stammered.

Jenson gave her a sympathetic smile. Then she let go of my hand, which she was still holding.

"So you and Starla aren't?"

"We're friends. Do you think just because I'm attracted to girls I'd try to steal her away from you? I see how your eyes light up immediately upon her arrival. It doesn't matter if it's in the hall at school or after you work out. You both have a thing for each other," she grinned. "No way Jenson, I wouldn't go there."

Owl started up the truck.

"Jenson, I'll drop you off first. If the girls want, well, I'll take them out for a night cap. Molly could probably use a drink right now. Starla, maybe you should contact your mom, let her know you'll be out later? I'll phone Rascal now."

Jenson didn't argue or get upset that Owl had offered to take us out. He laid a hand on my shoulder and squeezed it gently. I had to believe my mother would be as understanding if we needed to go to her. Molly's parents weren't bad people. On the other hand, when it came to church they were pretty serious. My mom had never been extremely religious. I'd been allowed to explore other perspectives.

We dropped Jenson off, and soon after pulled up to a placed called The Bar and Grill. The engine on the truck made a sputtering sound and then stalled.

"At least we're here," groaned Owl.

"True. How are we going to get back into town? My mother is expecting me home by curfew. It's about an hour and a half from now."

"Listen, we'll go in and have a couple of drinks. You will anyway. I'm not going to given that I'm your D.D. Later, I'll come back out to tinker with the truck. If I can't get it working, I'll call you and Molly a cab. Will that work?" he asked.

"Sounds good," said Molly.

Exiting the car I heard someone holler my name. I turned my head to see Shellena and Lance.

"Friends of yours?" asked Owl. He took the key out of the ignition, then jumped down from the truck and pushed the door shut.

"Kind of," I admitted. Molly stood close beside me, not sure what to make of them. Of course, they weren't in their vampire wolf hybrid form.

"Hey Starla, we have a table inside. Come join us!" They pleaded, straggling up to me.

"Um, I'm kind of here with Owl and Molly," I said, gesturing to my friends.

"Hi Owl, what's up? Do you mind if we all mingle for a spell?" jested Lance. He gave him a friendly slap on the back.

"I don't want to be rude, but we kind of have a private party going on," said Owl.

"If you decide you want to join us, you know where we are," Shellena sang. She winked at him as she strutted up to the entrance.

"We'll need to meet up sometime regarding the case. If you can, come to Hunters Park soon and bring your friends," said Lance.

I gave Lance a funny look. This seemed a bit out of sorts. Perhaps they were just being friendly? I might check with the ranger. I needed to meet with him to figure out our next step. Although I guess my being a big fox, ahh girl I should just maybe take care of it myself? I shook myself out of oblivion.

"I'll consider it, and get back to you. I have to get together with Mike at any rate," I replied.

"Good, good, take care now, Starla, and if you change your mind, you're welcome to join us," suggested Lance.

We trotted up to the bar door, and Owl opened it for Molly and me. Unusual, I thought, glancing around to see if we must seat ourselves or wait to be seated. The place was packed. An old juke box stood in the corner, singing a song about Jack and Diane. I smiled to myself. Molly appeared to be scoping out the place. For a bar, it wasn't too noisy. The stools near the counter had all been taken. I spotted several tables that overlooked a lake, or maybe it was a pond?

"Let's get a booth," I said.

"Alright," he replied.

Molly and I followed him to a large booth in the corner. I sat down, and Molly scooted in beside me. Owl seated himself across from us. Glancing over at the bar, I watched as Lance and Shellena chatted with a couple sitting on bar stools.

"How do you know them?" asked Owl.

"They hold an alliance with my clan. They're acquaintances. I haven't really gotten to know them yet. Ranger says they check out. I'm just not sure yet."

"Makes sense for you to be leery," he reasoned.

"So what are we drinking?" I asked Molly.

"Do they have fruity drinks here?"

"Yes, we're girly when it comes to drinks, no beer for us!" I announced.

The waitress trotted up to us, doing a little dance, all the time grinning. She was wearing a maid's dress, simply conservative, but it looked good on her.

"Hi there, what can I get for you guys, gals tonight?" she said.

"Do you have strawberry margaritas?" asked Molly.

"Sure do," she replied.

"We'll take two of those, and some chili cheese fries for all of us," I interrupted.

"Thanks, Starla. You know how much I love those!" Molly said.

"... And for you, sir?"

"I'll just take a Cherry Coke."

"Nothing in that tonight?" she offered.

"Nope, I am the DD tonight, well if our truck starts back up."

"OK, I'll bring that in a jiffy," she said, retreating.

I caught Molly checking out her bum and nudged her. She blushed.

"Are you going to be OK?"

Molly brushed her hair behind her ears and tried to smile. She rubbed her palms on her jeans nervously."I don't know what to do about the situation with mom and dad. I can't go on living with them this way. I should tell them," she sighed, her shoulders slumping down to the edge of the wooden slab. "Maybe I could practice on your mom first."

"It couldn't hurt," I answered.

"She just seems so open minded. Above all, she's the only one who ever suggested I try out other religious beliefs. I feel a tad more comfortable with her. She might have some advice on how to handle my parents," she said.

Molly was right about that. I'd seen my mom speak to other parents about their children when issues occurred. She was very helpful in getting them to see the positive points in difficult situations.

The waitress came back and set down our drinks in front of us.

"The chili cheese fries will be up soon, ladies," she said.

"Thanks," said Owl. The waitress turned away from us and walked to the bar.

"Rascal's dad seems really nice. A lot nicer than the ranger described him," said Molly.

"Yep, he's pretty spectacular. He just tends to be careful around strangers. At one time, he was the kind of man that would give you the shirt off his back until he was taken advantage of various times, by people in these parts," Owl confessed.

"Makes sense," replied Molly.

"So this Eva you brought up in conversation tonight, she didn't tell you anything else about Nuria?" asked Owl.

"No, I didn't give her a lot of time. I was in shock when she revealed she was my best friend's mother. When I lived in Los Angeles, I knew her as Kris. Cal, her daughter, is one of the missing kids. I have to decide if another meeting with my clan is necessary at this point."

He nods, and I change the subject.

"Do you think you'll go to the dance?" I asked Molly.

"Not sure yet, I'm not even certain they would let me go with Maine. I still have to invite her, and I'm not positive she likes me like that," she pondered.

"Ah well, you can at least ask. I don't see why you two couldn't go. I know that Lyana is attending with her girlfriend," said Owl.

"I didn't assume there were very many people out here," uttered Molly.

"We have a few brave souls," he replied.

"I've heard rumors about a support group at the college. Do you know if it is true, Owl?" I asked.

"I'll look into it," he said.

"Good, we could even start an alliance group like a P - flag, except call it F-flag for friends."

"You guys, I-I... didn't expect you to identify with..." replied Molly.

"We're your friends," Owl reminded her.

"I hate to interrupt but I have your chili-cheese fries," said our waitress, setting them down.

"Thank you!" said Owl.

We all dug in, silently eating til only a few fries remained on the large plate.

"These are the best chili cheese fries I've had in ages! I've lived here for a long time and never experienced such awesomeness!" exclaimed Molly.

Owl chuckled. "I'm glad you like them. I figured Starla hadn't ever been here since she just moved to town recently. This is a pretty good place to hang out. They also accept everyone. If you get my drift, Molly."

Molly blushed and smiled at the same time. Our conversation started to die down. I looked at my watch. "It's almost ten. We need to get going."

"Is it really that late?" asked Molly.

"Unfortunately, yes, let me get the check and then we'll jam."

"Nope, it's my treat tonight. If that's alright with you ladies," Owl offered.

"Thank you," we replied in unison. I almost wanted to say, jinx.

"You're welcome, now let me go see if I can get the truck started. If I can't, then we'll call a cab." Owl shimmied out of the booth and headed to the bar, to pay our tab.

I hoped these were Owl's true colors, that the person I'd seen before who showed me anger near the book club was gone. This Owl made me smile; he belonged to our group, our tribe. Why put so many labels on people? Why not just accept them as they are, I thought as we left.

Chapter 16

(Thursday evening)

I unlocked the apartment door and pushed it open. The night light in the hall was on, but it was barely enough to see to hang our coats. Mom and Megan must have already been in dreamland. I turned on the lamp on the table in the hall and set my keys and purse down.

"Let me have your jacket to hang up," I whispered to Molly. She'd just locked the door behind her.

"Thanks," she said. I took her coat and hung it and mine in the closet.

The quiet atmosphere relaxed me after the taxing day of new introductions.

"Ready?" I asked Molly.

She nodded in response, and we climbed the stairs to my room with no interruptions.

I opened the door. No dark shadows, nothing lurking about. Molly flipped on the light.

"We should get some sleep," I said.

"Yep, I'm just going to take a quick shower, change, and then crash," she replied.

I walked over to the closet and took out the flip couch and set it up near the window. The sound of the shower reminded me of rainfall, too bad we didn't live in Seattle. I went over to my bureau and pulled open my drawer. Yes, nice warm soft jammies. I pushed the drawer closed and got ready for bed. As much as I wanted to find out about what had happened to Du-Vance, my mind drifted, imagining myself running through the forest free in my fox form, nothing to hold me back, no parents, no mysteries, just a sense of overwhelming freeness released. Something about the moon made me want to sprint. I'd heard that foxes were related to the wolf, so maybe that was why. I went over to sit on my bed to wait to use the bathroom, but before I knew it fell fast asleep.

(Friday)

The bright morning sun shone through the curtains. I rolled over, pulling the covers over my head. I'd just take a few more minutes to myself before Molly woke up. My bed was warm and comfy, so I closed my eyes to float back to paradise.

Without warning, I discovered myself in a field surrounded by acres of wheat grass. The sun gleamed down on my strawberry blonde hair. A sense of serenity and peace overcame me. Then rushing out of nowhere a fox appeared. She skidded to a stop, staring at me. I lowered myself into a sitting position on the ground, beginning meditation. A warm, soft breeze blew my long hair behind me. Reflecting back to when I'd first met Star and Eva I tried to place the current fox in this dream. Who was she? Where did she come from? Feeling a soft object nuzzle my hands slowly, I opened my eyes.

"You must find her. The pieces will fit if you follow the trail. Owl, will guide you. Listen to him; go to the cabin in the woods. There, you'll find more clues. First, you must be at peace. You've always found a place in your heart for rebels, warriors and those defiant of the social norm. I have to go now. Take care, Starla," she spoke.

My eyes fluttered open, I couldn't tell if it had been a lucid dream or vision. I'd used meditation in my sleep? My eyes strayed to the flip couch, empty. I heard Molly in the bathroom. The clock read 11:46. If I didn't get up soon, the whole day would be wasted. Mom had probably already left for work. She'd be at the library stacking books and working on the computers by now. Surely Megan had left for school.

I got up to take a quick peek at my calendar, Friday. I had math class this evening around seven. I raised my arms above my head, stretching a bit. Molly spun out of the bathroom.

"Hey, so you finally woke up, sleepy head," she said.

"What do you want to do today? We could play detective, take a day off, or maybe even meet up with Jenson."

"Is your mom home?" she asked.

"You'll have to wait until tonight if you want to speak to her. She gets home around five. It was quiet when I woke up, so I assumed everyone had left," I said, grabbing jeans and a T-shirt off a nearby chair. "I heard you in the bathroom earlier then attempted to go back to sleep. It was pretty peaceful until my lucid dream. I'm sure that's what it was anyway, I'm going to take a shower. Last night it just didn't happen."

Molly walked over to the flip couch, putting it back together, then sat down. "Sure, math homework, ugh," she said, holding up her book she'd pulled from her backpack. "Then when you get done we'll consider what to do next."

"Good, it will give me a bit of time to think things over."

Closing the bathroom door behind me, I leaned against it and sighed. Eyeing my extra clothes I'd set on a nearby shelf, I wondered what Owl was up to today. Did Rascal give us an address to that cabin he talked about last night? I remembered him, saying it was in a park, no maybe a reservation? I turned on the shower, waiting for it to heat up, listening to Molly fuss over equations, ew math. I was not looking forward to homework. I'd have to finish mine before class tonight. Molly and I had the same arithmetic class. She'd been tutoring me. Would I go, or skip out? There was something I had to do for my lit class? Reading in our book, that's right. I'd almost forgotten about that. Thank goodness it wasn't due til Thursday. It was an introduction class I was completing at my own pace. Ah, I'd get by. Lit was easy compared to math. I felt the water spraying out of the shower head, just right, and then stepped in.

We'd decided to work on our studies given that it felt like ages since I'd cracked a book. I wasn't that thrilled, but after many attempts to contact Jenson and Owl had failed, we figured it would be best.

I saw that Molly had almost completed her art project. She'd been working on a few abstract drawings. I set my book aside for lit class. I'd just finished reading "*The Telltale Heart*" by Edgar

Allen Poe. I'd forgotten how much I enjoyed a good spooky tale now and again. Math had been the worst of it, and Jones hadn't given us much homework this week. The downstairs door creaked from below. I jumped up, then fell back down on the bed.

"It must be Megan home from school. It's after 3:30," I said, placing my notebooks and school things next to me.

"We didn't even break for lunch," observed Molly.

"True, but we did get a lot done. Do you want to go downstairs, get a bite to eat? We could catch up on Ellen if you want," I said.

"Your mom lets you watch that with all her rules?"

"It is, public-television we're talking about, and she loves PBS so if you're up for Sesame Street, Arthur, or maybe even Martha Speaks," I teased.

"Well, I did catch you and Jenson, watching Curious George that one day," she said, standing up from her spot on the floor. Molly gathered up her books, placing them, inside her backpack along with her overnight stuff.

"Yes, in January when I moved in after we'd set up the TV. I love my cartoons," I said optimistically as I put on my shoes and pulled on a sweatshirt. We made our way downstairs into the kitchen. My sister already had out the fixings for sandwiches.

I poked Megan on the shoulder from behind."What are you doing? Mom's not going to be happy if we ruin our dinner."

My sister points to a note on the fridge.

"Mom won't be home tonight. She has some sort, of meeting at the library discussing what new books should be brought in. You know how she is always fighting for non-censorship. What have you two been up to all day?"

"Homework, we woke up at about noon," I replied.

"Must be nice," Megan complained.

"It is, but there are other responsibilities that come along with it. I can make us the sandwiches if you want."

"Nope, I can do it. What kind do you guys want? I have cheese, ham, turkey, tomatoes, mustard, and mayo."

"Ham and cheese sounds good," said Molly.

"Yeah, same here," I replied, getting cans of soda out of the fridge.

"We should take our sandwiches into the living room since mom isn't home. She hardly ever lets us watch TV while we eat dinner," said Megan. She reached up on top of the fridge for the paper plates.

I laughed and picked up the bag of baked potato chips.

"Yeah, that does sound like a plan. Do you guys want to watch cartoons on PBS or Ellen on ABC?" I asked.

Molly looked at Megan, waiting for her to decide.

"Let's do Ellen today. Martha Speaks kind of, freaks me out," she admitted

"Who's freaked out by Martha? I think she's adorable," Molly interjected.

"I just have a weird sister," I replied, putting chips on all of our plates.

We picked them up, then headed out of the kitchen into the entrance hall, and then straight down a few feet to the right was our living room. I really didn't live, in it like most people. My mom expected me to do homework, sometimes housework and work at Denny's.

"So what do you think of Ellen?" asked Megan.

"I think she's got a good sense of humor, great guests and is more entertaining than Doctor Phil," Molly answered.

Megan chuckled, "Yeah, I like that she has some real life heroes on her show besides the usual celebrities. I used to watch Oprah."

Leaning over the coffee table, Megan turned on the TV. Once she sat down I placed our plates on it.

"Has mom, had her library guests over lately?" I pondered.

"Not that I know of, hmm, dad did come over last night, though. You were out. They seem to be getting really chummy," she said, nudging me.

"Well, I'm not jumping to any conclusions yet sis, oh commercial break is over," I said munching on my sandwiches.

We leaned back to give the talk show host, 45 minutes of our attention while in the 15 minutes, of commercials we'd be told what products to buy that would make our lives better. Man, my mom living in my head, weird.

It was seven o'clock. Molly had left for math class an hour ago. I should have gone. She didn't heckle me as she normally would. Instead, I'd done the dishes, picked up the living room, and cleaned my bathroom. What mom didn't know wouldn't hurt her. Now I wasn't at all sure what to do with myself. I considered calling my dad. It had been a while since we'd spoken. Mom would be home soon, then Megan would have to shut off the TV. She'd been glued to it all evening.

I got up from the kitchen table, prepared to head upstairs to either do some reading or call my dad. I went to take my cell phone out of my pocket, and it rang.

"Hello, this is Starla."

"Hey, it's Owl. I got your number from Jenson. I'd been cleaning up my room this evening, no biggie right?"

"I guess. Did you find something?"

"I came across a few pictures from pow-wows I've attended over the years. Nuria must not have known she was being photographed. During them, we have elders take pictures of our tribe members for the newspaper. Once in a while Martin would tag along with Rascal. There is clearly, a woman with him in this picture, and it's not Martin's mom," Owl blurted.

"This is good. Then we'll be able to identify her."

"Yes, have you come up with any clues, ideas, anything since we last spoke?" he questioned.

"Um, yes in a very unconventional way."

"OK, well go ahead, tell me," he urged.

"I had a lucid dream this morning. In it a spirit animal connected to me. I believe she is part of my clan, possibly a member of it or may even represent a part of me. The cabin Rascal was sharing, so little about, we have to go there! This fox told me we'll find clues there, to lead us to Nuria's whereabouts. The only problem is I can't remember the name of the park. If Du-vance does have a half sibling, then possibly he was searching for her and not Nuria."

"Let's all meet on Monday at the cafe before class. How does that sound," asked Owl.

"Good, it seems to be our official meeting spot. I'll call Jenson to see if he can join us there," I answered.

"What about Molly?"

"She and I usually meet up, before class. It should work," I reassured him.

"Anyway, how was your day?"

"OK," I answered, making my way to my room. "Molly and I finished some homework. I tried to get ahold of you, but got no answer, Jenson, too."

"He and I hung out and also caught up on some academics. We both realized we'd forgotten our phones once we got to the library. It was early yet, ten a.m.," he groaned.

"No way was I up that early. I didn't even wake up til around eleven, and then I tried to take a siesta, but was startled by that vision."

"Hmm, so nothing fun today?"

"Did Jenson ask you to give me the third degree," I answered him.

"No, but..."

"OK then, if it's necessary you can tell him that I look forward to seeing him later."

"Yep, well..."

"Owl, what is it?"

"Jenson... Maybe you guys should go to the dance coming up."

I smiled, "Yes, we almost certainly will. I'll talk to you both Monday."

I hit the end button on my phone, placing it on my nightstand as I heard my bedroom door open.

"Hey," said my mom peering in.

"Hi, how was work?"

She came over and sat on the edge of my bed.

She shrugged her shoulders, smiled, and said, "Eh it was OK. Did you get your homework done?"

"Yes, and Megan made us dinner. Ham and cheese sandwiches, then we watched Ellen, little sister treating big sister."

"Dad's coming over for dinner tomorrow night. Both you and your sister are required to be here. OK?"

"Yeah, sure, Mom."

She proceeded to give me a hug. I embraced her back.

Pulling away, I asked, "Is dad still taking me to get my moped license?"

"You'll have to ask him. Now get some sleep. I'm sure we'll get it dealt with soon," she said, closing the door behind her.

I began to ready myself for bed. My mind raced. I wouldn't be gathering with everyone til Monday. Why weren't we working on the case this weekend? I only worked on Sunday. Dad would be here for dinner. How were we supposed to discuss the case with Megan there? Me, being a fox would have to come out sooner or later. How long will they keep things hidden from her, like they did me? What about Lang Orion? Nothing had been mentioned about him. I found it rather bizarre unless he wasn't connected, to any of the others. I don't think Cal knew him. Eva and Star never even mentioned him when I was there.

Putting my clothes in the hamper, I realized I'd forgotten about the diary and pictures mom had given me. I rummaged around my top clothing drawer, fishing out the envelope along with the diary where I'd stashed them. I'd look through some of the pictures tonight, but the diary would have to wait until tomorrow. I was already having, a hard time keeping my eyes open. I put the diary in my drawer of the night stand, not sure why I feared someone taking it.

Myth

The manila envelope appeared old and worn. How long had my mother had it? I turned it over in my hands and then picked at the scotch tape holding it closed. Once the plastic was removed, I pulled out several photos of various sizes.

In the first set of pictures I scanned, it was difficult to tell who was who. I'd never seen mother in her fox form. Why hadn't she shown me? The picture was taken, in a field at Hunters Park. It looked like a moonlight meeting. I saw a few wolves in the photo. Turning it around on the back side, it said: "Meeting to admit Dan into the Clan officially." Other small snapshots I shuffled through contained several of a bride and groom. In them, my mother was in her human form. My father as far as I knew was human. The two larger prints were group pictures. One a mixture of many clans, wolves, foxes, wolf-hybrids, and a few humans were also standing beside them. Was that a park ranger? I wonder if it was the one that Rascal had spoken of.

Hmm, to me they were just photos. Nothing evident jumped out at me. Mother could probably tell me additional details. I should ask in the daytime. The diary I kind of wanted to go through myself. Was I born a fox or human? What did I, look like? Why didn't I ever see pictures of myself as a fox, only a human? Thoughts scrambled my brain. Recently my concentration was on Du-Vance's death. I set the photographs on my nightstand before turning out the light.

Anticipation of what was to come clouded my brain. I reflected on Owl's kind heart in spite of our first meeting. Then Jenson's arms engulfed me as I lay deep in fantasy. I almost fell asleep until I jolted awake, concerned about Molly's dilemma. Finally, when I thought sleep had arrived, I tossed and turned some more until I eased myself into peace, letting it go, giving it to the wind to sweep away my unsettled insecurities, into the night.

Chapter 17

My stomach rumbled at me as I got up to face the day. I slipped on an old pair of jeans and a purple sweatshirt, then went downstairs. The kitchen was empty. Mom and Megan weren't up yet. I lifted my face towards the sun. Its rays poured through our window overlooking the sink. A chill remained in the air from the freshly fallen snow. Shielding my eyes from the light, I reached up to the top cupboard. I pulled out the box of Honey Toasted Oats pouring them into my bowl. Then set them down on the counter briefly to grab the soy milk out of the fridge. What? An animal was outside our kitchen window, was that a fox? It was! Could it be one of my clan members? I opened the pane to get a better look, then called out, "Star, Eva, is that you?"

She or he didn't answer. I hoped it wasn't a shapeshifter trying to trick me. The fox began twitching, transforming before my eyes, into the form of my mother. Quickly a paw reached out, pulling her stashed clothes from the side of the shed. Shivering, I backed away from the glass. Was that truly mom? I was about to go upstairs when Megan hopped into the room.

"Hey, mom went on her morning run. She said she'd be back for breakfast. Did you think I was sleeping? I had a book to read, for English. Remember *Great Expectations*?"

Before I could reply my mother opened the back door, letting herself into our kitchen.

"Hey girls, that was quite a run. I didn't mean to startle you," she said to me, shutting the door.

My sister picked up the Honey Oats I'd left on the counter and grabbed soy milk out of the fridge.

"Want some sis, unless you're eating your cereal dry today."

I took the milk, pouring it onto my cereal and watched as my mom got her own bowl. She came to sit between Megan and me, setting her bowl down beside ours. Without a word she pulled us both into a huge bear hug. Then let go. She grinned, and then began preparing her breakfast.

"So sis, what did you think of *Great Expectations*?" asked Megan again.

"I really liked it, one of the characters spontaneously combusts!" I exclaimed.

My sister almost blew milk out of her nose. My mom laughed at us both. Studying her, I observed her take in a deep breath, then slowly exhale it out. I touched her arm, pulling up her sleeve tracing my hands over what appeared to be the same fox tattoo I had. I'm not sure what made me do it. The need to feel close to her, or was it instinct? How come I hadn't seen it before? Did she cover it with make-up? What about all the times we'd gone swimming in the ocean in L.A.?

My tattoo had not glowed in a while. Eva hadn't given me a lot of data on how it worked. She'd said it could sense things. What things did it sense besides my clan, as Molly had suggested? Mom took my hand gently pushing back down her short sleeve shirt.

"Yeah, I have one too. It's been really difficult to keep it hidden," she said.

Megan spoke up, "Mom, I don't have a tattoo. Did you and Starla go get them before I was born?"

The cat was out of the bag. I didn't think mom would be getting out of this one with my Lil sis.

Mom pushed her long strawberry blonde hair behind her ears before she spoke.

"Your sister and I were born with them. Your father and I didn't meet each other in L.A. We met while he was going to school here. I lived in Hunters Park. One day he came into the park to do some research for a plant biology class. I saw him as I was doing some hunting that day with my family. I know this all sounds eccentric." My Mom placed her hand on top of my sister's. She looked afraid. "I don't know how else to say this, Megan. I am a fox who has the ability to transform into a human. I was very young at the time, around sixteen years old. Your father was 19 when I first observed him. Every time Dan showed up in the forest I'd follow him. This went on for several months. Early on, my clan warned me to stay clear of humans. My father and mother, who have passed now, urged me to believe that this kind of relationship would complicate things. Still, I was infatuated with him."

My sister started to speak, but my mother held her hand up to hush her. "Please let me finish, and then you may speak." My sister's eyes grew wide with astonishment. She continued to sit silently, her hands gripped the table as if she was on an airplane flight.

"One day I came out of hiding in my human form to meet him. We began taking walks together in the forest. I listened to him discuss his interests. I'd been schooled by the clan, enough to get by. Struck by the way he carried himself, I was inspired to attend college. In order to do this, I would have to live amongst humans.

He'd said there was a test I could take if I wanted to enroll. The jolt is I never told him I was a fox. I deceived your father because I was terrified that it would end our relationship."

My sister had tears streaking down her face. She'd pushed her bowl of cereal aside. I tried to read her, to see inside her heart so that maybe I could help her understand. This was the first time I'd ever heard this story. I mean, I knew they'd met in college, but my mom had lived here! If all this had occurred, then why did we return? Had my father summoned us here?

"It became clear when I was pregnant with Starla that I must reveal the truth to your father. I honestly thought I'd end up raising you alone," my mother whimpered, gazing at me. "He was so many things that day, scared, furious, upset, yet he still held me, and kissed me before he took off. I remember that night so clearly. He left me in Hunters Park. Kris (Cal's mom) and I were best friends. She comforted me, keeping me sane til Dan came back. He was gone for almost 3 months. I still don't know what went on during his absence. I never asked, assuming he was working on his college degree, and he'd held a computer job at the school."

"Is Starla a fox too?" Megan interrupted.

"Your sister is half human, half fox. Your father told me recently that she'd discovered the truth about her heritage. I wanted to keep you girls safe from all this. The whole reason it was so touchy for me to be with your father at the beginning of our relationship is that there are people who do not want us to merge. Most humans and other species we know of accept each other, learn, take on each other's cultures, positive traits, learning and growing from our differences. We let these unite us instead of using them as tools of separation. The Bandits think otherwise. It's one of the reasons I alienated myself from the clan. Your father, he wanted us to exist with both at once. I didn't see the possibility of it," she explained.

"Is that why you and dad split? It wasn't about him leaving his teaching career to become an investigator?" asked Megan.

"It was a little of both. How are you dealing with this? Are you majorly freaked out?"

"I just want to know about me. Where do I fit in? Do I belong to you and dad?"

My mother moved her chair closer to my sister, wrapping her arms around her. She kissed her gently on the forehead."You do, belong to us. It's why your father and I are trying to work things out. We were going to talk to you about everything tonight," she stated. My mother gradually let go and brushed Megan's hair behind her ears lovingly.

"You and Starla are sisters unique in your own ways. I know you'll gain some of my abilities. I've been surprised nothing has happened yet, that I know of. If anything occurs, visions, an ability to move objects, seeing things clearer in the night when it's pitch black, anything let me know, OK?"

My sister nodded.

I got up, taking my mostly empty cereal bowl to the sink. Turning around, I asked, "So what's on the agenda for today?"

"I think we could all use a day out of this apartment. In fact, I've been a bit stuffy myself. Maybe it's just guilt, but do you guys want to go to the mall?"

My sister's eyes lit up. The mall was something she never said no to.

"OK, but we have to at least go to Music Radio," I said.

"I'm not going to say no, but I sense this is a bribe," proclaimed Megan.

"Kind of, you can't go telling your friends about this. The only exceptions to the rule are Jenson and Molly. I'm not sure who else is involved. Things are a mess since Du-Vance's death. I've stayed out of the assignment your father and sister are working on. Right now my job is to keep you girls secure. I'm hopeful after this is over things will be peaceful, or..."

"What is it Mom? Were we ever at peace? Did we ever live amongst humans, wolves, gypsies, wolf hybrids, and Indian tribes?"

"That's a lot to ask me right now. We'll discuss this in depth later tonight when your father arrives," she said.

"OK," said Megan as we got up from the table.

"Let's go get our purses and coats, and then we'll meet mom in the car," I said to my sister. I turned to exit the kitchen, heading towards our entryway.

"Sounds like a plan, Mrs. Star of Starlight. I demand to see you turn into a fox!" She grabbed me by the shoulder in a playful manner.

"Not likely, mom has us under wraps. What are you doing, stealing all my witty lines," I retorted. Then gently gave her a friendly bump.

Once in the hall I opened the closet door, getting our coats. My sister took hers from me and put it on.

Megan pulled me towards her, "Thanks, I just have an awful lot of questions. I don't want to ask mom everything," she whispered.

I gave her a quick squeeze of reassurance, "OK, but save it for tonight after dad has left and mom has gone to bed."

She nodded, and we headed out of the apartment to wait in the car.

Myth

Hours later...

Megan and I deposited our loot on my bed. She was all smiles. Mom had let her pick out a new outfit with accessories.

"Dad better get here in a flash. Mom's pretty edgy," said Megan, sitting on my bed.

"You think, she never lets us get Taco Bell, go to Dairy Queen, get new outfits and new music all in one day," I stated.

My sister pulled her knees to her chest and rested her face on them. I wondered if she'd always felt excluded, the odd one out. I'd thought I'd been the outcast. She had all the popular friends. Could it be I'd misinterpreted my sister? I had consistently run off doing my own thing in L.A. I definitely changed since we'd moved here.

"So you and Jenson, how is that working out?" she asked, running her hands over my bedspread.

"We've had one date so far. Our relationship hasn't altered too much yet. It's just the beginning," I sighed, recalling how his arms had felt as they'd engulfed me. I preferred to be in them right now.

"Do you have a boyfriend?" I asked her. She was in eighth grade, after all.

"Nah, not right now, I've got too much homework, and I prefer hanging out with my friends. I do admit some of the boys are cute. They just act like fools attempting to impress us. I don't buy it."

"I get it, been there."

We took our new outfits out of their packages. My sister had gotten a cute pair of jeans with a dressy pink shirt. I'd just stuck with jeans and a nice new purple hoodie. It was either that or a flannel to wear over my white T-shirts. I hung my new clothes in the closet. I realized if I was going to the dance I'd have to go on another shopping trip. There was nothing in my closet to wear. Dresses were not in this girl's dress code.

"Where are your green earrings? Can I borrow them?"

"Sure, sis, in my night stand drawer," I replied nonchalantly.

"Where did this diary come from?" Megan asked, pulling it out from the drawer. She examined the brown leather cover.

"Mom gave it to me. I still have to go through it. There are pictures also in that manila envelope. I forgot to ask her about them," I said.

"Can I have a look?"

"The pictures yes, I want to read the diary first. Mom gave it to me."

"But..."

"No buts or you can leave," I argued.

She sat down and leafed through the pictures. Maybe I shouldn't let her see them. It would only cause her to inquire further, yet she was going to have to meet the clan someday. I hoped my mother realized that everything now must come together. Whatever puzzle pieces she had torn apart to try to save us hadn't worked. I had to piece them back together. They wouldn't all exactly fit, not as they had before, but they would have to merge.

"Do you know who any of these foxes are?"

"No clue. I tried to find out last night. The others you know are Mom and Dad's wedding, right?" I asked.

"Of course, I do."

She continued to study the photos.

"So the others in these pictures: wolves, foxes, wolf-hybrids, I mean, who knows what else we are a part of." She tossed them down on my bed.

"I'm just"...

"Upset, hurt, confused, angry," I blurted throwing the words out for her to grasp.

"Yeah, but I still love mom," she gulped down the tears. I don't think she wanted to cry again in front of me.

"Look on the bright side, we went shopping today, I'm still your sister. You can't get rid of me, fox, or no fox, OK?"

"OK, but tell me what your tattoo does?"

I shook my head, grinning, "It might be a warning signal not sure. I have yet to see it glow, if someone should call upon me. Eva, one of the foxes in the clan says it helps me sense things, but I've about given up on figuring it out. No one wants to tell me," I replied, rolling my eyes.

"Ask Dad tonight, tell him you need to know. It could be useful in the case."

"I will, now can I have some privacy before it all comes hailing down on us?" I asked.

"What?"

"Mom and Dad, in the same room, I know you said they were lovely dovey last time.

My sister turned, leaving the room.

I glanced at the diary sitting on my night stand. I wondered if it said how in love they once were. They had to be to create us. That passion was only starting to form in me. I shuddered. It scared me to imagine it. Love, Jenson, even what Molly must be going through, I could not hide from it. It never did me any good in the beginning when I'd gotten my visions.

I opened up the diary to page one.

Chapter 18

Setting down the diary beside me, I placed a hand on the cover, tracing the symbol of infinity. My mother had gone through a great deal in her life. What she wrote made it sound as if my father was the best thing that ever happened to her. Pa and Ma were loving, but stern. It sort of oddly reminded me of *The Little Mermaid*. It started out as ordinary everyday adventures with her family, but as she grew older it became apparent she was intensely interested in the world outside her realm. There was no mention of any love interest inside the clan. My mother wrote as if most of them behaved like brothers to her, protectors of sorts versus anyone she could become romantically involved with. They weren't too keen on that. Eva remained my mom's biggest supporter. I neared the last page. Eva told my mother to follow her heart. What upset me was the diary contained nothing relevant to the case. Did I overlook anything? Had my mother given this to me to connect with her, or the clan?

If Megan wanted to read it she could, I thought setting it on my nightstand. Dad would be here eventually. I could almost imagine my mother calling me downstairs. Tomorrow I'd have to get up early for work. Ugh, so not looking forward to that. Hopefully, I'd be able to get my moped license soon. No more walking...

"Starla, come help me with dinner," my mom hollered.

Right on target I thought, seeing my sister waltz out of her room.

"I heard mom calling you. Did you find anything out in that diary?"

"I found out what are grandma and grandpa would have been like. They strike me as stern from the way Mom described them. If you ask me, we're lucky to have her. You can review it later tonight. Return it once you're done," I said.

"No problem, why wouldn't I?" she sassed.

I shrugged, heading down the stairway. Warm smells drifted from the kitchen. Peering in I observed my father taking cheesy bread out of the oven.

"Yum, amazing, are we having spaghetti again?"

"No, Mom left to pick up pizza. She thought she'd better holler at you to come down before it got here. I wanted to make an appetizer to go with it. I miss cooking. It gets lonely making dinner for one," he replied.

"I know, I hate eating alone after a work shift. It's why I usually pick something up there with one of the wait-staff," I answered.

My dad set the plate of cheesy bread on the table. I grabbed the plates out of the cupboard to help get ready for when the food arrived. Would she remember my pepperoni?

"Thanks, for helping. Um, mom discussed with me your conversation this morning. I'm glad she told you. I just wanted to be there," he assured me as Megan strolled into the kitchen.

"Can I have some of that?" she asked, pointing to the bread on the table.

"Sure," Dad said.

She quickly scooped one up off the plate, putting it into her mouth.

"Hmmm," she moaned.

Dad chuckled.

"We know it's good," I replied.

"Starla, why don't you grab cups for soda?"

"Sure." I took them down from the cupboard and then placed them on the table alongside the cola.

"I'm sorry we haven't been able to get you your moped license yet. How was your date with Jenson?" he asked me.

I sat down next to my sister.

"I really like him. Star said it doesn't have to be complicated. That similar to you and mom, it might work. She doesn't want me to worry."

"That sounds like Star. Megan, how are you faring with the news from this morning? Do you have any concerns you must discuss?"

"Mom explained most of it. It was worth the trip to the mall. Does it bother me that you hid it from us, of course, it does, dad!" she yelled and slammed her fork on the wooden table. It made a small indent where it had hit.

"Understand we only kept it hidden from you girls for your protection. We love you."

"I don't understand why you had to hide it for so long," Megan muttered.

"To safeguard you. There was a massacre in River Rouge years ago. A family from the clan was killed that contained half fox/half humans, vampire hybrids, and other half-breed mixes. Star, their daughter, and some others discovered them. They'd heard something was going down in the area. They didn't make it

146

in time. She found her parents' bodies. The other's they tried to help fled. We'd been cautioned by Star after she returned to Hunters Park. I wished to continue helping her. I owed them at least that. Your mother and I agreed on separating to keep you both secure. Then I arranged to assist the clan. After a few years of investigative work, nothing turned up. But now I'm concerned about all of us, especially since Du-Vance's death."

Megan gulped down some soda, "I understand dad, it just makes me sad. At one point in my life, I even considered I might be adopted."

I tried to stifle a laugh, but then remembered I had the same idea when my powers appeared. Mother and father weren't truthful regarding them so I had no clue where they'd come from, definitely a Clark Kent moment.

My sister continued, "You haven't been around much since I was born. It's so not fair. You appear in our lives when you want to, and then you're gone again. I sure hope this time things end up differently. Even if you and mom choose not to be together, I'd like my dad back," coaxed Megan.

Fritz barked from somewhere in the house. Suddenly he romped on into the kitchen.

"Fritz, are you looking for food?" I said. I stood up and walked over to his bowl, picked it up and then glanced at the door handle. It moved.

"Dad," I said.

... Click, click, click...

"Dan, can you open the door! My key isn't working," shouted my mother.

Pushing back his chair, Dad got up and opened it. I finished getting Fritz his food so he'd be distracted while we ate.

"Thanks, could you take the pizza?" asked my mom as she entered the kitchen.

"I got it. What toppings did you get?"

"Half is pepperoni and olives for you girls. The other half is veggie. I hope you don't mind hun," she blushed.

My dad took the pizza from her. "Come sit so we can eat. The girls and I have already begun discussing what happened this morning, and why," Dad explained.

"Ah, well how far have we gotten? What did I miss?"

"Dad said you kept Starla's identity as a fox a secret to protect us. It's all due to a massacre at a place called River Rouge," Megan repeated.

"That's true," she replied.

My dad took my mother's hand, holding it in his. I dished up our plates with pizza.

"Your mom and I have been trying to work things out, maybe I should have listened years ago. I just couldn't leave the clan unprotected, nor could I make her live a life she deemed would put you girls in jeopardy. Now that everything is out in the open..."

"It's alright, Dan," said mom.

"I've tried to stop caring for you so many times. I even attempted to date once, but you were there in the back of my mind. She kissed me, and I just pulled away. I couldn't," he stuttered.

My dad was crying at our dinner table. I'd never seen my dad cry, never! Our pieces of pizza sat untouched. I swore you could have heard a mouse squeak if one had been in the room. Was my mom mad? Dad had tried to kiss someone else, well on one occasion nevertheless.

"I want us to try and be a family again," Mom announced.

"Are you moving back in dad? When?" insisted Megan.

148

"That's up to your mom. We've in the process of getting on the same page, to try and see each other's views. It's going to take time," proclaimed our father.

"One day at a time that is what we promised ourselves, that we wouldn't rush, but that we would accept each other as our relationship comes back together," Mom explained.

"So," pushed my sister.

"So, give them time," I said.

Mom and dad both chuckled at that.

Things appeared to settle down after a short while. I'd wanted to ask my dad about the case all evening.

"Dad, a lot has been going on with the Du-Vance case. You said you'd keep in contact with Jenson, Molly, and me. Where have you been?" I pushed.

"Your mom and I have been catching up, so I've stepped back a bit. You haven't seen Ranger Mike, since you met the clan. I stopped by the other day, and he told me you'd met Owl at a book club. He took you, Jenson, and Molly to meet Rascal and question him. It didn't sound like anything new had surfaced, hence I wasn't too anxious. I did hear you revealed Eva had a sister, Nuria. I already knew this, of course, being Eva is Cal's mom. I wasn't aware that Rascal didn't know about her."

"Dad, we believe Du-Vance might have gone searching for Nuria, and that was why he was killed. Eva said she's a part of the fox clan. It wasn't as Rascal had suspected. He assumed she was part wolf. I'm surprised you didn't know this since it pertains to our clan."

My dad stared at my mom with his eyes. I could read them in an instant. It was as if he was saying, should we tell her? What? If he knew so much about the case, why did he hide it from the people who required the truth the most? It was blatant; the massacre in River Rouge, Nuria, Du-Vance, and an enemy all fit together.

"Part fox, part wolf," spoke up my mother.

"How can that be, and human? That seems impossible," I argued.

"We assumed so too. Honestly, I don't know why Starla. The only thing we know is she is physically a merge of a fox and wolf. The mental abilities, she has are united. It's kept her separated from us if someone sought to mark one of us..."

"Can I go eat in the living room?" interrupted Megan.

"You should stay. It's vital you recognize this. If something should occur, you ought to be well-informed. It may not seem significant, however you're a part of this family. Therefore, you're still part of the clan," pointed out our mom.

"I'm meeting my friends on Monday before class to discuss the investigation, is there anything else I should be aware of?" I pondered.

My mom smoothed out her long strawberry blonde hair and then pushed it off to one side of her shoulders. She appeared to be observing my father's features as I often did when admiring Jenson.

"The only people who truly understood Nuria are the natives she let in. Rascal, was probably the best person to go to for details. Owl led you in the right direction. I didn't know her; I saw her a few times in passing before we left, but never to chat. She attended a few clan meetings, but it was a rarity to see her unless it was an urgent matter," mom disclosed.

"Owl found a picture from a pow-wow of Nuria. He's supposed to share it with us when we meet. I'm confident though that we'll find clues in the cabin that may help us find out what is going on. I pray she's still alive, that they didn't get to her like they did Du-Vance. It makes me speculate if Rascal's son didn't have secrets too," I said.

Chapter 19

Sundays were crazy at Denny's. I'd already waited on several tables with crying children, one had spilled milk all over the table, and another screamed because we had no cherry topping left for pancakes. I was ready for the day to be over. Entering the wash area I put the dirty dishes in the sink and started the water for suds'.

"Hey, can you wash those? The dishwasher called in," hollered Don.

"Yeah, sure, I need a break from waiting tables anyway. Do we have enough staff to cover?" I asked.

"Just enough," he answered.

Marla swayed to the music behind me, as she snatched up the next breakfast order.

"Hey chica, I have to get this out, but we should talk," she said.

"About what?" I asked.

"Life, friends, and college. You could use some breakfast. Did you even eat before you came in this morning? You always have so much running around in that brain of yours," she added. Marla waved and continued swaying her way out of the kitchen into the dining area.

I hadn't eaten. I'd been a bit antsy. Jenson had not called me all weekend, and neither had Molly. It seemed as if things were at a standstill. I hated playing the waiting game. I'd also been working up the nerve to ask him to the dance. Had he even asked me yet? I didn't think so.

"Starla, there's a girl out here, looking for you. Says her name is Molly. She seems extremely upset," Don said, strolling up to me. "I told her she could wait til your shifts over. It's after one o'clock you leave at 2 p.m. right?" he asked.

"Yes."

"Well, your friend has perfect timing. I'll let Marla know you have to leave now. She's always, so chatty. I'm sure you two can hang out another time."

"Sure, thanks," I replied.

I finished up the dishes and placed them in our large drying unit. I'd stock up the food bar quick before I left. Ambling out to the dining area I glanced up, Molly sat in the booth near the entrance door. She looked miserable. I'd have to get her out of here. I didn't think it would be a good idea to stick around. Possibly we could go get a bite to eat at the Sunshine Cafe. I didn't want Marla to interrupt us. Molly hadn't looked this frantic about anything since her grandmother died. Marla approached me and tapped me on the back. I turned around.

"I've got this, just put away the dry dishes in the back. We'll chit chat another time. I can't imagine what's going on with that friend of yours, but she needs you," said Marla.

"Thanks," I replied.

I was putting the last dish away in the stack when I heard a loud crash. Peeking out, I saw a toddler had knocked over a pitcher of Coke, and it was all over the floor. The entire family stood up from the table as Marla raced out to the floor to try to calm the child and clean up the mess. This was why we told customers, we preferred them to let wait staff bring them more drinks. I needed to get out of here!

"Don, I'm punching out. I'll see you later," I yelled.

"Sure thing, I hope everything is OK with your friend," he said, waving goodbye.

Zig-zagging through customers, I stumbled to the booth trying not to trip over my own feet. Molly snatched my hand, giving it a squeeze, then let it go. She started wiping her eyes with a napkin.

"Sorry, I didn't know where else to go," she wept.

"Did they throw you out?" I asked.

"No," Molly said through her tears. She stood up collecting her purse and coat.

"Can we get out of here? It's kind of, crazy," she sniffed.

"I wanted to leave this place all day. It's been a madhouse from kids spilling drinks to them crying because we are out of cherry filling," I said. I tossed my hair tie into my bag, letting my curls fall loosely around my face.

Molly managed a smile.

"I was supposed to go out for lunch with my family, but left in the middle of church. I couldn't stay. I... I'd have gone postal on our minister. Done something regrettable," she stammered.

"What's that?" I asked. We left the building nipping near the main route towards the seven eleven.

"I almost got up in the middle of Pastor Joe's sermon to tell him off. I... You know how quiet I usually am about stuff like this.

In the past, I've just let it go," she said, gesturing almost knocking me in the face. "Oh, sorry," she said, bringing her arm back, holding her purse near.

"Tell me exactly what happened."

"I was sitting in the pew next to mom when he announced we'd be talking about the sins of the flesh. I just sat there thinking not this again! It's something they've been pressing in our parish recently. I should have known he'd bring the subject up, especially in the midst of the college dance. The whole time I felt this chicken bone forming in the back of my throat. I couldn't breathe. I kept contemplating what about unconditional love? Free will, judge not lest ye be judged and love, thy neighbor. They feed that stuff to us, and now this. I can't, take this anymore, no more!" Molly stopped in the middle of the sidewalk and stomped her feet on the ground. Abruptly losing control of her body gravity took over. She lost her balance and almost fell onto the cement, but caught herself.

"You almost fell, I'd tell you not to get worked up, but I'm right there with you. I'm proud of you."

"You should have seen, mom and dad's faces when I got up and zapped out of there! I should have stood up for myself, but then what? What would have happened?"

"It depends on them. Most likely they would have asked you to ask for forgiveness for your sins. Do you plan on going home tonight? Your mom and dad are going to know something is up." We linked arms and continued to hike on. "If you need to camp out at my house again, you can, but they do know where I live."

Molly laughed,"I'm not a little kid. I should have done this a long time ago just cut the ties," she replied, making a slicing motion at her neck by means of her hand.

Molly had barely noticed where we'd been strolling to. We stood outside the convenience store.

"Food," I said, pointing to the well-located store we'd just wandered up to.

"A slushie would be good with a giant chocolate chip cookie," said Molly.

"Great lunch choice," I replied, pushing open the doors. We moseyed on in.

"I don't want to be here very long, so I'll get the drinks if you find the cookies," said Molly.

"OK, but make sure you make mine a frozen half-cherry, half cola."

A few blocks down we sat on the swings at Springville Elementary sipping our drinks whilst nibbling on cookies.

"Can we not discuss this right now," she sighed swinging slowly back and forth.

"You're going to have to eventually. Are you going home tonight?"

"I don't want to. I don't ever want to go back," she muttered.

"Consider how many times you've run from this. You can't escape by ignoring it any more than I did by avoiding my feelings for Jenson. If you don't do something you'll burst! Think about your new friend, Maine, you, your happiness, not all churches are like the one you attend. I'm not saying they don't have a right to their opinion, but you too have a right to be happy, to your free will," I insisted.

"I'm used to being told what to do. Listen to others, in addition, follow the church," she mimicked. "I just want to be myself," she declared as she swung her legs back and forth sitting on the swing beside me.

"OK, I'm going to lay it out, give you my opinion. You don't have to agree or be fond of it. Believe me, loads of the social order won't," I said.

Molly got up from the swing, and we headed back towards the road.

"OK, advise me," she said.

"This is between you and God. It's not anyone else's life. You're my best friend. You deserve to be loved and happy. Although with my upbringing, your folks would call me a hooligan."

Molly chuckled through her tears.

"I'll be here no matter what. You can't get rid of me."

"And if the church gets rid of me?" she asked.

"Mom and I will help you find a new one," I answered.

I opened the door to our apartment.

"Starla, Molly's parents called, is that you?" she asked, peeking around the corner before she disappeared back into the living area.

"Yeah, mom," I said, closing the door behind us. I turned and hung up our coats. We'd just made it back from the playground. Molly had finally managed to stop crying for a third time. Now, I was afraid that there would be new tears. Traipsing into the living room, I saw my mother. She'd just sat back down, with the evening paper in her lap.

"Hey girls, Molly's folks want her to call them."

"I don't want to talk to them, Tri. I can't have a discussion with them right now," argued Molly firmly holding onto the arm of the couch as she stood.

"OK, you're old enough to make that decision yourself. So, do you want to tell me what's going on?"

Molly sat down next to my mom on the sofa.

"My mom will understand," I assured her.

"I want to go to the dance, but I want to go with a girl. My parents, they won't understand. I..."

"Is that why you have been struggling err, not wanting to go to church?" asked my mom.

"Yes, I can't do it anymore. I can't pretend. I should have left by now, moved out, but I love my family." Molly cast her eyes down towards the floor.

My mom moved closer to her, wrapping her arm around her shoulders.

"It's going to be OK. Here in our home there is no judgment. You haven't told your parents then yet," she asked gently letting go of Molly.

"No, Church today was dreadful, so I left. I didn't want to cause a scene or be, disgraced in front of the entire congregation who've known me for years. They won't see me the same way once I'm out," Molly proclaimed.

158

"You can't hide forever, but for now you can stay here."

"I'm going to start looking for a place of my own," replied Molly.

"I understand. You should at least give your parents a chance. Let them know what's going on even if you decide not to stay with them," my mother replied.

Molly nodded.

"College, will your parents stop paying your tuition?" I gasped.

"It might happen, but there are loans, and I'll have to get a job if I move out. I have a small amount saved in my accounts. I probably should take their names off of them before I tell them."

"Do you think they would do that? Not only stop paying for college, but empty your accounts?" inquired my mom.

"My parents have at all times followed the church. You've always let Starla make her own, choices about religion, given her options. I've envied that ever since we've been friends, even when I only knew her online. Not many moms would just let their daughter be friends with a girl she'd never met."

"I'm just starting to let go. It isn't easy. You girls, are growing up. It's hard for me not to see my daughters, as my little girls."

My mom smiled at me.

Chapter 20

(Monday)

When I had woken up, Molly had already left. Brushing off my worry, I got ready for the day. It was time we'd made some headway in this case, unearth some more clues and even maybe locate Nuria.

I examined my work schedule for the week. I hadn't gotten many hours. Oh well, extra time for detective work and friends. I lifted my jacket off the back of my bedroom door and took my backpack off the floor. I'd be hoofing it today. When would dad take me to get my moped license? It wasn't doing me any good in that shed.

A cold chill crept up my spine. Briskly, I strolled towards the college entrance. My knapsack felt like it had rocks in it, but they were only my books and supplies for the day. Earlier it had been dark and gloomy. The snow wasn't so bad if the sun was shining. I pushed the doors open into the large hallway continuing straight to Mr. Jones's classroom. Molly would probably be there already. I peered in through the glass window. She sat at our table writing in her notebook. Lifting my hand, I knocked on the plate glass to get her attention. She looked up and smiled. I waited while she gathered her things.

"Hi," she said.

"Hey, let's go get some coffee. Owl and Jenson will probably already be there. It's nasty cold outside. I cannot wait til spring!" I shivered, wrapping my arms around myself attempting to warm up.

"Good luck with that," she chuckled. We walked towards the cafe.

"Yeah, I've heard winter lasts roughly right into May. It's astonishing." I shook my head.

"You'll get over it," said Molly gently bumping my hip with hers as she smiled.

"You OK, after yesterday?"

"Yeah, I'll be alright. I just keep contemplating how to approach them," replied Molly.

"I get that. When do I, get to meet this friend of yours? The one you spoke of the other night?" I asked as we passed another classroom.

"Soon, I might suck it up, be gutsy and ask her to the dance. It's still nix-on telling the parents for now."

I frowned but kept silent.

"If I do go, is it OK to tell them it's as a group?"

"I don't see why not, but you know they're going to ask you why you left church yesterday," I replied.

"I know."

"Are you going to go back home?"

"I'm weighing my options," she answered.

Stepping, into the cafe, the atmosphere shifted. A maze of organized chaos, students chatted, mingled and caffeinated drinks were being purchased. I noticed Owl and Jenson, sitting at a round table in the corner.

"I'll go get us drinks. What do you want? My treat," I said, taking my wallet out of my backpack.

"A hot coffee with hot cocoa mix," she said.

"Coming right up," I replied, turning to the wonderful smells of freshly brewed Joe. Yum! I moved into the line. We had an hour before class started. I'd understood we were meeting Owl so he could show us the picture. Had he talked to Rascal about getting the address for the cabin? What would we do if it was locked, or maybe Nuria was still living there? I watched as the line moved closer to the student making coffee.

"Next," she said.

I stepped up to the counter, eyeing the list of choices.

"Can I have an Americano made like a Mocha, and then I'd also like a coffee Add in hot cocoa please," I said.

"Sure coming right up! Joe, did you hear that?" she asked.

"I'm on it!" he shouted.

"That will be a six-fifty."

I handed her seven bucks, got my change and wala! Joe handed me my drinks.

"Thanks," I said. I spun around, bumping into Mr. Jones.

"Getting a coffee before class I see. It's a great way to stay alert!" He stepped closer to the barista and pulled his billfold out of his pocket.

"I love my Mocha's in the morning," I replied.

"Well, I believe you'll enjoy our lecture today. It will give you more to contemplate."

"Is it more about foxes, or are we going to discuss werewolf's?"

162

"Nope, something much cooler, and I'll want to talk to you after class."

"You're almost up to the counter so I should go." I managed a weak smile. "Not only that my friends are waiting for me," I added.

"Catch you in class." He turned back towards the counter, and the barista began taking his order.

I noticed Molly had joined Owl and Jenson at the corner table. I hurried over to them trying not to spill our drinks. I handed Molly her hot coffee with cocoa and sat down beside Jenson.

"Mr. Jones was being mysterious concerning our next lecture. He requested to speak to me after class. I'm apprehensive with all the hints hidden in his current curriculum."

"He's pretty cool. Last year, our tribe had an exhibit at the museum. He included it in his class syllabus sharing stories of our tribal myths and legends. Jones isn't a likely suspect. He could be a great ally. We just need to be careful seeing as we're not sure who all the enemies are," explained Owl.

"Yes, but they could be anybody at this point. It could be the wolves who are living across from Starla's clan," Molly replied.

"True, but we haven't yet had any experience with them. Our primary goal is to find out what happened to the missing kids, why Du-Vance was killed, and now we are speculating he may have had a sibling. It's a lot to take in. His father seemed OK when we saw him, but he's just skating by," stated Owl.

"Can we see that picture you had?" I asked.

Owl opened up his pack and pulled out a green photo album. He skimmed the pages, then stopped.

"Here it is," he said, laying it out in the middle of the table. He pointed to a young woman with curly blondish brown hair, big soft brown eyes and a kind of slender build wearing a light-fitted floral dress.

"I can see why Rascal was enchanted by her," stated Molly as she examined the photo.

"Have you told anyone else about this?" I asked.

"No, I figured I'd let you guys know first. Maybe I was wrong to assume no one was looking for Nuria. I thought she'd left on her own accord," Owl said.

"A lot of this information and inquiry needs to be discussed with those involved, especially Nuria's sister Eva. She's missing a daughter. All of our speculations, could be tied in together, or maybe I'm reaching and they're separate events," I said.

"It would be great if we could head to the cabin, on our own. I've been to Outlook Point a few times. I'm sure if we drove around, we could find it," Jenson suggested.

Before I could mention Nuria, being a fox-wolf merged, I heard a voice.

"How many cabins do you suppose are out there?"

"Sit down Lance," ordered Owl.

He pulled out the chair the furthest from us and sat. I had no clue he went to college here unless he was just using the community computers.

"What are you doing here?"

"Stopping by to see how your investigation is going. No one is handing out information. I thought I'd drop some knowledge, on you. Shellena and I wanted to chat with you the other night at the bar," he said.

I played with the napkin in front of me sipping on my Mocha. Molly stared at the table behind us. It must have been someone she knew, or maybe Maine?

"It wasn't the right time for us to talk," spoke Owl.

"Well, I know where the cabin is. I've been there. It didn't come to mind until recently. I'd done some work for Nuria in the past, helping her fix her lawn mower among other things. She didn't trust many people out there, even Du-Vance's father had never been to the place," said Lance.

"We should at least let Eva know we're going out there. I mean, her sister knew where she lived, right?" I asked.

"Yeah, she hardly ever went there though. Nuria liked her privacy. I was quite surprised when she and Rascal got together, but who am I to judge. We all need companionship, at least most of us do," Lance responded.

"Um... I... I have to go. I'll meet you guys in class. Jenson, catch me up on all this later? There's somebody I need to speak to," Molly stuttered.

"Sure thing."

"Bye," we said.

Molly hadn't seemed too focused since we'd sat down, so I wasn't surprised when she left.

"She didn't stay long," said Lance.

"The girl has other things on her mind," Owl smirked.

"What sort of, things?" asked Lance.

"Ah, leave it alone. Let's get back to why we're here," said Jenson.

"I was going to offer to take you guys out to the cabin. If you want we can meet up with Ranger Mike, first that's fine, but I need to know what day we're all free," Lance answered.

"Wednesday, after Molly gets out of church, or Saturday are my only free days right now." I was shocked when I'd looked at my schedule at Denny's. I rarely got Saturdays off.

"By the way, Jenson I want you to come over for dinner soon. First, I have to make sure my dad's going to be there. Bring him up to date on the case so to speak," I confirmed.

"Sounds good. Wednesday would be the best day to assemble with Ranger Mike, as well as the other clan members," said Jenson.

"Great," said Lance.

"Has my dad spoken with you about any of this?" I asked him.

"We've touched base a few times. Last time, he chewed me out about scaring the crap out of you," he chuckled.

"Well, if you hadn't I probably still wouldn't know the truth."

Lance got up from the table surveying the scene around us. "I've got to get to the computer lab to work on my resume. This current factory job isn't cutting it. If I have to fill another applesauce, packet I'll lose it. There's this job hiring an auto repair place," he said.

"Fixing cars, huh? Well, I am going to get my moped license soon I expect. Things have been pretty crazy recently. I must get my dad to take me." I bunched up the napkin beside me.

"Well, make sure you do. I heard about Eva loaning it to you. A nice gesture, as it was Cal's and all," noted Lance.

"What time should we meet at the Ranger's station?" asked Owl.

"Two is good. I have a few errands to run. Oh, and bring donuts. Mike loves em!" Lance exclaimed. He stood up, then waved as he strutted away from the table exiting the cafe.

Jenson and Owl packed up their things. I grabbed my backpack and empty Mocha cup.

"I guess Molly will meet us in class," I said scanning the room for her.

"Let's go, better not be late. You know how he is, locking the door so you can't show up tardy," verified Jenson.

"Yep," I answered.

I'd have to tell them later what I'd discovered about Nuria.

"Why is the class half full? Where is everybody?" I asked Molly as I sat down next to her.

"Not sure I've been here a while," she said. Then pointed to Mr. Jones, who was setting up the power point.

I fished out my notes from my pack. My syllabus said we had a test Friday. We never held the class on Fridays?

"Do you suppose he'll put everything on the next exam? I mean we've gone over the Kitsune Fox, Unicorns, Vampires, and," I stopped in thought.

"It says here we are going over the idea that cross breed, species exist," said Owl who sat behind us.

"That's right, and today we have a small class. Some students are going to be in hot water when they decide to show up next week. The test is Friday. I can't be in class Thursday. If you need to take it that day due to work or prior engagements, see me after class. I'll work something out if it's acceptable say you work that day, for example. I can be a pretty awesome guy," he said.

Jones turned away, continuing to set up his equipment. He shuffled through papers placing them on his desk beside an envelope. Owl's name was scrawled, on it. What? Why would he have a note for Owl and want to talk to me after class? That doesn't make a whole lot of sense. I turned my notebook to an empty page prepared for anything Jones might decide to drop on the examination.

"We have to study this week," Molly whispered to me as Jones made his way to the computer. He turned it on to begin the power point.

"I'm not exactly sure how with all we have going on," I muttered, sighing. I felt Jenson, who was seated behind me, place his hand on my shoulder. He gave me a little reassuring pat.

"Look, we'll plan something after this cabin invasion. Lance will just have to understand," Jenson whispered.

"And if he doesn't?" I asked.

"Don't fret now. We need to focus on this power point, plus you can always study after work tonight."

Mr. Jones pulled down the screen used to display the power point, turned off the lights and the room fell silent...

The oration dragged on and on for a two-hour class. Carefully, I took notes as Mr. Jones presented an array of topics. So, much for just speaking about mixed breeds. He's not only discussed the merger of a human-fox and a human-wolf, but of doppelgangers who brought forward the definition of spirit animals. Some tribes believed particular members had the ability to transform into an animal. If they were spiritually connected to one another. Shapeshifters could transform into anything assimilating themselves, for either good or evil purposes. It wasn't a short lecture. I lay down my pen as Mr. Jones turned the lights back on.

"Why can't we just study Greek gods?" Jenson blurted. People in our class chuckled around us.

"I prefer to teach on the fun side! I'm not boring or comparable to other professors on campus. We will get to the Greek gods. In this unit, our focal point is on mythical animals in film, stories, scripts, and a few I've speculated may have existed at one time here. Yes, right here in Springville."

Owl's eyes got big. I pushed my chair back near to where he sat.

"Hey, are you OK?" I asked, whispering.

"Pretty much, but you know there's some truth to what he's saying," Owl replied.

"Yes, but it's all speculation, he said so himself. I wouldn't panic much unless he comes creeping into Hunters Park."

Mr. Jones cleared his throat, taking his place back at the podium after organizing some notes on his desk.

"Now, you'll need to know everything we've discussed in this unit for the test. Remember, it will be on Friday unless you make arrangements for Thursday! I expect you to be able to identify mythical creatures, where you might find them, how to defeat, or merely stun them. If they live in a mythical place or on earth, I want you to distinguish that too. At the end of the test, there will be a chance for you to gain extra credit. You'll make up a story. Reflect on which mythical creature you most relate to or interests you. Write about that," he concluded.

Everyone started to get their things together. You could hear whispering behind us. This didn't seem like an ordinary group of students. Did I not pay attention to my class or was I falling into the trap of pushing everything together that might relate to the case?

"Starla, I'd like a word," said Mr. Jones.

"OK." I collected my book and lecture notes.

Jones stepped up to my desk setting down some note cards, a magazine, and a report of some kind.

"Extra homework, this is why you wanted to talk to me!" I was flabbergasted.

Mr. Jones acted like he didn't know what to say. He stood there silent. Then shook his head, as if he was waking himself up from a micro-nap.

"What was I doing?" he asked.

"Giving me some materials, are they for extra credit?"

"Oh no, I want you to use the note cards to study for the test. The magazine is a special edition of spirit animals, and the report is from ages ago. It has to do with Cal Summers. The report given speculates what might have occurred. Crazy accusations I must say. For example, she joined a fox tribe the other stated kidnaped by bandits. The most bizarre rumor was she'd been seized for her safety."

If this was true, why wouldn't her mother know? Could the urban legends be accurate, mixed in with her disappearance? Du-Vance's death genuinely got me thinking.

"So, are you expecting me to find out what happened? What do you know about this?" I demanded.

"Do some research, write a story based on what you believe may, or may not have happened, for the extra credit on the test. That's all I'm asking for," he stated.

"OK, but you're, being pretty cryptic," I replied rolling my eyes.

"Yeah, you're being really weird. I hope that no one, put anything other than cream in your coffee," speculated Jenson.

Mr. Jones just grinned and chuckled. I couldn't determine if it was an evil chuckle or a friendly one.

"See you in class on Friday," he said, slipping an envelope into Owl's backpack.

Chapter 21

"I have no clue, how I'm going to put together this report for Mr. Jones and tackle all this crap for the case," I told Jenson. All four of us were sitting in a sandwich shop eating our lunch.

"We have the meeting on Wednesday. You could privately talk to Eva about it."

"She doesn't know what transpired. You read the report. Cal wandered off, running after a dog that could, possibly, have been a wolf. We don't know anything after that," I said.

"My advice read that report Jones gave you scour it for any clues," suggested Molly.

Owl, took a big gulp of his cherry cola then let out a huge burp!

"Sorry, about that. I agree, going over that report first before assuming there are no other leads is something we must do," Owl added.

"We?" I demanded.

"Yes, we're in this together. It's rather complex," he stated.

"How is it complex?" Molly inquired.

"Finding Nuria, that is step one, if they are all connected, then either she or the clues might tell us if the reason for her fleeing was to protect Rascal and his son. If so, then whoever was after Nuria, may have been after Du-Vance. They might have even killed him," Jenson responded.

"What about the missing kids? Do you suppose Cal and Lang fit in with this case? Star a member of my clan told me, a group called the bandits didn't like half-breeds or merged species. There was a massacre years ago at Rogue River. I'm pretty sure they're involved in all this!" I said.

"We can add them to our suspects list, but we shouldn't jump to conclusions," advised Owl.

"We'd better take notes. That way we can present them at the meeting. It'll make it a bit easier," Jenson suggested. He pulled out his notebook and flipped it open.

"Take what we know to Mike," recommended Owl.

I finished up the last bite of my turkey delight, smearing a bit of mustard on my sleeve. Ugh! I hated stains.

"Nuria is a blend of half wolf, half fox. I wanted to tell you when we were having coffee today. Then I was reminded again by the lecture in class. One of her parents had to be a wolf-human, and the other a fox-human. If not, then how did it come to be?"

"Who told you that?" asked Owl.

"My mom, Tri," I replied.

"When?" asked Molly.

"Saturday night, my dad came over to have dinner with us. We had an open family discussion about some things and the case."

"The idea of merged species ties into Jones class again." Jenson banged his hand on the table.

"It may simply be a coincidence, but I have been wondering about that as well," I answered.

"Keep your mind open to the possibility that either Jones is feeding us information or trying to get us to solve something that could help the case. Why that is, I don't know. He's a nice man. Awfully strange, though," observed Owl.

I got up and emptied our trays into the waste basket, then sat back down.

"What happened after you went back to Rascals?" Jenson asked Owl.

"What night was that?"

"When you took the girls out for drinks," replied Jenson. We all got up to leave.

"Nothing really, I prodded him for more clues, but he didn't seem to have any. It was a lost cause, pressing him for more facts."

"OK, well, I should go. I want to get to the DMV," I said.

"I ought to go home and face my folks," said Molly, standing up from the booth.

I shielded my eyes against the glare of the sun hitting the freshly fallen snow. Fox tracks? Was someone watching us, keeping tabs?

"Weird," I pronounced, pointing to the tracks as we left the building.

"Make note of that," said Owl.

Jenson took my hand. The snow crunched under our feet as we trudge to his car.

"Molly, you want a ride home," he asked.

"I'll take her," replied Owl.

"I'll see you two, Wednesday. If anything happens, I'll call you," said Molly.

"OK, sounds good."

"See you later," said Jenson. We strolled hand in hand to the car.

The DMV was packed. I tried to contact my dad, no answer, so I'd left a message on his cell.

"You really didn't think this could wait any longer?" asked Jenson.

I gave him the evil eye. Really, did I want to depend on everyone else for transportation? Eva had given me the moped, so I could go places.

"It will make life a lot easier. I know you love hauling me around, but I like my independence."

Jenson smiled, squeezing my hand. He knew better than to argue with me. It had been a while since we'd fought. It was during our friend period. I began to blush thinking about how only a few days ago we decided to modify things.

"You didn't study for this test, did you?" asked Jenson.

"How hard can it be? I mean I have my driver's license."

Jenson started laughing uncontrollably...

"What, what's so funny?"

"Your dad and you truly have no clue, do you?"

"What do you mean?"

"Here in Springville if you have an operator's license, your driver's license, then you can legally drive your moped. You just have to get it registered in your name. That means, Eva has to give you the paperwork. You can most likely get it from her. It's a common mistake, don't fret about it," he said.

I folded my arms a crossed my chest. I felt really silly. I constantly wanted to appear smart, being a feminist, after all. How could I allow a boy to know more than I did? Jenson got up from his seat extending his hand to me. He helped me up as if I was his maiden princess. I guess, he was trying to be nice.

"Come on, I'll buy you a slushie."

I picked up my purse slinging it over my shoulder. He opened the door for me as we made our way out into the parking lot.

"So are you going to give me more details on what I need to do to register it? Is there a fee?" I asked.

He opened the passenger door to his car, and I slipped inside buckling up.

Jenson got into the driver's seat, placing his keys in the ignition. Then gazed at me, "In life there are always fees for things, but the good things are free."

"And what is that?"

He leaned over, gently placing a kiss on my lips. It took me a minute to register, exactly what he was doing. *Slightly awkward, but not bad* I thought pulling away slowly.

"OK, then," he said.

"Yeah, I'm definitely OK," I replied, a bit flustered.

"What are your plans for tonight?" he asked before driving out of the parking lot.

"I'm not really sure. Study for Jones class, then ponder the report he gave me or maybe veg in front of the TV for a bit, if mom allows it." I sighed.

"You don't seem too pleased right now. Earlier today you showed enthusiasm," he said.

"I'm just a bit overwhelmed," I replied, taking his hand in mine.

"Was it the kiss?" he asked.

A tingle, that is what his kiss felt like, thousands of them. I smiled. "No that was actually, amazing even if a bit clumsy for our first kiss."

"Was it that bad?"

"No, I just wasn't expecting it, is all," I replied.

Staring out the window I watched businesses fly past us. 4:45 p.m. was it really that late? My stomach began to growl.

"We probably should pick up some Nachos too."

Later that night at Jenson's....

I stared at the four names that appeared in the report of suspects in Cal's case. I couldn't wrap my head around it. Jenson sat next to me on his bed, Molly had recently joined us, and Owl was absent. Apparently he'd promised to help Rascal shovel his driveway.

"I just can't figure it out! How did Mr. Jones get his hands on this," I said, holding it up to them. "Mike didn't even know the names of the bandit members. The only one who may have had any clues is Star."

"You haven't had any disturbing visions again, have you?" asked Molly.

"Nope and my tattoo hasn't been signaling me. You'd think the clan would want to keep closer tabs," I said.

"Or maybe they actually, trust you," Jenson commented.

"It's peculiar I've only met women from my clan. No men? Is that a creepy, coincidence, or what?"

"And you only just considered this now," stated Molly.

"Yep," I replied.

Glancing to the side, I saw Owl step into the doorway.

"I wouldn't worry about it. I'm sure you'll be introduced to others, in good time," he said entering Jenson's room soaking wet from head to toe.

"Are you alright?" I asked.

"Sure, I had a lot of snow to clear out of Rascal's driveway. I should have stopped by my house to clean up. It sounded pretty urgent earlier this evening when you called me from the phone."

I handed him the report.

"Sika Gem what kind of name is that?" Owl asked, holding up the photo of a tall dark-haired, skinny wolf. He stood next to a motorcycle in the snapshot on his hind legs.

"I didn't see any photos when I observed the reports. Where did you find them?" I asked.

He turned over the report to show me, four photos that had been, gently adhered to the back with two sided tape.

"It's easy to miss, but now we have faces to go with names," said Owl.

"The other names are very different too, Minder, Garvin, and this last guy, calls himself the Gladiator. Minder is the lone female in the gang," I stated.

"Minder is kind of cute," said Owl holding up a photo of a girl wolf, whose fur was long, and brown with blue eyes and a medium build.

"She may be cute, but probably pretty dangerous," I replied.

"Read the report," Owl said, looking at me.

The suspects Minder, Sika, Garvin, and the Gladiator, were called into question after Cal Summers went missing. They had been charged in the past for assaulting humans whom they suspected held traits of the mythical or mystical nature. Mr. Dun one of our former Police Chiefs, ensured us there was some truth to these unusual ideas. In spite of this, the other units laughed it off as a joke. They just couldn't take it seriously.

"I wonder if Mike knows who this Mr. Dun fellow is and was there anything they found on these creeps that could have been Cals? Did they ever have contact with her, or was it another massacre mission they decided to abandon?" asked Starla.

"I would bring this up at the meeting. When you encountered them, it was extremely brief. You barely know anything but bits and pieces of a few members' lives. Your association with them has been limited so far," said Molly.

"I do have a lot to learn. They told me after the case I could choose to either stay living with my mother or choose to live with the clan."

"Does that mean they would shun you if you choose not to live in their territory?" asked Jenson.

"No, I could choose both. I'd just have to be more cautious about who I interact with, those who might press for knowledge about the fox clan. If they still want me to be a guardian, then living between both species might be the better choice."

"Why is that?" inquired Owl.

"A balance must be maintained between humans, the fox clan, mixed species and other peaceful divisions. Those that wish us harm need to be kept at bay," I answered.

"Where did all this come from?" asked Molly.

"Since I met Eva and Star it's something that has been in the back of my mind. It's not something that can just be jumped into. I have to take it all in steps and then decide, what is going to be best for me."

Owl sat down the two remaining photos not yet inspected. The Gladiator was blonde, husky, green eyes, and rather large even for a wolf. I picked up the picture to observe it closely.

"So this group, are they all wolves? How do they drive motorcycles, if they are not half-breeds?"

"They are extremely intelligent. I heard Rascal talking about them once with our tribe. They use to hunt in our territory. It was an ongoing battle between us until they finally left the area," said Owl.

"How would these wolves have gained the ability to rationalize like humans and still have the body of the wolf? How can they be prejudiced against those who share other forms or merges of various species? When they themselves contain an ability outside of their own kind?" I asked.

"No one has been able to reason that out," Owl grumbled.

Gavin was the last photo. An odd-looking fellow with a long stripe down his middle, a mow hawk. He stood beside a tree near a river. I pointed to the photo, looking at Owl.

"Is this River Rogue?"

"Not sure, but it does look similar to it," he answered.

"Once we meet with the clan, I may be able to write my reply to Mr. Jones query about what happened to Cal for the test. Can I trust him Owl? How much do I tell him," I asked, rambling on.

"This is what you should never do, don't ever give specifics concerning where the clan is located, unless instructed by your dad or one of the other members. You can state what occurred and names. We only use first names, so we're not easily detected," said Owl.

"Are you a part of our clan?"

"No, but I am part of a tribe and we are very protective of one another, so make sure you honor your relationship with the fox clan. You don't want to lose their trust. The same goes for each and every one of us. We must be careful what we say and do around others. We have done well so far, but let's try to step it up a notch, OK?" coaxed Owl.

We all nodded at him and gave O.K.'s.

I got up from Jenson's bed to walk around the room. Antsy after the chat concerning the report. I scoured all of the pictures he had from grade school up on his wall, and those we'd taken together since I'd moved here.

Owl walked up beside me to observe what I'd been looking at. "Ah, so pictures from when you were young," Owl said to Jenson.

"Yep, those were the days. In grade school, I was the king of the computer. That's when they were real monsters with plastic discs," said Jenson. He stepped up alongside me observing over my shoulder. He leaned his chin on me, his arms finding their way around my middle.

"Hey, you guys are making me feel really old," I said nudging his face with mine.

"Have you had a chance to skim over the spirit animal magazine Jones lent you?" asked Molly. She was still seated.

"No, do you want to go over it now or..."

Sage sprinted into Jenson's room, her curly hair bouncing behind her as she jumped up and down.

"Hey, you guys come down and have a snack with us? We are watching a great show on snakes! Get it snakes and snacks?" she stated.

We all just laughed.

Gently I took Jenson's hands off of my waist, and he allowed me to pull away.

"I could use a break from this," I said, gathering the contents of the report back into its envelope.

"Sounds good," stated Molly.

"I'm in," replied Jenson.

"Sorry, I need to take care of a few things. Also, get out of these wet clothes. Thanks anyway, Sage. I'll have to take a rain check," said Owl parting.

The rest of us gathered our things to go meet Jenson's family in the living area for snacks.

"Hey, Molly," I said.

"Hmmm, what?" she asked before we headed to the living room.

"Have you talked to your folks yet?"

"Mmm hmm, let's not talk about it now, later at your house, maybe tomorrow after you finish your shift?"

"How about milkshakes on me?" I volunteered.

"All over you, now that would be funny," Sage laughed, overhearing us, as she continued to stand in the doorway.

"You know what I mean," Molly said, rolling her eyes.

"OK, around three then?"

"Sure," she agreed.

"You guys, let's go, get our snake and snack on!" hollered Sage.

Really, she was cute, even if sometimes annoying.

"OK, we are on our way," I answered.

Chapter 22

I'd just gotten back from Jenson's. No one was home. Mom and Megan were probably out eating, a late dinner or shopping. I took advantage of it, kicking up my feet on the coffee table in the living room. It was only eight O'clock, but Jenson and his folks had plans with relatives. It sounded like some kind of family movie night. Why wasn't I invited? Had he not told his parents, we were dating?

I opened my backpack taking out the magazine Jones had given me. Why not get some reading in, after all, it might help me with the case and my academic issues. I'd only gotten glimpses of my clan, and my parent's lives prior to my existence. As a human, my spirit animal had to be a fox or was this spirit animal thing only for tribes resembling Owls? I knew people's beliefs differed but couldn't one adopt another's values into their own life? I mean, why would that be so offensive to them, and would it be? Ugh, maybe my mentality is all mixed up.

Flicking through the pages of the booklet, I turned until I found the fox. It read:

"If you happen to meet this spirit animal it can be a guide or a trickster. You may want to pay attention to the people around you and your or their circumstances. Gain the ability to adapt to observe for you may have to take action of some kind to overcome obstacles in your way or a problem in daily life."

It reads like a horoscope, not what I expected of a pamphlet type mag on spirit animals. I had been thinking more of the kind that legends of tribes claimed could transform from a human form into an animal. I guess, maybe that was more of the shapeshifter variety?

Owl's eyes had gotten really large in Jones's class the other day. It made me curious. Quickly, I leafed through the article till I found the Owl staring at me. It was a regular one too, not a White, or a horned. I was curious if this summary pertained to all Owls.

When the Owl is your spirit guide, a veil is lifted. You're able to see the true reality of things, past deceit and illusions, others may place before you, finding what is hidden not only by others but from them as well. The owl is wise and must use his knowledge carefully.

That did resemble Owl, but how could he be a spirit animal? Did Owl give him visions akin to my fox clan? Well, one of the members, from the past or someone from our clan sent me that revelation about the cabin. Logically, even though I am part fox, wouldn't a fox be my spirit guide? It seemed so at any rate. What could, Molly's spirit animal be or Jenson's? Did it have anything to do with their personalities? Owl, would know! I got up from the couch rifling through my bag to find my cell. I unlocked it. I had two missed calls both from my mother. She hadn't left me a voice mail. I hit the call button, one ring, two rings, three rings...

Come on mom pick up!

I heard a click, then nothing, then click. Maybe her phone was dead? It had happened before. If Megan was with her, she'd have her phone. I dialed that number.

After a few rings she answered.

"Hi, sis, what's up?" asked Megan.

"Mom tried to call me twice. When I called her, she didn't answer," I replied.

"Her phone's dead. The Library is having a special showing of "*Great Expectations*," the film. It was made in 1946."

"Mom's letting you see it then. Have you finished the book?"

"Yes, just the other day. Did you want us to swing by to pick you up?" Megan asked.

"I am kind of in the middle of something for Myth class. Then I have to go over my notes for the test on Friday," I replied.

"Oh, I was just sort of hoping we could do that sister thing, you keep promising. We hung out at the mall, but that was mom's idea. This kind of is too. I just thought it would be fun since you said how much you enjoyed the book," hinted Megan.

"I could put studying on hold for the rest of tonight. Tomorrow evening I'll ask Molly over to cram. Just don't bother us.

"But you need to study," Megan interrupted.

"Yes, I do," I admitted. "Studying will happen tomorrow, tonight my Lil sis comes first."

"YES! I'll tell mom you said OK, we'll pick you up say... in about ten minutes. The movie is starting at nine-fifteen," she blurted hanging up.

I pressed the red button on my phone. I'd be attending a vintage film tonight. The last time I'd seen that old B&W was in high school. I pranced into the kitchen and patted Frits on his head. He was sitting next to his water dish.

"No one gave you water today?" I asked him.

He made some growling noises at me as I took his dish over to the sink. I filled it with liquid and placed it back on the floor next to him.

"There you go, boy. Now, watch over the house when I'm gone."

He made a few sad noises at me. I gave him some more pets before heading out of the room into the hall. I took my coat off of the hanger and put it on. Then stood looking out the front door waiting for them. I'd hoped that Megan had some of her candy stash with her. I could use some sugar. The library sometimes served refreshments with features. Perhaps they would have popcorn?

I shielded my eyes as the headlights approached the curb, illuminating our small porch. My mother pulled up into the driveway in her blue bug. I rattled my keys, yep, they were still in my coat pocket. I shut the door and locked it behind me. Afterwards, heading to the car. I'd certainly sleep well tonight. I would be surprised if we got home any earlier than eleven. There was sure to be a discussion on the film later for students. My sister loved stuff like that!

I'd been right, the discussion had gone, a bit longer than my mother had intended.

"Can we get going?" I asked impatiently.

"Soon, your sister needs to finish up so she can prepare for the essay. She will have to compare and contrast the two different media's," spoke my mother.

Myth

I gathered up my coat and went to sit in the back of the room to wait. It had been a nice evening. My sister and I giggled at the right parts of the film. Mrs. Havasham was our favorite character.

"I didn't realize you would be here tonight," said Mrs. Porter.

"I hadn't either, but Megan wanted me to be here, so I am," I answered.

"Did you like the film?" she asked.

"I did, and we both laughed and got sad at the right parts too."

"Your sister is an excellent student."

"Why thank you. She's getting much better marks than I did in school."

"That may be true. Your sister thinks rather highly of you. She told me, you have a gift with words, that is," she said, patting me on the back and winked before she walked away.

I went to stand, when my sister inched towards me dragging a boy behind her with curly, dark hair.

"You have to meet my sister," she demanded.

"But I am not your boyfriend!" he retorted.

"No, but you are my friend. I'd like you, to at least say hi," pushed Megan.

"My name is Chaz, your sister and I are in English together. She sort, of has a crush on me," he said standing beside her.

My sister blushed.

Then he turned, waved, and said, "See ya round, Megan."

"He's cute, I'll give you that."

My mom headed towards us away from her group of acquaintances. "Girls, let's get going. It's almost midnight. Megan, you will be going to school tomorrow."

"I have work, so I am more than ready to leave," I replied raising my eyebrows at her.

187

She linked her arms with ours, gently guiding us out of the building. I kept looking around, occasionally glancing back.

"No worries, Suzie will lock up," my mother stated when she saw me peering back.

The ride home was fairly silent. I listened to mom and Megan talk. Sitting in the back seat I tried to keep my eyes open, but kept fading in and out of consciousness. Eventually, we made it home where I managed to, literally, crawl into bed. Sleep it had never felt, so good.

(Tuesday)

The milkshakes tasted delicious. I smiled, glad to be done with work for the day. Molly sat across from me munching on French fries.

"I am so ecstatic to be out of the house," she beamed.

"So, what is going on? Did your folks totally spaz?"

"If they had I'd probably be staying at your place. The whole thing to them is a choice. They're convinced I'm using my sexuality as a way to gain attention. I tried to explain to them that it's simply not true," she said.

"Are they playing the neutrality card?"

"Basically, I'm not allowed to bring any girls home. I presume, they don't want me to date them either. The matter is, we're adults," she responded.

"Have you threatened to move out?"

"No, but I do know, I'm going to the dance with Maine whether they like it or not."

"Stick to your guns, but be prepared for the worst."

"They did the whole, we still love you routine, and maybe this is just a phase, you're going through. I asked them, how many guys have I dated?"

"And their answer was?"

"You didn't find any of them attractive, really, didn't you at least try to like them? My parents are set in their ways. Perhaps, I'll find a job on campus at the bookshop. Who knows, maybe I could find a paid internship," said Molly.

"It could work. I've contemplated moving out myself. Mom, won't be thrilled about it. I don't really, want to live in the forest. Catching some Z's on the frigid earth, even in fox form doesn't sound comfortable. I need my independence from family nevertheless I don't want to be too far away," I said.

"We could get a place together."

"Bingo, splitting the rent would be a lot easier than paying, on our own," I admitted.

"How are you and Jenson?"

"Pretty good, we haven't had a lot of alone time recently. He made me furious at the DMV the other day. I don't need a separate permit for the Moped. My dad had Eva contact them. He put my name on the registration so I can drive it now. He called me this morning to let me know."

"Great! Could take me on a ride sometime?"

"Sure, but you have to put on a helmet."

I took my coat off the back of the booth. I began to put it on when Marla came over with our check.

"Here, and your discount was added," she said, handing it to me.

I smiled, "Thanks."

"Now make sure you leave me a nice tip," she added, winked then sauntered towards the kitchen.

Molly blushed.

"Does she like you?"

"Not like that, she's always teasing me about Jenson. She calls him my boy toy," I smirked.

Molly rolled her eyes.

"Yeah, exactly," I replied.

"So are we going to go back to your place to study for this big test or would you rather go to the library?"

I made a funny face, squishing up my nose.

"Not sure?" asked Molly.

"Not really, going home would be fine, but at the same time, I'd rather not."

"Is Jenson home? We could visit him. What is he doing tonight?"

"Not sure, we could give them a ring. Do you want to call or should I?"

"Call Jenson, first, then he can contact Owl. We'll meet them at the library. Sage is a sweet kid, but we need to study."

I nodded in agreement and dialed Jenson's number. It rang and rang, nothing.

"He isn't home. I'll try Owl," I said.

Again, the phone just rang. I shrugged helplessly.

"Well, maybe they're at the library and forgot their phones. You know boys, that's what happened last time we couldn't reach either of them."

"Let's go, do you have everything?"

"Yeah," I said, lifting up my backpack off of the booth beside me.

Molly stood up as we got ready to leave. I put down fifteen bucks for our treats. That should cover the tip too, I thought.

Molly put on her scarf, hat, and mittens. I already had mine on.

"Do I owe you anything for the meal?"

"No, it's on me. Don't you remember milkshakes all over me?"

She laughed and playfully hit me in the shoulder.

"Come on, it's going to be a cold walk to the library," I said.

We took a steep stairway leisurely descending into the basement of the library. Molly stared at the rows and rows of discarded books that occupied the shelves surrounding us.

"Are these all surplus books?" she asked.

"All of the stories they were unable to sell. The librarians don't like to throw them out. The city prefers they get rid of them, but what they don't know can't hurt them," I answered. I touched the book bindings that lined the walls, before finding an adequate place to sit.

We set our bags down on a table near one of the shelves. I just loved the smell of old musty books.

"This is out of the way of distraction," said Molly sarcastically. She clearly had seen me eyeing the books.

"It's OK, here." I pulled out the cards Mr. Jones had given me. I handed them to Molly, watching as she scrolled through them. Pictures of the mythical creatures, urban legends we'd studied were on one side and on the other definitions, strange symbols for each, and what was that?

"Hey, what is that in the right-hand corner of each card?" I asked.

"Just a trademark," she said, laying the cards down flat so I could check each one more closely. "I don't sense, it's anything, we need to scrutinize."

The Kitsune Fox's card contained a paw print, for the Owl a feather, the wolf an eye, and it went along like that. Each piece, of the animal, was depicted in the right-hand corner on the opposite side of the card the image was printed on.

"They're only flash cards. I'm not sure why you want to make this into something more," said Molly.

"It could mean something about each animal, a symbol they go by. I have that fox tattoo, so maybe these are the ones the other clans have, or tribes depending on how they refer to themselves," I stated.

"These little clues are driving me nuts!"

"You have to admit, little by little we're gaining an understanding. The main problem is the lack of conclusive evidence. Let's anticipate that whoever bothered Nuria, left us various clues back in her cabin," I stated.

Molly handed me the cards, and I began to quiz her. We had a lot of reviewing to do. I couldn't just wish for a good grade and get it.

Chapter 23

(Wednesday)

The blustery wind whooshed by us. The cold air, hitting my face. Chilled, Molly and I stood along the curb outside the apartment complex. A few seconds later, my father's car pulled up next to us. Molly leaned over as my father rolled down the passenger side window.

"Hi, how are you?"

"Good, it's nice to see you, Molly," he said. She opened the door climbing into the back seat. I grabbed the handle on the other side of the car and pulled the front passenger door open.

"Dad, can I drive?" I asked, holding out my hand for the keys.

"No, but I'll buy you both coffee."

"Bummer, what a master manipulator," I said, giving him a weak smile. I sat down in the car.

"Is something bothering you?"

"No." I strapped on my safety belt. "It's been a while since I drove. I miss it. When I get a chance, I'll have to take the Moped for a spin."

"She's been thirsting to get out, on that thing ever since she drove it back from Hunters Park," Molly interjected.

"Be careful with that," he replied, pulling out into the street. "So, what's going on with you and Jenson? Do I need to worry?"

"Dad, no, we've been dating for a few days. What do you take me for?"

"I'm just asking, after all, you are nineteen."

Molly tried to keep from snickering in the back seat keenly aware that the farthest Jenson and I ever had gone had been hand-holding and cuddling. I don't' think she was even aware we'd kissed each other.

I patted my dad softly on the back."I'm grateful you realize this. Jenson, he's a good guy."

"Coffee, you're passing Joe's," Molly complained.

"I'll have to pick up a cup for Jenson, Dad."

"Please, get me a regular, black, then we'll pick up your main squeeze," my dad said with a huge grin.

I cringed, parents!

When we arrived the ranger's lodge buzzed with excitement.

"This is crazy! There are members I don't even know here yet," I said to my father as we stepped into the station.

"It's OK, let's all just sit down and get started. I'm glad Molly stayed at the house last night. Did you two get a lot of studying done for Myth class?" he asked.

"Yes, we spent most of our time at the library. Mom brought us home around ten after her shift. The staff adores her. They allowed, Molly and me to stay after hours to finish up," I said.

"That basement is kind of creepy," said Molly taking a seat next to Jenson. I was sure the meeting would be starting quite soon. Everyone had helped themselves to food and coffee. There was a lot of chatter. Glancing around, I noticed Lance and Shellena had not yet arrived. They'd better show up. They were supposed to lead us to the cabin.

"Hey, how are you Starla?" asked Mike.

"I'm full of questions I'm hoping you can answer," I replied, taking a seat.

He chuckled at that. "So you're going to give us the third degree? Lance and Shellena should be here shortly. I understand they are taking you out, to Nuria's cabin. No one's been there since she disappeared. None of us considered it a possibility she was involved, in this."

"Look, I'm pretty sure Nuria isn't behind Rascal's son's death. We suspect she may have been threatened by someone, thus leading to her quick departure. We're not sure who at this time caused it. We have suspensions, but no evidence or documents to back it up. The thing is we have to verify that the Bandits are involved," I tested.

Mike flinched falling backward. He braced himself against the wall.

"Are you OK?" asked Jenson, moving from his seat, he helped him up.

"Yeah, we need everyone to get comfortable, so the meeting can begin," said Mike. He then sat down.

Shellena and Lance strutted into the room seating themselves near Eva, and Star. I saw a few male foxes; Owl was here, no Rascal, though. My dad stood up looking like he was going to take the lead. Really, the ranger wasn't going to be in charge of this? Then again, dad was the detective.

"Starla, please present the clan with the information you brought here this morning. Include all of the questions you came up with since your last meeting with Eva and Star," he instructed.

I stood up, "If I may address you there are several things I'd like to clear up first. This way I might be able to further, identify with you," I finished.

"Starla!" My father exclaimed.

"It's alright, go ahead," said the ranger motioning with his hands for me to continue.

"First of all, my tattoo, what does it mean when it glows? Is it a warning, a signal, or does it mean you are tracking me?" I inquired.

A small elderly man with graying hair spoke, "Therein lies your answer. We use all three methods you've mentioned. Did you discover this on your own?" asked the male fox.

"I pieced it together with what Eva and my mother told me. I noticed some fox tracks, the other day outside this sub shop. Molly, Jenson, Owl, and I, decided to get some lunch after class, and when we left we saw them in the snow. Who are you anyway?"

"My name is Cavin. I'm one of the elders. I watch over the clan with my wife. She can be a bit bossy," he said smiling. "Today Kaya is looking after some of the young kits. Our place is to guide, and protect our clan family. Over the years, I have met and trained with Wiccans, and Shamans, learning how to cast spells. Please forgive me, the day you came to meet us our men were protecting the perimeter of the park. It's something we've started doing more regularly since Du-Vance was killed," he replied.

"Are you, and were you aware that Nuria, Eva's sister's missing?"

"Yes, why do you ask?" he questioned.

"When I met with Eva, I told her I suspected that Nuria and Du-Vance were, somehow, tied together in, all this," I replied.

"What is the all this you refer to," he responded.

"The death of Du-Vance, one of them must have known something that got him killed. We don't know why Nuria fled before this happened to Rascal's son. Was she trying to protect them or herself? Whatever they knew or she knew the enemy didn't want it brought to the surface. Cal and Lang seem to be intertwined in this also. Cal, was half fox-half human like me and Lang? After what Star told me about them along with information on my mother and father. It seems plausible that it's, them. If not, the only other suspects we have to talk to would be your wolf friends sharing this state park. I need to know what you know, now," I shouted.

Hushed voices filled the room. The members spoke amongst themselves. Were they trying to figure out if I was worthy of them or something? Maybe we should have just continued without their help. Wait, I was supposed to be helping them! It seemed as if I was doing all the work for them and my father.

"Remember when I said, I would feed you clues that you were on a need to know basis, for your protection?" asked my father.

"She wasn't there for that," Jenson interrupted. "She'd gone to the diner, but I recall it," he replied.

"OK, well, we did speak with the neighboring wolves. They, of course, claim they were out that night hunting in a different territory," said Dan.

"They are allowed to leave?" I asked.

"Yes, as long as they plan, confirm, and hunt in authorized areas," spoke Mike.

"So they have an alibi, that doesn't mean they're not involved," I concluded.

"She's right, one of them could have stayed behind, snuck up on Martin and attacked him. He was alone with no weapons unless you count the backpack," said Shellena.

"What, a backpack? No one told me about that. It wasn't in the report," I cried.

"No, because it was shredded when they found it, leaving no evidence," countered Lance.

I put a hand in the middle of the table, sliding out the report, and photos Jones had given me. I positioned them so everyone could see.

"These photos and this report were given to me by my professor Mr. Jones, who teaches my Myth class. I find it odd he would not only have them, but in addition, be teaching, about urban legends that pertain to us. All of you should take a look at them. Are they familiar to you?"

Each constituent carefully examined the report and pictures sending it on to the next individual. It stopped at a placid aged fox. It was unusual, that the Park Ranger or my father hadn't introduced me to the new parties. He was all fox, and I had not heard him utter a word from the time we had entered the station.

"This, this can't be right!" he said, stopping with one of the photos in his paw. "Can it?" he asked.

"What are you referring to," said Star, who sat beside him.

"In the photo do you see it?" he asked, pointing, "A shadow, a shadow of a girl!"

198

"What, we never saw any shadows when we went through them. How can that be? You an elder have better eyesight than those in our youth?" asked Owl.

"Sonny, with your experience, alongside the spirit of an Owl. I'm quite surprised you did not take notice, look again," he pushed the photo towards him.

Owl picked it up, holding it near the sunlight squinting to pick out an odd shape. Behind the gladiator lay a faint shadow. The only way you could claim it was a girl was her ponytail.

"How do we know it's Cal? It could be a different girl," said Owl passing it along to be observed by other members.

"There is a way," spoke up Star.

"Give me the photo," Cavin demanded.

The picture had made its way into Mike's hands. He reached over the table giving it back to him.

"There is a way to enhance the shadow bringing out her spirit form. It won't be perfect, but we should be able to tell if it's her or not," he said.

"How?" I asked.

"Starla, you were pretty close to Cal. Eva you're her mom. You both need to step over here, touch the area of the photo near the image and concentrate on a specific memory you had with her. One, where you connected to each other's spirits. Then hold on to it and push it into the photo. If this works, it will bring out her human and fox features. It will be hazy, but it will serve its purpose."

I was reluctant to do what he said. Playing with magic? I was warned of the aftermath, if it backfired.

"Go on," said my father, urging me to start the proceedings.

"Give me a minute. I have to concentrate. It's been ages since I saw Cal," I replied.

Eva moved to stand on the other side of Cavin. She reached out her hand towards me. I thought maybe she wanted me to take it, but she was motioning me to join them.

"It's time you trust us. We had faith you would provide us with new documentation, and you have," said Eva.

"Yes, but, it is old evidence in which new data has been found."

"If it helps us to find Cal, and Lang, who cares!" exclaimed Star.

She was right. Why was I being so hesitant, to comply? Shaking off my self-doubt, I joined them on the other side of the table. Without being asked, I touched one of the sides of the photograph, bowing my head, to begin.

"Be calm, let your past, guide you. Now push your memory into the photo," urged Cavin.

Lucid images flashed in my brain on and off. The time, Cal and I met until it stopped, at a single memory. We are darting and dashing in and out of trees in a forest setting. The sun's shining through golden leaves drifting down around us from the magnificent Oaks. I looked just about five years old. No, Ok, yeah, this was behind our old elementary school, I'm not sure where our parents were at.

"I'm a fox," said Cal

"No, I'm the fox," I replied, as we tagged each other and fell laughing on the ground.

Is that a tail I see, am I imagining this? My mother would never have let me show my true form. I don't remember this. I opened my eyes, pulling my hand away from the photograph.

"What was that?"

"Your mind focused on an important incident you experienced with Cal. There you united as clan members. You didn't know you were linked, but you sensed it. This opened up your mind to a part of you that was lost. An episode that had been concealed until now," said Cavin.

Shoving the photo aside, I gave my father an angry glare.

Eva took my hand.

"Calm down now, it was only done for your protection," she pleaded.

"Was that the only time?" I asked.

"The only time I'm aware of," Eva replied.

Cavin picked up the print, examining our results his eyes teary.

"It's her."

Everyone peered at the snapshot sitting in the middle of the table.

"What do we do now?"

Cavin's eyes met mine. A quick shiver crawled down my back. I breathed in and out sensing the emotions of fear, contemplation, grief, acceptance, and at last optimism. They were depending on me. I was supposed to be the hero, but I couldn't do it alone.

"You're not alone," he replied reading my thoughts. "Owl is a good guide, but you're a guardian. The fox that followed you to the Sub-shack was sent by me. I thought you might be being pursued. No one was detected, though."

"Which Fox was sent?" I asked.

"Nayla, a rare white fox, and close friend of my wife's. She habitually visits once a year. This time she made an exception due to our circumstances."

"She's not here because?"

"Large groups of people make her uneasy. When she is traveling, moving, roaming about she stays invisible preferring not to be seen. She enjoys her anonymity choosing only a few relationships with others," he said.

"Will we be introduced?"

"That is highly unlikely. She may shadow you if needed," he stated.

I stood up and gave a little huff. Was this clan run, by men? Did they make all of the decisions for us? If so I wasn't going to fit in well.

"I prefer to make my own choices," I spat.

Owl wore an expression of shock at what I had just said. Cavin pushed his seat back appearing as if he were about to exit.

"That's OK; we'd rather have strong females in our group. I didn't mean to offend you by my sternness. I'm trying to act in your best interest. Right now a meeting is not a necessity, but if it comes down to it, we can set one up. If that's what you wish," offered Cavin.

My father motioned for me to sit.

"Minder, Gladiator, Gavin, and Sika, what do you know about them?" I asked.

"We never had names before. We'd catch glimpses of their figures in raids of violence. Flags rose with the name Bandits appearing at each site they overtook," said my father.

"What!" I exclaimed, standing up.

"I didn't want to alarm you, and we didn't even know if they were involved. Now we have proof!" said my dad.

"Proof of what? It's just a picture. She could have been standing behind a tree watching, for all we know. It's still not clear," I spoke.

"She's right. It still doesn't prove she was taken by them, but it definitely makes me more suspicious," said Eva.

"What are you hoping to discover at the cabin?" asked Mike.

"Notes, clues, threats, home invasion, anything that could be seen as foul play," said Jenson.

"And this Jones character?" asked Cavin, speaking to the Ranger.

"Jones is only aware of what happened to Cal, and her mother. He's been a professor at the college for years. Strange, I might add that he doesn't seem to age. Urban legends and myths are his specialties. From time to time, he's proved helpful to me. Dan and I have never had a reason to see him as a threat," Mike responded.

Lance gave a low growl in the back of his throat as his ears shot up.

"What's wrong?" said Molly.

Shaking off the bad vibe, he relaxed again.

"Nothing, probably a few rabbits, and I smell a squirrel roaming about," he muttered.

"Control yourself, hunting can wait until after this, and then we have to take them to Nuria's," replied Shellena.

I laughed, nervously wrapping my arms around myself, feeling suddenly chilled. Jenson took his coat off wrapping it around me.

"Speaking of Jones, I found this stashed in my coat pocket the other day," said Owl throwing down a long envelope.

"What's in it?" asked Mike.

"Don't know, haven't had the guts to open it," he answered.

"If it's anything like that Spirit animal magazine, it will just leave you pondering if what you think is true," I said.

"What's, to question?" asked Owl.

"If you have an animal guiding you, that is, a spirit can you take the outward appearance of that animal?"

"It's possible, but highly unusual for that to occur. They're meant to guide you, not possess you. If you belong to a clan, or a tribe the animal may choose to unify with you in battle," Owl replied.

"Alright, now what's in the envelope?" asked Cavin.

"Why don't you open it? I'd really rather not," Owl answered.

"Men," Eva and Star, replied in unison.

I snatched up the packet, rapidly opening it before anyone could object. I pulled out a heart shaped locket by its chain careful, not to damage any prints that might be on it. Then I took out the note.

"Read it," said Owl.

My hands trembled as I unfolded it. Cal's handwriting, but it looked aged as if written exactly after her disappearance.

Dear Mom or whoever finds this,

I am in a safe place. They are looking for me. The dog I chased turned out to be a wolf sent to protect me. At least I think he is. I have not been harmed yet. There are rows and rows of apple trees here, and I often play in the fields. They don't let me go to school. Half-breeds, saving me, most of it, I don't understand. XOXO

Love Cal

"Can I have the locket?" asked Eva.

"I have to take it in for prints. Please, place it all back in the envelope carefully," said Dan.

I did as he said, and handed it to him.

"At least we know she's safe," said Star.

"It can't be the bandits," I said.

"Or one of them went rogue," interrupted Molly.

I gave her an inquisitive gaze.

"She means maybe one of them got fed up with the killing and turned against the others. Consider this, if one of them decided that this killing was senseless, that the peace treaty was something they wanted, what would they do?" asked Cavin.

"It's pretty obvious. They would separate themselves from their current race, to protect those their clan would target, but how would they do that?" questioned Jenson.

"Change their appearance... I don't know..." I responded.

"This is a lot to take in, Owl you and the group get ready to head out to the cabin. Shellena and Lance go, pack up some of those left over's in the fridge and take water and soda," said Mike.

Cavin came over to me, setting his hand on my shoulder.

"You'll do fine; I hope you'll consider joining us after all this is over. If not, at least remain an ally," he said.

My stomach was empty, lightheadedness took over, and I passed out. That was the last thing I recalled.

Chapter 24

Something nuzzled me. "Fritz, is that you?" What had happened? Where am I? The last thing that occurred what was it?

"Are you OK?" asked the voice.

"I don't know where I am? What's going on?"

"Open your eyes, you're fine. You just passed out," said a girl.

My eyelids fluttered, but they didn't want to open as if something held me back.

"Jenson, where is he? Molly? Owl? Did they desert me?"

"They left to put supplies in the van just relax," said the stranger.

I began breathing deeply in and out as she'd said. Afterwards, I managed to place my legs up to my chest in a sitting position.

"Look at me, you have sleep covering your eyelids. How did that happen? Tsk, Tsk," she spoke.

Her paws slowly rubbed gently at my lids, and I heard her shuffle aside.

"Now try opening your eyes dear. You should be able to see now."

Slowly, I opened them. There before me stood, Nayla?

"Where did you come from? Cavin, said you prefer small groups, to be on your own, that you're not comfortable around others." Looking around I didn't see anyone else but the two of us. A white fox how had she?

"Dear one, it is an honor to finally, meet you. You're correct, I don't particularly fancy large crowds. Cavin warned me coming here today would not be in my best interest. In spite of that I wanted to meet you, having heard you're a part of the investigation concerning the Du-Vance fiasco." A sly smile spread a crossed her lips. She tapped her right paw on the floor, "You are a smart one. I admire that in a girl. These men don't often give us the time of day." She placed her paw back down firmly on the wood floor and moved about the room.

"Can I go now?" I asked.

"You wanted to meet me, so here I am."

"Are you going to watch over me? How did you wipe my eyes with your paws?"

She stopped pacing and sat on her hind legs, paws up resembling Fritz.

"Here and there, we keep track of our members, monitor them and their contacts. Background checks are performed to ensure that no damage will come to you, or us. We determine with this who means us harm and those who are trustworthy."

"And..."

"Loyalty is in your veins, Strong, naive but strong. You'll have spells to master, thought speak might be possible, and your willpower is beyond measure. I don't see you letting them stop you."

"Who?"

"Those who wish us destruction, the ones you've been trying to pinpoint, in, order to find Cal and Lang. Nuria, she was an amazing woman."

"I don't think she's dead. Where are my friends? I should be leaving," I replied, standing up. The door to the lodge swung open.

"The van's all packed up and ready to go," Mike said, shutting the door behind him.

"OK, are you going with us?" I asked Nayla

"I've planned to follow from afar. If something should go haywire, I'll ring the clan via their tattoos. If yours goes all glow crazy, get back to your home base," said Nayla.

"Why? What does it mean?"

"Enemies are close by, danger."

I laughed, "We haven't seen any peril since I started this investigation. I've been startled a few times, but nothing too rash has taken place."

"I advise you begin, observing, the area's around you. Now that you're on track extra caution must be taken I'll be here as a guide, but my ability to protect you is limited. Please, we don't need another River Rogue," she stressed.

"You were there?"

"Yes, now go with your friends. They're waiting for you outside. I'll be right behind you invisible to the eye. If you need me, try saying my name in your head. You'll have to master this. You don't just wake up a guardian you require training. Did anyone tell you this?"

"No, only that, I had a choice of where and how I would live," I replied.

"Hmm, well, it seems they have left it up to me then." She turned around with a wink and disappeared.

"Mysterious one she is," Mike said.

"I'd better go." I stood up and opened the door to leave.

Mike nodded at me as I left the station.

Jenson wrapped his arms around me. I snuggled into his warmth, to take pleasure in a few moments of peace. He pulled away slightly, gazing at me.

"Are you alright? We're all packed up. Owl and Molly are in the back seat of the van. I counted on you preferring to ride up front with me."

What I most wanted was a long, slow kiss; I reflected, staring into his blue eyes. I touched his face with my hand and leaned my forehead against his. OK, get your mind where it ought to be. Concentrate on the case girl, I told myself. Moderately my heart rate calmed, and the flutters in my chest subsided.

"Yeah, I'll be fine," I replied, untangling myself from his embrace.

He opened the passenger side door, and I stepped in, sat down and buckled up. We didn't need any cops pulling us over, safety first!

"Where are Lance and Shellena?"

"They're right in front of us in the blue van," he said pointing. "We're going to follow them."

Molly gently touched my shoulder, and I turned to face her.

"What happened after we left?" she asked.

I leaned back in my seat while Jenson started the car. He put it into gear and lurched forward.

"Sorry guys," he said, waving his hand.

"Just focus on driving for now. You know how traffic can get at this time of the day," snapped Owl.

"Will do, I'll just be the chauffeur," Jenson joked.

"Only until we get there, then you can use your remarkable skills to uncover clues," I teased patting him on the back. It never hurt to indulge the boyfriend.

"Will do," Jenson replied.

"Okay, Molly this is what happened after you left. I woke up, and Nayla was there. The white fox I insisted on meeting. Pretty strange if you ask me. I couldn't even open my eyes. She somehow wiped away the goop. I found her rather crafty implying I needed training to advance as a guardian. I'm not sure I told you, but Star revealed this to me when we met. At the time, I was honored, but didn't give it too much consideration. I'm not sure when or where lessons will begin."

"It probably has a lot to do with what Cavin spoke with you about earlier," theorized Molly

"Learning to speak to someone without being heard would be an advantage when protecting one's clan," I admitted.

"Yep, pretty obvious and you'll need some coaching in, order to gain the ability to control and handle, spells," Owl piped up.

"My mother is going to love this. Remember when I e-mailed you about that book I took out of the library on Wicca?"

Molly laughed. "Yeah, your mom flipped her lid. Afterward, you had to promise you wouldn't try to use them unless it was to solve a mystery."

"And I bet she said only in life and death circumstances!" Owl exclaimed loudly.

"Come on guys I'm trying not to lose sight of the van. Keep it down a bit," said Jenson.

"Okay, let us know when we get there," I insisted.

"How should I know, I've never been out this way before," Jenson remarked.

"Good point," I snapped. "Now about learning spells, Mom almost certainly didn't want me to recognize my capability to perform them. She already knew how much I admired Willow on that Buffy show," I giggled. "Now there isn't much she can do. I'm in the middle of it all. It makes sense that I find a way to embrace it."

"Weren't you upset with your dad and mom over all this?" asked Owl.

"I was for a bit. Mom shared pictures from her past and a diary from her youth. Dad has been over a lot more which makes Megan really, happy. She's optimistic we'll be a family again. It's a possibility, but not a guarantee. I'm still not ecstatic about finding out the way I did. It was shocking, after all. I'm just glad to move forward. It will be even better after Cal is home."

"Without a doubt. Owl, how do you wager Jones got a hold of that note from Cal?" asked Molly.

"I'm not sure, but it's exceptionally odd it was delivered to him instead of, Mike."

"If what my clan says is true, he almost certainly discovered it alongside a path in Hunters Park. I've seen him strolling in the early morning there near the college," I said.

"I'd say it was bizarre if my own, mother didn't get up early to jog," Molly interjected.

"True, but there has to be more to Jones than he's telling us hints, clues, our class. It's as if he wants us to uncover his true identity," I said, as I glanced out the window watching pine trees fly by on either side of us. I hadn't even noticed we'd left the city. I was too busy discussing current events.

"I assume we're almost there. I keep seeing all these trees, and we passed a small gas station a few minutes ago," said Jenson tapping the steering wheel. He'd turned on some low, music. I couldn't tell who the group was singing la la la.

"It can't be too far out then. We've been driving for about twenty minutes," said Owl.

Molly played with the necklace Maine had given her, and then set her hands back to her side.

"You alright?" I asked.

"Yeah, just a bit nervous about this," she admitted.

The van in front us of slowed down. We turned right onto another side road, made a left, then right again and pulled up to a tiny log cabin surrounded by pine trees.

"This is it," said Jenson, pulling into the drive and parking the car. We unbuckled our seat belts and then got out to stretch before beginning the search.

Jenson stepped out of the car opening the door for me.

"Thanks," I stated, hoping down onto the snowy earth.

"Welcome, we'll figure this Jones thing out," he said as he shut the door. "Let's only hope he's not an enemy, directing us into a trap," Jenson whispered in my ear. Odd, perhaps he didn't want Lance or Shellena to hear? I spotted Lance jumping out of the other van.

"It's good to see we all made it here safely." He slapped Jenson on the back in a friendly manner. I smiled. Hmm, maybe he would be a good addition to our team.

Molly and Owl stood, off to the side waiting.

Shellena got out of the van and slammed the door shut behind her. She trotted up to me as if I was her new best friend.

"You look better. Less pale than when we left the park. Any word on your guardian status?" she asked playfully punching me in the shoulder.

"Nayla, says I have a great deal of knowledge to obtain. I presume she'll guide me until I'm up to speed on things."

"Sure thing kid, you're probably right."

"I may be new, but I'm not a kid," I prompted her, gesturing for the rest of my friends to join me.

"I have the key so you'll have to step aside," Lance said behind me. We entered the small open porch that led up to the door. Jenson stood beside me.

"How do you know it's locked?" he asked, tugging on it.

"Nuria never left it open being paranoid about privacy. She claimed in the last few months she was here, she was being tracked. The clan was never able to prove it," said Lance.

"She constantly had me monitor her mail. I couldn't tell who sent it. No return address. We, all kept our distance for fear if we tried to interfere with her business or secrecy that we'd be expunged, from her life altogether," Shellena explained while Lance unlocked the door.

It swung open, and we shuffled inside to escape the cold. Lance closed it behind us latching the lock by the chain above the door.

"That should do it. You never know who might show up," he said.

The small living area contained a desk, on the far left corner of the room with a chair tucked under it. It must have been where she wrote her notes, letters, I observed. On top of the desk laid several books, letters, stamps, and a small lamp. In front of us sat a faded gray couch, next to that on the right an old blue lazy-boy. The only other item, in the room, was a coffee table, where a small radio and several magazines, had been placed.

"No, TV?" I asked.

"No, she just had the radio out here. I don't even think, she could get reception, for the local channels, if she tried to," said Owl thumbing through several books, then setting them down.

"Anything there?" asked Lance glancing at the books.

"A few spell books, "Portrait of a Lady", and a dictionary," replied owl.

"Is this it?" I asked.

"What do you mean?" said Lance.

"Are there other rooms, I'm not seeing any."

"Come, let me show you," he said.

We followed him straight to the end of the room on the right-hand side. He placed his hand on an odd looking button concealed in the wall. Gradually the wooden panel slid open, revealing a bedroom, which joined a bath.

"Check the bathroom? See if there are any unusual items in there," I demanded.

"Give me a minute," Owl mumbled.

Pushing past him, I shoved the door open, revealing a black and white tile floor, a sink with a cabinet above it, next to it the toilet and an over-sized bathtub. Man, I would have loved a soak in that! I peered into the cabinet above the sink, empty. No toothbrush, soap, or any toiletries. The bathtub had been cleaned, and no shampoo, soap, or other products remained.

"Nothing, it's spotless," I said making my way back into the bedroom. It was simply furnished with a full bed, nightstand, a dresser, and shelves of books.

"This is the main room, her sanctuary. She never allowed me in. The rules in place being, enter only if an intruder, were to appear on the premises. It was vital that I respected her wishes. No one ever asked Nuria why, about anything. Even Eva rarely spoke with her except for clan meetings. It's not something you'd expect from one seeking peace," said Lance.

"If she sought serenity outside of society, it would make complete sense to me," I said, sitting down on her bed. My eyes made contact with a picture on her nightstand. Nuria and Eva, they were quite young. A diary laid next to it with a few letters tucked in-between its pages. I picked it up as we heard a ruckus outside, a raccoon's maybe? They were scavengers.

"Shhh, Stay quiet, and in this room, don't make a sound, and don't come out whatever you do!" said Lance.

Then I heard it, revving or maybe an engine that wouldn't turn over. How could that be with no neighbors, garages or other outbuildings? Still, it seemed far away.

"What? Don't you think we could handle facing an enemy?" I asked, trying to hone in on my fox audible range.

"There could be more than one," Owl pointed out.

"Let them take care of it," Molly whispered shivering as she sat down on the bed beside me. Jenson stood, near the door, we'd entered.

The revving of motorcycles or a vehicle of some kind, grew louder. Were they going to ride right through the cottage?

"Just let Shellena, and I deal with this," spat Lance.

"What about Nayla? She told me she was going to track us. Wouldn't she have placed some, kind of barrier or protection spell around us?"

"She'll do what she can to distract them," Shellena clarified.

"Your job right now, is to collect as much information as possible. Let us deal with whoever is outside. Once you have the data study it, save it and keep it close. If we don't come back in twenty minutes, I hope one of you has a good mobile plan."

Jenson held up his phone. He was still getting two bars, and had a full charge. Lance patted him on the back.

"Good man, now Shellena and I are going to take care of this."

My body urged me to transform. All of my senses were telling me to merge into a fox and here was the bro/sis team telling me to collect data, stay behind and play the mastermind. I took a gulp of air asking myself what Willow would do and then sucked it up, taking out the letters inside the journal. Owl and Molly gathered near me as I read it out loud.

Dear Nuria,

It's getting worse. I sense the need to take Cal away from here. I didn't imagine the bandits would get this hostel. I only wanted to keep our species divided for our well-being. After River Rogue and all that death, I'm unable to continue. At the time, I thought it was right. Now that they want to start an anarchy, I can no longer be a part of this. I've realized it was a war of hate. The only achievable success I now seek is through compromise. For now, I'm taking Cal into hiding. She never knew why she was kidnaped. We made her believe it was for her protection. That her clan had a plan, to sacrifice her to your gods and it's such a mess! I'm asking for your alliance. I'm leaving today. I know it's been years since her disappearance. I've observed you among your people. You have a gentle kindness, warmth; along with that I admire your ability to protect your life, keeping it off the grid. Make sure you avoid getting close to anyone. If you already have, please end it. We must stop them from destroying what tranquility you and your tribe have found.

Sincerely,

Minder

After reading the correspondence out loud, I set it down on the bed beside me. Molly and Jenson wore expressions of concern.

"So this is why she broke it off with Rascal. There is no mention of a sibling or a child. It could mean we were wrong assuming she may have been pregnant."

"True, but there are other notes, can you hear what is going on outside? Are they, OK?" asked Molly.

"I hope so," I replied surveying the room once more. I noted, it was windowless and stepped towards the wall, to press my ear against it.

"You need to leave! I don't care who you work for or your intentions. This is private property," shouted Lance.

"Others like us will be arriving. We cannot allow the mergers you've created with the outside world," said the man.

"Mergers protect us all, keep us safe. It's when you are divided, splitting up clans, humans, and hybrids into categories that the evils begin. Death, bloodshed, hate, and prejudice all over the vengeance you seek," Shellena shrieked. It sounded as if there was more than one of them.

"What's happening, are they fighting?" asked Owl.

"Shhh let me listen, unless you want to go out there."

"This land belongs to Nuria and our clan. Blood, will not be splattered this evening. You will leave!" argued Lance.

Glancing over, I saw Molly. She'd opened up the next memo reading it silently. Her eyes got big, yet she kept silent.

Listening, I heard, a padding of feet. I closed my eyes, trying to tune myself into the beings outside of the building. If I could just align myself with one of them to see what was going on. Was it possible? Could you do that with current events as I had with the past at the meeting?

Nayla, is she out there? I thought.

Then it began...

"Into the darkness you shall subside, leave this land go back to your pride. I Scorn those who wish to inflict harm. I come in peace while you have come armed. Our love here is for all now. I banish you into the night. Leave now or there will be a brawl."

I took my ear away from the partition. Molly came over to me with a note in her hand.

"They are in a hilly area, maybe mountains? This letter doesn't give a good description. It would have been before Nuria

218

left. In it, she asks them to meet her at a place called Great Lakes edge," she said.

"Did she include any pictures or hints of how far away this place is from Springville? It's not in another dimension, is it?" I asked.

"They cannot hide everything. This postcard is stamped, from a place in Michigan. It can't be too far away. We are already residing in a Northern town," stated Molly.

She handed me the memoir along with the mail. I placed them in the large tote I'd brought with me.

"Think it's safe to leave?" Jenson asked taking my hand in his. I pulled him close, leaning a bit on his shoulder. He kissed my cheek. Molly smiled at us.

Abruptly the entrance slide opened, before us, stood Shellena, Lance, and Nayla.

"I heard you perform a spell. Did it make them disappear?"

Nayla trotted over, nuzzling my left hand that lay at my side. I detected sadness in her big bright green eyes.

"All is well now. The spell will keep them at bay, till dawn. If we leave now, I can mask our scent. Have you gotten what you came for?"

"It's difficult to say yes confidently," I replied

"Then allow me to go foxy on, this place," she snickered swishing her tail.

A white spot darted from one end of the room to the other, in madness. It looked as if a ray of light bounced off the walls. It reminded me of the clubs in L.A. I'd gotten into one once. Mom had not been pleased when she'd found out.

"It's clear, we should move now and get back to Hunters Park. Transport what you've collected. Come along now," she said scowling.

Following her out into the cold, it was ironic. Things were heating up, and this ice burg was about to melt.

Chapter 25

Dead air filled the van like an unexpected visitor. Sitting in the back seat, Molly rifled through letters we'd found. She'd pushed me to grant her the authority to search through them, hoping for a hot lead. I hadn't heard a peep since. Jenson's eyes remained on the street. I dare not even attempt, a romantic gesture. . Frowning at the gray sky, I stretched my arms over my head and yawned. It was overcast, not a night for star gazing. I shivered, it had become bitter cold. Slumping back down in my seat, I fought to get comfortable. The long drive that now seemed shorter on the way to Nuria's became an irritation. We had been right, and then we'd also been wrong. Jenson took his free hand and squeezed mine. Reassurance, leave it to Jenson. I squeezed back and then ran my fingers over his.

Finally, Owl broke the silence.

"Want some," he said, pushing the pack of pink bubble gum over the center console.

"Yeah, sure I'll take some bubble gum! That way I can blow away my worries on the way to the Ranger's station," I said with a weak smile. I took a piece out and popped it in my mouth.

"Jenson?" he asked.

"Nah, I need to concentrate on what just developed. I'm curious if Nayla will advise us on training for the next mission."

"You mean, as a group alongside Starla?"

"Yes, that's precisely, what I mean. We are alliances in this. I'd like to consider us protectors. Peace seekers. What else would you call us?" he demanded.

"We are a rather odd bunch," I responded.

"It's what drove us together in the first place," Molly said closing the journal.

"Did you find anything in that?" Owl asked, pointing to the red book.

"Wouldn't you like to know!" Molly replied.

"Why, aren't you getting sassy? I'd think that you're trying to take my place," I said to her. She smiled mischievously.

"Really, can you, at least, tell us one item or subject that's in the book?" I urged.

"This is rather relevant, a map. It's on the last page at the end of the journal. The rest is the usual stuff, for example, her day to day life with Cal up, until her disappearance. Then she grieves for her daughter. There is a bit about the bandits, but not much to go on otherwise. If you want to look it over to see if I missed anything you can," Molly replied.

"Pull out the map," I insisted.

She opened the diary to its last page and unfolded the map stapled to it.

"Michigan, hadn't Star talked about a place there?"

"Are you familiar with it?" asked Molly. She traced the bodies of water surrounding the land in the drawing.

"Yes, Star mentioned a few places there. Her, folks were involved, in a massacre in River Rogue. She lived in Charlevoix for a while before it happened," I said.

"Hey! These markings weren't here earlier. Perhaps they appeared when I touched the paper? Someone drew a path from

Charlevoix to Thunderhead Bay. I'm not sure how Great Lakes edge fits into it," Molly replied.

"It is on a corner, maybe they just simply called it Great Lakes Edge," Owl observed.

"Maybe, but I'd like to take a look at it and the journal once we get back," Jenson suggested.

"Ay, ay, Captain!" I teased.

Molly and Owl laughed. I then realized we'd entered Hunters Park.

"This map is the one I gave Nuria when she mentioned being interested in learning about Michigan. You know it's a tad north of here," he said, as we gathered around the table in the main room of the station.

"I believe we live in a pretty northern region, already," stated Molly boldly from where she sat.

"We do for Illinois that is," Mike responded. He'd been shuffling pamphlets into stacks before we arrived. They sat in a large pile on the wooden table.

I rubbed my arms chilled.

"Do you have any hot cocoa?" I asked.

"In that cabinet over there, why don't you make yourself some?"

"Anyone else want Co Co?" I asked, standing up.

"Me, please," said Molly.

"Us too," Owl and Jenson replied.

I walked over to the tiny observation area with the sink and microwave to make the drinks listening to the discussion.

"What else did you uncover, besides the map? What's in the diary and those notes there?" he asked.

"From what we read, Minder has Cal. She's protecting her from the bandits. They manipulated her into accepting the idea our clan would sacrifice her to their gods!" Owl asserted.

"That's some messed up brainwashing," Nayla replied. She trotted forward near the table where they sat.

I spoke up as I put the second cup of cocoa in the microwave. "Minder left the group when she realized what happened at River Rogue wasn't a one-time thing. She stated she agreed with keeping our species divided, but was against increased bloodshed. The letter made it sound as if she seeks to compromise."

Nayla paced back and forth. "Still, we must be careful young ones. Starla, you need to prepare for this additionally. If all of you intend to back us, then we must organize a gathering for you to study our ways. We have a short time to lay out the groundwork. Cal's been missing for years, and this cannot wait," she pleaded.

"How are we going to trace Minder?" Molly asked Nayla.

"We just have to use that map. We know she is somewhere near Thunderhead Bay. I can get the wolf clan across the way to head over, see what they can track down for us," she replied.

"Do we trust them?" I asked, placing the hot chocolates on the table in front of my friends. Then sat down to sip mine.

"I have no reason not to. I would have heard from the group out east, or west if anything odd, or violent had been occurring within our allie lines there. We try to keep each other informed. They were, notified when Du-Vance was killed, and your father was put on the case."

"Good to know."

"Now do you young adults have anything pending right now? I apologize for referring to you as children, but to me you are adolescent," she confessed.

"We have a big test pending in our Myths class for Mr. Jones," replied Molly.

"He gave me a pop quiz extra credit essay I need to write. It has to do with the investigations, but I need to dig out my notes to find it," I added.

"Do you have it with you?" Nayla asked. She trotted over and sat down beside me.

"Not sure, let me go through my backpack. It could be with me, or at home. I packed pretty quickly this morning." My tummy rumbled. I had to stop skipping meals for this. Molly, Jenson, and Owl hadn't eaten either. Unzipping my pack I pulled out my notes from class. I'd scribbled down what Jones had told me.

"Here it is," I said, giving her my notes.

"I have paws, therefore, I cannot turn pages."

Opening my notebook, I figured I might as well give her a condensed version of what Jones wanted.

"Write an essay based on your knowledge of what happened to Cal Summers or did not happen referring to rumors: She joined a fox clan, was kidnapped by bandits, or may have been taken in for security reasons," I muttered pushing the papers aside.

"Do we give Jones what he wants?" asked Owl.

"As an enforcer of our laws you must answer his questions."

Nayla and I looked up at my dad who stood in the doorway. He strutted over to the table, slammed the papers onto the desk and sat.

"Security, safety, higher powers, have been established for some time. Jones must be one of them. Rascal and I have shared the responsibility of the tribe. He is working from a distance. Mike, did you know about this?" My father demanded.

"No, who assigned him the task?"

"Why would I, ask you, if I knew?" Dan hollered.

Nayla jumped onto the table and sat down facing us.

"Now, let's not sit here and argue. You confirmed Jones hadn't looked as if he'd aged, at the meeting. Perhaps he's immortal. If so, he may have anonymous contacts. He could be playing both sides or safeguarding all of us. We don't know. Clearly he's not a threat thus far. The worst that occurred was those dang bandits at Nuria's house! They were probably there to try to capture Starla," she spoke sternly.

I sat straight up in my chair.

"Why would they want me? You said yourself I need to be trained, as a guardian. I can't just have a vision whenever I want, and do not yet fully understand how the rest of my abilities work. If I did, wouldn't I have established a way to get Cal back by now?"

"Leverage my dear. One of their's went rogue to protect our side. Wouldn't that piss you off, if you were a bandit?" she remarked.

"Definitely, a friend, doing an 180 or would it be a 360?" I contemplated.

"Doesn't matter, I want all of you back here tomorrow to start training. In the meantime, Dan, you and Rascal will keep an eye on Jones. You say he's an enforcer, but to me, he's still a suspect."

"Whatever you say, I'm beginning to believe that the women do have the upper hand in our clan, after all."

"Do I write the essay?"

"Yes, write what you know. If he's an allie as he has currently been acting, a protector, he'll give you more clues. Don't let on that we're training for Thunderhead Bay. I have to find out if Minder and Cal are, actually there. I sure as hell hope, Nuria is with them."

"Do you presume the bandits have her?" asked Molly.

"If they did, they would have sent us a ransom note by now," responded Nayla.

"Or they are waiting for the right time to attack us, separate us and pounce on us one by one," I reasoned.

"Three p.m. tomorrow we'll train physically for endurance, speed running, dodging, tumbling, and the use of sticks. After that, a few mental tests to see where your skills lie. If you need to Starla, let Denny's know this is an emergency. You'll be needed this weekend. The trackers should be back by Friday, relaying what they've discovered. Any problems, let me deal with your boss. I'll put him in a trance," ranted Nayla.

I felt like I was in a cheesy movie. My life kept getting stranger and stranger. I sunk into my seat, as Nayla, bounced off the table, disappearing into a fog-like mist. Dad got up collecting our mugs and placed them in the sink.

"Make sure you wear something warm tomorrow. I haven't checked the forecast yet. Have you Mike?"

He shrugged, "It's supposed to warm up a bit for a few days. They say the forties, which is bizarre for February."

"We can always stash our stuff in here if it's too warm better to come prepared rather than freeze," Molly spoke up.

"Darn right about that girlie. I despise the chill during this time of year."

I gathered up my notes sticking them back into my pack. Jenson leaned over giving me a quick hug. The dance would be at the end of March. I hoped this would all be over by then. Molly and Owl were getting their coats on when Eva shuffled in.

"Nayla just told me about Cal. Star and I want to assist with training. We have experience."

"Yeah, and what about the men in our clan, are any of them going to help us?" I asked.

"Cavin is getting up there, and someone has to watch the little ones."

I laughed. "So are the roles reversed here? It's usually the men that go off to war, and leave the children with their wives," I stated.

"I can probably scrounge up a few of them. You won't be getting away from Shellena and Lance. They'll fight tooth and nail to come. They love a good brawl!"

I stood up and took my coat off the back of my chair preparing to leave.

"And I thought we were a peaceful clan," I sighed.

"We are until one of our own is killed. Cal and Lang went missing ages ago, and Nuria takes off. It's not as if, we didn't strive to get them to sign a peace treaty before all this."

I put on my jacket, then picked up my backpack pushing passed Eva to leave. My friends followed behind me. Before reaching the doorway, Eva grabbed me by the arm stopping me. I thought she was going to throttle me to the ground or something! Instead, she pulled me into a hug.

"Now there is hope. A light shines again brightly in a mother's heart. If you feel anything, get any kind, of signal I want to know," she said.

I pulled back a bit from her hug. "OK, but I haven't heard from Cal in years, not since you left L.A. I didn't know she was missing nor did I realize she'd lived here until I read those files." I shook my head. "I wish mom and dad never kept this from me. Then maybe this wouldn't have taken place," I said, trying not to let my emotions show.

"No, don't look at it that way. If you had known, you could be right beside Cal at this very instant. You're our light, our guardian, and we'll start preparations tomorrow. Nayla will lead us, and we'll begin again," she said, letting me out of her embrace.

I nodded, not sure exactly what she intended.

"I hope this means this war if it is one, or ends up one, will lead to tranquility. I'm not one for bloodshed."

"Neither are we," said a gal standing in the doorway.

Perchance, it was Star in her human form?

"Star?"

She grinned mischievously.

"See you all tomorrow," she said then turned away, Eva trailing behind her.

"Let's go," I said to my friends.

"Are you, forgetting something?" asked my dad.

"What's that?"

My dad dangled the keys from his hands. "You forgot I drove this morning. Here," he said, throwing them to Jenson. "Drive safe, I'll pick it up tonight at your house."

"Thanks," he said to him. Then turned to me, "We need to get some food. I heard your stomach growling loudly, overall this crazy chaos."

I said goodbye to my dad and took Jenson's hand in mine. We shut the lodge door behind us, allowing Molly and Owl to walk ahead.

"I'd ask if you were OK, but that might seem macho," he said pulling me a bit closer.

"I have you, Molly, Owl, and the others. I'm pretty strong."

"I never said, you weren't, but if you need anything..."

I didn't answer him, instead I, kissed him right there, quick, soft and sweet.

"What was that for?"

"Because it was what I needed," I said, looking up at him. Owl and Molly were almost to the car.

"Come on, I'm starving!"

"Alright, alright," Jenson answered, as I began running towards the vehicle. He ran behind me. Molly and Owl were now sitting in the back seat waiting for us. I tagged the car first.

"When are you going to start driving your moped?" asked Jenson.

"When we don't have to carry passengers," I said giggling.

"Hey, lovebirds, where are we going to eat?" Owl broke in.

"How about the diner Rascal met Nuria in," Jenson suggested as he opened the driver side door.

"Sounds good," he nodded to him.

I opened the passenger's side door and sat down. Well, he wasn't going to be a gentleman every time, I contemplated. He hadn't opened the car door for me.

Myth

Later, that evening Jenson dropped me off at home. I sat at the kitchen table observing big snowflakes as they fell outside. My books were strewn, about the table. Math class, I'd turned in assignments, but when had I last attended? I couldn't even remember. Mom never asked me either. My grades were falling, and I only had three classes! Mom had made me promise I would take the whole college thing seriously. Maybe I'd make it through in less than four years.

"Hey, what's up," Megan asked, waltzing into the room. Yes, literally, she waltzed. I shoved aside my homework sighing. I placed a hand on my head trying not to cry.

"Is it math class again? I can help you."

I started to snicker, and then the tears began to fall.

"It isn't that bad is it? I've managed to help you with this class before when it's trying to kick my big sis's butt."

"I've missed one class, but turned my last assignment in. I haven't attended, since this whole fox stuff happened," I replied, getting up to get a glass of water. I filled my cup and sat back down. Megan pulled out the chair across from me and sat.

"Have you missed any tests?"

"Not yet, we have one this Monday. I'm sure it's not going to be fun, and this is just intermediate algebra!"

Megan patted me on the back, "Ok, let's look at your syllabus. Have you picked up any of the assignments you turned in?"

231

"No, just put them in her office mail. Afterward, I hightailed it like a sissy."

"Molly has this class. I thought she was your tutor?"

I gave her the look.

"I know, I know I sound like, mom."

"Molly has had her own, dilemmas to deal with. She knew I'd skipped class, but never talked to me about it."

"That's rather odd, even for her. Maybe she's skipping out now too," she said, pulling my math book towards her. She began to look it over.

"No, she went to class. It was the same day she watched Ellen with us."

"Hmm, why don't we finish the next two assignments, then you'll be a bit ahead of the game. You should take the practice test. I think you know you need to call Mrs. Price. Tell her we had a family emergency. Hopefully, that will do the trick. If not, talk to mom," my sister suggested.

We went over several polynomial problems and other crazy equations. Myth class was my thing, English, Art, sociology, but math class was parallel to waking up, in a nightmare and realizing it was real.

I completed the next two assignments on the list with Megan's help. After that, I took the practice test.

"What are her office hours? You need to call her. I know this, and I'm only a seventh grader," she said sternly with an aggravated stare.

I got out my cell and found her number leaving a quick, but brief message. Thank goodness. If I remembered correctly, the mission was taking place on a weekend. At this point, I might have to give up college and my job. How the heck was I going to live? If this is how it was, maybe I shouldn't be part of the clan. Then again, maybe I was just, being my drama queen self.

"Are you going to be alright? Can I leave you alone?"

"I'm just going to call Molly. I would contact Jenson, but..."

"Girl time," my sister said, getting up from the table. "Well, I am going to make myself a snack and head upstairs. Mom should be home soon."

"Yeah," I said as she exited.

I didn't know how I could be so irresponsible. It wasn't like me, to not go to class, nor was it like Molly not to rag on me about math. She'd been the instigator that pushed me to sign up for it. My mother was right beside her at the time. I collected up my books, notes, and other miscellaneous materials that had cluttered the dining table. I picked up my cell off the counter to dial, Molly's number.

I listened to it ring till she picked up.

"Hey, um, didn't I just see you at the meeting?"

"Yeah, but..."

"What's up?"

"I just finished up the assignment I missed in Math class, and the next one. Plus I studied for the test. Megan helped me," I stammered.

"It's OK, you only missed, one class. I'm not sure right now what I'm going to do. It's like the-the battle of the bands here. My dad is on one side, my mom on the other."

"You lost me. Whose side is who on?"

"Mom says that she's going to stick with me. That she doesn't care what the church will think, but dad, he just isn't handling it well."

"What changed her mind?" I asked.

"She had a girlfriend once."

"You mean!" I exclaimed.

"No, not like that, but a girlfriend of hers back in college was gay. So now she decided she can deal with it. I did find a job. I'm supposed to start Monday. I just hope I can. I hate to back out of all of this now..."

"If you, really need to I'll understand. Nayla said we didn't have much time."

"Too bad I couldn't live with the clan," Molly pondered.

"If it gets worse, you could stay with us. I'm not sure how much mom would want to charge for rent. Maybe you could do the dishes?"

"Yeah, your mom is, down to earth nice. I wouldn't want to impose on you guys, though."

I sat back down at the table. I'd been staring out the window for a bit as the clouds covered up the stars.

"I don't imagine she'd look at it that way, OK?"

"Alright, is there any reason you called besides math?"

"Not really. Megan said girl time. I don't have any plans this evening unless you do with Maine?"

"Nah, we did talk on the phone for a bit. I'm, we're kind of in the gray zone."

"Friend zone?"

"No, gray zone, you know nonchalantly bumping hands, or a slight suggestive gesture that you like him or her more than friends."

"Ah, as Jenson and I were a few weeks ago."

"Yeah, but you and Jenson, you'd been playing cards for a while on that one."

I laughed, "You're right."

"Hmm, so have you seen Buffy the Vampire Slayer? The film, not the TV show."

"Oddly enough, I haven't."

"Say, that I have it. Do you want me to bring it over, say slumber party?"

"That is tempting, we don't have to be at training til 3 p.m."

My mom walked in the back door. I mouthed to her "Can Molly come over?"

"Sure, sure, I just have to get a few things done for the library."

"Was that your mom?"

"She just got home from work. I'll see you in a few," I said hitting the end button on my phone. I got up, proceeding into the living room.

"Mom, Can we watch a film in here tonight?"

"Hmm, sure, let me grab my things. I can take care of this in my bedroom. Is Molly, OK?"

I shrugged, "Not really, her folks are now fighting over if she stays, goes, or if it's right or wrong," I replied.

My mom picked up her book list and put it in her tote. "If she needs a place you know she can stay here."

"Yeah, I did suggest it, in exchange for rent or dishwashing."

My mom picked up her glasses and put them back on. She stood up and then touched my back as she walked around me to get to the hallway.

"Tell Molly for now, no charge. If she needs to stay with us dishes, chores, and she has to finish college."

I smiled, leaning against the wall of the room. I loved my mom.

"Thanks," I said.

"Now enjoy whatever it is, you're watching tonight. Don't forget you have Denny's in the morning. I know you're an adult, but no eye rolling!"

I rolled my eyes anyway, after she left the room.

The movie and popcorn had been what we both needed. Molly's parents arguing over their daughter's sexuality? Why couldn't they just love her? I accepted Molly already fast asleep on the flip couch. She was way more comfortable here than at home. Maybe I'd get to meet Maine soon. It would be nice to put a face with a name, and see why Molly cared for her so.

Gazing at my nightstand the clock read, 11:57 P.M. almost midnight. I pushed myself up and leaned to look out the window. The moon was full, the stars filled the sky, and I breathed in the cool air. It seeped out of the cracks in my window pane. I yearned for my fox form, wishing I could just transform and go out for a run as my mother did. Perhaps tomorrow I'd get a chance to train in that structure. Right now running wasn't risk-free. Even if it was, would Nayla allow it? I snuggled down further into my quit. My shift at Denny's would start at 10 am. I only had to work til two, but I'd be talking to Don about taking a little time off. Too bad Nayla hadn't given me a time frame. I couldn't quit my job.

Chapter 26

(Training day, Wednesday)

That morning, Dad and I went to Denny's, to break the news to Don about my aunt. We used the excuse of her being deathly ill, a white lie I kept telling myself. Nevertheless, the chicken bone rose in my throat from guilt. I was glad to be wearing layers as the chill hit my face the second we'd stepped out of Jenson's car. It was then I noticed Nayla, Cavin, Shellena and Lance standing at the edge of the forest motioning for us to accompany them. I wasn't sure where Eva and Star were.

"I guess, we're going into the clan territory," I said over my shoulder to my crew. Owl, had his hands in his coat pocket, Molly held her scarf tightly around her face, and Jenson tried to catch up as we made our way to the path. The one I'd first seen when we'd searched for answers on our own about Du-Vance.

"And why didn't your dad come today?" Molly asked.

"He and my mom want to spend time with Megan. She's been left on the sidelines of this whole clan thing. I'm actually, psyched they're not holding my hand on this. They trust me, my choices, and where my clan will lead me now and in the future," I replied a little more confident than I felt.

Nayla waved to us off in the distance. "It's OK, come forth at once! Ranger Mike, did give you the clear. He told you to come here right?" said Nayla to us, as we walked forward, into the forest. Were we supposed to go left or did we go right?

"On your right Starla, come on now and escort me on the trail. I'll guide you and your friends into the training area. You talked to your job manager, didn't you?" she asked.

"Don, I spoke with him this morning. He expressed concern for the aunt we told him had taken ill on my dad's side of the family." She nodded, and we advanced deeper into a forest of thick trees. I could barely see the sunlight.

"No need to fret. There's a clearing up ahead with obstacles, equipment, and huts. Star helped build them and Cal when she was here. Lang Orion, he did most of the work. It's such a shame. He was an excellent builder at age 13, very rare quality. We thought he might become an architect one day," she said, shaking her head.

"Are we going to do any of this training indoors?" asked Molly. She rubbed her arms with her hands

"I'm afraid all of our physical exercises, will be performed outside. Once we get started, you should warm right up!" Nayla exclaimed jogging towards an obstacle course. Four huts made of clay and brick lay behind them.

Jenson gave me a concerned look while we sprinted towards the drill area. It reminded me of an old army film. One with tires you would run through, sticks in the ground you would dodge, and instead of crawling under wire they had used tree stumps with logs set on top of them. I stood, surveying the lay of the course.

"Starla, you'll be doing most of these in human form. I don't want to assume that you'll remain that way should we become engaged with the enemy. A reminder for all, force is only to be used if we have to battle," said Nayla.

"Is anyone else here," asked Jenson beginning to run in place, to fight off the chill.

Looking back, I caught a glimpse of Shellena and Lance. In an instant, they flashed forward skidding to a stop in front of Nayla. I did a double take at their acceleration. That was some super speedy wolf feet, I thought.

Star stepped out from behind a pine tree, "Really, you must start showing up on time. Both of you, are constantly, using your strengths to cut corners. It will catch up to you. Then when you most need it, you'll put us all in danger."

"Were you hiding from us?" I asked.

"No, just got here. I, on the other hand, was tending to the young kits with Kaya. I think you two ought to try it sometime. We can always use more hands, or should I say paws on deck," Star replied.

"Yes, however, we're wolves not kits. Anyway, as a guardian shouldn't Starla, be teaching them how to control their morphing?" offered Lance as he quickly made his way ahead observing the challenge.

I shifted my body weight from side to side not sure what to say. I was just getting started on this whole gig hands on!

Catching up to him I shouted, "You, I've only been in this group for a week and a half. Give me a break! Let me find my ground, get through this case. After that, we can debate my role here. I haven't even decided if I'm going to reside among the clan, or if I wish to continue living in-between, or even maybe..."

"Don't let them scare you off," interrupted Nayla. "At present, there is no time to agonize over your guardian duties with the younger generation. Let's focus on the tasks at hand. Molly, you look awfully cold. Why, don't you do the first official run through?"

"Are you, going to time me or, do I just go?"

Shellena, who was, standing by Lance got out her sports watch, "The goal is to get through the challenge in less than 5 minutes. After you go Owl, Jenson, and Starla will trail behind you. Others from our clan are arriving to lend a hand. Don't let it distract you from this task just keep going. Are you ready, Molly?"

She nodded to Shellena.

"OK, ready, set, go!"

My eyes were on Molly for a few moments. Then other clan members started to arrive. Most of them were unknown to me. Cavin and Kaya had shown up. I could tell it was him. He was the only elder with a white stripe on is forehead proceeding down his muzzle. They sat side by side viewing Molly, who had just finished the obstacle run. Jenson, gave her a high five, Owl threw her a thumbs up, and I quickly delivered a brief smile. My ears perked up as I heard the crowd behind us discussing how we might be saving the clan from future threats. One thing I couldn't understand was how this was supposed to be undercover? Everyone was here. Wouldn't they be drawing attention to themselves? We were not that remote from the city. I turned my head to see Owl racing into the tires. Man! He was supercharged! I rolled my arms back, my hips, and then stretched out my legs. It would be my turn, before long. I couldn't help but gawk at the new arrivals. If it was my kinfolk, it appeared fairly mixed. Hmm were any of them the wolf clan we were at peace with?

"Starla, Go," hollered Nayla.

I had to move fast, plodding through the big old tires I made an effort, not to fall flat on my face. Then I swung quickly around the sticks in the earth heading forward getting geared up to do a version of the Limbo. Ungracefully, I hit the ground, rolled over, and started shimmying on my back under the logs. After about four of those, I got up running to jump over another four hurdles in front of me. I was never good at those in school. I managed to hop over two of them. The other three, well, I knocked two down, and after that the other fell on top of me. I got up, dusting myself off and headed over to Nayla. A bead of sweat dripped from my forehead. I never thought myself overweight, but I sure did feel out of shape.

"I guess I'm going to need a lot of work. Hopefully, I'll be better at mind speak, spells, and whatever else the rabbit decides to pull out of his hat," I confessed.

"We'll toughen you up," Lance said, jogging over to me. He gently slapped me on the back. I shuffled aside not sure what to say. He hadn't been particularly, nice earlier.

Jenson strutted over clearing his throat.

Oh no, I thought don't do something stupid, don't fight.

"I'm not, really sure if you're trying to be brotherly, or if you're flirting with my girl. Now up until this point I thought you were cool helping us go out the cabin, scaring off those bandits with Nayla's assistance. It seemed incredibly honorable of you," accused Jenson. He stood his ground, arms crossed.

"I'm not going to steal your girl. We always have rattled up the newbie's a bit. Do I see her as a sister? Sure I do. We're all family, well, maybe not biologically, but so what?"

Jenson took in a few deep breaths laying his arms at his side managing a bit of a crooked grin.

"The goal is to create emotions of conflict and anger in order, to use it towards defeating the rival. With any luck, we won't have to use physical force. It would be great if we could just find Minder so Cal can come home," determined Lance.

"Too bad, in all probability it won't be that easy," replied Kaya walking up to us with Cavin by her side. "Do you imagine she'll immediately be willing to hand her over?"

I shrugged my shoulders, "You're right, we don't know. She sounded fed up in the letter. It might be possible to get her to unite with us," I replied. Glancing over my shoulder, Molly and Owl were whispering to one another as they stood beside Star. I was ready to go inside to start our mental discipline unless there were more workouts in the lineup for today.

"Do you have news? Why all, the spectators? It seems odd if we want this under wraps," spoke up Shellena.

"Let's just all gather inside," said Cavin. "Now, as for the rest of you anyone here that is not attending the mission to Thunderhead Bay, go back and guard the park."

"Hut one, then?" inquired Nayla.

"No, Hut 3 the sweat tent. We are going to hold a quick meditation. We'll start by introducing our new affiliates to some of our basic knowledge, speak thought spells, among other control development," suggested Cavin.

"What about stick work? Jousting?" interrupted Lance.

"Never mind that, now, come!" ordered Cavin.

No one hesitated. We filled the hut. Cavin didn't speak, but pointed us in the direction of where we should sit urging us to form a tight circle, some of us with fur, some in their human forms, a few wolves, one fox, a fox-wolf merger, and a few I was a bit unsure of. I didn't ask.

Inside the tent, the tension rose. A fire pit sat in the middle of the spacious hut with wood ready to be burnt. Would I have to smoke peyote as the Indians had, or go on a vision quest? Jenson sat on one side of me, then Molly, and next to her Owl. I observed as Kaya, and Cavin stood off to the side. Star, Shellena, Lance, and Eva entered the circle. Where was Nayla? I tried to relax, closing my eyes as everyone began to sit down beside each other entering the ring. Something fuzzy nuzzled my hand, Nayla?

"Let me sit beside you," she said.

Molly and I moved over to make room for her.

"Won't you get awfully sweaty with all your fur? I've never seen you in human form. I mean, you're not part human are you?" I asked.

"No, I'll be fine. I've attended a few of these. I'm a rare one. I can sense things, speak, and perform spells. I'm here to guide you on your journey. Please don't fret, just sit back. Cavin will speak, and we'll get started on this next lesson," she whispered.

"Now that I have everyone here who'll be assisting us on this expedition I am going to begin the ceremony. If you've never done this, just follow along. Any questions will be, answered during these proceedings. Do not speak unless necessary. If, at any time, you sense you're going to pass out, raise your hand. I have room temped water sitting in a compartment in case of that. Now, there will be periods when you want to address the group. Raise your hand, err paw if it pertains to the mission, a vision, or anything else that may be relevant to the case, or Thunderhead Bay," announced Cavin.

Kaya pranced forward as a fox and then began her transformation. She faded in and out, facing us. A woman with long brown hair, green eyes, and a silken white dress emerged before us as if she'd stepped out of a fairy forest. A minute passed, then she spoke.

"I do not transform as you're used to," she said directly to me. "I am a Kitsune as your mother is, Starla. It means I may use my powers to seduce, if I wish, but I choose not to. As you can see Cavin is my husband," she said nodding to him. "We though have not been properly introduced."

She stepped into the circle and walked towards me. Then stopped and kneeled down beside me on her knees taking my hands. "Your mother was an important part of our clan. The day she decided to leave we experienced great sadness. You, however, are her most treasured gift. Keeping you from harm tore her from us. The love she shares with your father is strong. I see into the future," she claimed.

"What does that have to do with?"

She placed her finger to my lips.

"Silence child, let me speak. You're going to be a great warrior of peace, simplicity, and love. I see an aura around you that emaciates out to us." She smiled at me, stopped for a bit then continued. "The light will shine today, you'll burn bright child as the fire among us," she said gesturing to the pit.

"My mother and father will they stay together?" I asked.

"Yes. Shh," she backed away, sprinting out of the circle to stand again by Cavin.

"My mysterious one," he said, kissing Kaya softly on the cheek. "Now if I can have you close your eyes so we can give thanks to the higher power. The one who watches over all people. Please, bow your heads taking just a minute to realize how lucky we are to have one another, to love, to live freely, for all we have fought for in peace, and when in despair, and desperation the violence that comes with it."

We hung our heads low in complete silence, eyes closed. Time felt as if it did not exist. A warm sensation spread slowly up my body like a tree, my feet as its roots, a tingle of heat growing, moving up my stems into into my chest then a feeling of escapism outside of my torso.

"Open your eyes, everyone! Look to the middle; see our strength in unity. What we created together! This is love, peace, hope, and the labors of friendship, relationships, and growth. It forges a fire within us spreading out as either goodness or hate. Open your eyes, do not fear this," he shouted.

In unison, our eyes popped open to see a great fire in the pit. I started backing up, seriously, we did that! Our love, emotions, hate, peace to the god above sparked life? Fire, also brought death and life a part of a whole, all this inside me?

"Do not be alarmed, this happens, when we work together. We also have to learn how to work apart. In this venture, we may become separated. If so those who are new here must be taught how to protect themselves. I am relatively concerned about Jenson and Molly. You both are brave ones."

Kaya stepped up once more, moving over to Molly.

"I see your pain, the hurt, of prejudice you've suffered. Here, you're welcome to fight beside us in harmony, for our clan, for friends, and to increase the confidence you desire to carry on. May this guidance and light inside us sprint out into you. I see a radiance you hold and have all along. Keep your faith and stay true," she advised.

"Yes, for eternity," Molly agreed.

Kaya turned to Jenson, "You're valiant, gutsy and comprise a great deal of devotion inside of you, if not you wouldn't wish to stand beside her. Unconditional love is an immense gift. You transmit it boldly," she declared touching his hand. "May I sit?"

"Um, sure, yes," he choked.

"Starla, given you are one of us. You do desire to be one of us, correct?"

"Yes, but I can still be me, still be with my mother live outside of this?"

"As always, we have said, it is your choice where you reside. We've already pulled you into us, receiving you, and now you must receive us. Is this what you want?"

I gulped down the lump in my throat sweat dripped from my forehead. I wiped it aside using my sleeve and proceeded to take off my jacket. Others did the same around the circle. Why were they mimicking me?

"Go ahead, speak," Molly urged.

Jenson kissed my shoulder and gave me a reassuring squeeze even in the heat of the hut. Owl looked, a bit smug as if he was used to this type of thing.

"I cannot say I've always felt alone, nor that I've been unloved. I just speculated why I could do certain things. My mother finally told me the truth. It wasn't simple to grasp. Now, that I've seen what took place here, I understand. A bit anxious; my emotions tend to rule me. I find myself in anger running away, at least in Springville. Whereas in L.A. I took the lead. I played the part of a character I wanted to be only to find out. I was her; strong, a leader, yet a bit wacky, sarcastic, that's me. How do I receive you?"

A stifled laugh came from the crowd.

Lance stood up to speak. Cavin nodded at him to go on.

"You must pick a name. Tri is Tri, but since you've been living in the territory of humans, your name is defined by them. I do admire Starla. Its unique charismatic, charming!" he exclaimed.

I blushed even if, he, was, more, akin, too, a pain in the butt brother he still made me a tad frazzled.

"Picking a name is not to be taken lightly. Give her a few minutes to reflect on her life. Let her go back to the beginning in her mind. Let her start there," Star spoke.

Eva moved swiftly to my side taking my hands in hers. I shivered; this meeting felt like it was all about me. What about the others?

"Don't worry about that now. Once, your name is chosen we'll be as one, all of us. Now find your center as you did when you initially entered the clearing. Go to that safe place within taking yourself higher up the steps; climb them until you reach elevation, deep breaths in and out."

Lifting flying, tranquility led me back to the field where the rain poured over me onto the ground. I saw her, or was it, he? No, it was a girl, a fox slowly trotting towards me. A mare was further out in the field of golden wheat that grew larger and larger. I could hear her in my head, her voice. It was, similar to the power of mind speak spoken by my clan. You will grow tall, strong and able to bend like the wheat in this field. You will not break for the rain renews you, and your speed is as fast as a mare. You have more than two paths for many, branch out if you let us step in. Do you choose to be Araina, or would you rather be Amare?

"Araina," I whispered, out loud. "That is who I wish to be spirit fox. Who are you?"

"Amare and I will be a part of you now forever. Should you need guidance, clear your mind and our hearts will meet. Your mom has a spirit guide inside of her also. It's been, hidden dormant for years. Now find serenity again, awaken to your clan. Begin my child, start once more, and fear no defeat, but let the ripples direct you."

My eyes fluttered open.

"You saw her didn't you?" asked Eva.

"In my mind, we spoke, as you've told me, I need to be, taught. Where is she, who is she?" I blurted.

"A part of you, Nayla would tell you that," she said, gazing in the direction of the white fox. She let go of my hands, scooting back to her spot in the hut. She then curled up lying beside Star.

"Gifting is something, Shellena, is able, to do. I've asked her at present to do so for our honorary members. Those who stand by you Araina," said Cavin motioning for Owl, Jenson, and Molly to rise.

"So I will be referred to as Araina while here, instead of Starla," I said speaking out of turn.

"You will, now let us advance."

Shellena leaped into the circle, scrunched down, and kneeled, staring upward at the peak of the hut. "I ask you give me vitality to bestow gifts on those who seek to aid us in integrity, truth, justice, and to bring our own back to the clan, amen." Lifting herself up a book appeared in her hands. She opened it, and the words poured out of her mouth.

"Burning bright I give you our light, to heal the damages, torment, and hate. Our hearts encircle yours in complete unity."

Shellena stood up, "Molly step forth, into the circuit we've created. Lance, I'm going to need your help here, please."

Molly marched into the ring. The fire, in the pit, grew stronger. Lance joined them.

"Our souls will unite, and in it will spark your ability to heal the wounded, to care for those who cannot do so for themselves. Standing here near your physical form you're emitting a potent ability yet to ignite you must let us in. You've hidden too long, your strengths as you did love."

I turned away to see Nayla smiling. She trotted up to Molly, grazing her hand with her head. Molly leisurely stroked her fur.

"Your bravery speaks without words," beamed Nayla. She sat on her hind quarters repositioning herself in front of the three of them. "Molly do you accept us? You're forever welcome here."

"Thank you, you have my heart," she said.

"And it is a gift," replied Kaya prancing in beside them.

In the union, eyes were closed. An immense light filled the inside of our circle, and we outside the border kept it in, pushing it back into those that were creating it.

"You gave us the gift of your open heart that widens eyes once closed. The three of us bestow upon you directly the capability to restore physical wounds, to elevate anguish caused in a battle. A protective ring is placed on you to repel enemies when in combat. Now let us embrace giving thanks to the ones above, gods and goddesses that shield us," Kaya spoke into the sky.

Those in the interior held one another twinkling like stars briefly. Afterward hands lay on each side of those before us.

"Molly, you may be seated," said Lance.

249

Cavin brought forth cups of water passing them out to us.

"Sip slowly, or you'll get sick," he affirmed. He finished up handing out the cups, seating himself beside his wife.

"Jenson, and Owl your offerings are more intricate. We are unable, to magically beseech you with them. Lance, could you take them to the arena. Hut number two. Where the fencing materials are at. He'll coach you, both there."

Lance got up, giving a sort of bow.

"I suppose, it's time for me and Lance to make nice," Jenson muttered.

"You'll do fine," I said, ruffling his hair a bit.

Owl gave his arm a playful punch. "Let's go, it will be fun. You'll get to fence with Lance. Prove to him you're worthy of Araina," he chided as they made their way out of the hut.

"Araina, you'll stay here. Memories can be used, as weapons. We'll start with that. Star is going to work with you," said Cavin.

Molly looked up at Nayla.

"Your fine Molly. Stay put," she said soothingly.

Chapter 27

(Jenson)

I wasn't sure what awaited us. I tagged along with Lance and Owl to training hut #2. Why weren't the girls coming with us? Starla, errs Araina, is an independent girl. If she even suspects she won't be allowed to participate in the altercations at Thunderhead Bay, it would be a disaster. Lance turned to me as we came upon the hut.

"Now is the occasion to notify me if you want out. Do you have any qualms about going on this mission?"

"No, I'm in 100%. I'd like to keep Starla err Araina safe. She, however, won't see it that way," I said, kicking up the snow in front of me.

"I sense you're wrong. She came to you when she turned into a fox and didn't know what to do," Lance reminded him slipping a key out of his pocket.

"You keep it locked up now?" Owl inquired stepping back.

"Someone broke in, last year. They didn't steal anything, but we suspect they were sleeping here."

"I guess you can never be too cautious, especially since you've had enemies about," I said.

Lance unlatched the padlock. The door flung open, revealing a large room with a cement floor.

"This is it, come on in," he said.

"What do you think?" said Owl.

I sauntered into the spacious area. "It sort of, reminds me of our old high school gym," I remarked jogging over to a basketball that lay on the floor. Lance spotted me as I was going to retrieve it.

"We're not here to shoot hoops." Lance intercepted. "Now if training goes well, maybe later. We'll need mats, which you'll find to the right of you." He pointed in the direction of some lying against the wall. "If you could, please take them, unfold them and place them in the middle of the room. Okay, here is what we are going to do. First, we're going to learn how to spar with sticks. This way we can defend ourselves in case of an ambush, it's vital. I'll grab the Kali sticks we'll be working with today," he said strolling towards a large black trunk.

I dragged two mats over to the middle of the room beginning to lay them side by side.

"How many do you suppose, macho man wants?" I asked.

"We'll grab two more, and see what he says when he returns. Look, Jenson, try to be nice. Lance, is a good guy."

"Actually, it irritates me that he flirts with Starla Araina," I said in a huffy manner, pulling over the second, mat.

"No, you're just convinced he is, because, you're, being an overprotective boyfriend," Owl mused. He slid his mat next to mine.

Lance, came back carrying a few sets of sticks. They appeared to be made out of bamboo. I'd seen them used in movies but never had any experience with them. The last time I'd entered a gym was for wrestling class. That had been what eighth grade? I shook off the memory of being taken down by someone twice my size.

"Here," said Lance, handing us each one of the sticks.

I pondered if we would only learn how to yield one stick. They didn't feel that heavy. Were they built to take someone out? Maybe just detain them for a bit.

"Shouldn't we have protective equipment?" I asked.

"Do you think we'll have gear with us on the mission?" Lance rebuked.

"Probably not," Owl chimed in.

"No, so we are going to have to watch ourselves. Pay close attention to me," Lance directed. He held his stick loosely in his hand. "Now I'm sure you've probably seen films with these types of artillery. Owl, has had a little familiarity with them."

"I learned, slightly from a demonstration we received during a pow-wow. They were used in an interpretive native dance," explained Owl.

"This time it's different. We'll be using them to protect ourselves." Lance, spoke raising his eyebrows.

"Is there a special way I need to hold the sticks, or do we just use them as we would swords?" Jenson prompted.

"No, you definitely, do not use them, like swords. If you hold them in an improper manner it could get you killed," Lance growled at me.

I stepped back, giving him room to demonstrate.

"Watch how I hold it, and then try it yourself. You should consistently have one fist length open at the bottom of your stick. Never cover up the bottom. When fighting make sure you keep it moving. Don't allow your opponent to grab the stick away from you."

Standing there, Owl and I did as he said.

"Good, now that is the correct way to hold it. Remember that."

"OK," we replied.

"I'll demonstrate a move. Then you both repeat after me."

We practiced several varying moves the long stick technique, short, and close combat. I worked up a sweat as Owl had sat out on the last one on one. Then, as I wiped the perspiration from my brow, I noticed Cavin had snuck in.

"How's it going Lance?" he asked.

"Good. I do have one question. Are the girls going to know how to act in combat? We cannot go into this with them only knowing spells, and speak talk. Molly can only give out so much healing before she becomes weak. She has to learn how to yield it and to regain her strength," admitted Lance.

"True and the girls are working on those things," he replied.

"We probably should practice tumbling, avoiding contact and diverging away from the opponent. You know, like you were teaching the young male kits the other day," spoke Cavin.

"You're right, now this is simple," he said and turned to us.

We tumbled and stood up against one another, even Cavin joined in. I had to admit Lance was a pretty good teacher. I wondered how the girls were getting along with their instruction.

(Starla)

I observed Jenson, Owl, and Lance exit the sweat hut unsure of how everyone would get along. I just hoped Jenson and Lance didn't go to wrestle mania, on each other before the real thing.

"Everything alright?" asked Nayla. She placed a paw on my back.

"I'm not sure how those two are going to manage to get along in combat. They seem to snap, at each other, easily," I said, annoyed.

"It's just male dominance. Men don't know how to act when a pretty, girl is around," she said, winking at Molly.

"Don't look at me. I'm more apt to consider Eva attractive," Molly muttered.

"Well, anyhow let's get out of this damp tent. I'll take you ladies to the dining hall. It's the one hut containing various rooms. One being a meditation area without the heat! Grab your coats now, as it's still frosty outside."

We put our coats on and trailed behind her to the first tent. There were lights on, so I assumed Star was waiting for us. Would Kaya be present? I hadn't spent much time with her. She gave off a motherly radiance during the gifting ceremony.

"Are we going to be allowed any hands-on combat, or is that against clan rules?" I challenged trudging towards the building.

"If you're asking if we frown upon women in our tribe defending themselves no. You'll learn how to push an attacker away rather than engage him in a fight. If it does get to the point, where you have to take him out, we encourage it. Do you suppose it's so abnormal that women and men handle things differently?"

"Men and women are like night and day," said Kaya as she walked up to us.

"I didn't know you were joining us," Molly spoke. We hiked on nearing the hut.

"Eva, isn't going to be able to make it. Some urgent matter with one of the young girls, love sick I think?"

"Not again, the wolf across the way," prodded Nayla.

"Yep, old Jinx, is up to it again," Kaya said, shaking her head.

"Who's that?" asked Molly.

"Oh, just this mid-aged wolf, he has the best intentions, of course. What he doesn't realize, is now is not, a good time to be intermixing. I would be a hypocrite if I didn't allow outside species to date. After all, that's what started this nonsense. You know that, right?" Kaya asked, turning to unlock the hut.

"Yes, it's what Du-Vance had been working on, and Nuria was involved also," I replied.

"The peace treaty," claimed Molly.

"Here we are, it should be pretty cozy once we get into the reflection area. This is the mudroom," she said, shutting the door.

I noticed pegs on a wall for our coats, a cubby underneath for shoes, and off to the right a closet. We put away our things and followed Kaya and Nayla.

"This way down the hall to the right is the meditation room," Nayla said as we passed photos of other clan members.

I stopped to examine one of them. A young girl with the ears and tail of a fox, but stood with human legs and hands. "Who's this?" I asked.

"One of the greats she's long gone now. You would have liked her gutsy, strong, independent, and incredibly witty," Nayla admitted. We moved along towards the door. Its sign read, reflection space.

"It isn't that big of a hut," said Kaya, opening the door for us.

There was a fireplace lit, illuminating pillows placed in a circle a few feet away. Several candles glowed. I counted five in the center of the circle all a variety of colors.

"Are those what I perceive them to be?" I asked pointing.

256

"What are they?" retorted Star, who'd been waiting for us in the room. She sat on a white pillow adjacent to a white candle.

"Magic candles, the ones that aid in spells, protection, and steer us to the future, or reveal the past," I answered stepping towards it.

Star nodded in response.

"Molly, why don't you sit on the blue pillow adjacent to the blue candle?" Kaya motioned with her hand. This will aid you in conveying, the healing power, we gifted you. We're going to strive to maintain a balanced circle."

I leaned in to look at the other candles inside the ring.

"I should be seated on the blue pillow to be open to using memory as a weapon," I stated, easing myself towards the area. I waited to see if anyone would protest against it. When they didn't, I sat.

Kaya took her place on the silver pillow near a silver candle. Then proceeded to give further details.

"We each have a dominant trait that stands out among us. We hold a weighing scale, playing a part to achieve one desired goal. When the correct element is achieved, I should be able to predict, a little of what is to come at Thunderhead Bay..."

"Let's not get ahead of ourselves," said Star to Kaya.

Nayla nodded at them and then spoke.

"A moment of silence, then I want to show Starla how to push her memories into the minds of others while using their own against them."

I shuddered, feeling a chill crawl up my back, a memory of its own, creeping. Bright white lights being pressed into my brain. I could no longer see them, anyone. No, it had just been a reoccurring dream, and they had halted. Had they not?

"Dear, are you remembering something, a dream, lights, noises?" Nayla demanded as she sat back behind our circle.

"Why aren't you in the ring?" I asked.

"Observing and protecting those inside. You may still see my thoughts and visions merge with yours. All of us will remain connected. We must always have one outside the circle in case something misguided, gets in. It rarely occurs, so breathe in and stand down, OK? You look like you've seen a ghoul," she commented.

"No, just a memory," I replied. "A white light I used to dream about, feared it, and I'd awaken in sweats."

"Prior to your move here, how long ago?" pushed Nayla.

"It must have been after Cal left L.A.," I retorted.

"The usual warning signs of one of purity being taken by evil hands. Did the dreams stop?" asked Star.

"Yeah, I just never figured them out."

"The past is past, let us begin," whispered Nayla.

One by one we took each other's hands without words. I could hear my watch ticktocking, my heartbeat, the breathing of my friends near me.

Each beat, I felt, pulsed. Memories old and new traveled from one of our minds to the next resembling one complete circuit. First, I saw Star in her childhood racing her mother in human form. Kaya leaped up to grab a fish out of a stream, while, in fox form, Nayla lay nursing a pup, and then Molly sat in a class gazing at Maine. What did all these memories mean?

We lifted our heads slowly, and Star ended the silence.

"Those memories were of us at our most vulnerable periods. If, in a split second you can pull those out of the enemies, then you can find their weakness. Hit them hard with an image of the future.

Once, we have all bonded, it's then we'll be able to use our powers jointly."

We focused on each of our strengths, concentrations and guided each other through the steps.

"Can you hear me?" I whispered internally to Star, Molly, Nayla, and last Kaya. They had me continue till I was heard and could identify each of them through their thoughts. Afterward, Molly practiced healing not only physical wounds but mental and emotional ones. It took a form of mixed emotions and concentration. She would let the feeling brim up to the surface and touch a part of the infected area. It didn't work for everything. It had to be something inflicted on other species through hate. It would not cure anything, biological or genetic.

"Will I ever be fully efficient at this?" asked Molly after she'd made several attempts. She'd achieved two of them.

"If you decide to remain an honorary member, subsequently you'll struggle less with it occurring, encountering more successes than failures. Two out of five isn't bad. Realize that Nayla created the image, the situation, and you were able to heal two out of the five species. That's impressive for a beginner," Star praised.

It only seemed as if minutes had passed yet mentally I felt burned out. I had not even taken a shot at attacking anyone with memories. Who would I target? I barely knew anyone except Molly. How could I hurt my best friend? I gulped down the saliva stuck in my throat.

"Molly, we need to be able to have Starla use a memory against someone. You have, known her, the longest. If Eva was here, we'd ask her. May we try it?" asked Nayla reluctantly.

Molly appeared a bit sullen, "I know she won't in actuality mean the attack, I guess we could attempt it."

I repositioned myself on the blue pillow. My butt had started to fall asleep. Man, I didn't expect I'd miss being out in the cold running an obstacle course. In, addition, my nerves twitched, as I ran my hands down my legs, striving to calm myself before, I began.

"Now just relax, bring to the surface a recollection you had of an occasion Molly made you furious. And so you're working to get a hold of that negative energy. Drive it towards her. Molly, you'll experience a slight jolt. It shouldn't be too painful," cautioned Star.

Molly winced, but looked as if she was attempting to stay strong.

My mind was totally blank! Molly and I had, in no way, any serious battles. The worst thing I ever thought of her was Jenson. I bowed my head low because this shot would be, below the belt, particularly knowing that Molly didn't favor men. I grabbed the sides of the cushion I sat on, digging in hard bringing myself to the instant they pulled up in her parent's car. When I alleged, she'd taken him from me.

A flash of light pierced out of the middle of the inner circle where the candles sat shooting towards Molly. I didn't see what I'd initiated. My eyes being closed and all.

"Stop!" shouted Kaya.

Star seized me.

"Control, deep breaths, will it down inside of you. Calm as an ocean, soft sand beneath your feet. You are no longer there learning to control this is critical. You have to be able to pull yourself out of the memory as well as in," she instructed.

I started to hyperventilate and tried to catch my breath. Vibrations pulsed throughout my body. I shook violently. Then it stopped.

My eyes fluttered open. I gasped at the sight of her. Burn marks up and down her arms. How could she, or Maine who I hadn't yet met ever forgive me?

Nayla huddled near Molly.

"Have you already failed to recollect the ability we bestowed her?" Star glimpsed at the two of them.

I didn't reply, just sat there, taken back at the power I had to deliver pain to others.

"We can't let this injury set in, or else you'll not be able to rejuvenate from this. Even though, it was gifted it's also, learned. Touch your affected area, imagining a bright healing light radiating over your arms. Now take your hands lightly running them up and down on the infected area. Concentrate, breath, gradually," instructed Nayla.

"Good, good, it's starting to fade out," said Star.

The burns gradually disappeared from my sight.

"I don't believe I can do that again, not to someone I care for." I stammered, hugging myself.

"This is good, it's needed Araina," said Star. She eased herself off her pillow. Then blew out the candles and retrieved them one by one.

Molly came over to me offering her hand to help me up.

"Look, it's OK, they're almost all gone now. I don't want you to be bothered by minor burns."

I touched her arms, observing leftover red marks that remained. "I hope Maine isn't too angry with me when she sees them. I haven't even met her yet I've already managed to get you hurt before the operation."

"I'm Ok. In fact, I need to ask you something Nayla."

"OK, go ahead."

"How much healing will I be able to do, before I run out of juice?"

"We're not certain. Since you are a beginner, I'd say you could probably heal up to ten minor injuries, major ones maybe two."

"I've also been apprehensive about what may occur when we invade the outskirts of Thunderhead Bay. Have the wolves you assigned yesterday left yet to scope it out?"

Nayla pranced in the circle as we stood up gathering the pillows off of the floor.

"I've spoken to them. Four of their members will be on the way there tonight. I told them to remain till morning, but they said, the night would be a much better occasion to monitor them without being noticed. Personally, I believe they are nuts. Don't they know that's when the bandits tend to roam about causing the most trouble," she said, shaking out her fur.

"Where do I put these?" I asked Star.

"Set them over on the shelving unit next to the fireplace where I put the candles if we should need them again," she replied.

I did as she had asked. Afterward, I returned to the middle of the room near Nayla, Kaya, and Molly. We stood in peace until Nayla Nudged me onward.

"We'll be going to dinner with the rest of the clan members," she urged.

"So we get to meet up with the boys, witness what they learned. I bet they got to do some actual hands-on fighting! What happens if my memory weapon doesn't work? We didn't even apply any physical fighting techniques," I grumbled to Star.

"You will. There will be one last session before you go to Thunderhead Bay tomorrow. You don't have anything planned do you?" spoke Kaya.

"No. Molly, any plans?" I asked.

"It won't matter much if I'm gone. Mom and dad have been frequently arguing if I should be permitted, to date Maine. Mom's more understanding," Molly said, directing it towards me on our way into the dining hall.

I patted her gently on the back and smiled. "It means a lot to me you're here you know."

"That's what best friends are for," she replied.

Once in the dining area mundane chatter filled the room on the subject of what we might have to eat. We sat down at a large table. Half of a log had been cut to create a serving area.

"Is that where we'll get our food from?" I asked sitting down.

"Yes, the young adults will bring out the fare to form a sort of buffet for us. We have about fifty people in our clan," announced Kaya.

"Wow, I'm not sure I can handle them all at once," I replied.

"Now what were you going on about earlier? Ah, you said, we were going to find out what may arise at, Thunderhead Bay," Star interrupted.

"I sought to invoke a spell, but after, you were burned Molly, I thought it better to wait, til tomorrow," responded Kaya. She played with her fork next to her napkin, "Maybe, or we could try..."

"No!" shouted Cavin, stepping into the room. "I don't want you trying to foresee the future. The bandits can read minds. It would put us at great risk. We can't let them know our intentions to attack. If we're lucky we'll only have to deal with Minder, and it will be peaceful if luck is on our side."

Kaya hung her head in remorse as if she'd been slapped. Star placed a hand on her back.

"The wolves will return soon. They'll tell us what's going on. We'll do our best with that," Nayla spoke trotting up to Kaya.

Cavin stood on the other side of her, gazing up at her face.

"Everything else is going as planned?" she asked him meekly.

He sighed, "The boys will be here soon. They were messing around throwing snowballs at one another. One of them hit me. I told them I'd had enough fun tumbling and avoiding on the mats today." He placed his muzzle in Kaya's lap, and she patted his head half-heartedly.

"I'm just watching out for the tribe. We cannot let anything slip out, to the opponent. They already have Lang, Cal, and Nuria; they killed Star's parents and many others to prove their point. I've yet to understand their method," he said in a harsh tone.

"If someone tried to do an experiment, on me, I'd be pretty angry too," argued Molly eyeing Cavin.

"You're right, but they should have gone to the authorities or another clan for aid."

"Did they?" I asked.

"No, Personally, I don't know the circumstances. Minder is the first person in the group to contact us. Well, Nuria I mean, given that you've found the note."

"What a mess, these scientists could still be out there. Each step we take, I keep gaining knowledge of truths kept!" I exclaimed stomping my feet on the ground.

"Araina, it will be alright," assured Nayla.

"No! When we get our members back, we cannot let this rest! As a guardian, I refuse to allow those corrupted bandits to remain free."

A loud crash echoed in the hallway. I began to get up to see what happened.

"Wait here," instructed Cavin his fur stood on end as he crept forward towards the entrance way.

Kaya leaned near to me, "My dear, you are taking on too much. Do you realize what kind of danger we are already in?"

"Better to get all the knots untied, then to leave something undone. If we can bring them over to our side, we might be able to join together to find these foes," I whispered.

Cavin was now outside, in the hall, he had to be. Minutes passed, five, maybe, then footsteps approached. I started to stand up only to see the boys playfully stumble into the doorway.

"What the hell happened?" Owl choked. He leaned against the door frame. Lance and Jenson were behind him."

"You tell me, we heard a crash. Cavin went out to see who, or what was there, and now he's gone," Molly blurted.

Nayla trotted to the doorway. "You boys better get in here, sit down, and take off those wet coats. You should have left them in the mud room," she scolded.

They took off their gear, leaving them in a pile, then came to sit with us at the table whereas Nayla stood off to the side.

"Did you see anything out there? We heard something smash, then a scuffle perhaps you passed him on your way here?" she asked.

Lance averted his eyes peering into the kitchen's open window. Clan kits had sauntered in silently beginning to prepare our meal. The smells wafted over to our table.

"What?" he asked.

Jenson shifted in his seat, and Owl took something out of his pocket. I thought it was important, nope only some gum.

"He was headed towards the Rangers station. He only told us to get to the dining hall, eat, and afterward either head home or stay in the guest rooms for the evening," said Jenson.

A rather large hybrid Fox, half human interrupted our conversation. He waltzed up to our table, placing large goblets of water next to our plates. "My name is Raze; Tonight I'll be serving you warm vegetable soup with hot bread. The desert will be an apple crisp after the light banquet. Please go on with your meeting," he said, turning away back to the kitchen.

"Kits huh?" I said.

"They are preparing the meal. That is our server. They do not have hands Araina," said Star, placing her own on her head shaking it slightly.

I slouched down in my chair. This had been, a lengthy day. I was ready to go home and curl up in my warm bed. Turning my hand over, I looked down at my wrist watch. It read 7 p.m. I still had Jone's class to deal with. When the heck, would I study or write that damn essay?

"Araina, I want you to know I'll discuss what we spoke about with Cavin. I'll see what he thinks about us finding a way to pursue these scientists, for now though we must focus on getting Lang, Cal, and Nuria back home safely," said Kaya standing.

"Where are you going?" I asked.

"To find Cavin, stay, eat, and rest. You'll need to be ready for the dawn. I suggest you stay here tonight if possible."

"Can't, Molly and I have to study for that test in Jone's class."

"Me too," spoke up Jenson.

"Well, then I'll see you all bright and early, say six a.m.?"

I about hit the floor! Six am, I guess we'd probably all be up all night. If I'd have my materials for the class with me, I would have stayed put. We just nodded to Naya as the soup was brought out, and she exited the lounge.

Chapter 28

(Thursday)

Last night, when I'd come home, mom had been working on book orders for the library. Briefly, I regurgitated the daily events. She was anxious about me going into the field. Jenson had sadly returned home. There was no time for a late night rendezvous or sneaking him into the house. I couldn't find the flip couch, hence I'd slept on the floor, allowing Molly my bed. Forcing myself up out of the scattered blankets, I floundered making my way to the bathroom. The soreness in my backside made me bend funny. My head was a pounding mess. I couldn't believe I had managed to write the essay for Jones class. It wasn't great, pretty rushed, if you ask me. Molly and I had gone through our notes until we crashed. No time for girl-talk either.

Stepping into the shower, I cranked up the hot water. It eased the pain and soothed me. This case was full of loose ends, maybe instead of untying knots we should be tightening them. I laughed, and it echoed against the walls. I placed a hand, on the tile. Gosh, I was a disaster. I needed one night alone with Jenson. Stop! I told myself, one night of passion wasn't worth it. Jez was I that stressed? Turning off the water, I dried off and dressed myself. Glimpsing in the mirror, I considered myself rather attractive.

"Hey, we need to get moving," said Molly, pounding on the door.

I opened it, letting the steam escape into my room.

"Mind if I take a quick one?" she asked, grabbing her clothes.

"Sure, we have about half an hour before Jenson picks us up. Did you call your mom, last night?"

"Hmmm, yeah," she said tightly holding her conditioner in her hand. "Dad just flew off the handle again, with me staying here. Now he thinks you and me..." she rolled her eyes, and then continued, "are an additional item."

"Your dad has such a stereotypical view doesn't he?"

"Sure does." Then Molly shut the bathroom door behind her.

"Dang, it's early!" Jenson affirmed standing in my kitchen.

"Yeah, mom and Megan are asleep. I don't imagine I'll see them until the twilight. After this session do you want to stop by, study a bit before the big test tomorrow?"

"Sure, Molly?" he asked.

She'd been quickly devouring frosted turbo rings while she sat at the table.

"I ought to go home tonight. I need to work some stuff out with my folks. It's mostly my dad, I'm concerned about. Mom's being supportive, but dad just assumes that staying over at someone's house implies a relationship."

Jenson chuckled, shaking his head. "Oh man, so now he's assuming that you and Starla?"

"Yep," she said.

Jenson slapped his hand on his knee and tried to control his laughter. "Your dad is a piece of work."

"No, he only wants me to be, well what he considers normal. Let's jet, OK. I don't want to talk about this anymore," said Molly, placing her cereal bowl in the sink.

"OK, get your coats, and I'll meet you in the car," Jenson said, pointing to the curb where he'd parked. He opened the front door and went outside. Molly gave me my coat, then put her's on.

"Jenson wasn't trying to hurt your feelings, you know. It's comical to him, that your dad just can't love you." I put on my jacket and grabbed my gloves and hat.

"Yeah, but not so for me," Molly answered, pulling open the door.

The cold wind hit my face, and I wanted to turn back. One more session, the test with Jones, then we could go to Thunderhead Bay. I just wanted Cal and Nuria back. Lang, I wasn't so sure about. I didn't even know him. Is he even still alive? Damn, those scientists! I wondered where they were, if they were dead, or in hiding? Perhaps the bandits had already killed them, but continued to seek revenge. I hoped I wouldn't have to miss math class. Wait, did I just think that! Gah, the clan and mystery were taking over my life.

"Wake up Starla-Araina, this is your life," I heard Cal whisper. Cal where are you? And how does she know my fox name?

The snow had gotten worse while we drove. Jenson tried to keep his car on the road. The tires were having trouble gripping as we slid in the slushy snow.

"I wish I'd have gotten snow tires," he grumbled, as we slowly pulled to a stop at the last light before entering the park. Molly and I had been hanging on to the car door handles fearing for our lives.

"Yeah, I wish you would have too," I replied. The light turned green. Jenson eased the car across the road, into the parking lot nearest the station.

Molly jumped out of the vehicle racing to open the passenger door for me. I fought a smile and tried not to laugh. Obviously she was going to give Jenson hell for what he'd said to her this morning.

"Considering you, like my dad think she's my lady I might as well treat her as such," she remarked smugly. I hugged Molly, giving her a small peck on the cheek. Jenson shook his head at our silliness. At that instant, he linked his arms with mine and Molly's. We trekked along to the cabin with the snow crunching under our feet and the sunlight peaked out of the clouds.

Nayla and Kaya ran up to us out of the wooded area in fox form. They were puffing and out of breath.

"Did you find out what happened last night?" I babbled stopping a few feet from the lodge. Jenson and Molly huddled against me for warmth, the wind bitter against my skin.

271

"Bad news, Lang is dead, has been for over a year. A postcard came notifying the ranger with no return address last night from Nuria. She said, she couldn't give the precise location where she and Cal are staying," said Kaya.

Uneasiness swept over me. Cal had contacted me this morning. Had she not?

"Did it say anything at all about how he died? Did the bandits kill him?" Jenson asked.

"Nothing, hopefully, Cal and Nuria will clue us in," she said turning towards the Ranger's station.

"Let's go. Star has set up the lodge for our last minute training sessions. I figured with the test in Jone's class you'd want some time for that. Did you get any studying done last night?" Nayla said, with a smirk.

"We crammed til midnight, and Starla, ah Araina finished up her extra credit essay," Molly said as we advanced towards the structure ahead.

"Did you find it, complex trying to put the pieces together without giving away specifics?" Kaya inquired.

"It was a tad unnerving, but I managed to play it safe," I responded.

"Good, good, Cavin is meeting us along with Star. We'll focus on Jenson learning various spells. Lance and Shellena pretty much have most of the spell stuff down pat. Although, with their abilities as wolf-vamps they can hold their own so to speak," Kaya said as we moved along.

"Will Mike be here today?" I asked nearing the lodge door.

"Yes. He'll be handing out the hot cocoa and donuts. You didn't eat yet did you?" Nayla interjected.

"I had frosted Turbo rings, but I could eat a donut with chocolate frosting!" Molly said energetically. She opened the lodge door.

"How about you, Jenson?"

"I never turn down free donuts."

Molly turned, shutting the door behind us.

Eyeing the conference room to the right, I noticed Mike had moved the large table out and mats had been placed on the floor. In front of us where he checked monitors sat a box of donuts and hot cocoa in paper cups.

He turned from the viewing area, "Hi guys, go ahead help yourselves to the goodies and warm up before you get started. Star and Cavin are on their way back from a perimeter check. It will just be a few minutes."

Walking by we patted him on the back each taking a Dunker to dip in our cocoa. I took a seat adjacent to him on the bench and the others joined us.

"Yesterday was successful?" he asked Kaya.

"All of them did fairly well. The focus today has to be on Molly and Arianna's self-defense skills. Jenson should be learning spells."

"Araina?"

"Yes, that's my given surname as a fox," I replied with a mouth full of donut.

"I like it. It suits you quite well." He took a sip from his coffee mug.

"Where's Owl? Has anyone seen him?" Nayla observed.

"Not sure, strange. He didn't tell me he wasn't coming," Jenson said.

"He'd better show up today," she sighed, shaking out her fur in a frenzy. "If we're attacked by the bandits or other enemies, we'll need to make sure everyone knows the basics," she said in a huff.

"He'll be here, probably was just up late studying for Jones's tests like the rest of us," said Molly.

I finished up my last donut cake chunk with a bit of chocolate. Then threw out my napkin in the waste bucket below the monitors when a strange tickle gradually crawled up my arm. I pulled my shirt sleeve up. My paw print was glowing! Could it be, Cal? She talked to me this morning. Why would she be making it glow instead of speaking to me with thoughts?

Star marched into the room with Owl and Cavin in tow, "Araina, your tattoo!"

"And what am I supposed to do now?"

"Sit on the mats to meditate. It may possibly be important information."

Quickly I entered the big room and sat in the middle of the mats cross-legged. Shutting my eyes, I turned inward, reflecting on what had materialized in my mind at daybreak.

"Concentrate on Thunderhead Bay; imagine a big body of water with a forest behind it. Afterward, put yourself in it, look for clues, listen for any signals, smell the air around you, and get your bearings. Then see if you can sense any of our tribe among you," Star instructed.

The air blasted sharp against my face as I combed through the forest. Finally, a lake appeared on the outskirts, pines, oaks, and a few scattered fallen tree branches lay on the ground near a bush containing red berries, a perfect place for deer to munch.

Abruptly, a multitude of birds flew out of their nest towards me. I ducked out of their way just in time. I continued on, til the screeching of crows surprised me. I hit the ground once again covering my head. At least mentally I did. I couldn't really be here, right? I was there, though, in my head, or maybe I'd traveled without my body. I shook it off moving deeper into the woods. It was getting darker in spite of the daylight behind me.

"Cal, you called to me this morning. Where are you? I need a location. Have you met up with the wolf clan allies? Do they know where you are?" I projected. I listened not only with my ears but my eyes and heart. Something was moving amongst the trees. It leaped behind them, hiding briefly, and shifted so fast I could barely see its form.

"Follow me," it whispered.

Steadily I ran through the woods, passing trees trying to keep track of which way I had departed. I was losing sight of the shadow! Gah, I couldn't lose Cal, not now! My whiskers pushed through my cheeks, ears sprouted into long pointy things, and my feet well they jutted out, and I took off straight into the trees. The shadow veered north, then northwest. I followed it until I reached the cave.

"Welcome," it cooed at me. "Don't be shy, come in. I've been waiting for you."

My small fox frame shook as I enter the enclosure. I couldn't tell what the entity was that sat in the corner, hunched over almost hidden. It sure as heck didn't look like any of the Bandits to me! Cal and Nuria huddled together, holding each other for warmth. Why were they in their human form? What had happened to them?

"What is it, what's going on? Why are you in human form? Both of you..." I uttered out loud.

"Bring them. We don't have much time," shrieked Nuria.

Damn, what was that protection spell? Freaking out, the last time I'd messed with spells had been ages ago and two had come from a lame documentary. "No time Starla-Araina..." I said to myself, pressing onward. I tried to get a better glimpse of the bizarre silhouette. It could be a hybrid wolf. I saw it had ears and pointy teeth. It glared at me with its lustrous eyes. Shiznit! I spun around accessing the cave.

Where was Minder? Was she dead, held Captive, had the note been a trick?

I screamed, "Gods of my clan! Surround Cal and Nuria in protection, push away the evil darkness with love and light. I'll return with friends in tow. We'll fight amongst the winter snow! Straightaway, I must go."

Reversing back to the apparition I gave it my best sneer, and then sprung out into the forest towards the water.

"Breathe Starla, Breathe," shouted Molly, petting the fur along my back.

My eyelids fluttered, and my paws grabbed the mat. "Oh, not this again!"

"You're OK, just in fox form. I contacted your dad. He's bringing you some clothes, no need to worry. We simply need to know what materialized," said Star.

"I sense a location," I stuttered.

"Alright, so we'll deal with this first. Afterward, you'll observe Lance, Owl, and Jenson with their Kali sticks. After hearing you on your quest, I've decided it best you be prepared as the men are. I can't have you getting sucked into whatever it was you have seen without any combat experience," Cavin instructed.

"You heard everything?"

"Most of it, you were outwardly vocal as you entered another territory or dimension," Molly said, rubbing her arms.

It was a bit cold in here, even with my fox fur to shield me.

"How exactly did I change into a fox on my quest and here?" Had everyone seen me naked or just parts when I turned?

"Don't be embarrassed. It's happened to all of us, who can change shape," said Star.

I nodded, glancing around to see everyone sitting down on the mats.

"Come on, up off of the pad," said Jenson. I rose on all fours in my fox form letting him pull me into an embrace. "Now, tell us exactly what occurred before we start training."

"Nuria and Cal are being held captive. I'm not sure what exactly happened to Minder. She wasn't there at all unless..." I pulled away from Jenson, who was still hanging on to my furry fox body.

"Who is it, which bandit?" inquired Cavin.

"It's not a bandit. It's something else. All I could make out were glowing eyes, pointy ears, and sharp teeth. It could have been a new breed for all I know," I said, sighing. I stretched out my legs in a yoga position I once viewed on TV then sat on my hind legs.

"The location?" Kaya asked, trotting near me.

"Thunderhead Bay, is located near a body of water on the edge with forests behind it. I ran through the woods, not knowing where I was headed. I went north one way, near some berry bushes, then northwest soon after that. It's still somewhat foggy. I didn't just come across it myself. Something called out to me. A spirit, it wanted me to find them," I said.

"Maybe it's a trap," Nayla pondered.

"Even if it is, how can we leave them there? I placed a protection charm on them. Not sure, how great it'll work out," I said. My ears perked up, eyes diverting to the entrance. My dad stood in the doorway.

"Mike," he said, scanning the room. "Ah, everyone is here. Starla, is that you? I'm curious to hear your fox surname. What did I miss?"

"You have a lot to catch up on if you plan on attending this mission. I for one think it's better if you let Araina do this on her own," Cavin urged.

My dad shrugged, "Araina? That's a good name. Is that what you want?"

I wasn't sure what I wanted. Having my dad by my side wouldn't be all that bad. He stood up for me when Mom said, 'No, I don't want her involved with the clan.' Now neither of them really had a choice because I was in a deep snowbank trying to swim!

"We need as many able bodies as possible. I don't believe anyone should be asked to opt out or be opted out," I glowered at Cavin.

"Starla, ah Araina, is correct. Now we need to start instruction. Please allow her to get changed," said Kaya, directing me to the bathroom.

Molly and the others gazed at me. How freaked out were they? I deliberated as Kaya nuzzled the door, shutting it behind us.

"You, OK? I wasn't expecting you to go on your first vision quest, so soon," she said.

"Yeah, a bit frazzled, especially when a bunch of birds flew out at me. It seemed so real. Was it?"

"It's called astral travel. Your essence left your body traveling to where you were being called. It doesn't happen too often for newbie's. I'm quite impressed. You handled it superbly. What spell did you use?"

"Like I said, I'm not sure if it even worked. I got it from a documentary on witches, then I added to it."

"Ah, let's trust it holds for a few hours. I'll talk to Cavin when we get back. We must expedite this assignment. We'll possibly leave tonight."

"Tonight," I choked.

"Yes," she answered, then started chanting.

"What, what are you doing?" I snapped. She leisurely walked around me.

"Helping you with the process, so you don't have to panic to switch back," she replied.

"Will I be on a need to know basis, for the rest of my life?"

Kaya chuckled, "You'll adjust to our ways and how matters are managed as you work with us. We'll be preparing you for such after this mission is dealt with. Then maybe, you won't feel so left in the dark."

Chapter 29

Transitioning wasn't painful at all. In fact, it was rather quick compared to the last few occasions. Kaya, now in her human form opened the door. Peering into the room, I discovered the boys had gathered large sticks from a black trunk. Cavin motioned us to join them.

"I see your back to your human self," said Nayla, sitting amongst the others.

"Hey, Araina, why don't you, and Molly come over here? We'll show you the proper way to hold these bamboo sticks. Then teach you some moves that could save our hides," chided Lance.

Jenson winked at me, then formed a short side swing at Lance, who stopped his move with a swipe of his stick, catching it in mid-swing, in the air.

"You have to be a bit faster than that, Jenson," he snickered.

Owl strutted over to him and they began to battle in a similar manner. Jenson warded him off, pushing Owl's stick up against his throat.

"Mercy, I give up!" he screeched, backing up into the wall.

Jenson backed away, "Sorry bro, just attempting to get out some aggression, learn a few things. No hard feelings?"

"None, why don't you pair up with Araina, ah Starla, and I'll pair up with Molly. We'll start there.

"Call me Araina, when I'm with my clan. Outside it, though, I prefer Starla, you see it's kind of like a secret society. That is, unless we can convince the uber villains they should join our side," I said smugly.

Molly stood up, "Right over here, then Owl?"

"Yes, over here by me. I'll show you how to clutch the Kali stick. You see how I'm gripping it?"

Molly and I nodded, making a note of it in our heads.

Once, she joined him on the mat Owl put the stick in Molly's hand. She ran her hands upward where she'd seen him place his.

"Good, that's great. Now watch Lance and I exhibit sparring. He was showing off a bit earlier with Jenson," said Owl.

We stood back as Cavin shouted out each move.

"Let's see it boys, short stick, long stick, mid-stick, and again!" Cavin hollered. They cycled over it about five times before they would even let us try. Nayla placed some protective gear out for us to use.

"We'll be armored in combat?" I asked and picked up the elbow and knee pads.

"It wasn't the plan, but I urge you to use them. The boys didn't think I'd make them wear these. I was reluctant due to it restricting them in battle, but after what you experienced it would be best."

Molly and I put on the equipment. I paired up with Jenson, and she again joined Owl.

"OK, now take it slow; follow your leader as he has experience. Go!" shouted Cavin.

I jumped forward moving my stick towards Jenson's. I pushed him back then he pushed me. It was similar to a game until one of us ended up with either a stick near our throats or backed up against a wall.

Angela K. Crandall

I couldn't see Molly, but I could hear her. It sounded as if she was doing better than I.

"Molly, keep-at-it, you have him cornered! Now one of the clan members who is not involved would run up, and take him from behind. We'd use the cuffs. The goal is to take these guys in alive," requested Star, clapping her hands together.

The sparring went on for a few hours before Nayla called it. She claimed we had to get things packed up quickly.

"I realize we haven't had time for magic, or to teach counter spells. Here," she said, handing Jenson a book. "All of you need to look this over. I suggest you go, see this Jones character. You almost certainly won't be back on time for that mythology test. Find out if you can get an extension. If he's at all connected with our clan, maybe he'll reveal something more than, what he has previously, got it?"

"Got it," I said. I helped Lance pick up the sticks that lay in a pile. I handed them to him, missing one. It fell onto the floor next to me.

"We won't have a problem will we?"

"What problem?" he asked.

"Are you and Jenson good? I need you to be for the clan's sake. I can't have you off sparring against one another. Well, because he," I said, pointing to Jenson "thinks you like-like me," I stated.

"For now, we're cool," he replied.

"OK, make sure it stays that way," I said, aiming the stick at him before placing the last one back in the trunk. I took my coat off the rack, putting it on, then my gloves, mittens, and hat. I'd always be sassy, a bit quirky so learning to play, no, to be the leader was imperative to our survival. I had to pay attention to my

282

peers. I could get a bit arrogant, not always my strong suit but hey...

"You ready to take off?" Dad asked.

"Are you guys ready to face Jones?"

"Seriously, you're acting as if it's a takedown. Not a meeting with our professor," said Molly, easing on her coat and buttoning it up.

"True, but I never anticipated when I moved here I'd gain a whole new family. My world is full of super fun surprises, why, stop here?" I asked them.

Lance smirked at my comment. Cavin held his lips together, trying not to laugh, Nayla and Kaya didn't seem amused, Star stood quietly, and Owl pulled me aside. The ranger well, I didn't know where he was.

"Playing with fire little lady?"

I shrugged, "It's what I've always done best, why, quit now?"

"Let's go, Dan, are you coming with us," Owl asked.

"Yeah, I'm right behind you."

"Where's Mike," I asked.

"Left, he had to retrieve some paperwork from the police station. It's a few blocks from here. There are details that must be added to Lang Orion's file. Nothing, for you to worry about," spoke up Cavin.

"OK," I stated, shifting my foot from side to side.

"It's alright, you can go, just be back here by seven p.m. tonight. That gives you five hours to get it together. It's almost two o'clock, go before I get upset. If we can pull this off we can pull anything off as a team," he said motioning for us to leave.

We hurried out into the frigid cold afternoon. Maybe we should walk, the college was merely a few blocks away. Molly,

Jenson, and Owl trailed behind my dad and me. He took my hand as if I was still his little girl. What might be racing through his mind at this very moment? How were he and mom doing? Did I dare ask him? No, not now we needed to get this Jones stuff dealt with.

Chapter 30

On our way to locate Jones, we shuffled through the newly fallen snow. A part of me believed he might help us. Was it possible I, was being silly to even, consider him part of this, fiasco?

"He might not even be in his office today. You're aware that he changed class to Friday for a reason," hollered Jenson, catching up with me. Molly moved alongside him, keeping pace.

Almost there, only a block more to go, I thought.

"I'm not sure, but his office hours in our syllabus say he's available Monday to Friday from two p.m. to four p.m. perhaps, we can catch him. Otherwise, I guess we just miss the test. What choice do we have?" I insisted.

"At least leave him a note. Plan B along with some studying up on that book Star gave you," suggested Dan a bit out of breath. "I never expected this to escalate so rapidly."

"Neither did the clan," I replied. "The plan was to depart tomorrow after the test, but we cannot leave Cal and Nuria in a cold cavern with the enemy! We must be ready for an ambush. My logic says the other bandits will most likely surround the area to protect the cave. They may have even rigged up booby traps. We won't just be able to go sprinting in there," I remarked.

"You may be wrong, how will they know we're coming? That is, especially if they assume our attack was, meant for tomorrow evening and not tonight," stated Owl as we reached the campus.

Molly advanced ahead. In fact, she ran as if her life depended on it.

"Jones, wait, we have to talk to you! It's urgent," she shouted chasing after him. He'd just come out a side door exiting the building, his briefcase slapping against his thigh. He stopped, looked up, and began to walk over to us.

"Hey, guys, there's no class today. I came by to check my e-mail and urgent messages, from the dean. He's been on me regarding my teaching habits. He's never favored me," he said. Then covered his mouth with his hand. "Oops, I'm not supposed to speak to students about that. There I go breaching confidentiality again!"

"You haven't changed a bit! It's like a flashback from my college days," said Dan punching him playfully on his arm. "I'm Starla's father," he explained, extending his hand. Professor Jones took it, shaking it wildly.

"Yes, yes, it's good to meet you. Now, what is so imperative?" he asked, opening the entrance door for us.

What was I going to say? I didn't want to lie to him. No, I wasn't going to fib. If he knew all about this predating stuff, why couldn't I trust him?

"Jones," I said, glancing at my friends. "I have an emergency. It, can't wait. My family has to leave tonight. You see two of them are in great danger. If we don't, they could perish! Molly, Jenson, and I are working with my father on the investigation of Du-Vance's death."

"And what does that have to do with your family young lady?"

On the spot! I was on the spot! Fudge, did I tell him that I could get all foxy. That all these years, what he had been teaching and speculating was the truth? Damn it!

"Dan, what's going on? You and I have been friends for a very long time. I've got a few secrets in my closet too. Maybe we could step into my office. You can fill me in on what this pertains to. If it's, what I presume, it is then I'll give them an extension. "Starla," he said, turning to me. "Do you have the essay completed?"

"Yes, of course! Math is what my mother has to prod me about."

Jones pushed open the door to his classroom, allowing us to enter. "Now I have about forty-five minutes before I have to take off," he said as we advanced into his office.

"Here, let's just sit down." He guided us to a small cubicle. "I don't have enough seats for everyone so you'll have to stand."

"That's OK," said my dad.

I pulled out the essay from the back pocket of my jeans. "It's kind of, rumpled," I declared, handing it to him.

He unfolded it and scanned its contents. "Good, good, this is very conclusive on who you suspect may have been involved in killing Du-Vance. Most would find it far-fetched alongside your allegations of this group you claim, were experimented on by scientists, but it all makes sense to me," he added.

"Huh," we said, looking at each other.

"You didn't assume I was that naive did you? I'm a member of the alliance," he boasted setting down the papers on his desk. "All the times you had your meetings in the cafe, or library I observed you, your tendencies, and interest in the Kitsune fox. I planned on revealing myself eventually. Even your father wasn't aware I knew. I saw when he and your mother fell in love. I just chose not to expose it, who would have believed me?"

"I certainly wouldn't have if you'd told me on the first day of class," I replied.

"I'm sorry if I rattled you. I'm only letting you in on the most pertinent activities. I don't even know, who in the clan is aware of me. I like to call myself a silent observer. If I perceive something going on that shouldn't be, I report it anonymously to Nuria. Since she's left, I haven't tried to make any further contact. Owl, your father Rascal is among us. I considered contacting him a few times," he responded.

"What kept you from doing so? Why spy on us?" Owl screamed practically throwing over Jone's desk.

"He's only trying to help us, push us, get us to grow. Now let's not start a war. We have another situation to deal with at Thunderhead Bay!" I exclaimed.

Molly sat crossed legged in the corner, appearing as if she might bolt at any minute. Her hands trembled flat against the carpet floor.

"Simmer down, you're all scaring Molly," Jenson piped in.

"If I can't handle this, then how am I going to be able to handle healing people?" she asked me.

"It's going to be OK, we just have to go over that book, Star gave us," I said.

Jones pulled out a stack of documents from a nearby filing cabinet. "Here's the rest of the paperwork on the bandits. I'm not sure, how much time you have, better get back to the clan."

"You're not coming with us?" I asked, my eyes diverted to the floor.

"It's not my fight, and while I appear immortal to others, it's only the slowing down of age. My story is for another occasion. I must go. I've said all I can without putting myself at risk," he replied getting up from his chair.

"Dan, it was nice seeing you again, hopefully, it will be on a lighter note when we next meet," he said exiting the office.

Stunned, should I be? My own, teacher had been stalking, us!

"He was protecting you Araina, let it go," spoke Nayla pushing into my mind with her thoughts.

"OK, fine, for now," I replied.

"Now go, open that book Star gave you, gather up some things, warmer clothes, perhaps, and then meet us at Mike's. We're all leaving, together," thought Nayla...

Jenson shook my shoulder bringing me back to reality.

"What?"

"You spaced, come on we need to get to the library. It's almost four. That gives us an hour and a half before we have to get back," he explained.

"And eat," said Molly. Her stomach grumbled.

I stood up, from the hardwood floor and rubbed my butt. That had hurt! Time to get my Willow on!

"What are you pondering?" spoke my father in a rather needling manner.

"I have to merge with Willow," I mumbled.

"Who the hell is Willow, there is no one by that name in our tribe!"

"She's from "Buffy," said Molly as we left the office, making our break for a secluded spot in the library before it closed.

"Ah, I bet your mother loved that you watched those shows," he snickered.

"No, not at all, in fact, when she found my spell books she threw a hissy. She took them away. Afterwards, I was stuck getting my advice from the history channel and documentaries hence, the reason that my spell probably won't last long, if it works at all."

"I bet you're more talented than you give yourself credit for," chided Molly as we passed the Cafe.

"Oh, coffee, Please come on," I pushed, grabbing my dad by his shirt.

"Your not two Starla, but I'm sure the library has a no coffee policy. All of us will get something quick before we go back. It's time to learn spells, your mother, has no say. I assume she'd rather have you and I come back alive."

I shut my mouth thinking it best. It had a way of getting me into trouble. So far I'd been a good girl listening, following instructions, even if, I was a bit bossy. Ah, no independent I considered smiling to myself. We waltzed into the stacks as if we owned the place. We practically did, my home away from home three days a week out of five.

"Our usual table," Jenson said to Dan pointing out seats near a window. There was no one in sight.

"Perfect, now let's get cracking!"

I laughed at my dad's slang, and he grinned at me.

(Nuria&Cal)

Meanwhile...

"You'd better hope they come for you," it hissed. Nuria and Cal were cowering against the cave wall, shivering, still unable to transform. Nuria thought, that with all the stress converting would be possible. She couldn't explain it. She'd inspected the enclosed

290

area various times, as it guarded the front of the cave. Its evil eyes darted back and forth, teeth protruding from its mouth as saliva poured out of it onto the floor.

"We'd better keep quiet, child. They'll be back, they said, they would. The light she left around us should protect us for a bit longer," she, mind spoke to Cal.

The thing tossed them a blanket, "Here this will keep you warm. I don't want you to freeze to death." It laughed. "The bandits want you, delivered alive! That Minder was so easy to deceive. I held on to the hope that she, Cal, and you were hiding, close by. Bulls-eye! You see, us, shape-shifters have our advantages. Unlike the Bandits, I hate everyone, not for what they did to me, but because I can!"

"Don't listen to it, keep focused, stay in-tune, try to connect," I told myself, looking down at Cal. It was my job now to keep her protected until that girl came back. Starla, I think that's her name. The one, the clan, talked so fondly of. The individual, Tri kept from us.

Chapter 31

(Magic)

"Now some of these spells are specific. The best ones for our use would be..." my dad paused skimming through the book of contents. "Hmm, let's see temporary paralyzes your victims. Quite conveniently called paralysis. I'll write that one down."

"Arc wc going to try and capture this thing?" I asked, peering over his shoulder at the book. There before me appeared a location spell. "How come, we didn't use that to find Cal and Nuria?"

My dad patted me on the back. "We tried several times to use that incantation long-ago. It didn't work something blocked Star's powers. She's the most talented in her craft given she's a half-gypsy," he reflected, drumming his fingers on the table. "A few of us have managed to learn some of these, but we are limited unless one of you is, able to pick up the ability quickly and precisely."

I wondered if anything televised on Buffy was true. Shouldn't Star be here teaching me this instead of my dad? What did he know about Wicca?

"Starla, you ought to give one of these spells, a whirl. You were successful using your intellect as a weapon during the candle magic ceremony," Molly reminded me, adjusting the book towards her observing it more closely.

"Yes, all of us will play a part in this. Dad, how many enchantments are we discussing here?"

"The highest ranking ones, are our top-line of defenses paralysis, protection, and banishment. If this entity is not of this world, and a demonic force we'll need to send it back where it originated," he added rifling through the pages. "Ah, here it is. The paralysis spell. You pour salt around the attacker next soak them in white vinegar, oils, thus purifying their soul," he read.

"Why would you purify someone's soul who's harmed you? Wouldn't you banish them to hell?" Jenson pointed out as he chewed his gum rather loudly.

"I'm not sure, this is what the book says. It also speaks of asking, our gods to take our enemy into his or her own hands. It depends on who your god or gods are." My dad blinked his eyes twice staring again at the chant on the page we were to use. "A very odd book for one of wizardry," he said.

"A little too moral for you," sassed Star. She'd crept up behind me. "Magic is only to be used sparingly. It's why, each of you has been taught to defend yourselves in combat. Now, the spells you're looking at here," she said, gazing down at the ones Dan had jotted down. "Right, these are the only ones we should need. You must go over paralysis first." She said and sat next to me

It was peculiar, to witness Star in her human form. I hadn't grown accustomed to people shifting from one shape to another. I'd have to do so myself. I brushed it off, struggling to focus on the task.

"Paralysis takes a bit of concentration. It's basically, freezing your victim in time, so you can get passed them. Your opportunity to escape is limited purifying their soul is optional. It's trickier since one has to have this as their chosen gift," she said looking straight at Jenson.

"Me, how do you know, I can do this?" he stammered.

"Kaya told me prior, to coming here. Remember, she can see the future?"

"Yes, but Cavin said..."

"She experienced a vision when she gifted you individually at the ceremony. A lot was going on. We figured the best thing to do was contemplate it when the issue came up. Rushing things is not our style," she reasoned.

"So, who exactly is he going to paralyze?" Owl said.

"Why not you, go ahead Jenson."

"Just like that, on the spot, no training needed!"

"Shh, just do what she says boy," said my father.

Jenson squinted as if he was in deep agony, and then flicked his hand towards Owl. He froze. Well, he half froze.

"Waa di you jusss do too muh," he responded.

"Don't worry," she said and placed a hand on Owl's shoulder. "It happens to beginners. Jenson will learn how to completely freeze someone sooner or later. For now, it will suffice. We could try again at the end of this session."

"Rally, whhh mu?"

"Hang in there, only two more spells to learn." I tried not to laugh. It was pretty funny. Nevertheless, Owl had to have a variety of special gifts. Why hadn't he shared them? It wouldn't surprise me if, in the middle of an attack, he transformed into his namesake. Sigh...

"Protection is pretty much Starla's area, isn't it? Since, she used it on her vision quest?" Jenson asked.

"Protection spells can be used by many; however, how potent, depends on the one's passion for protecting another. It's inwardly produced such as adrenaline. I can give you basics as the book does, but overall it must emerge from your spirit pushing it out towards the ones you wish to shield. We are hoping for slight fatalities here so no one, go rogue hero for us OK? While, on this mission, we work as a team," Star ordered.

"You know, you're using all my lines, and I'm the father," Dan said sternly. He looked as if she had hurt his pride.

"Finish up telling them about banishment," Star instructed, pushing away from the table. She stood facing us. "Now I'll meet you in a half -hour. Dan, please brief them accordingly. We don't know what this thing is. It could be demonic, a ghost or even a brand new..."

Dan put a hand on her arm, "I'll advise them, and we'll be on our way. Thanks, I'm glad you came to facilitate," he admitted.

"I was passing through and remembered about Jenson. I thought it imperative," she offered. Then turned away dissipating into a fog.

I shook my head twice clearing my brain of what I'd seen.

"She knows magic, don't be shocked that she can just, poof!" whispered Molly. She turned the banishing spell page back towards my father.

(Megan & Tri)

"Mom, stop pacing. They'll be fine," she said as we sat down to eat dinner.

"If, it wasn't her first assignment with her clan. I wouldn't worry so much. It's exasperating, things have gotten so erratic." I picked at my rice and chicken. Then brought it to my mouth and chewed.

"She said she'd be home this evening, if she isn't, she should call, if not ground her." Megan stabbed pieces of veggies with her fork.

"I'm sure your dad would love that. I imagine he's confident that I'll reunite with the clan."

"Will you?"

"I don't desire my life to be so solitary. Secretive..."

"Mom, you're still hiding parts of who you are, just like you were hiding them from Starla. You guys are lucky to be part of something so cool," she responded.

"Cool, isn't the word for it. When you have bandits hunting you down," I snapped.

"Oh, the same people you let run you out of town?" Megan put down her fork. "Why did we come back?"

"Your father made me promise Starla would go to college here. That way you both could reunite with him. I never planned on, us falling back together again," I answered, wiping my hands on my napkin.

"How come you never got a divorced?"

"There's no such thing in our clan. Marriage is possible. Then there is the separation, but we don't call it a divorce. It's more about cutting ties, and you have to have a ceremony. We never did."

"Why not," nagged Megan.

I began stuffing myself with mouthfuls of veggies and chicken. It was too painful to reply. My life was finally starting to come back together again with my girls and Dan. I had to make my final decision about the man I loved, my truth, and if I'd go back to it all. If I did I'd have to acknowledge the way things were, would I have to fight? How would I fit in? Now that I was a librarian, could I?

"Mom, are you OK?"

"Yeah, I'll be fine. After we finish up, I'll contact your dad. There may be some complications. Nothing for you to agonize over."

My daughter pushed around the chicken and rice left on her plate. Setting aside my own, I got up, taking hers and mine to the sink. "Do you want some dessert?"

"No thanks, I'll go, wash up. Let me know if you reach Starla," she replied, getting up from the table. "I'm going to go, do some homework in the living room."

"OK, let me know if you change your mind about dessert," I shouted as she left.

I picked up my cell siting on the counter. It was one of the things I'd compromised on when it came to technology. In truth, it had saved our lives many times when one had forgotten their homework, we needed milk, or in case of an emergency, which was rare. I began to dial her number, then stopped. What was I doing? Didn't I trust my daughter? No, I had this right. I was concerned. Buck up, you're still the parent I told myself then returned to, dialing.

"Starla," I said as I heard a click.

It's mom, she mouthed to Dan.

"Hey mom, I was going to call. Dad and I are at the library. It seems as if we are," she paused...

"Are you leaving tonight, did something transpire?" I asked, leaning down to pet Fritz on the head. He'd entered the kitchen in search of treats.

"A vision, Cal, and Nuria. They're being held captive by an evil entity. I'm not sure what kind. I administered a protection spell, but we don't know if it worked, or how long it will last. We're departing tonight. I've spoken with Jones, and we can retake the test. You need to tell Molly's folks, she's with me, or us," Starla stammered.

"You want me to lie?"

"What will her parents say when you tell her she's on a mission with a girl whose half fox?" Starla answered.

"OK, you know I dislike lying, it's why I left the clan," I replied.

I was in a tight spot. Molly's parents were already upset about their daughter, revealing her own secret and here I was putting her at risk by not telling them the truth about my offspring. Jenson's parents let him do what he wanted pretty much. Double standards, damn societal norms!

"I'll talk to her folks, now please put your father on the phone."

"Hi there."

Hastily I interrupted him."Do me a favor, keep our daughter alive. That's all I ask, get this mission completed and get her home unharmed. After that, we'll re-evaluate our status. Presently, Megan is worried about her sister but won't say so. I'm rather upset about what Molly's folks will assume, however, I know I need to let this come to pass," I said.

"Tri..."

"No, one more thing, no matter what, do not let the bandits take our daughter, or that monster," I insisted sharply.

"I'll call as soon as it's over," he vowed hanging up.

I hit the end button on my phone setting it on the counter. This would be a long night. I'd better brew some Coffee. Perhaps I'd allow Megan to stay home from school tomorrow. That way we could watch films together this evening. I needed to get this off my mind. I never let my kids stay home from school.

(Starla)

We'd left the library and were making our way back to the ranger's station. The coffee dad had promised long forgotten. It wasn't far, but it had begun to snow rather rapidly. Jenson held my hand, which was doing little to warm me up. It's not like we could just stop in the middle of a snow storm to cuddle. Molly, Owl, and my father paraded in front of us.

"I can scarcely make out where we're going," I complained to Jenson. The wind blew right through my jacket surpassing layers of clothing. Could it get any colder? It felt as if it was negative two degrees. I was, iced!

"Keep moving, there's a beam of light further ahead. Mike probably hung a lantern on the post so we'd find our way back," he said, giving my hand a reassuring tug. Pushing against the wicked wind, I propelled myself onward. Meeting Jenson's speed, I neared Molly, Owl, and my dad. Once we reached them, I let go of Jenson's hand to pull my hat down to protect my ears.

"My fingers are frozen," Molly shouted trudging on.

"Mine too, I sure hope there's hot coffee," I said, trying not to slip on the ice. I shuffled my feet to stay upright on the frozen ground beneath me, almost sure I would fall. After a few more steps, my front leg slid out, in front of me and my back leg followed. I tried to stop myself placing my hands out to lessen the impact. Bam! Right on my butt, Jenson and Owl reached down and helped me back up.

"You've got to be careful! It might be best if tonight you use your fox form when in battle. Your claws will help you grip the ice. Please be more cautious," Jenson insisted. We ventured on. I could make out the glow of the lantern that hung from a post above the station. Nayla sat next to it. I noticed her tail twitched.

"She's on watch. I wonder, what has them spooked," I asked.

"It's hard to tell. It could be a number, of things better to find out for ourselves, instead of pondering," said my father. He gave us a stern look. One that said, don't jump to conclusions.

"Something's up." Owl pointed to the window. Inside elders had gathered around a table in the makeshift room we'd used for training earlier that day.

They seemed a bit agitated, unsure, and restless. I could feel it radiating off them.

"Everyone's here," I said nearing Nayla. She trotted up to my father appearing sullen, sad, and worn as if we'd already met defeat.

"It's best that we all go in. A major event took place while you, were gone," she softly whispered.

"Did someone die?" I stammered.

She gestured to the lodge window. I moved closer, peering in to get a good look. In the middle, of a table sat a wolf crossed legged with human qualities. Minder? Could it really, be? She was a female, and they had her in cuffs.

"What? Why would you handcuff her?" I asked, freezing my butt off while the snowflakes froze my face.

Molly placed her hand on my back. Jenson on the other side of me reached for my hand, and my dad shot me an ugly glare.

"We should face this, maybe Minder will be able to help," said Owl impatiently.

"Go," Nayla ordered. "I must stand watch in case the Bandits or anyone else arrives searching for her."

"Alright," I responded. I stepped up to the station's door with my friends and father in tow. Pushing the wooden door open, a warm rush of air met us as we tiptoed into the lodge. I removed my boots and placed them on the mat, off to the side. Slowly I took off my wet winter coat.

"Here, let me help you with that," greeted Kaya. She took our coats placing them on hooks near a register. "There, now they should dry before you have to run off again. You'd better sit down. I'll bring you coffee with cream. Cavin and the crew are interrogating Minder. It hasn't been good. Mike is out on watch with Lance. They'll be back soon."

I grabbed the wall to stop myself from falling, but the room spun even though I stood still.

"We'd better get something to eat too," Molly said to Kaya eyeing me.

"Yes, we can't have you passing out. Mike has some cheese and crackers stashed somewhere around here. I'll make a plate up."

A few seats were left open side by side. Molly and Jenson helped me to sit beside my father who'd already joined the group in the middle of the chaos. Minder appeared disoriented, tired, and dehydrated. She wouldn't be any use to us in her current state.

"We're interrogating her to find out if she's going to help us, or if she's lead them here," Cavin spoke directly to me.

"She isn't going to be any good to us dehydrated, tired, and disoriented. At least, give her some food, and water," I demanded.

Cavin huffed, "We tried to get her to talk, but she refused. You're the only one she wants to address."

Kaya sauntered in, placing a large plate of cold cuts, cheese and crackers on the table. Then she left to grab the tray with glasses of water for everyone. No coffee? I'd definitely need to get some on the way to Thunderhead Bay, or I'd be sleeping through the battle!

"Sorry, Ranger is out of caffeinated coffee," Kaya sulked pouring water into our glasses. I pushed mine towards Minder and started fixing her a plate of food while eating cubed sized bites of cheese and bite-sized crackers. I took a large gulp of Jenson's water. He didn't say a word. Kaya refilled it and set it back down.

"Can you take the cuffs off so she can eat?"

"Are you mad? She might run!" exclaimed Shellena.

"Do I look like I am in any shape to run," she hissed.

No gentle lamb, definitely feisty.

"Shellena, you saw the notes, all of you know the clues we received. Why would she come here to hurt us now? What is in it for her?" I badgered.

"You have no clue who, or what you're up against," pressed Minder.

"Tell me, I want to know." I slammed my hand down hard on the table.

"First water, then food, after I'll tell you," she replied.

The elders all stared at her. I mean all of them Cavin, the gray fox, and a few whom I'd never seen, Shellena, and Kaya. When would Lance and Mike be back? Would they witness anything?

"OK guys, cuffs off, or I'll feed her myself," exploded Kaya.

"Dan, stand guard at the door. Owl, please join him. You'll both have enough strength if she tries to run."

Oh please, I thought. You saw the letters. If, anyone was going to come after us, it would be... one of the bandits, wouldn't it?

Cavin undid her handcuffs and allowed her to sit across from me next to him. She ate mouthfuls of food ravenously along with large gulps of water. Once done a loud burp escaped her lips.

"Excuse me," she said. Hiccupped, and then proceeded to address me. "Be prepared for them. I wasn't. I tried to defend your alliances. I assumed we'd be safe at the old shack, but they discovered us last night. I managed to get away, except that entity got Nuria and Cal," Minder shuddered.

"What is that thing? How do we fight it?" I asked.

"It's frightened of fire, but it will try to leap over it, you cannot touch it. I saw it sideswipe some trees turning them to ash as I ran into the woods. I'm surprised it didn't threaten to do the same to Nuria and Cal."

"Why did you wait so long to come to us?"

"Wait? I've been wandering in the woods for hours. I was coming to warn you. Thunderhead Bay will be swarming with Bandits in a few hours. They've picked up a few new members since I'd abandoned them. That's what they called it. I left with Cal in the middle of the night. I had managed to keep them at bay for years til now."

"Do you know anything about these scientists. The ones who experimented on you?"

"We never saw their faces. They wore masks," she said, shrugging her big furry shoulders. "I can change if you like, so I'm more appealing?"

"What is your true form," spoke up Cavin bravely.

"True form, I lost that a long time ago when the experiments started. Now I can either be a makeshift human or a hybrid wolf with great strength. I'm able to move large objects and run twice as fast as your clan members. I can see from one city to another, pinpoint them actually and people. It's quite frightening when you first realize it," she said shaking. "I recognize you must think me odd to feel this way. I was one of them, very vengeful til I understood that it would never end as long as we fought each other."

"We should be fighting the scientists," Molly interjected.

Minder pawed at the table digging in her claws leaving marks. "Smart girl," she said.

"Nuria and Cal are our first priority," Kaya said, joining the conversation. "That's what we need to focus on. Will you assist us?"

"If you trust me, no cuffs or I won't be able to defend you. I was once a part of the Bandits. I know how they fight and their weakness. Let me tell you about them," she said.

Chapter 32

"So, what you're saying is they have no magical capabilities," spoke Kaya refilling Minder's, coffee, mug. I smiled, watching her do so. Mike and Lance had returned about an hour ago. Lucky for us they brought coffee.

Kaya turned to me, "More Coffee Araina?"

"Yes, please!" Around me, my friends and a new kind of family chuckled.

"Thought your name was Starla kid," said Minder roughly.

"When I found out I was an, ahh sort of human fox. I was asked to choose a surname."

"Well, you might want to go with Starla Araina it's a little less confusing. As I was saying all of your magical training will give you the upper hand. The best bet is to combine magic and Kali sticks. Are any of you yet familiar with that?"

"Shellena and I, are," Lance spoke up. "I'm sure it won't be a problem intermixing them. I just have to put spells in place for Molly and Jenson. Starla, Cavin and I already discussed this, you and Nayla's job will be to get to the cave."

"Good idea, the enemy will be spread out in the woods guarding it if they know we're coming. That is if it's a trap," said Minder.

"That thing told me the Bandits want Nuria and Cal alive. Have you taken it into account they may have experimented on

305

them? Perhaps they have joined the scientists, after all, to make us all hybrids?"

Minder's Coffee she'd been sipping sprayed out of her nose as she tried to hold back a laugh. She picked up her napkin and wiped her face. "No way would they do that! I mean, after all, they've been through to keep everyone separate who wasn't a full bred mythical creature yet they, themselves were altered by, mad scientist humans! In a way I find it quite hypocritical as well as ironic," she said, drumming her fingers on her coffee mug.

Cavin turned up his arm, glancing at his watch, "It's almost nine p.m. We need to start heading out if we're leaving tonight. Mike, did you drive the two vans over from the garage?"

"Sure did," he replied.

"Aren't Star and Eva coming with us? They put a lot of elbow grease into our preparations. Where are they, Kaya?" I pondered.

"Eva is too great a risk, and Star lost her whole family to these monsters. Literally, putting her in the middle of this doesn't seem fair," Kaya stated.

"Yes, but she is part of the clan. You did tell her what was going on, right?"

Kaya sighed.

"Right?"

Molly, Jenson, and Owl tried to calm me. I don't know why I hadn't thought of Star or Eva. They were both at my training sessions. They knew we were going to fight. How could they stand back and do nothing to help us?

"Wait a Sec. Cavin, who's protecting, the kits and juveniles when we're gone?" Kaya asked.

"Not sure, why?"

"The bandits could be leading us away from our home base, making the rest of our group susceptible to an attack."

Kaya glanced up to address the issue. "I could stay behind. I'll appoint the oldest male and female youth to monitor the area during your absence. Star and Eva can help guard the park. It is a risk, but far less of one than if they go. Cavin, please, warm up the vans, and grab the coolers just in case we end up stuck somewhere. I don't want to even, think about the last excursion we took without provisions just in case."

He nodded, stood, and the Ranger handed him his keys as he whispered directions. Jenson, Molly, and Owl put on their winter wear and exited the lodge.

"Nerved up are we?" asked Cavin.

"A bit, I'd like to consider that I'll kick some major bandit butt. However, my role will be getting to the cave without being attacked."

"Minder and Nayla will assist you. If, for some reason you end up in there alone, heaven forbid just go with your gut instincts. They are usually never wrong."

I nodded to him turning away to put on my coat and gloves. I wasn't going to wait for them to make any more decisions. I was about to head out the door when Kaya stopped me.

"Here, take this pack. It has some first aid stuff in it, food, a blanket, a notebook, and a pen. It may seem extreme, but you might need it."

"Thanks, it could come in handy," I said, throwing the pack on my back. She opened the door. The others were already in the van. Nayla trotted up to me, "Ready to go?"

"As ready as I can be," I replied.

Molly held the van door open for me. Nayla and I jumped in.

"Put on your seatbelt, this is certainly going to be a slippery ride," my dad said, looking back at us.

"Is everyone here?" I asked.

"Yes, Cavin, Shellena, Lance, and Minder are taking the other van. Owl, Jenson, and Nayla, can I see some hands?"

They raised them, and Nayla her paw.

"Alright then," Dan smirked. He started up the engine. "I'll be tailing them. If there are, any problems Lance will blink his lights twice, and motion for me to pull over. Sit tight, discuss the plan if you must, but most of all, do not distract me," he sternly ordered.

"OK, dad, how long is it going to take to get there?"

To this, my dad sighed deep and long, a sigh that said a hell of a long time. I spotted a pack of cards lying halfway underneath the seat. Reaching down, I picked them up.

"Cards anyone?"

"Good idea, now who wants to play 52 pick-up," asked Owl.

"No! No! No! Not in the van when I'm driving. I don't know what, you kids are thinking. You should play poker, Rum, or even that B.S game I hear kids talking about!" exclaimed my father.

"B.S. It is," hollered Jenson.

I shook my head, here we were about to go after bad guys, and we were going to spend what might be the last hours of our lives playing bullshit! Thanks, dad, I thought. Jenson grabbed the cards out of my hands shuffling them. He passed us around seven each placing the rest of the pile in the middle console.

"Now let's hope they don't go flying everywhere when I hit a curve," noted Dan, eyeing us while he maintained the wheel.

"No worries, we have it under control," Owl replied.

"Nayla, did you want to play?" Molly asked.

"With these paws, no thanks. I'll watch and laugh. I've heard about this game!"

... After three rounds of B.S., we'd grown tired, and my stomach screamed for food.

"Did we bring anything to eat besides what Kaya gave me in my emergency pack?" I asked Nayla who sat on the floor.

"There's a cooler in the back. Ranger Mike, packed it with soda and energy bars. There should be enough for each of you to have one can and one bar. We're taking precautions. Don't go overboard," she demanded.

Owl smirked, "Of course, sit tight guys I got this covered!" He leaped up from the seat scuttling back to the rear of the van where the cooler, sat.

"Grab me water and see if there's a container back there," ordered Nayla.

"Got it, and for the rest of us cola, that is our only choice unless you want water?"

"We need our caffeine," Molly interjected.

Owl carefully made his way back to our seats, handing out the drinks and energy bars collected. He then knelt down next to Nayla. "Water and a paper cup will have to do," he said, pouring it for her and allowed her to drink.

"Did you happen to get me one of those energy bars?"

"Sure did," he said, unwrapping it, for her. She ate it out of his hand gratefully and nuzzled him. He got up and sat back down next to Molly. We opened our cans of cola and unwrapped the power bars. Silence filled the van with munching, chewing, and the slugging of soda.

My dad spoke up, "I want you to spread out once we get to the forested area at Thunderhead Bay. It will be deeper into the forest passed the lake. Starla, Araina, you're probably more familiar with it, seeing that your astral spirit traveled there. Molly upon arrival, you'll join Cavin in the other van. Later, once positioned we'll need you to back us. I cannot allow you both to sit tight as you could become easy targets."

"Truthfully, I thought about us staying behind near the lake area, but then we'd be too far away to heal the injured. Then what good would either of us be?"

"It will all work out. I'm sure of it. We've trained and have a plan of action. Kaya is guarding Hunters Park. Everything is covered, except, the actual, encounters," Owl grimaced.

"I got your back. It's too bad we all couldn't have ridden together. Next time we'll rent, a tour bus," Jenson joked, trying to lighten things up.

"Once I get the signal from Lance, we'll stop and touch base. I'm sure they've been contemplating what will happen upon our arrival," announced Dan.

Everyone, including myself, was beginning to realize the actual conflict, we'd be facing. Molly rubbed her hands on the armrest and stared out the window.

"Hey," I said, touching her arm to get her attention.

"Oh, sorry, I was listening to your dad. I have loads on my mind. Maybe, after all, this is over, my Mom will convince my dad, I'm not going through a phase. Then I can go home. If not, I might end up at your house for a while."

"It wouldn't be too bad would it? Being stuck hanging out with your best friend, staying up til midnight studying, watching TV, or talking about our love lives."

Molly's face broke out into a smile, "It would be great to stay with your family. The problem is my mom would get lonely. If I had a brother or sister, it might not be that hard, on her. Dad's, always been harsh. It wouldn't matter much to him," she muttered tapping her fingers on the seat.

"Don't say that, remember when he helped you with that volcano experiment in sixth grade, for the science fair. He was so proud of you!" Jenson exclaimed.

She leaned over and playfully gave Jenson a gentle shove. "Yeah, that was, sixth grade, and I took Harvey Mill to the dance. Dad was all for it. Kissing Harvey was utter grossness. I didn't think he was going to stick his tongue down my throat." She shuddered at the memory.

"Ah, it couldn't have been that bad," my dad interjected.

"You didn't know Harvey," replied Owl, rolling his eyes.

" So did you two know each other then?" I asked. They shook their heads.

"No, not personally, but we did have a few classes together," Owl admitted.

I leaned back in my seat and closed my eyes drained from the day."We probably should get some sleep," I suggested.

My dad turned back to us, "We have an hour before we hit that rest stop, Lance, and I talked about as we left the park. If you want to rest do it now," he said then turned back to the road ahead.

Owl grabbed a book out of his backpack as I laid my head against Jenson's shoulder shutting my eyes. Could I sleep? What would happen when and if I reached Cal and Nuria? This thing

311

could turn people into ash! I had to destroy it. I'd flung fireballs at Molly using memories against her. I had no history with this entity, but if I could trigger anger, then I should be able to prompt the fireballs again. I contemplated this drifting into a deep sleep.

Suddenly the van jerked to a halt, and I bolted upright in my seat. "What's going on? Why are we stopping?"

"Rest stop, everybody out!"

Ok, I knew we were going to stop, but he didn't have to get pushy. Jenson and Molly unbuckled their safety belts, then stood up to stretch from sitting in the not so comfy van seats.

"Go, use the restrooms if needed, if not wait in the entryway. We'll have a quick meeting there," he affirmed.

Owl opened the door, and we jumped out. My friends hurried off to the bathrooms while Nayla met up with Cavin. I noticed Minder milling about outside the main entrance. I took it upon myself to find out if she had a plan.

"So," I said, walking up to her, "Do you know of any enhanced spells because I'm sort of, freaked out about taking on this entity? Do you think if I could shoot fireballs at it that it would die? What if it backfires scorching me?"

"We only have a few options, and none of them, are guaranteed. One sure thing is once we are in there, it's not going to let us escape. Your vision gizmo you had or astral travel allowed you to disappear as you were without your body. Otherwise, you would've been stuck like Cal and Nuria are. Nuria is clearly, smart so, her cowering means we're in deep poo," she answered.

"What are these options?" I pushed.

"Option one, you let me handle it. Two, I distract the entity while you and Nayla, get them both out of the cave. Three, we leave it up to Cavin to come up with a plan," she said.

"You leave what up to me?" he asked, trotting up to us.

"The plan to attack the entity. We were discussing options," Minder informed him.

"Hmm, I see let's get inside and warm up. Dan is buying everyone hot cocoa from the vending machines. I'd sure enjoy some myself," he said prancing through the doors.

Minder scoffed, and we followed Cavin inside. My dad was handing out hot cocoa. Yum, chocolaty goodness before certain death! I took a cup from him joining the circle that had formed in the little alcove. Nayla and Cavin were already, seated in the middle of the circle. They waited, for the chatter to subside. Shellena and Lance stood off to the side discussing spell options to use with the Kali sticks. Jenson and Owl were horsing around with a Hacky-sac they had found in the hall, and Molly stood next to me silently sipping her drink.

Cavin stood up to speak. "Now, this isn't going to be an easy mission! We may have causalities. I'm hoping we can keep each and every one of you safe. Molly, you'll be placing yourself in great peril. Jenson and Owl get with Lance. One last training session before we leave, pair up while I go over things with the girls."

I watched the boys leave the building. Huh, guess they'd just do some drills near the picnic area. That would be quite the site to any onlooker.

"Pay attention now. Do not be afraid to make up spells, chants, to use anything found in the woods. Thunderhead Bay is, lightening territory. You may be able to hone its power against this entity. I heard you, Minder, when you were speaking of choices. I'd like you to try this if all else fails. It's risky. You could pull the bolt towards yourself or another clan member. Only use this if necessary. Now I'm going to leave you with Nayla and join the men," he said turning away.

"That's it! That is all he is going to tell us," I huffed spinning into Nayla.

"Calm down now, you have me," she winked.

"And what will you do?" I paced back and forth in front of the girls bathroom. Molly walked up beside me and gave me a few reassuring pats on the back.

"I'm, your secret weapon," stated Nayla.

"Tell me then, what will you do?"

"I can't, then it wouldn't be a secret. We have to have an upper hand in this. Please trust me Starla-Araina. I don't want to see you hurt. You're our guardian. Once we get through this, there will be more training," she sighed already exhausted.

Molly patted the top of her head, "I trust you, come on, you trust her to don't you?"

"I do, I mean what choice do I have?"

"Starla my dear, you always have a choice, remember that," she said nuzzling my hand.

"Come now," said my dad, stepping out of the men's room. "It's getting late, go touch base with Shellena and Lance. Then get Owl and Jenson back in the van."

Exiting the building, I spotted them sparing near several trees to my right. Jenson was pretty fantastic! Dang, he had Lance by the throat. Oh, how the tables had turned. My heart pounded. All I could imagine was wrapping my arms around him to pull him close.

"Come on," said Molly, urging me to run to him. I lagged behind, weighed down by the idea of facing, not only the entity but the bandits. Gladiator appeared pretty strong in those pictures. Sika, and what was the other guy's name? Plus Minder said they now had more members! How many were there?

I stepped up beside Jenson as the sparing ended and took his hand.

"Hey, I think Starla's heart skipped a beat," Molly chuckled, trying to catch her breath.

"Oh, yeah," he gazed at me with his cute smile. My heart was melting, I leaned into his shoulder and allowed him to embrace me. After a quick squeeze, he pulled back, staring into my eyes.

"You have a lot on your mind," he said, tracing my face with his fingertip. "All of us are going to protect you, help you, and guide you. I know you believe you're Miss thing that you have to be tough for everyone. Remember, we have your back," he softly reassured me.

"You have all of us," Shellena insisted as they gathered near me. Me! As if, I, was an oracle or an awesome version, of Buffy herself. I hadn't even taken on the monsters yet! Way to go, guys, make me feel extremely, important before I slip up. Would I, or did I have this in the bag?

"We're going to target the bandits that will try to stop you from getting into the cave. All you have to do is run for it," Lance explained to me.

"I guess we can try that. Typically, though, the enemy tries to block those who attempt to gain access to a prisoner so you may have to track me," I said.

"Right," Jenson said, aiming his finger at me.

Shellena nodded at this.

Molly cleared her throat and elbowed me. I looked up at my dad standing beside me. Well, he was sneaky. I usually could tell when he was present. A sort of emotion I'd never thought of as being a power, mythical or magical. He didn't seem happy. The gaze was more of, worry, than anger. I'd seen it before when I'd worked a few cases in L.A.

"Cavin said there was news, of a few of the bandit members trying to enter the park. Those individuals, have been apprehended. Kaya has them in a holding facility. Jones is there. I'm not sure who contacted him, but he's helping her and the others who stayed behind. Now I need everyone in the van. Cavin is waiting," he said, glaring at Shellena, and Lance.

We proceeded to the van. Shellena and Lance went in the opposite direction to where Cavin had parked. I held Jenson and Molly's hands in mine. We were going into battle, man I felt like a care bear. What was I going to do? Put my care bear stare on them? Willow on Buffy would have laughed at that.

"Deranged thoughts?" prodded Owl opening the van door to let me in.

"My childhood coming back to haunt me. You know all those cartoons with powers, backed by emotions, meant for good," I replied.

"Not the Care Bears again! I was getting used to Buffy," complained Jenson, who'd know about my past since forever.

316

Myth

"Kids, now just get in the van," Dan said aggravated. "Jenson, Molly, Owl, and you Starla, please focus. We have a half an hour til we reach Thunderhead Bay. Meditate at the task at hand, pray, ask for guidance to your god, gods, or, whatever it is you derive strength from," he sputtered getting in the driver's seat.

Once buckled up, I took my friend's hands in mine. In silence, we said our own, prayers for the journey that awaited us. The tight knots in my stomach began to ease up, but I knew it wouldn't last.

Chapter 33

(Thunderhead Bay)

I heard knocking. Where was it coming from? Was I dreaming? Awakening, I opened my eyes. No, Molly, Jenson or Owl anywhere! Don't panic, maybe they went out to get some air. They couldn't have been captured this quickly.

"Hey, is anyone here?" I called out.

No one answered. I peeked outside the van. We were parked, in a scenic area. I stood up to get a better view out of the windshield. No snow? Had I just entered a different dimension or had it melted overnight? Get a grip Starla, I told myself. What would Buffy do? I wasn't powerless.

I sat down in the center of the vehicle taking in calming breaths. I tried honing in on my ability to call my clan, via my tattoo. Did any of them have tattoos, in addition, Cal? If so, was it assumed I knew because we hadn't discussed it?

A sudden rush of air crept up over my body warming me. A hug was I being, hugged! A tingling sensation erupted in my toes igniting my torso throughout my small frame. Relax, you can't turn, just relax! Was this what they wanted? Is this why the clan had left me? No one told me this was part of the plan! Whiskers emerged out of my face. My fox form began to take shape virtually painless. My ears sank into my head while my pointy ones jutted out. My legs and arms sprouted fur. The van, how the heck, would I get out of here? I didn't have any hands!

I jumped up, nearly hitting my head on the ceiling. Study your surroundings, what could I use to get out? Could I, push my paws under, the door handle and pull it open? I moved up front to the driver's side door. The handle curved with openings at the top and bottom. I might be able to push my paw under, then pull. If I had enough strength, I could get out. OK, can't hurt to try. I'd probably end up dead meat if I stayed here.

My paw fit right under it! I pulled it towards me, slipping my paw out from under it quickly before it, swung open. I hadn't been trapped, after all, just panicked! I hopped down to the ground. No sense in closing the door. Hunching down, I inched underneath the van scanning the area undetected. Outside it appeared a lot like Hunter's Park only a lake was near; behind it was the forest I'd seen in my vision. I spotted Nayla under a tree, her eyes closed. Was she dead? Her body moved up and down. No, only sleeping. I would have to make it fast. I could either race to her or creep towards her. If no one was here except us, it wouldn't matter. If they'd left, and she was guarding me, then I was screwed!

Suddenly she vanished, then appeared peering underneath the van.

"What are you doing under there?"

"What am I doing? You left me alone. Where are the others? The plan was for them to distract the bandits then we'd make a run for it into the cave," I said shaking myself furiously.

"Come on, we need to take our positions," she ordered trotting into the trees.

"You didn't answer my question," I prodded.

"You were being protected, in case, we were tracked. The other issue, we couldn't wake you. I don't know Starla Ariana. Owl tried to rouse you. Then Molly, after that Jenson, kissed you. Nothing worked. We suspected you were in a kind of, trance. Do you recall, anything?"

"No," I said, trailing deeper into the wooded area. I hoped I wasn't being led into a trap. Was this Nayla? It could be a shapeshifter. I stopped for a Sec, and she glanced at me funny.

"You don't trust me do you?"

"How do I know you're not a shapeshifter?"

"You called me from the van earlier. I responded by assisting you in your transformation," she snapped. "Sorry, I'm on edge. When you plan things out you're confident about them, now, it's different. Owl, Jenson, Lance, and Shellena have spread out along the outskirts of the forest. The dirt path, do you remember this?"

I shook my head no, as we continued along.

"Molly heard you utter it in your sleep while we tried to awaken you. Minder's meeting us up here a ways."

"What time is it?"

"3 a.m., let's hope the bandits assume we gave up," she chided.

The trees appeared to fly by us as we ran. She sped up, I sped up, nothing, no sign of anyone. My legs burned as if on fire! I wanted to stop, needed to stop, but no, I had to keep going. Did I really, run this far last time? Out of nowhere Minder dropped out of the trees joining us.

"Keep moving, they've started to arrive," she growled. It played out like a slow motion movie. Owl and Jenson appeared to be playing monkey in the middle with a large wolf hybrid of some kind. It was trying to get their Kali sticks. Jenson would throw his sticks to Owl, then Owl to Jenson, and it kept jumping for it. Well, so much for a challenge, I pondered.

"Stay back, run go!" Owl shouted to us. Too late, Gladiator charged at us! He'd grown tired of the game. Now, we were his targets. Move feet move! I was almost far enough away when something grabbed my leg. I hit the ground!

"Ha ha, I caught a foxy!" shouted the large brute. Straining to see my attacker, I peered over my shoulder at his golden blonde hair and smug grin. He had the same smile in the pictures I'd seen. My tail was in his hands, and he tried to pull me along. I, on the other hand, dug my clawed feet, into the ground, holding my place.

"Jenson, help! I don't have any memories to attack him with," I hollered. Geez, now I was the defenseless girl. Damn, it wasn't supposed to work this way.

Jenson scrunched up his face. It looked like he was trying to poop! Oh my gosh, really?

"Is it working, is he frozen yet?"

The gladiator, seemed, unable to move his legs at the moment, still my tail remained in his hands.

"Jenson, open your eyes and stop scrunching. You've managed to freeze his bottom half at least."

"Keep your paws gripped deep in the earth!" hollered Minder.

"What are ya gonna do girlie? I got my crew coming to back me up," Gladiator taunted.

"Owl, work some of that Mojo or whatever Cavin taught you," Minder said skidding into the dirt. A medium sized wolf with large protruding fangs held her down.

Who the hell, was that? What about her super fast speed and great strength?

Nayla pushed Gladiator from behind dropping him to the ground.

One hand lay on the soil the other gripped my tail tighter. It appeared as if he was gaining mobility little by little back to his legs. I'd better take a chance while he was weak. I had to act fast! I arched my back swinging my body outward, flinging him into the trees. It wasn't far, but he flew, landing against a tree trunk with a whack! I didn't wait for him to get up. I ran over to Owl and Jenson, who were now chanting.

"Go, go," he prodded.

"Minder, I can't leave without her!"

"That's right, she's not going anywhere. Minder belongs to us," spat Sika. He stepped out of the woods, onto the path. I watched him slither over to where Minder was being held captive. "Do you think we'd stand for this? My power has grown much stronger. I've been waiting, for years to drag you back! Was, my love not good enough for you? Everyone wants to make sacrifices for the humans! Look at me! I can never believe I was once one of them. You let Nuria put foolish ideas in your head. No, tonight this ends! No alliances, none, they join us or become our prisoners. The last is death. Gavin is on his way."

Minder whimpered, "Leave, Gavin, will execute you." She pushed up against the animal crushing her to the ground. Behind a tree, was it Lance? Putting his finger to his lips, he swiftly snuck towards us.

"What is the point of all this? Why bother us?" I shouted.

Minder shook her head at me, "Big mistake."

"Yes, she is a big blunder. You're an abomination like us! Don't you understand, you're stuck, neither able to exist in one world or the other! This, is why we don't mix. It's the reason we stay hidden. Look, at me!"

I froze. All, I'd learned now, gone.

Powers? What powers?! I turned away from him, to see someone peeking out from behind a tree.

"Lance?"

Putting his finger to his lips, he swiftly crept in our direction. I had to think! Fire, I needed to start slamming it at them!

"Now my man Gladiator, is going to wake up. I can call him off now, surrender to me," he demanded. "Join us, give yourselves to me. Then no harm will come to you. In fact, we could end the human race. I never knew, we were so destructive until betrayed by one of my own."

Rapidly, the wind picked up behind us.

"Chant," shouted Jenson!

What the hell was I supposed to be chanting! My irritation climbed, up and over the garden wall. A surge of adrenaline pulsed inside me screaming to be let out. My back arched. I leaped at the creature holding Minder down, forcing him off of her.

"Why you," it spat, trying to corner me. Lance, had crept up behind him with his Kali stick. Sika, didn't notice his pal about to be, attacked. He was too busy gazing at Gavin, attempting to bust through a sort of force field. That must have been why Owl and Jenson were chanting, I reflected. Every time he hit it, he'd try again. These guys were definitely, Sika's sidekicks, really dumb ones at that.

(Tri)

I couldn't sleep. Instead, I tossed and turned. Dan, better take care of our daughter. Often he'd let her take on more than she could chew. I sat up, pushing off the covers. All the doors in our apartment were locked. I'd checked every one of them before bed. I'd be damned if I lost her to the insanity of my clan. The clock on my nightstand read 3 a.m.

No, I couldn't use my visions. That was a clan thing. I'd be drawing them back into my life if I did that, better get up and check on Megan. I pressed my feet down on the cold wood floor, stood up and proceeded to the doorway. I pushed it opened, nothing, empty. What was I expecting to see Monsters?

The door across the landing stood ajar. A light shone out into the hall forming an eerie shadow. Perhaps Megan was still up reading or attempting one of those Sudoku puzzles she loved. Starla hated them. I cringed at the thought of how different, my daughter's were, yet somehow, managed to get along. I felt along the wall cautiously moving towards her room. Then I peered in. Yep! She was at it again! Well, I shouldn't scold her too much, I couldn't sleep either.

"Hey Megan," I said, pushing the door open slightly.

Megan set her game down looking up, "Oh, I was just getting ready to put it away."

Myth

"No, no, it's fine. I can't sleep, anyway. I'd try to call Starla, but they are probably in the middle of a mess. I can just imagine your sister getting tackled by one of those thugs!"

"You mean the bandits, the ones you told us about?"

"Yeah, those guys," I said, sitting down next to her on her bed. She still had her posters up, of Winnie the Pooh and Piglet. I smiled, glad she was maintaining some of her childhood past.

"Did you ever consider going back? You could be there right now fighting by her side."

"And what would happen, if your father and I were both killed? I don't want you to end up in the system. My job is to protect you girls, not lead you into danger."

"Oh, Mom, come on- the clan would take me in wouldn't they," she complained.

Intelligent and smart, I couldn't get anything past my girls. I pulled myself up onto the bed getting ready to snuggle in.

"Mom, really," she replied to my claiming her domain.

Then I pulled my daughter into me in spite of her complaints and kissed her on her head.

"I love you, and Starla. Let me hold you tonight, ease my mind that at least one of my daughters is home and safe.

"Ok," replied Megan, leaning against me.

I couldn't bring to mind when I'd last needed reassurance. Usually, I dished out the hugs, compliments, and encouragement.

"What now," Megan asked.

"We get some sleep. In the morning, we blast dad's phone," I suggested.

"Mom, sometimes you think like a teenager."

"Good night, Megan."

"Night Mom," she replied.

(Starla)

Dodging the creature was a chore, comparable to basketball. I recalled playing a few games as a kid. I'd wanted to join, but wasn't coordinated, enough. Would Gavin, ever give up? I stood there while he continued to attempt to break through the force field. How much more ridiculous could this get? I actually, felt sorry, for this lunatic!

"Join you? I'd rather eat dirt!" shouted Minder to Sika moving closer to me.

"Get out of the way," he spat. Yes, literally right, on her face. She wiped it away getting ready to throw a punch. Lance, sprang into our area grabbed the creature from behind and shocked him. He fell limp in his arms.

What? Fire bolts? I'd never seen Lance use them before.

"At this second, the ball isn't in your court. You'd better plan your next move. Gavin isn't getting in," Lance sneered at Sika, pushing the creature's body aside.

"Attacking my minions means little to me. I'll immediately call in more," he retaliated.

Gavin sat outside our protected circle. It reminded me of a small child, waiting for someone, to let him enter. Minder grabbed my hand, and instantly Nayla was at my side. Squinting her eyes, she appeared as if she was concentrating rather hard. I could feel myself slipping into human form. "No! I have no clothes. What are you doing?" I reflected.

"You'll be fine, Molly and Cavin are on their way here," Nayla reflected back.

"But, Gavin, he'll attack them!"

"It will be fine, you're over-reacting," she speculated sending me a stern look.

Hit by an overdrive of simulations I wanted to rip Sika and Gavin apart. I stood on my hind legs or were they my human legs? My paws shook as I lifted Gavin into the air.

"OK, Starla Araina, please keep him there. The boys will bring down the shield long enough for them to pass," said Nayla.

I held him steady, deep in fury. I don't think it had anything to do with concentration, but more with the anger that kept him off the ground. I noticed Lance, who slowly inched up to the area Sika inhabited. He closely eyed Minder, a scrawl on his face. Then I saw them approaching from both sides. On one Cavin with Molly, and on the other three small animals similar to bats rapidly flew towards us.

"Don't bring up the shield yet, entrap them!" yelled Nayla.

Sika jumped forward in front of me and grabbed my arm trying to force it down.

"Let go! Stop, get him off me!" I screamed. He continued to twist my arm close to the ground. Minder grappled for him, but he shoved her aside.

"You're not going to keep them up there! They'll enter the ring to swallow you whole. Then you'll wish you'd joined us. When I gave you, the chance," Sika spat at me.

Lance eased up behind him ready to pelt fire into his ass. Unexpectedly Jenson sprang forth, striking him on the forehead with a Kali stick. Sika stumbled a bit, then repositioned himself upright.

"Ha," he said, and then tried hitting Jenson with his fist. Owl stepped in tripping him to the ground. Sika struggled to get up acting as if his bones had been crushed. Minder held him there with her stare.

"The force field, Jenson, keep chanting, we're not ready for it to shut down. Shellena, what the hell are you doing? Use your powers to entrap them! Starla, can't do this alone! Where is Dan! Has anyone seen him?" Lance shouted.

My dad, damn, I hadn't even thought. No Starla Ariana, focus, hold him up!

Shellena knelt on the ground, placing her hand on the earth. A ripple of waves spread out onto the trail nearly reaching where the bats stood. As it was about to hit, they flew into the air, avoiding the electric currents.

"Well, that worked like a charm!"

"Try again," I said, "this time one hand to the earth the other to the sky. Then aim at them using your hand, like a gun."

Shellena pushed ripples into the earth as two bats settled down onto the ground. After paralyzing them, she moved her arm upward and caught the third one in mid-air. It fell smack into the earth!

"OK, now drop the field!"

Cavin and Molly raced to Nayla. I let go of my hold on Gavin. He slammed into the dirt.

"Darn it!" he said, scrambling to get inside before the barrier sealed up again.

"Close it," shrieked Molly.

Jenson and Owl fatigued from chanting stood back. I detected venom dripping from Lance and Shellena's, lips, or was it saliva?

"Get down, in case he enters!" shouted Lance. Spittle dripped from his mouth and sizzled onto the earth. It made Sika cringe, digging into the earth below him.

Shellena joined Cavin close to the front of the encircled area. Gavin was closing in on our territory.

"Use the fireball thingy like you did earlier!" I demanded, backing away.

"Can't, firepower is only good once every hour," he replied.

This was it. I had to save my family. Mom and Megan most likely were expecting me home by now.

Leaning over, I whispered to Nayla, "We have to get out of here! Can't you project a memory mentally to me so I can kick some hybrid wolf butt?"

"I can't hold Sika, much longer," Minder piped up.

"Let me. Nayla, Starla Araina, and Minder, you must leave now," pleaded Lance.

"What about Gavin?" I asked.

"What about him?"

I looked down at myself, still a fox, whew! At least I hadn't changed yet...

Nayla placed her paw in mine. Intensity, a rush filled my body brimming over with pain.

Fire everywhere, my kind running to escape Sika, who stood in a circle igniting them with flames. What? How? Why we're, we so safe? Why was this so easy?

"Use it Starla, Araina, use it!" pushed Nayla.

My heartbeat quickened as if it would explode out my ears. Thump, thump, ba-bump, louder and louder till I thought I was bleeding out my ears. When I couldn't take it anymore, a horrific sound bellowed out of my mouth. The one I'd used when Shellena and Lance first visited me! Damn, why didn't I think of it before? The super hybrid baddies cowered as low to the ground as they could covering their ears. I didn't have time to say goodbye to Jenson. I stole a quick glance back before the force field came down, and we dove into the forest.

Chapter 34

(Cal and Nuria)

I ran through the thicket of trees deeper into the forest, almost out of breath. My paws barely touched the ground before I leaped up again, into the air with my super fox body. Well, maybe it wasn't super. It did give me time to reflect on the ideas running wild in my head. If Shellena and Lance were Vampire hybrids, why hadn't they just sucked out these bad-asses blood? Why did we need to hold them? Why not just kill them?

"Starla, we do not just kill," Nayla said invading my mind. "We have to hold them accountable. They'll get a trial first, then placement or banishment. The elders will decide. Now that Cavin is there they should be contained."

"Should Be?" I stopped, gazing at Minder. I guess she'd served her purpose, but after the lack of abilities I considered she had, I was rather disappointed in her strength to reprimand her once clan, now enemies.

"Starla, give her a chance! She's right beside us! Who knows, she may be able to read our minds."

Minder stood still a few feet away, her ears perked up, listening for something. Cautiously, she pranced up to us.

"I thought. I heard something over there," she said, pointing her long black nails in the direction of a train track.

Nayla provoked movement in the trees. She flicked her tail up and down in a fast motion, creating wind, pushing its large branches out of the way. Nothing but some Squirrel prints. A few nuts lay scattered on the ground.

"I don't see anything suspicious. It's best we keep going. How much farther is it Starla?"

"We should be about half way. It's beyond those red berry bushes. I'm not exactly sure how I know that. Last time I..."

My arm was vibrating! Did that mean Cal was near? I touched my arm.

"Are you OK?" asked Minder.

"My arm, my tattoo, it's going all haywire on me. Someone must be in the area trying to signal me! Maybe it's Cal! Do you suppose," I said, turning to Nayla.

"It could be your dad. I didn't want to worry you, but as soon as he parked the car..."

"What... -what happened?"

"I saw him exit the van, and then he just walked into the woods," said Minder.

"And no one went after him? What were you thinking?" I shouted.

"That your dad is capable of taking care of himself. It isn't like this hasn't happened before in these situations. Come on, let's keep going, perhaps daddy-O will come to our rescue at the cave," Minder joked.

I rolled my eyes at her and flicked my tail against the itch on my back.

"Starla Ariana, I'm sure he'll turn up, now move!" Nayla prodded me with her nose.

I felt like cattle being herded by a master, not as if my instructor was pushing me to find myself via this mission. We knew, the bandits killed Du-Vance, due to this treaty thing Nuria and he had devised. In turn, Minder left the group seeking redemption by keeping Cal and Nuria safe, yet never returned them. Eh, maybe it would have been risky to our clan, but wasn't it more so now?

"Starla, first we get Cal back, then put the bandits in their place. Afterward, we'll investigate the scientists that started this entire fiasco. It cannot happen all at once!" Nayla thought, poking into my brain.

I shook off her warnings. A headache began to form from the brief mind invasion. My paws pounded on the soil, my breathing quickened, as I tried to keep pace with my companions. I was falling behind. My tattoo now bore into me, burning my skin as we closed in on the cavern. Minder jogged up to the base of the entrance.

"It's urgent, get over here," she shouted.

My dad sat near the cave opening holding his arm to his chest. I observed a few deep gashes near his midsection, but none of them appeared fatal.

"I thought that thing, just set stuff on fire! Why did you come here! Did you presume you'd take it on yourself? Look at what it did to you!" I exclaimed crouching beside him.

"I was trying to protect you. Mom called me worried sick. I figured maybe if I could get to it before you did, well then we'd just get Cal and Nuria and go home."

"What planet are you living on mister," Minder remarked. She held his arm out examining it.

"There's no time for this! Minder, take his shirt and wrap his wounds," I ordered, standing up.

Nayla nodded at her to proceed.

"You can't go in there," my dad shouted.

"Minder, stay with him. Dan, it has to be dealt with!" Nayla insisted.

Dan slowly tried to ease himself up to stop us; subsequently, he fell back stumbling to the ground.

"Whoa, buddy. You better listen to them. I've seen Nayla in action. It'll be fine," Minder reassured him.

Dan grimaced, as she tied the torn cloth around his left arm.

"That's what I thought," he said.

"It's not just going to let us waltz in and save them," I whispered to Nayla surveying the inner darkness.

"Child, it's called the element of surprise! Remember when I disappeared, leaving you alone after our first meeting?"

"OK, what's the plan? Minder back there didn't exactly tell us how to destroy this ghoul." I nodded towards where she sat with my father.

"I'll transport us into the cave. If we try to walk in there, it may push us right back out. You were in your astral form before so it couldn't harm you," she said setting her paw on my shoulder. "Ready?"

"Do you have any advice before we pop into this death trap?" I asked.

"You contained it previously and showed great courage escaping the clutches of the foe. Try to use your connection with Cal to capture it. It might work with a spell, possible, but not guaranteed," Nayla pondered out loud.

"Alright, and if that doesn't work, what then?"

"Improvise! Use those Buffy skills, or was it Willow? Kicks some butt!"

"That was just a TV show," I prompted with a stare.

Nayla gripped me with her paw, and a sudden shudder ran through my body. The sensation grew stronger until I'd felt as if I'd jumped out of my skin! Landing on all fours at the base of the cavern, I glanced deep into the darkness.

"Where are they? I'd think if that thing attacked my father it would hone in on us like a dog on bacon!"

Nayla gave me a stern motherly look, "Did you think we'd just be right where you found her? It's not going to be that simple. Last time Cal called you, pulling you into her vortex."

"It still doesn't explain why it was near the entrance when it attacked my dad," I replied.

"Suppose, it was searching for food, or it heard him? It could be a number, of things really," she admitted.

We trotted further into the cave. My eyes adjusted, little by little, enabling me to see shadows. A slight fluttering from above spooked me. Backing away, I looked up at a few bat inhabitants. Thank goodness they weren't the bandit bats! All at once my vision went, wacko! It was as if I was staring down the light in the tunnel. The one, in a near-death experience, but I'd never had one of those!

"Are you good, should we keep moving?" asked Nayla.

I opened my mouth, but nothing came out.

"What is it? Do you see something," she asked, trotting to my side.

"My vision, it's kind of, gone cray cray. If I'm seeing, things correctly, they're straight down this tunnel. It's hovering over them, right now. I'm not sure how or why I've lost my voice. Maybe it has some, kind of power over me, is its nerves?" I thought to her.

"Possibly, we need to proceed with watchfulness,"

"No, duh," I responded automatically.

Nayla pushed ahead, reminiscent of a ghost urging me to stay out of harm's way. I followed close behind tracking the entity ahead of us.

"Now, when I get up there it's going to take a lot out of me. I'm going to play with it. Cat and mouse so to speak, keep it busy. If this works, once it's distracted enough take Cal and Nuria out of here. Don't worry about me. If I'm lucky, I'll have enough power to transport myself out of the cave."

"What do you mean? We have to destroy this thing, or at least, entrap it! I could try to throw fire at it. You know, like I did to Molly accidently."

Nayla turned around facing me, "Please trust me, it could dust you!"

"I know, but we're already going to be dealing with the bandit issue. It would be nice to have one nasty baddy, out of the way permanently!"

"Ok, Ok," she muttered. "If you think when I'm confusing it you might be able to take a hit then, take it. It will be one less thing we have to deal with back at the park."

"Mmm K," I whispered, my voice gradually coming back to me. Crouching down, we crawled in the direction of the villain.

My throat was dry. I licked my lips with as much saliva as I could muster.

"There," pointed Nayla towards the back side. "Go slow, stay behind me. I'll disappear and then reappear attempting to get it to catch me. If it should catch a whiff of who you are, we may be in trouble. Let me do the talking. I want you to work with Nuria and Cal to trap it."

"Yes, I'll do that."

I hung back, shadowing Nayla. She swished her tail at my nose. Gee, that, tickled! I tried not to giggle. Nayla flashed me a concerned look, and we trotted on. A sudden jolt of energy pushed me forward briefly moving me ahead of her like a chess piece. Nayla bounced forward throttling me to the side, but not before the entity leaped in front of me.

"News is, you're the new guardian. If we mix, then you could be surprisingly powerful," it hissed floating back and forth in front of us.

Turning my head to the right, I saw Nuria and Cal. One of them was pointing to a pendant of some kind.

"Go to them. I'll try to hold him here," mind spoke Nayla.

"And if you can't?"

"Girl, please, take out that can of whoop-ass!"

I leaned back on my hind legs, getting ready to run eyeing Nayla the whole time.

"Ah, ah, ah, I don't think you're going anywhere. You wouldn't want to end up a pile of ash."

"Why are you helping them?" I asked.

"Power, Sika promised me I'd be their new leader. All I needed was to gain access to you. Once you're in my possession, I can harness your powers. Your clan will have no choice but to join us."

I scoffed, "No way that's happening. I'd rather be cinder!"

"Really? I could make it happen right now."

Nayla sprang forward.

"What are you doing? Do you want to play a game? I'm all for that. I love games, and I always win!"

"Do you presume you can catch me?" cackled Nayla. She dashed from one side of the cave to another.

"I bet I can!" The entity smirked.

Nayla winked at me, then vanished.

"Where the heck?" He turned his head from side to side, trying to guess where she'd gone. Then randomly began to pounce.

Nayla reappeared near the left of the cavern and then disappeared as he surged ahead!

I scurried to the right where Cal and Nuria huddled.

"How do we get rid of this thing? Can we banish it? I've seen it done on TV in supernatural shows lots," I commented."

"We've got to contain it. I've been teaching Cal how to use her abilities. Minder aided us prior to our imprisonment. We had to wait for you to be physically here. We needed three people for this spell. Come on, before it tires of this game, or it squelches her," advised Nuria wincing. Nayla reappeared near where the crazed creature had dropped to smash her.

"Now, you have to do it now!" she screeched before she vanished again.

Nuria and Cal scooped up my hands, "Listen, follow along, and chant what we do."

A whoosh of air hit my face. Nayla dove to the side, redirecting it away from us.

338

"You are after me, remember," she shouted.

"Spirit of hate and haste frozen in a sapphire. Cold bold women of three, bitterness we rage on thee. Frosty winds whisk, you into this pendant for eternity!"

I watched the sapphire necklace on Nuria glow.

Just then, it sped up dive bombing me. I hit the ground, bringing Cal and Nuria with me. I smelled smoke! Fire?

"It's fine. You're only singed. You'll be fine," Nayla choked, coughing from the fumes. "Three times, repeat the mantra," pushed Nayla. She was wavering; growing tired. She wasn't the only one. I watched the monster lose its balance. It stumbled, falling off to the side.

"What are you doing to me, witch? Or should I call you charmers and gypsies?" It continued to spit out accusations of who we were appearing, now disoriented, out of sorts as we chanted in unison.

"Spirit of hate and haste frozen in a sapphire. Cold bold women of three, bitterness we rage on thee. Frosty winds whisk, you into this pendant for eternity! Spirit of hate and haste frozen in a sapphire. Cold bold women of three, bitterness we rage on thee. Frosty winds whisk, you into this pendant for eternity! Spirit of hate and haste frozen in a sapphire. Cold bold women of three, bitterness we rage on thee. Frosty winds whisk, you into this pendant for eternity!"

A tremor of vibrations grew, fluttering from Cal's hands to Nuria's and then reaching mine. Our bodies emitted a bitter chill, forcing it outward.

"Push it out of yourself; aim at it, now!" Nuria stood away from its withering body.

We directed the element out of our bodies. The Wind formed inside our circle.

"Release your hands, direct it to it, before it regenerates!"

What? Regenerates, what was this thing!

We lifted our hands and pushed! It engulfed the entity in a bitter chill. The gusts pushed against it despite the fact that it struggled to break free.

Nayla lay slumped over in the corner, not moving but continued breathing rather heavily.

"Concentrate, you're almost there," she whispered her eyes closing.

As the matter before us, chilled the entity, it grew smaller until it crystallized stopping all movement. Time slowed down for me. Nuria and Cal moved closer huddling in.

"Now we have to push it, don't stop concentrating force it into the pendant," Cal whispered into my ear.

Speeding up, the crystallized villain jolted to the side, zig-zagged and then zapped into the necklace transporting Nuria a crossed the room.

"I'm still here, just a bit sore now," she stammered pushing herself up. "We'd better get Nayla back. Do you have a healer on hand?"

"My friend Molly, she's a beginner," I added.

"Gifted," Nayla coughed weakly.

"Save your strength," soothed Nuria.

"I might be able to help," I replied.

"If you were in human form, right now we have no clothes for you. It would be rather embarrassing if you showed up without them," Nuria answered.

"We can't let her fade," I gulped nuzzling her with my long fox nose. I breathed, what was left of my power, into her. She began, to slowly revive.

"Starla, let's go," said Nuria.

Stepping back, I sat on my hind legs.

"It will do for now. I sense it's best, for you and Cal, to get re-acquainted. I'll carry Nayla."

"What happens next?" Cal inquired.

"We'll exit the cave. Dad and Minder are waiting for us," I replied.

"Good, the rest of the clan is?"

"Where I left them, or in the parking lot near the lake. They were holding off the bandits so Nayla and I could locate you," I answered.

"I hope that's all under wraps. It would be nice to present them to the console."

I shrugged, not sure who they were; Cavin was one of the members. Perhaps they would be the elders to give the bandits, a trial? Reaching for Cal's hand with my paw she accepted it.

"Miss me?" I asked. My voice was a bit squeaky as a fox.

She pulled me into a bear hug.

"I knew we were connected. I sensed it when you showed up, but my mom?" Cal, leisurely, let go of me.

"She had to stay behind, guard the clan with the kits. I wanted her to be here too, but they insisted."

"Did you talk to her a lot, since you've found out about us?" she mused as we began to travel.

"No, not really, it's been a wild ride so far. I have a long way to go and plenty of decisions to make." I gazed back at Nuria, making sure Nayla was stable.

"Everything's fine, keep going," she reassured us.

I turned back continuing, "What did you do all the time you were gone?"

"The bandits treated me as their, own daughter. They told me an astonishing story. My clan, our clan, would sacrifice me, to their gods, so they rescued me. I was foolish to trust them. It was fine for a while until they threatened Minder. After that we left, when Nuria came to us. I just... I didn't know what to think. I almost didn't go with her, but something told me to. A gut feeling at first, then my tattoo glowed. I saw Nuria had one also. Have you seen it?"

"I was too busy helping you both, trap that phantom. Nuria, I'd like to get to know her," I said looking back. "We have so much more to do in order, to make things right. The entity is contained. That is one evil, dealt with. It doesn't end here. You were told what they really, wish to obtain. Were you, not?"

"Minder spoke of killings of half-breeds. It's why my mom left Springville. We moved back, but you stayed behind," she said, strolling towards the sunlight that beckoned us. The opening of the cave gradually appeared ahead.

"Almost there," said Nuria. Minder raced up and peered inside, "is everyone OK?"

"We're going to be fine. Nayla is a bit out of sorts. She needs to be healed. Is Molly with you?"

"I'm here. Cavin dropped me off."

"What happened?" I asked as I exited the cave into the daylight. Cal and Nuria followed behind me with Nayla.

"Your dad is healed," she said, motioning me to where he stood.

I frowned, eyeing the scars left on his arms.

"Well almost, I couldn't quite stop the scarring. I'm not that advanced yet," she confessed.

"Minder, where is she? What about Jenson, is he OK? Gosh, I wasn't even thinking about him at all. He could be dead!" I shrieked.

"He's fine. Minder left, when she got the signal to go. As far as we know all the bandits are in custody. Jenson was banged up a bit, Shellena and Lance, being Vampire hybrids, got a taste of Gavin. He wasn't as scary as Sika had convinced us," she laughed shaking her head.

Nuria walked up to Molly holding Nayla in her arms. She carefully set her on the ground. My dad came closer to me. Then pulled me into a bear hug.

"Dad, I'm no hero. Cal and Nuria instructed me and knew what to do," I protested, pulling away.

"Yeah, but you showed up," answered Cal.

Molly knelt down next to Nayla. She placed her hands on her body. Lightly she ran them a crossed her fur in a soothing motion. Nayla shivered a bit before shakily standing up on her own.

"Can you make it to the van? Everyone else is at Hunters Park," said Molly.

"Should we head back there, then?" I asked my father.

He glared at me, then again at Cal, "I imagine your mother expects us home. It's almost nine a.m. She's probably pacing the floors. I know, and you know, how old you are but..."

"Mom still thinks I'm her little girl," I replied.

"The clan can wait. I'm starving, and besides your mom makes great pancakes!" blurted Cal.

"Just a Sec, your mom is waiting for you at Hunters Park. It's been how many years? You don't seem that distraught by it," my dad pointed out.

"She's probably still in shock," concluded Nuria, standing up for her.

I turned back and took one last look at the cave. Not really, sure why. It's not like it was a huge part of this case. After all, Du-Vance was only a small portion of it. We still didn't know who had killed him. I sighed to myself turning to my tribe. I hoped Jenson and Molly would remain in the company of me here. Maybe, I could be a part of both worlds. We'd just have to wait and see.

"You ready to go, or are we going to live in the cave now?" asked Nayla.

I shook out my fur and gave her a grin, "No, let's get going."

"Alright, Cal, we'll drop you off first, and then pick up Jenson at the station. He's gone, to help, but you'll need to be home, Starla. I promised your mom you'd have some time off. If, you wish to train you must finish this semester of college at least."

"I plan on finishing my degree," I chirped as we trotted along. I could see the others lagging behind us.

"You will, but I have plans for you. If you wish."

"My friends, Jenson, Molly, and I have Jone's test and the dance!"

"You'll get to those things, patience is a virtue," she added.

Chapter 35

(Breakfast Aftermath)

Jenson, Molly and I rushed out of the van. We scrambled up to the apartment complex. My dad trailing behind. As soon as I stepped onto our front stoop, my mom opened the door. She greeted us with Megan at her side.

"Glad to see you in one piece." She exhaled a sigh of relief and patted me on the head. I nuzzled her hand a bit, then pulled away. Megan just ogled me in awe.

"I'd like to go up and change. I'm afraid if I stay a fox much longer I won't be able to be human again," I muttered.

"We all need showers," observed my dad staring at the lot of us covered in dirt and grime.

"Well, the girls can head upstairs. Jenson, and Dan, go clean up in my bathroom. Megan, and I will get breakfast ready. We've been on the edge of our seats ever since last night," she said, nervously touching my father on the arm.

"Heading up now. Molly, could you get the door for me?"

"Yeah, come on," she replied, glancing back at the others.

"We'll see you at the breakfast nook. No worries, I've spoken to your mom," said Tri to Molly. She nodded back, and we headed in. I raced up the staircase.

"Wait up! I don't have foxy speed. I'm drained, from the healing I did," said Molly.

Once we reached the hallway, Molly opened the door to my room. Everything was as I'd left it. I walked in and sat down next to my bed. Molly shut the door behind her and strolled over to me.

"I'll shower first that way you can transform. Do you mind if I borrow a shirt?"

"Go ahead, you have a pair of jeans in the bottom drawer of my dresser," I said.

"Oh, I must have left them the last time I stayed," she shrugged. Then calmly waltz over to my dresser and opened the drawer, shuffling about until she uncovered them from my mess.

"Found em! Good thing I forget them," she said, shutting it. Molly stood up casually sauntering to the bathroom and then pushed the door closed behind her. I waited until I heard the shower running. Twitching my whiskers I closed my eyes, bracing myself. Would it hurt this time? Did I have to panic as before or was I able to now control it?

"As a guardian you'll need to learn to change without panic," Nayla mind spoke to me.

"So I just imagine changing, and poof?"

"It will take work, but yes, something similar to that. Now, do what you must. I'll contact you again near the end of the semester. The console will be putting the bandits on trial. We'll need you there. No worries, we'll keep your father and mother informed. She still has yet to decide if she's coming back to us."

"And between those times, what do you want me to do?"

"Keep your friends safe, we'll contact you, after the dance. Now try to shift before Molly has showered," she instructed.

I laid down placing my head on my paws conjuring up my own, image. I'm a girl, short, medium built, strawberry blonde hair and hazel eyes. I'm infatuated, with Jenson. I'm not sure if it's love, but warm tingles are nice, so foxy you have to go. Let me go. I thought of Jenson's warm arms, his kisses, and bit by bit felt myself return to human form.

The door to the bathroom sprung open.

"You know, coming out of the shower, I hoped you'd put clothes on," Molly stammered, turning away.

"Sorry, it took a bit longer turning back. Can you grab me my jeans, a shirt, and ah, you know?" I stammered.

"Of course, I just try to stay clear of naked people. You know seeing your best friend nude is awkward. I'm sure Jenson would find you striking," she teased.

I grinned at her, muffling a laugh."Are you going to leave me huddled here?"

"I could... Nah, better not."

Molly opened my dresser drawer searching for an outfit. She held up a pair of old, ratty jeans with a gray sweatshirt.

"Here," she said setting them beside me.

I picked them up. Scrambling to the bathroom before any more embarrassing comments were made.

Standing in the shower, Jenson filled my head. Truth, be told I needed to go on another date. This hero stuff had been pretty spectacular, but a real date that included a movie, hand holding, popcorn, and maybe a bit of kissing. If things happened, clan things, no you've already committed yourself; I thought as I banged my hand against the shower wall. Nayla had promised me, down time. Plus, I could pick up a few of those books now, at the library on Wicca and magic! I finished rinsing the conditioner from my hair. Then turned off the water and grabbed my towel that hung over the shower curtain. Soft, fresh and wonderful! I stepped out onto the mat. The mirror covered in steam. I wiped it free staring at myself, *the fox or the girl?*

"Nice of you to join us," said my mom, putting down a plate of food in front of my father. "Sit down, eat something. You have that test you need to take for Jones anyway. He called you'll go, after, this."

"And Denny's, am I going back to work?"

My mom laughed, "Yes, but not today. You don't look up to it."

"Are you sure the test can't wait?" asked Molly. "We were up all night catching villains. Jones knows this right, given that he helped Eva at the park."

"Yes, but he'd feel better if you'd just get it over with. You only have two more before the end of the semester. Then you'll be prepared," boasted my father.

"Are we going into battle again? Because the bandits have been captured." Jenson questioned holding his fork in midair.

My father cleared his throat as my mother pulled out the chair beside him. She seated herself rather close and held his hand.

"No, first of all, we still need to interrogate the bandits, find out which one of them killed Du-Vance. Unless, the entity that held Nuria and Cal was the culprit. However, the dance is in a few weeks. I want you kids to focus on that. Jenson, afterward the clan would like to give you an assignment if you choose to accept it. Starla will need to complete her guardian process before joining us. Can you handle being on the board to locate the scientists?"

"What!" I slammed down my fork like an angry child.

"Now, you'll be training dear. We need all the aid we can get," said my mother.

"We?" asked Molly.

"Yes, your father and I believe it's best to gradually intertwine ourselves back into the tribe, especially now that the threat is contained."

"I think it's great! Does this mean you and moms are getting back together? Do I get to be a part of this now?" blurted Megan.

"One thing at a time. Jenson, Molly, are you game?"

"Me?" spoke up Molly.

"Yes, you're a good healer, and not only Starla's best friend. Now your family," added my dad.

"I'm a bit confused," Molly replied.

"You've proven to us you can be trusted. Both you and Jenson. I'll speak to Nayla and Cavin. You'll be official members."

"Finish up, Jones will be waiting," urged Tri.

Jenson and Molly helped me to clear the table. Afterwards, I turned to get my coat and noticed my dad standing beside me.

"I've grown rather fond of Jenson. I know it didn't start out that way."

I nodded at my dad.

"Did he ask you to the Dance yet?"

"Yeah, I think I'm old enough to say yes, right?"

"Right," said my dad hugging me.

"Come on, let's jet," Molly interjected. I pulled away from my dad, and she handed me my coat. I put it on ready to face my new reality.

Author's Note:

Thank you for reading Myth book 1. If you enjoyed this installment in the series, please leave a review at http://www.amazon.com/dp/B016P42VXI or the site at which this book was purchased. I'm currently in the process of writing book #2 in this series. As a new author, I appreciate helpful feedback from my readers. I look forward to continuing writing for as long as the world will permit me.

Sincerely,

Angela K. Crandall

Made in the USA
Charleston, SC
10 April 2016